FAME

A HOLLYWOOD MAFIA ROMANCE

FAME

A HOLLYWOOD MAFIA ROMANCE

by

GINNA MORAN

SUNNY PALMS PRESS

ISBN 978-1-951314-80-4 (soft cover)
ISBN 978-1-951314-81-1 (hard cover)

Cover design by ZoneArtz Design
Cover images copyright Depositphotos

For Inquiries Contact:

Sunny Palms Press
9663 Santa Monica Blvd Suite 1158
Beverly Hills, CA 90210, USA
www.sunnypalmspress.com
www.GinnaMoran.com

1

The Looking Glass

Stacia

"Hurry up and cover your tits, wild child. This is where His Majesty said to drop you off." Talon keeps his gaze toward the string of traffic before us.

In Hollywood, sometimes a ten-minute drive could take an hour, especially on Sunset Boulevard on a Saturday night.

"You're teasing me too much tonight," Talon adds, drawing my attention away from the long line of scantily clad women and sophisticated men in suits waiting to enter Daddy's club.

It's a hot mess and not my first choice for where I

1

spend my free time, but my dad, His Majesty, insists we gather at his precious nightclub for our chapter meetings. The location used to be one of the first Hollywood movie studios but now fronts for his darker business endeavors, including running Hollywood's most powerful and corrupt business enterprises.

Anyone who secures representation by one of Daddy's many firms, they're guaranteed stardom. But it doesn't stop there. The St. Germaine empire cultivates businesses across all fields—from entertainment to medical—and darker, illegal activities I try to avoid.

And with our wealth and power comes thousands of people yearning for just a taste of the Looking Glass. Daddy loves fucking with Hollywood's finest. Even a name or money might not get them into the VIP section some nights. He designed it that way to make people crave more. Try harder. Flock in droves. It creates an exclusive environment built on people's desperation for attention and stardom. The Looking Glass can and will deny most celebrities from entering its VIP. The speculation as to why and who gets special treatment keeps the tabloids spinning.

But to gain access to the second level of the club, where dreams come true and people can change lives with a simple call, a person must be a member of the Looking Glass chapter, and becoming a member is nearly impossible. The Esoteric Society only lets in a very few of the most elite men and women by an initiation many can't pass.

"Come on, birdie. Enjoy the show. You just keep your eyes to yourself because of Daddy." I cup and bounce my boobs on the palms of my hands, cackling as Talon's jaw twitches. I love teasing the hell out of him. He's the one man I shouldn't flirt with, but I've never been much of a rule follower.

"I don't mind if you peek." I soften my voice, toying with the line Talon constantly shifts between us. "You know you want me. It'll be fun. I haven't been laid in. ..two weeks." It takes everything in me not to break my attempt at seduction. A laugh bubbles in my throat, my body heating at the idea of fucking my dad's business partner. It would serve Daddy right after sleeping with half of my sorority house the moment I graduated from Duke Carrington University, the private college my family has attended for generations.

"Fuck yeah, I do. I like my life. You're too damn hot for your own good, Stacia, and I only have so much resolve. You're not ready for what will happen if I decide to give in to your sexy little ass." Talon grips the steering wheel, his face remaining expressionless, his voice a smoldering rumble.

"Keep telling yourself that, birdie. My sexy ass might currently have a gemstone-studded plug since everyone will be watching me walk up the stairs." I lean forward between the seat, caressing his cheek.

His muscles cord, his body tensing under my touch. "Goddamn," he utters, licking his lips.

"Just imagine what I'd let you do..." I lick his earlobe and fake moan, hoping to shock him right in the balls in a good way.

I've only gotten him to break once over the last four years, and I'll never forget how hot he was to kiss. How big his cock felt through his pants.

We can't help it if we both find each other attractive. I don't know if it's because Talon is off-limits or what. He's not only Daddy's business partner, but he's fifteen years older and the enforcer of our society's chapter, meaning he does a lot of shady shit I've only heard about.

But I swear he gets hotter every time I see him. It's been a month since he's come over, and I'm pretty sure it's because Daddy fired both our driver and my bodyguard for something or another last night. Talon offered to take me to the Looking Glass, so I wouldn't have to call for a car since there's no way I'm driving in this traffic. He's a bit overprotective...or possessive. He swears he can't have me, but I know he might not want anyone else to either. It makes this game we play so much more fun.

"Fuck, Stacia." He groans, snapping out of his lustful haze. "You love torturing me. I have to meet your dad around back. He demanded you're dropped off out front. He wants the paparazzi circling." Talon stops in the middle of the street, not even caring that horns blare behind us. I hesitate, smiling at him as he finally looks at me in the rearview mirror. "Now put your tits away and get out. You have five seconds or you're coming with me and ensuring I die a happy man."

I laugh and pull on my glittering crop top, messing with my boobs until I have a perfect amount of cleavage showing. A diamond glitters for my navel piercing, and I spread my legs just enough to show off my lack of panties, proving I wasn't joking about my additional bling.

I catch Talon stretching up in his seat, flicking his

gaze up and down my body in the rearview mirror. I knew he'd look. There is just something about this man that I can't help being attracted to. It's not like I'm starved for attention. I'm about to get plenty.

More horns sound through the air, and I squeeze between the front seats, even though I could exit from the back door. I close the space and press a playful kiss to Talon's cheek before licking him and scrubbing my fingers through his neatly combed hair, making him grumble.

"Don't plan to take me home after the meeting. I booked a hotel nearby, so you don't have to worry about me. I think I can handle a ten-minute car ride with a stranger. Who knows. Maybe I'll invite them to the penthouse." I smile at him again. "Though if you want to join me..."

He narrows his eyes, leans across me, and flings the door of his Audi open. "Don't tempt me, wild child. You've given me some massive fucking blue balls that I can't even take care of."

I touch his thigh, drawing a circle. "Too bad we have a meeting, huh?"

He groans and points out the door. "Just get your ass out of here before I yank you onto my lap and give the paps a real fucking show."

"Only after you spank me, right?" I grin and wink.

"Until you can't fucking sit," he responds.

I laugh and slide out of the car, bending over just enough to give him a peek of my ass in my short skirt. "Let me know about the penthouse. If it's not you, I'll find someone else."

He narrows his eyes. "I'll kill the fucker, so don't even think about it."

I twitch my fingers, ignoring the agitated yells from the cars stuck behind Talon. "Oh, I will. Lots. Thanks for the ride, birdie. Muah!" I slam the door and blow another kiss, laughing at his glower.

I know how much he hates my nickname for him, but I can't stop using it. From the moment I knew his name was Talon and he said like the talon of a bird, I have called him birdie.

Twisting my torso, I wave at him once more. He hits the throttle and does a burnout, sending a cloud of white smoke into the air, obscuring the view of the line of pissed-off drivers behind him.

The sidewalk sparkles under the fluorescent lights of the digital billboard across the street, displaying a preview of the next Hollywood blockbuster. I check my makeup with my phone camera and smack my lips together, making a popping sound. The huge line of club goers wraps around the building like always, and I hear someone complain about the fact that I stroll straight toward Tony the bouncer. Turning toward the girl's group, I wave them over. It never hurts to show off my pull of power.

"Come on. Tony will let you in with me," I say, smirking at how excited they become. The more women in the club, the better, according to Daddy. It gets the men to pay and play.

"Stacia! Stacia, look over here. Ladies, you too. Show us how happy you are to be Stacia's charity case. Give us that red carpet smile." The flash of a camera sparkles in the side of my vision as one of the club's most notorious paparazzi snaps a picture of me.

I lift both of my hands and flip him off. "Give us something to fucking smile about, asshole." He's so obnoxious but Daddy would never send him away.

"If you don't want me to show off your charity work, then how about you give me a nice tit shot? It'll land on the cover of starlight magazine." The paparazzi snaps another picture. "It's been a while. Work hard to find?"

This fucking asshole.

Tony grasps my shoulder, drawing my attention to him. He's more than just a bouncer at the Looking Glass. He's also one of my dad's long-term security guards and only takes the shift twice a month. Security is always vamped up when His Majesty's court is in session. But it's not what it sounds like. This isn't like the court in the judiciary branch of the government. This is the Looking Glass Court of the Esoteric Society, one of the most prevalent, exclusive, find out-and-die type of associations. The Looking Glass requires all members to meet at Daddy's club to discuss business and our Hollywood empire—from who to influence, which political parties to back, what celebrities to bring on board, which businesses to build or destroy, and so much more.

And because of who my dad is and how I followed in his footsteps and attended Duke Carrington University, I was invited to participate in the yearly initiation and accepted right before graduation. I'll be a member until I die. Or until one of the society enforcers like Talon kills me for fucking up. I've seen it happen—only once—a few years ago, when I attended my very first meeting with Daddy.

It was enough to scare me into compliance, but now that I've immersed myself in the Looking Glass chapter, I realize it's not all that bad. The man murdered even deserved it for using his influence to sex traffic aspiring actors. It might be acceptable for some bastards, but not with our chapter. Such a scandal could jeopardize our empire.

For me, the perks outweigh the dangerous side of the business and make it easy to not think about the scary shit. I've been able to get out of every illegal shortcoming I have faced. Underage drinking. Trespassing. Indecent exposure. Drug use. Shoplifting. Assault on a catcaller... Talon wasn't wrong about me. I was, and still am, a bit wild. That's what happens when your mom is a failed actress with a drug problem, constantly absent and in rehab, and your dad owns a massive empire that also entails underground business endeavors among Hollywood's finest. But she doesn't know. She's not a member and never will be. I think the secrets strained my parents' marriage and also pushed her into spiraling.

"Don't let him get to you, Cia," Tony says, shielding me with his hulking body. He waves the girls I took from the line inside, letting the other bouncer check

IDs. "He thrives on getting a reaction." Tony's older than my father and very loyal. He would knock the paparazzi's teeth out if I asked him to.

But Daddy likes the attention and free exposure that comes with the paps. So do most of the celebrities that come here. For some, it's their sole reason, considering they can't get into VIP and need to get attention. It helps keep them in the ever-moving spotlight.

I smirk and pat Tony's cheek. Straightening my shoulders, I hold my head high. "Don't worry. He doesn't. I was just considering his offer. It's been a while since—"

"Don't you even think about it, Cia. I don't want to have to break his camera again. There's no way I'll ever let that bastard put my sweet angel on the front of one of those gross tabloids and all over the internet. I know you think it's fun now, but if it happens, it'll stay around forever. I don't care if you're twenty-five. You're like my own kid, and I'm gonna treat you like that. Now get inside. You're not being added to any mother fucker's spank bank." Tony nudges me toward the door.

"I'm sure I'm already there. You know Daddy doesn't give a shit," I tease, letting him guide me toward the entrance of the Looking Glass.

"Exactly. Which is why I have to. Have fun tonight and be safe. Make good choices. Don't think I won't be watching out for you. Try not to drink so much." Tony waves me away with his attempt to parent me a bit too late in life because he knows no one else wants to, especially now that I'm an adult. He's one of those guys that considers his children as his babies until the day he dies, even if they're seventy years old.

"You're going to have to let me grow up sometime, Tony." I grin at him, appreciating his words, despite enjoying teasing him about it. "You know Daddy is already prepping me to take over the business in all its twisted glory."

Tony tightens his jaw, looking ready to argue with me. Someone shouts my name at the top of their lungs. I recognize Bianca's voice over the loud, thumping music playing a mix of the current trends at the top of the charts. The club is divided into four sections, each with a different genre of music, drawing in tons of people because there's so much to choose from and enjoy.

I blow Tony a kiss and rush toward Bianca, spotting her in a mini dress barely long enough to cover her pussy. I'm sure she doesn't wear any panties ei-ther, making it easier for her to fuck whichever hot guy she chooses. Unlike me, she has free range. She doesn't have every bouncer and security guard trying to interrupt. She also doesn't have my dad's reputation hanging over her, creating not only a cock-block but a cock fucking fortress. As soon as anyone finds out that I'm Stacia St. Germaine, heir to the St. Germaine empire, they either immediately back off or try to take as much as they can from me.

So sometimes I use an alias.

But not tonight. Tonight, the VIP is filled with members of our society chapter.

"Bitch, you took fucking forever to get here. I've been having to hang out with Cinnamon." Bianca crinkles her nose, mirroring my own expression at the thought.

Cinnamon is the trophy wife of one of Daddy's closest friends and business advisors, Jefferson Garni-ca. She's younger than we are and still going to college. She was initiated into the Esoteric Society just a few months ago at DCU and married Jefferson soon after.

"All she talks about is Jeffy, the non-existent weath-er, how boring her classes are, and how she doesn't get why she has to graduate when she's already initiated," Bianca continues, looping her arm through mine.

Cinnamon acts like she's special because she was chosen to join because of Jefferson's love of college freshmen instead of being entitled by birth. She comes from wealth with her family's tech company. Something to do with medical software or some shit. I don't really know or care. I tune her out.

"That's exactly why I'm late. I only have time to wave at her now." I stick my tongue out at Bianca. "Maybe you'll learn for next time."

What Cinnamon doesn't realize is if dear hubby decides he doesn't want her anymore, our chapter doesn't allow divorces. With Jefferson's position on the King's Court, he could make her life hell and send her away or worse...

It's one of the things I'd love to change when I take leadership. I just have to prove myself first. These men can't run our chapter forever and with the way they've been initiating more women the last few years, I know they won't. I have to appreciate men like Jefferson. Thinking with his cock, which might not turn out so well for our newest member.

I shiver.

"Says the lucky bitch who doesn't have to live on her family's time. You know my parents take this shit seriously and insist we come together." Bianca pulls my thoughts away from Cinnamon. Unlike my parents, Bianca's were high school sweethearts and initiated together. Half of our member's spouses only hear whispers about what goes on. They think it's some alumni organization when it's far from the truth.

"At least you didn't fail to seduce Talon. His Majesty fired our driver, so he brought me, looking extra fucking delectable tonight. We were this damn close." I hold my index finger and thumb an inch apart. "He would've given in had there not been a meeting."

"Damn, Cia. I wish I had someone to fuck with like that. My mom's at it again with the dating apps. You should see all the men she has lined up for me. Apparently, I should be married already and not whoring around. She's decided she wants to approve of anyone who gets to take our name. She even plans meetings with them beforehand. Like a fucking date me to date my daughter. Super cringey." Bianca rolls her eyes, her words tumbling from her mouth. It's only been a couple hours since I've talked to her, but she always bursts with shit she can't hold in for long.

"Are you serious? What the fuck?" I glance around the club, catching the gaze of a couple men staring at us. I recognize a local drug dealer Daddy sometimes gives free range in exchange for a cut. A few women crowd around him, vying for his attention—or probably paid to. He's so damn sleazy.

"Right? She just makes it so I don't want to date anyone. I'd rather die alone than have her seconds, even if it's supposedly for me. So gross." Bianca grimaces.

"I bet she'll ask them for a demonstration. Make sure they know how to find a clit," I tease, crinkling my nose, regretting my joke immediately. The last thing I want to think about is Marge-Louise's sex life. It's bad enough that she and Juan constantly grope each other in displays of public affection—no, just displays of public porn. I once caught them fucking in the women's bathroom and wanted to bleach my brain.

Bianca fake gags. "Seriously, Stacia? I didn't think about that. She probably would. Her and Juan are open."

I shrug. "Mama Marge might just want the best for you."

Whacking me with the back of her hand, Bianca

then swipes a colorful shot glass from the tray of one of the servers heading to the booths that come for table service. It's the closest anyone who isn't a member of our chapter can get to VIP treatment on a meeting night. The server knows better than to say anything, because drinks are always on the house for us.

Bianca downs the shot and shakes her head, releasing a yell. "You're lucky we have a meeting or else I'd tell that dude over there that you want to hook up and were too shy to approach him first." She fake-glares at me.

I roll my eyes and grab her hand, pulling her toward the stairs to the VIP lounge. I'd feel bad for the poor soul she'd give hope to, because usually, they're intoxicated enough to summon the bravery to talk to me. And if they have an ounce of hope, most of the douchebags here assume that playing hard to get is a yes for them. They'd end up on the floor, cupping their balls if they even tried. They'd be lucky to deal with me and not one of the bouncers.

Because Daddy has a reputation to maintain and doesn't want to deal with paying more to the authorities than he already does to keep them away from his business. He ensures that no one is ever declared dead on our property, and if someone gets drugged, it's in the back alley. This is one of the most notorious clubs in Hollywood, which is why it's one of the most popular. Every night is ladies' night, which the men love.

Everyone considers Daddy to be progressive with his supposed punishment to men caught doing bad deeds, but I know the truth. He's just as capable of being pervy as many of the other men in positions of power. A lot of shit goes down here.

And tonight, is one of those nights.

Bianca twirls next to me, making me dance with her to the stairs that'll take us to the VIP lounge which leads to the meeting room. I don't know what to expect tonight apart from the boring chapter business shit. I don't have any sort of influence yet. I'm not on the King's Court. I'm considered just an heir and member until I'm worthy enough to take on any of the tasks available.

"Ms. St. Germaine, Ms. Perez. It's nice to see you both." The familiar voice of William Blackstone sounds through the air. He's from another chapter, but it's not uncommon for different chapter heads to travel and participate in meetings. It's how everyone knows everyone in the Esoteric Society. We were founded in England in the 1800s by men who went on to rule Victorian Britain...and the world. Hollywood and the Looking Glass are only a tiny part of the Esoteric Society. Being so vast is the only way our network works.

"Billy! Daddy didn't tell me you were coming." I throw my arms around the man and kiss each of his cheeks, showing my respect in the form of affection. It's instinctual and has been trained into me my whole life.

"Because he wasn't aware. You know how much I like to surprise the old bastard. I brought a couple of heirs with me, who are moving into your area. I wanted to introduce them and make sure they felt at home here." William hands me a ceremonial robe.

I pull my masquerade mask from my purse. It sparkles with real diamonds and matches Bianca's. When the meeting starts, we're unified as one and our identities, despite being known amongst each other, remain protected from any sort of scandal. We never know who to trust. Some asshole could've hooked up a camera. Some paparazzi could've snuck in. And we can't risk the world finding out.

"Oh, fresh meat," Bianca says grinning. "Do we know them?"

William chuckles and shrugs. "Maybe you ladies can do the honor of welcoming them during the introduction ceremony. One of them has traveled from Mexico City. The other just got back from a sabbatical in Greece."

"Ay, papi. You know I'm always happy to...if they're single and not fifty. Do you think Juan would approve of them?" Bianca asks, using her dad's first name instead of one of endearment. It's always been their thing.

I grab her hand. "There's only one way to find out. Come on, Bianca." I pat William's cheek with my free hand. "It was nice to see you again."

"Always a pleasure." William turns away to welcome the Bordeauxs, one of Hollywood's power couples.

I don't want to get caught in another conversation, so I tug Bianca away. We put on our robes and adjust our masquerade masks, heading across the VIP lounge and toward another door. It's a secret room that only members of the Esoteric Society have ever been in.

Another set of stairs takes us into the basement,

where dozens of people hover around, waiting for my dad to arrive. He is the King of this chapter, and nothing will begin without His Majesty. He's always the last to arrive and the last to leave.

"I need to say hello to Juan and Marge-Louise. I'll be right back. Why don't you grab us a seat?" Bianca motions toward the circle of chairs lining the room, where we'll sit as spectators, only participating in the ceremonial vow, since we're not at the level to voice our business opinions.

I only nod my head and watch her stroll away, heading toward where her parents wait by the altar. I gaze around the room, trying to put faces to the figures covering their identities with their masks. I should recognize everyone by now, but I haven't put much effort into it. Some of the elders must speak for me to know who they are. It doesn't help that some of them I rarely see without a mask.

Not that it matters.

"Hello, astéri mou. It's been a while." The familiar voice turns my blood cold, and I stiffen in my seat. "Do you mind if I sit with you? I don't know anyone else, and you know the rule about showing a transferring heir a warm welcome. I need someone to introduce me during the ceremony, and I'd rather it be you. I've missed you."

My heart pounds as a dozen memories cross my mind. I can't believe it. Christos is here. He's really fucking here. I haven't spoken to him since our initiations, and I thought I'd never have to deal with him again. He's reached out a ton of times over the years, but I've always denied his calls after what happened between us. I was hoping I could forget it. Treat it as if our year of dating was nothing but a nightmare.

"We have a lot of catching up to do, now that I'm in town, astéri mou." Christos hums under his breath, gliding his hand over my knee. His use of the nickname he'd given me, my star, ignites something warm inside me. It feels as if no time has passed at all.

A part of me wants to lean toward him. To rest my hand on top of his and remember what it was like to be touched by my first love and first heartbreak. But I know better. I can't open myself up to him. The warmth turns into blistering fire.

I smack his hand and stand up, crossing my arms over my chest. "Are you kidding me? I don't want anything to do with you, Christos."

"Careful, Stacia. You know it's against the rules to

speak my name. I could reprimand you right here for it." Christos gets to his feet, towering over me.

"You can try, but you just broke the same damn rule." I shift on my feet, peering around for Bianca. She can intervene. She can be the one to welcome Christos.

But the lights go off, and Juan sets the candles ablaze.

Fuck my life.

I can't even run. I can't hide.

I'm at Christos' mercy, and once again he manipulated me for his gain.

With Christos, I always lose.

"Astéri mou, please. It's one night." Christos grabs my hand, sliding his fingers through mine. "I want a second chance."

"Then don't make me do this." My chest clenches with my softening voice. "Pick someone else."

His brown eyes flicker, the candlelight dancing in his gaze. "I can't, Stacia. It has to be you. It's always been you."

2

White Queen's Kiss

Stacia

Something as little as a kiss shouldn't be the cause of my undoing.

I stumble to my seat and plop down, my knees weak from my swelling emotions. The Welcome Ceremony has been a tradition at the Looking Glass chapter since it was founded in 1921 with the founding of Duke Carrington University and the rise of Hollywood a decade before. Alice Steinbeck, nicknamed Princess Lily by Gene St. Germaine, my great-great-grandfather and the founder of the Looking Glass chapter. Princess Lily was the first woman and starlet to be initiated into the chapter, and she always welcomed the new heirs—both gentlemen and ladies alike—with what was coined the White Queen's Kiss. It's been a tradition carried on but with a twist since she passed away in the 1960s.

And now, here I am, handpicked by the man I despise the most in the world, to kiss him and offer my services, which means I can't escape him for weeks. He's allowed to shadow me, call upon me, and basically own me for the entire night.

Something that makes me cringe even thinking about. I loved this man, and he destroyed me. He destroyed us. He'll use this against me.

The thought of kissing him cuts open the scars he left behind, turning them into fresh wounds.

I pull at my robe, the fabric feeling constrictive. "I hate you," I mutter, my voice cracking. "I fucking hate you."

"I want to fix things. I've changed. I'm not the same man." Christos towers over me, his gaze burning my skin, though I refuse to look.

Since he asked me to be his companion for the meeting, and I failed to immediately find someone else to play the role in his Welcome Ceremony, I'm stuck. He obviously planned this. I know he did. I wonder how long he's been in town. I have so many questions that I don't want to ask, because I need to shut down and murder whatever it is he's trying to do.

"Astéri mou, come on. It's only a kiss." The nickname, which means my star, prods at my heart. He had given it to me when we met on Spring Break in Greece during college. Christos made it so easy falling in love with him, his charm just as lethal as he is and even more destructive.

"We can't break tradition. It'll feel utterly wrong to do it with anyone else. Please, join me at the center. Everyone's watching." Motioning toward the altar, Christos points to Bianca waving at us with a hooded and masked figure by her side. It must be the other heir William talked about. I'm sure Juan asked her to do the same thing.

Sliding his fingers through mine, Christos tugs me to my feet, taking advantage of the paralyzing emotional whirlwind spinning through my mind. The double doors to the King's chambers open, revealing Daddy in his decorative mask and robe, the design made to show off his superiority. He doesn't say anything as he strides into the meeting room. Talon follows behind him, carrying a wooden chest with the dagger used to blend blood between His Majesty and the new heirs.

Our eyes lock from across the room for a split second. Even with my masquerade mask, I'm sure my emotions show clearly with my uncontrollable pout. He's always been ultra-aware of my feelings, considering our attraction and constant flirting, pushing the boundaries of our friendship.

"Help me," I mouth, resisting stepping forward.

Talon squares his shoulders and turns his attention to Christos. If I could see Talon's expression behind his mask, I bet I'd spot him glowering. Talon would much rather cross the room and punch Christos in the face rather than follow my dad to the altar. He's protective like that. Probably jealous of the idea someone chose me for the ceremony when there are dozens of others to choose from.

My silent request for an intervention goes unanswered, but I had to try. I'd do anything at this point not to let Christos do this to me. Unfortunately, Talon would never break tradition and risk punishment. Not for anyone, including me. An act of disobedience, especially from our enforcer, guarantees not only degradation and humiliation, but it also guarantees a shit load of work he probably wouldn't want to take on.

I force my mouth to smile, trying to cool Talon down now that I riled him up. It was unfair of me in the first place, especially because he doesn't know what went down with Christos…at least, I think. He'd have to go through the collateral our society has on us, and something like that must be requested and proven necessary to share in cases of controlling our chapter's members.

Christos is a lucky bastard and basically untouchable when it comes to his indiscretions with me. He's far too good with his business endeavors and now one of the most sought-after money launderers, which is the only reason I bet he's here.

But despite his worth to the St. Germaine empire, I will never forgive Christos for what he did. There is nothing he can do to make up for using me as part of his initiation in his chapter. And now coming here? I'm pissed Daddy didn't warn me. He knows our history. He knows Christos broke my heart and betrayed me. He obliterated my reputation to get ahead.

I shudder at the thought and yank my fingers away from Christos, my rage intensifying.

I can't do this. I can't pretend his presence doesn't

mess with me.

I'd rather be punished than welcome him into our chapter.

I steel myself for what I know will not only embarrass Daddy but will also cause a conflict between chapters. This could fuck up whatever agreement William has with the Looking Glass. The repercussion could hurt our chapter as a whole. I can't see another way around it, though. I'm about to disobey Daddy's authority in front of another chapter leader, and nothing will change my mind. This could have more than the usual consequences, but I'm done.

I'm fucking done.

I have to prove to Christos that whatever he's trying to do in coming here, trying to fuck with my head…it's not going to work. He claims he still wants me and that I'm the only one for him but I know there's more to it. It's been years. Why now? Why come here and try to fix something broken beyond repair?

Because he's a twisted bastard. This has to be some sort of power move.

Silence fills the air as everyone gathers into position for the Ceremonial Vows which always open our meetings. Daddy lights another candle, and he uses it to set the altar ablaze, creating brighter light.

Everyone chants their welcome to His Majesty in unison, holding a fist to their hearts with the recognition of his leadership and our promise of eternal loyalty to the Esoteric Society.

"And I vow the same," Daddy responds, raising his glittering cane. "Court is now in session." His voice booms through the air as he smacks the cane to the hard floor, calling order. "We have several things on our agenda tonight, but first, it has come to my attention that a welcome is an order. His Majesty of the San Diego Rabbit Hole chapter has kindly joined us tonight, bringing new blood with him."

A round of calculated, soft applause fills the air as William heads to my father and joins him. "It is always an honor to join the Looking Glass chapter, Your Majesty." No one uses real names while we're together in session. We all have nicknames, and Daddy owns the king title here because he's the leader, which kind of made me Princess, my nickname in honor of Princess Lily. I know it's lame, but it kind of just stuck.

"I would also like to introduce you all to the newest members of your chapters coming in from Mexico and Greece. They have been in the San Diego chapter for a couple months now, but after an SOS His Majesty put out for another business expansion while waiting for the next initiation season, they have kindly decided to transfer."

"They will be utilized to the fullest and become some of our greatest additions." Daddy waves his cane, acknowledging Christos and the other new heir. "To show our appreciation, we will proceed with an official welcome and a vow in the form of the White Queen's Kiss. Please step forward with your companions, and we will begin the blood-bonding ceremony." Daddy's voice sends my heart sinking into my stomach. If he knows Christos transferred, he doesn't react. I thought he would show just as much anger as Talon. Maybe he'd even deny the transfer.

"We're up, Princess," Christos says, tightening his fingers around mine, forcing me forward.

I dig my feet into the floor, refusing to move.

Christos sighs. "Don't be shy. We've done worse. Maybe you'll remember why you were so in love with—"

"Fuck off!" I yell, ripping my hand from his. "Get away from me. I'm not fucking doing this."

Audible gasps sound from the other members, but

I don't let it stop me. I ignore Daddy as he yells my nickname.

Spinning on my heels, I run toward the door. I elbow Talon and step on his foot before he can snatch me off my feet. I kick another guy between the legs. I dodge around a woman, trying to block the door.

"If you leave here, there will be some serious consequences for disobedience," Daddy snaps, remaining in place. It is above him to chase after me. He has others to do it. "Don't be stupid."

"I don't fucking care." I point at Christos. "I'm not welcoming him. He can screw off. I'm done tonight."

I don't wait to find out what else Daddy yells. No one will follow me once I'm out of the room. They won't stop the meeting on my behalf.

It gives me at least an hour to myself to decide what to do.

I know I should run, but I don't. I refuse to show that my dad's threat scared me.

So I head to the bar, setting my gaze on the first hot guy I see.

I rest my elbows on the bar next to him as he waits to make his order. He eyes me in his peripheral vision, checking me out without giving me his full attention.

I lean forward a bit more, accentuating my cleavage.

"What are you having?" I ask, turning slightly to meet his gaze. "The bartender won't serve new people. I'll buy you a drink."

"How about you order, and I'll buy?" The man taps his fingers on the bar top. "It's the least I can do if you're going to help me out. I should've known she wouldn't serve me after the sixth time she's walked past and served everyone around me."

I laugh and shrug my shoulders. "I'm surprised you even got in. Do you know someone here?"

"I'm meeting a client. They picked the place and put me on the list," the man says.

"I guess that means you'll turn into a regular." I smack my hand on the bar top and wave toward Kitty. "Kitty Cat, don't leave us hanging. We need some drinks."

Kitty drops what she's doing and heads toward me. "Baby doll, I wasn't expecting you here for another hour. Do you want your usual?"

I turn toward the guy. "I'll have whatever he's having."

"Bring us two Drink Mes. My friend told me they were the best shot, and you're the only one who can make them." The man smiles wider at me. "If that's okay with the lady."

I laugh and clap hands, my energy returning as I redirect my focus away from my dark thoughts. "That's perfect. Two Drink Me Elixirs, Kitty. And keep them coming. I had a long fucking night already."

"You're an incredible dancer," the sexy, mysterious man says, sliding his hand across the small of my back. He pulls me closer, swaying in beat with the pulsing music. Sweat sparkles on his forehead, his easy-going smile filling me with life.

I lean in close, tilting my head slightly, waiting to see if he'll close the space to kiss me. Drawing his hand up my back, exploring the smoothness of my skin with his rugged fingers, he combs his fingers into my hair, pulling me in. Our lips meet in an electric caress, warm and inviting, and just as sensual as our dancing. If clothes didn't separate us, we'd be fucking right here on the dance floor.

Gliding my tongue over his, I reach between us and stroke my hands over the hard length pushing against his pants. He's so turned on for me that I want to test him and see how far he's willing to go.

"I know a place we can go," I murmur, flicking my tongue over his earlobe. "I mean, if you want."

I don't even know his name, but I don't care. He keeps my mind off everything, his attention exactly what I crave after the shitshow tonight. My adrenaline runs hot, mingling with the intoxication of the alcohol, making me feel invincible.

Christos can fuck the hell off.

So can Daddy.

Talon.

The whole Esoteric Society.

"Whatever you want, beautiful," the man murmurs, kissing my neck. "I'm not afraid of getting caught."

I giggle and bite my lip before I lace my fingers through his and tug him in the direction of the storage room just off the side of the bar. Kitty winks at me as she serves another patron, unfazed by my behavior. When Daddy is stuck in a meeting away, I'm going to fuck and play with whoever I want. If I'm going down, might as well have some fun.

"Do you work here or something?" Bar Guy asks, peering around the shelves of supplies.

"Or something." I curl and uncurl my fingers, luring him closer with a smile as he decides if he's really all in or not. "I just know a lot of people. Don't worry. Just have fun."

Spinning around, I hike up my skirt enough to flash the fact that I wear a jeweled plug while I shift some boxes in front of the door. He releases a deep hum and steps closer to grab my hips from behind.

"Damn, beautiful. That's so sexy. But I'm curious as to why. Were you meeting someone?" He grazes his fingers over my ass cheek, standing close enough that all he'd have to do is whip out his cock and align our bodies.

I'm normally not as bold, but everything tonight pushed me over the edge, and I happily spiral into this oblivion. "I was betrayed," I say, stepping back to push my ass against his pelvis.

"And you want revenge?" he murmurs, rubbing his fingers from my ass to my pelvis until he can slip one inside me.

I moan and lean against him, my heart racing in excitement. "I just want you to fuck me."

Spinning me around, the handsome man pushes me against the shelves and kisses me again, his tongue gliding over mine with enough passion to make me moan. I tug at his belt, helping him unfasten it enough to pull his cock free.

And then he's inside me.

The pressure of his cock stretches me in incredible pleasure, zinging heat across my skin. He props me on the metal shelf, knocking tumblers over in the process. Neither of us stop as glass shatters on the floor. He holds my ass with one hand and uses the other to strum my clit, igniting a wave of tingles through me. It's the first time a man plays with me this way during a one-night stand, considering the few others were more concerned with themselves. I moan and cling to him, gasping as his body hits mine over and over, rattling the shelving unit. He's as good a lover as he is a kisser, and I arch and squirm with my building orgasm.

"You're so sexy, beautiful," he murmurs, thrusting harder and deeper, ravishing me in a way I haven't experienced in a while. He's unexpectedly attentive, and I can't get enough.

"God, you're so fucking good. Right there. Keep doing that. I'm going to come again," I say, groaning and squirming. I gasp and kiss him, nipping his lip and enjoying his company. He smiles against my mouth, drawing perfect rhythm over my body until another orgasm explodes through me and I scream in pleasure.

With a grunt, he pulls out and finishes across my bare thighs, his handsome face puckering with his lust. I snatch his face and kiss him again, tempted to never leave this room. The handsome stranger grabs a new bar towel from the package and helps me clean off.

I dance around him, intoxicated on lust, and grab his tie. "Another drink?"

"Fuck yeah, beautiful. Whatever you want," he says, hugging me.

I smile. Finally. Someone who won't tell me what to do or fuck with my head. This is exactly what I needed. One last celebration before who the hell knows what. I don't even care anymore.

"That's what I love to hear," I tease, entwining my fingers with his.

I drag him back into the club, the music and lights blurring as he spins me around and hooks me by the waist.

"Let's get that drink," he says. "I still have some time. My client's running late."

I grin and kiss him again. "Abso-fucking-lutely. Nothing sounds better."

3

Hot Mess

Stacia

Bitch Babe: WTAF? Are you crazy?

I stare at the text message flashing across my phone. Bianca's risking a lot, texting me during a meeting. Not that I'm being an obedient heir, considering I left altogether and have been taking shots, fucking strangers, and preparing my escape before the end.

Bitch Babe: I thought you'd come back. There's still time to beg for forgiveness. Things are taking time with the new heirs. As long as you return before the meeting ends, it'll be okay.

Blinking the haze from my vision, I ignore Bianca

and tuck my phone away. Bar guy smiles at me, holding up his shot glass. The bass thuds through the speakers, shaking the tall table, and I suppress my regret and grin.

One of the male servers sets two more shots in front of us. I don't recognize him, but it's not like I know everyone here. Bar guy hands him some folded cash, and he vanishes in the crowd in the direction of the bar.

"To serendipitous encounters, good music, and beautiful strangers," Bar Guy says, his gaze traveling from mine to give me a slow once-over. Our knees touch as we sit alone in one of the bottle service booths.

"To hot sex and handsome strangers, too." I clink my glass to his, letting the beat of the music fill my soul. I haven't had so much fun with someone besides Bianca in a while, and definitely not here at the Looking Glass.

The cloudy blue liquid of our Drink Me Elixirs swirls around in the glass, glittering in the colorful strobe lights. I tip it to my lips and drink it in one swallow.

The alcohol burns going down my throat, and I release a breath. I scoot closer to Bar Guy, laughing with my excitement. My body continues to buzz, growing hotter with another shot and his smoldering eyes devouring me.

"Want to get out of here?" I ask, sliding my hand up his chest, feeling his chiseled muscles through his suit jacket. "I'm over this place."

His lips curl into his easy-going smile, drawing my attention. He nods his head without a word, sliding his hand across my side and to my back, the heat of his palm electrifying against my bare skin.

I don't hesitate and kiss him again, tasting the sweet, spicy alcohol on his lips. He hums against my mouth, kissing me deeper, devouring my continuous affection. I slide my arms around his neck, sitting on him so that I can feel his desire for me again. Our tongues graze against each other, the kiss more sensual than passionate. I can't get over how amazing a kisser he is, and if I can keep him around, it'll keep Talon, surely commanded to be the enforcer, away for at least tonight. Because Daddy won't risk exposing us in front of a stranger.

I break away from his mouth, gasping a breath. "I know you said you were meeting a client—"

"I'll let him know something came up. He'll under-stand, considering he's late. Let's get out of here." He scoots to the edge of the booth with me on his lap and helps me stand. Sliding his arm around my waist, he pulls me in close like he can't get enough of me.

"I'm staying in the penthouse at the Silver Screen Hotel," I murmur, caressing my lips against his ear.

"Funny. I'm staying there too. I'll get us a car." Bar Guy pulls out his phone from his suit jacket pocket.

I don't even know his name, yet I don't care. All I can think about is losing myself to the night. I want to forget about the meeting and Christos. I want to forget about any sort of punishment that comes from my behavior.

"I'm Leandro, by the way." It's as if he reads my mind. He smirks at me, flicking his phone up, so I can see the truth for myself in his details on the car ride app. Leandro Ramiro—a sexy name for a hotter man. "I know it's a little late for introductions, but I'd prefer to know you as something apart from 'beautiful' in my mind. Also, I want you to have my details in case you're wondering or want to tell a friend you're leaving with me."

I've never had a man mention something like this

before. I don't know if I should be a bit concerned, that maybe he's suggesting it as a way of getting me to trust him or what. But I have worse people to fear.

"Leandro, huh? I like it. And that's sweet of you to suggest, but I'm good. You can just call me whatever you want." I wink at him, the alcohol flowing through me, warming my skin. Another server comes by and offers us two more shots, Kitty keeping them coming like I had asked.

"You're a brave little thing, aren't you?" he teases, shooting the drink in one swallow. "I could be a serial killer or something."

I hold my shot up. "So could I."

I tip the small glass back, feeling the blue liquid burning down my throat to heat up my stomach. The lights blur around me, and laughter escapes my mouth. I can't control it. Whatever is in these shots is hitting me harder than usual.

"Fair point. So let's make a pact. If either of us is a serial killer, we'll take the night off. Let's just have some fun. What do you say?" Leandro smiles, his dark brown eyes reflecting the colorful lights. Rainbow haze falls over us, and I bob my head, giggling as I take his hand.

"I say yes. A night off sounds amazing." I flick my attention to the VIP. It could be the last night off I ever get.

I guess I have to live in the now.

Leandro twirls me around and envelops me in his arms, tugging me back to press his lips to mine. "Good, beautiful. Let's get out of here."

"You know, I've lived in LA all my life and have never been here." I weave between two glowing lampposts out of dozens outside the Los Angeles County Museum of Arts. Starbursts crowd in my vision, but I push through the intoxication. "It's incredible."

"We should come when it's open." Leandro follows behind me, his gaze drinking me in. I can't tell if he's wobbling or if it's the entire world.

I beam him a smile and trace my fingers around one of the light poles, circling it to come up behind him. Traffic lines the street in front of LACMA, and I spot tourists snapping photos from several vehicles. The Petersen Automotive Museum across the street glows red under the metallic structure, creating quite the sight, even blurry with my foggy gaze.

"Are you asking me on a date?" I ask, sliding my arms around his waist from behind. My face rests between his shoulder blades, and I inhale a soft breath of his woodsy, citrusy scent. The cologne smells familiar, but I can't place it.

"A second date." Leandro turns in my arms to face me, his easy-going smile only curling up a little. His eyes sparkle in the light, the glassiness of the alcohol affecting him as much as it does me. I feel free—like my soul is about to flutter away from my body. The edges of my vision remain shadowed, making the lights almost eerie.

I caress my hands up his taut chest and to his cheeks, pulling him toward me for another kiss. "We'll see about that. I'm not much of a dater. I can't exactly be tied down right now."

Leandro chuckles against my mouth, grazing his hand lower to the small of my back, pulling my hips against his. I feel the hardness of his arousal press against me, and I kiss him again.

"I'm not asking for anything serious, beautiful. I just want to take you out, feed you, and do whatever you want. You know, a good time." Leandro hums against my lips, brushing his mouth softly to mine, inviting me to kiss him more so I don't have to respond.

My body zings, a cooling sensation crawling from my stomach and up my arms. It also travels down my legs and to my toes. I wobble on my feet as exhaustion threatens to send me to the ground. It's as if the intoxication of the alcohol intensifies the longer I stand here with Leandro. Or maybe I'm drunk on his affection. Either way, I'm turning into a hot mess.

I ease away first, blinking my eyes. Leandro grips the lamppost, stabilizing himself. I'm not the only one now feeling off. I can see it in his shifting eyes. He rolls his shoulders and composes himself, offering me another smile. But this one's different. Something else lines his face. Worry, maybe.

I open my mouth to ask him what's wrong, but my tongue numbs, feeling as if someone shot a burst of Novocain into it. My heart races, and I can't calm down my quick breathing no matter how hard I try.

Dread crashes over me, my sudden need to get out of here intensifying. Panic tenses my muscles. I can't focus. I can't get myself to move from Leandro's arms.

And then his eyes widen, the glowing of a glittering

lamppost above us sparking flames over his skin. I startle and pushback, my thoughts racing as shadows and lights dance around what used to be a handsome man. What the fuck?

"Stacia, what's wrong?" The voice sounds like Leandro but comes from a figure made of fire and darkness.

I hold my hands up. "Stay back. Something's wrong."

"Try to stay calm. I think we were slipped something at the bar and it's hitting us now." Leandro steps closer, and the fire and light disappear as he moves out from under the glowing lamppost. I gasp in relief and rush him, just needing to hold on to someone. To something. I don't feel so great.

"I'm sorry. I'm scared. I think I'm hallucinating." I lick my lips, touching Leandro's face, praying to the universe that he doesn't morph again.

"I know, beautiful. I'm tripping too. I promise I'll get you back to your hotel, though. Just stay close to me. When we get a car, try not to say anything. Even if things look fucked up, just remember it's not real. Focus on something. Let me see your hand." Leandro lifts my hand, inspecting the onyx and diamond ring on my index finger. "If things start to get weird or terrifying, I want you to study this ring. Count the stones. Remind yourself what you like about it. Touch it. Just focus on it."

I swallow and bob my head, squeezing my eyes shut. "Can you take me back to my hotel? I just want to get out of here."

"Yes, of course, beautiful. Anything you want. Just don't let go of me." Leandro guides me through the lamppost exhibit and toward the street. The lights mimic strobes, blurring in a light show as if I'm traveling fast.

A horn honks, startling me. Leandro pulls me closer to him until I hug his side. He manages to hold my weight, but I know he's feeling the effects of the supposed drugs that were slipped into our drinks. I should've known better. I usually only trust Kitty, but I was distracted with Leandro. This high feels different than any time I've taken something else. More intense. I feel as if I might have a heart attack at any second, my heart smashing around my chest in chaotic beats.

Leandro steadies me in place. "The car is just around the corner. Try your best to remain composed. Say hi and then let me do the talking."

Because if a driver sees that I'm far too fucked up to even comprehend what's happening, I'll be in a lot of trouble.

I open and close my mouth. "Okay—"

"What the fuck are you doing with my girl?" The familiar baritone of Christos snaps in my ears. "Get your fucking hands off her."

The world spins as Leandro twists me around, shielding me protectively. It doesn't stop Christos from charging and grabbing Leandro by the back of his suit jacket. My knees weaken, buckling on me. I don't even have a chance to reach out for anything as I fall to the ground.

"Christos!" I'm not sure if my voice even sounds out or not, but I know I'm screaming at him in my head. "Christos, stop!"

I watch through my blurry vision as Christos swings his fist, missing Leandro's face by inches. A figure stands over me, and I tilt my head up, meeting the hazel gaze of an unfamiliar man.

He reaches down and grabs my hands, hauling me to my feet. "You okay, Princess?" he asks, his voice a low murmur with a hint of an accent dancing on his words.

Shit. He's from the Looking Glass.

I try to pull away from him, but he only tightens his grip on me. "Let me go. Get your hands off me, asshole."

He obeys my command and releases me. I stumble and fall back to the ground. A small cry escapes my mouth, and I scramble back until I hit one of the lampposts. I grab it, trying to pull myself to my feet. My vision dims despite the light shining in my eyes. Fuck, I feel sick. I feel out of control. But mostly, I'm terrified.

And then I see them.

Leandro straddles Christos, punching him in the face again and again. The other guy rushes over and grabs Leandro, dragging him off. Someone hollers from a distance, and Leandro gets up and jogs to me. He lifts me in his arms, cradling me like the small child I suddenly feel like.

"Put down my girl. You're making a huge fucking mistake. You don't know who you're dealing with," Christos snaps, his voice deep and guttural.

"Fuck off. She doesn't want to be with you. I promised her I'd get her back to her hotel, and I don't break promises. So back off or I'll beat you unconscious." Leandro shifts his jacket, showing off what I think might be the hilt of a gun. Holy shit. The fight might've sobered him up more than me. I can barely process what's happening.

I'm too out of it to care.

Christos and the other guy don't come after us.

Leandro carries me toward the street and waves down our ride. I thunk against the backseat of the car and listen to him confirm the address of the hotel. I lose myself to the blurring lights.

<h1 style="text-align:right">4</h1>

What the Fuck

Stacia

Pain pulses behind my eyes, and I groan. I rub the heels of my hands into my eyes, scrubbing at my fake eyelashes. Damn. I feel like utter and complete shit. I squeeze my eyes shut, pinching my false lashes between my fingers, and peel them off.

It takes me a moment to realize that I have no clue where I am or how I got here. The last thing I remember was staring at the city lights with Leandro. I was so shaken after the confrontation with Christos, I asked him to have the driver take a detour in case he was following us. After that? I have no idea. It's fuzzy.

I sit up in the dark room, my stomach twisting with

the movement. The comforter falls away, showing off my naked body. Shit. Well, at least this went how it was expected. Too bad I can't remember much, considering how good a lay he was at the club.

"Leandro?" I whisper, my throat tight and parched.

No one responds, but I spot him sprawled next to me, hidden under the fluffy comforter. I recognize the pattern. It looks like we did make it to the Silver Screen Hotel, after all. Now that my vision adjusts to the darkness, I spot my belongings scattered across the vanity table.

I groan and stretch my arms over my head, my body feeling as if I was hit by a bus. I shimmy lower under the sheets and scoot toward Leandro, spooning him.

That's strange. He's fully dressed.

I sit up and shake his shoulder. "Hey, wake up. Leandro?" Something about his lack of reaction digs into my soul. I pinch his chin, trying to turn his head, but he doesn't budge.

I recoil at his cold skin. There's no way he can be freezing in the heat of the room. I straighten my back, sobering even more because of the weirdness. Grabbing his arm, I struggle to pull his stiff body over. And not stiff as in muscular. The guy feels solid. Unmovable.

"Leandro?" I ask, kneeling on the bed to better grasp his arm.

The second I turn him over, I gasp as panic erupts in my chest. Holy shit. Holy fucking shit. This isn't Leandro. I remember what he looks like. No matter how drunk or high I was, I'd never forget his handsome face and easy-going smile. How his dark brown eyes captured me in every moment, keeping my attention. This isn't even a case of alcohol vision. I met him sober and my hazy memory stops after we spent at least an hour gazing into each other's eyes. But this guy? His lifeless blue gaze stares at nothing. He's dead.

I scramble to get up, yanking the comforter with me. "What the fuck! Fuck!"

I spin on my bare feet, searching the room for signs of what happened. The desk lies on its side, and one of the framed pictures is shattered. Everything that was in my suitcase now lies scattered around the room. It definitely looks like a fight happened here, but I don't remember whatever took place. I inspect my hands, catching sight of blood under my fingernails. Fuck. It's the only word I can really process.

I can't get caught up in this bullshit.

I rush to the bathroom and look at the messed up wall where the towel rod was supposed to be, I think. I'm not exactly sure. It's been a month since I've stayed in the penthouse. Things could've changed.

I wash my hands and stare at my face in the mirror. My blue eyes shine red, completely bloodshot. Combing my hands through my knotted, deep brown hair, I try to separate the tangles. My diamond necklace must've broken off at some point, but I still wear my earrings and ring.

I rest my palms against the counter. "What the fuck happened?" I ask myself, hoping that my reflection might come to my rescue and respond.

Gathering my bravado, I tug on my bathrobe and carefully step back into the expansive four-bedroom suite. I make a wide circle, avoiding looking at the bed and the stranger in it, and I peek into each of the rooms and then into the living area.

I spot my phone glowing in the dark, the vibrations turning louder as I stroll closer. Reaching down, I try to grab it off the floor, but I lose my balance and land on my knees. Glass digs into my skin, sending burning pain over my legs. This is too much. My stomach twists again and I dry heave. This is worse than any hangover

I've ever had, and I know I didn't drink that much. A couple of shots would've made me loosen up. I wouldn't have been blackout drunk. And the sickness clinging to me? Something else is up.

Drugs. That's right. I remember Leandro suggesting someone slipped us something at the Looking Glass.

I flutter my eyelashes, clearing my vision the best I can. It's as if my gaze has been coated with something, and it's hard for me to see through. It doesn't help that I just want to go back to sleep. Maybe if I do, I'll realize that none of this is real. Maybe I'm having one hell of a nightmare.

My phone buzzes again, and I look at the screen.

Unknown: Bitch, I hope you're okay. I've been banned from communication with you until you turn yourself in to the King's Court. I'm using a stranger's phone, so don't reply back. If someone finds out that I broke the rules, they'll punish me. Love you, bitch. Do the right thing. Christos isn't worth it.

Of course, my society chapter would bar communication with me. I fucked up. I really fucked up.

It takes everything in me not to call Bianca, but I can't do that to her. It was my mistake, and she shouldn't have to pay for it. But I shouldn't have to pay for it either. It was so fucked up of Christos to put me in this position. The bastard.

I stare at my phone for another couple minutes, trying to think of what to do. Most people would call the police, but what would I say? I just woke up naked next to a dead man? That'll cause all sorts of suspicion. It's in our chapter's bylaws to contact His Majesty first. Unfortunately, that's my dad. And I'm in a shit ton of trouble.

Fuck my life.

Maybe I can get someone else to take pity on me. Someone who can talk my dad down.

I just hope Talon answers and doesn't immediately turn me in for punishment. He's not as hard as my dad, and at least he likes me a little bit. I can't imagine he'd be on Daddy's side if he found out why I ran out during a mandatory meeting, breaking protocol and denying participating in what is supposed to be an honor with the White Queen's Kiss.

I squeeze my eyes shut, listening to the phone ring and ring.

Voicemail.

Goddamn it.

My heart crashes into my stomach with my desperation. I don't know what I was expecting, calling Talon. Of course, he wouldn't answer. Why would he? Like Bianca said, I've been barred from communication until I face the aftermath of my rash decision.

My phone buzzes in my hand, startling me. I stare at the unfamiliar number. A frown pinches my brow, and I watch my screen flash for almost a minute. I hate not knowing who's on the other line. I hate talking on the phone altogether and prefer to text message.

I exhale a long breath and accept the call without saying anything.

"Stacia, it's me." Talon's familiar base tone murmurs through the line, sending my heart fluttering. "You're in a hell of a lot of trouble, wild child. What the fuck was last night about? You know you shouldn't be calling me—"

A sob escapes my lips, cutting off his words. "I'm sorry. I'm so, so sorry, birdie. I didn't know who else to call."

"Are you hurt?" Talon asks, his tone changing, growing softer. "Where are you? I'll come and get you."

I hiccup and wipe my arm across my face. "At the

penthouse. I don't know what happened last night. I had a drink with a guy, and I...I don't know. I can't remember much after leaving the Looking Glass. I feel like shit." I know I should tell him about the dead man in my bed, but I'm afraid to say the words out loud. If I say them out loud, they'll be real. I don't want to risk him denying me and leaving me to fend for myself. Or worse. What if he turns me in to the police as part of my punishment on behalf of my dad?

"Fuck. I'm on my way," Talon says.

"Please, don't tell Daddy. He's already pissed off." I sniffle and say a silent prayer, hoping he gives into my pleas.

Talon groans. "We'll discuss things when I get there. Just hang tight. I'm coming."

Except I feel as if I'm free falling with nothing to grab onto.

My life crashes around me before my eyes. Fucking Christos. This is his fault.

He should be the one to pay for this. Not me.

If only life could be so easy.

A masked man towers over me, holding a knife. My heart races as I stare into familiar eyes I can't place. I knew I'd have to pay the consequences for my insubordination, but I was hoping to put it off a little longer.

"You're an embarrassment to our chapter, Princess. It has been voted that you are no longer worthy." An indistinguishable voice booms through the dark room. Shadowy figures chant incoherently, and I scramble back.

"Please, I'll do anything. I'm so sorry. Please." Tears burn in my eyes, and I slap my hands to the icy floor. "Just give me another chance."

"There are no second chances, Princess. Now, stand up and face me with dignity or die in shame." The figure glides forward, seeming not to touch his feet to the floor.

I gasp and push back, feeling around for something, anything, to protect myself. My hand slides across a cool and sticky substance, and I cry out as blood coats my fingers. A bright light flashes on, the spotlight shining next to me. My body freezes. I can't believe what I see. Bianca sprawls out dead beside me, blood coating her skin. What the fuck?

"Bianca!" I scream, twisting to grab onto the front of her dress. "Bianca, no!"

"This is your fault, Princess. She wouldn't have had

to face the same punishment as you had she made better choices. You're both disgusting, shameful heirs." The masked man stands over me, threatening me without actually proceeding. I don't know what he's waiting for. Maybe he's trying to torture me with anticipation.

But I'm no longer scared.

I'm pissed off. I'm enraged. How dare he murder Bianca. All she did was text me. How did they even find out?

"Let me do the honors," a familiar voice says, striking me to the core. Christos materializes from the shadows, his handsome smile getting to me the same way it had the first time I laid eyes on him. But something wicked lingers in his gaze. He's not the same man I remember.

He's worse. Much, much worse.

And it looks like I'm about to die by his hands.

I guess I should've known this would always be my fate.

Hands lock into my hair and yank me to my feet. I reach up and grip Christos's wrist. His golden, light brown eyes sweep across my face and down to my lips. I bite my cheek to stop from reacting. I won't give him the satisfaction. He's already ruined my life once before. He will not take pleasure in ending it now.

I spit in his face.

Christos's eyes glow bright red, startling me. This is impossible.

The room heats up, and I thrash, trying to break free. More red eyes decorate the room, illuminating from within the shadows, and I watch as a wicked smile stretches across the wall without a body, glowing like the Cheshire cat.

A loud banging resonates through the air. It distracts Christos enough that I can swing my leg out. I kick him in the dick hard enough to get him to let me go. I fall from his hold, bracing to hit the floor. But it doesn't come. The world spins around me, the shadows and light blending, and I scream out. There's nothing to hold onto. There's no world around me.

I free-fall through an abyss.

I manage to flip over and stare beneath me. At least I think I'm facing down. Smoke wafts below, and I spot another pair of glowing red eyes.

And then I see a face.

It's my own.

Blood covers my skin, and I scream without making a noise. My reflection morphs below me, growing bigger and bigger until my mouth is just a gaping hole. My teeth sharpen and I stare in shock at the monstrous figure I turn into.

I can't do anything as I dive down, closer and closer...

I jolt upright, my body thrashing as my nightmare releases me. Gasping, I scrub my face, trying to orient myself. I must've fallen asleep again. I still feel hungover. Sick. My head spins, and my heart doesn't stop racing. I want nothing more than to curl up on the carpet.

"Stacia! Open up! Don't make me break down this mother fucking door." Talon's voice rises with the thud of his fist pounding the door.

Groaning, I push to my feet, wobbling. Talon bangs excessively, harder and faster. He might actually break down the door.

"Coming," I croak, my voice hoarse with sleep.

I stare through the peephole, making sure he's alone. Talon's silhouette fills the space outside my door. A rush of relief washes through me, and I fling it open. He doesn't get a chance to brace himself before I jump at him, forcing him to hug me. He doesn't push me back or anything, just takes a step forward and closes the door. It's as if my mind and body know he's safe. He'll protect me. He'll help.

"I'm so glad you're here," I murmur. Trembles shake through me. "I was scared you wouldn't show."

"Of fucking course I'd come. Now, be honest with me, wild child. What am I dealing with? You can tell me anything. Do you think you were assaulted?" Talon's voice deepens with his question, and I feel his worry as if it's my own. It's one of those things. Always assume the worst, because the worst tends to happen a lot around here.

"I don't think so, but I can't be sure. I woke up naked next to..." I wave my hand toward the master suite in the penthouse.

Talon's eyebrows furrow as he follows my line of sight. "He's still here? I'm going to kill him."

I laugh in exasperation, but not because it's funny. It's the only response my body knows how to give to his threat. My voice rises and pitch, sounding maniacal. "You can't kill someone who's already dead." I sob and shake, my admission striking me on a soul-deep level.

Talon sets me on my feet and gives me a once over, realizing I'm only wearing a robe. Taking a step back, he blinks his eyes as if he's trying to process what I had just said. He scrubs the back of his neck and turns away. "Stacia, what do you mean he's already dead? You're fucking with me, right?"

I lick my trembling bottom lip, sucking it between my teeth. Shaking my head, I answer him with silence.

Swinging his arm, Talon punches the wall, leaving a crater behind. "Fuck."

"I don't even know who he is. He's not the man I left with last night. Things are so fuzzy." I take a step closer to Talon and touch his arm. "If you don't want to help me or if you want to call the police—"

"No. I'm absolutely helping you. We can't get the damn police involved. There's no need to if we can cover this shit up. It's less work and cheaper." Because there are members of the police department and local government that our chapter buys off. You can get away with a lot if you have enough money.

"I'm sorry," I say, knowing that Talon doesn't deserve this kind of shit. "I would've called my dad, but...you know."

"He's not happy with you, Stacia. You're going to have to deal with it, you know. I don't understand what got in your head, but I'm sure you had a reason. I hope it was a good one to risk your stance and freedom." Talon meets my gaze expectantly, silently asking for me to explain myself without demanding it.

"Christos is my ex. He used me as part of his initiation into his chapter without letting me know and without my consent. They have a video." I lift and drop my shoulders, trying not to relive the humiliation. "I didn't want to be a part of his Welcome Ceremony. There was no way I was going to give him even an ounce of respect or my attention."

Talon stiffens, curling his fingers into fists. "Does your father know?"

I purse my lips, nodding my head. "Yes. He accepted the same collateral as part of my initiation into the Looking Glass chapter, so I didn't have to do anything else."

Some would think it was lucky of me, but I still cringe thinking about it. There were options and my decision was stolen from me. Daddy thought I got off easy. Maybe it's why he didn't think things through. He doesn't care about how I feel and will probably holler at me to get over myself since it was years ago.

"And he still insisted you welcome the bastard?" The question isn't intended for me. He's more likely speaking his thoughts out loud.

"None of that matters right now." I take his hand

and tug him closer, just wanting him to help me. I don't want to think about the body anymore or what could've happened.

He shakes his head. "It does matter, but you're right. Let's see what's going—"

A loud knock on the door startles me, and I hear a woman call out, "Ms. Saint Germaine, room service."

I grimace and look at Talon.

He brings his finger to his lips, silently asking me to be quiet.

"I have orders to leave it on the table if you don't answer." The woman says it for security reasons, obliging by whatever instructions she was given.

Talon growls, storms to the door, and opens it. "We canceled that," he lies, filling the frame.

The woman peeks around him, her eyes darting from mine and then behind me, where the room lies in shambles.

Fuck.

"Yes, sir. I'm so sorry for the mistake." She remains professional because she's afraid. I can tell. The moment she gets back downstairs, she's going to alert the management, who might alert the police.

Talon knows it too, because he slams the door in her

face. "Grab what you can. We need to go. I'll see if I can find an ID."

"Are you sure we should go? It'll make me look guilty." I bounce on my feet.

Talon dips his chin in agreement and nudges me forward. "You damn well might be guilty, wild child. Now pack your fucking bag."

5

The Bodyguard

Stacia

"**Y**ou need to shower. Make sure there isn't a chance in hell that the fucker's DNA is on you." Talon hands me a stack of towels, far more than I need. "Inspect yourself for bruising. I'm calling in a friend to draw some of your blood. I want to check for drugs."

Drugs. That's right. Leandro mentioned the possibility.

I wish my head would catch up. I hate knowing that I'm missing chunks of time.

Clutching the sink, I remain still, facing the mirror. Talon treating me like a criminal makes me feel like one too. I don't want to delve into anything more until we have concrete answers. The phrase 'Don't answer any questions without a lawyer' comes to mind, even if Talon isn't a cop. Does he truly think I'm capable of murder? I've heard the stories about how people get initiated on the King's Court and the price they pay, but I had never been faced with testing my morality for loyalty.

"When we're done, I want you to go about your day as if nothing happened." Talon reaches out and grasps my shoulder. "It's going to be okay. I got you, wild child." Without another word, Talon closes the bathroom door.

I hover in front of the fogging mirror. Steam fills the air, dampening my skin. I know I should hurry, but I'm desperate for a moment to just catch my bearings and breathe. Closing my eyes, I rest my palms on the cool counter, trying to imagine the events of last night. Only bits and pieces surface—Leandro's handsome face and beautiful dark brown eyes, how amazing it felt fucking him in the storage closet, but then I remember the blurry glow of the lampposts at LACMA...and Christos. Fuck. He was there. He had followed me with another guy.

Oh, God. Was the other guy the dead man in my bed?

The only way to be certain is to look at the evidence that Talon collected, but he won't let me see it until I've cleaned up.

So I gather myself together and hop in the shower, washing away the grossness of the last few hours. Tears burn my eyes. The hot water washes them away along with my remaining makeup. I scrub my hair and wash it three times with shampoo before I slather conditioner in it. I take extra care to scrub my hands and fingernails before moving to the rest of me before finishing with my feet and toes. I don't exit the shower until my skin turns pink from scrubbing, and even then, I linger a few minutes more until my skin prunes.

After getting out of the shower, I swipe my hand across the foggy mirror and stare at my reflection. I look like shit. Even worse than before. My puffy eyes ring with mascara residue, and I take a moment to scrub it off the best I can. Talon doesn't have everything I need, but it is what it is. I brush my teeth with the travel kit he gave me, and finally, I dress in his too big T-shirt and boxers. They smell fresh like lavender, and I use the fragrance to push myself forward.

Voices murmur through the bathroom door, and I crack it open just enough to see the back of a man speaking with Talon. The man rubs the back of his neck, messing with his dark hair. Veins flex in his arms, cording along his well-defined, bulging muscles. Dressed in a tight shirt and jeans, the man wears casual well. What am I thinking? I shouldn't be checking out a stranger.

Talon catches my gaze from over the man's shoulder, slowly giving me a once-over. I've been caught. He lifts a brow and narrows his eyes, his jealousy flaring despite the situation. My distracting Talon doesn't go unnoticed because the man shifts and turns to peek over his shoulder at what has stolen Talon's attention.

The man's jaw slackens as his mouth falls open. I blink a few times at the realization. I've been thinking about those dark brown eyes all morning, and I can't believe they stare at me now—in shock instead of desire. Maybe even a blip of fear. I guess a one-night stand might've been too much to ask the universe for. I didn't expect to ever see him again.

"Leandro? Holy shit. You're friends with Talon?" I hug my arms over my chest, wishing I had known because I would've tried harder not to look like complete shit. Talon has seen me without makeup and trashed a dozen times, but everyone else? The only other people beside him to have seen me in this hot mess state are my parents and Bianca. And Christos.

"Wait. You know each other?" Talon steps past Leandro and moves between us. I can't tell if he's trying to block me or if he's trying to get in Leandro's way.

"Not really." Leandro tightens his jaw.

"We met last night at the Looking Glass," I say at the same time Leandro speaks.

Talon smacks Leandro on the shoulder. "You weren't supposed to introduce yourself to her until after our meeting, you asshole. You didn't even know if you had the job."

"She never gave me her name. I didn't know she was the client. That's why I canceled our meeting. She's the one I escorted back to the hotel. We were slipped Juggernauts into our shots." Leandro pulls at his shirt collar and rolls his shoulders. "I told you that. It was a shitshow."

The surprise melts off Talon's face, morphing into anger. The series of fine lines deepen around his eyes and furrow his forehead. I don't even have a chance to react before Talon swings his fist and punches Leandro in the jaw hard enough to knock him back.

Talon snatches Leandro again, stopping him from falling. He smashes him to the wall and locks his fingers around his throat. "She's the woman you were with? What the fuck? You better not have touched her. I will cut off your fucking—"

"Talon!" I screech. "Stop!"

He jerks his attention to me. "Did he fuck you?"

"That's none of your goddamn business," I snap, my hands trembling with his wild emotions. "You have no right to ask. You don't own me."

Leandro growls deep in his throat, managing to sock Talon in his stomach, getting him to release him. Instead of tackling Talon, Leandro put space between them, raising his hands in surrender.

"I didn't fuck her," Leandro flat out lies, his eyes catching mine, silently begging me to follow along.

I feel bad for him, so I close the space to Talon and wrap my arm around him. "It's none of his business," I repeat, resting my chin on Talon's shoulder. "But he's telling the truth. He didn't fuck me." Because I totally seduced him.

"We had a couple drinks," Leandro adds, not breaking eye contact with me. "She asked me if I wanted to get out of there, and I didn't want to say no. You know I hate the idea of buying a lady a drink and not ensuring she gets where she's going safely. Too many fucking pervs."

I didn't know I could find Leandro even more attractive.

"And then what?" Talon calms down enough to listen instead of trying to throw another round of punches. He probably realized that he can interrogate Leandro to see if he knows anything about the dead guy.

"We stopped at LACMA for a bit, but things get fuzzy from there. It was then I realized something wasn't right and suspected we were drugged. I helped her get back to her hotel and made sure she was safe. That's when I met up with you. You saw me. Did I look like I got fucking laid?" Leandro flares his nostrils, refusing to look at me now.

It takes everything in me not to react. Because I need to do a better job at ensuring a fuck session is evident for days.

What. Am. I. Thinking?

Talon studies Leandro without responding for a minute. He flicks his attention to me and back to him before flicking his neck. "You have a fucking hickey."

I guess that works...except I don't want him questioning it even more.

"So what?" Leandro sighs and shakes his head. "Don't you think you should've told me you were involved with my potential client?"

I hate how they argue about me as if I'm not here. I pinch Talon's side, trying to redirect him again. He stiffens under my touch, but I don't back off.

"Who I'm with is none of your business, Talon. What happened at the Looking Glass doesn't even matter. You should be asking him about the fucking dead guy." Because I thought it was Leandro, but he's standing in front of us. What if he was the killer?

As if Talon can read my thoughts, he slams his fist to the wall beside Leandro's head. "Was it you? If you were so fucked up, maybe you did it. Stacia isn't capable of murder. I've known her for years, and she can't even kill a fucking bug. I doubt some drugs would've changed that about her."

"You can't be certain," Leandro says, remaining frozen against the wall. "She has some spitfire in her. I went back to my room immediately. You can confirm it with the hotel. We even talked on the phone, remember? I don't know anything about a dead guy. What does he look like? Maybe it was her boyfriend. We had a confrontation. He was a real possessive ass."

My heart sinks into my stomach at the mention of Christos. "I don't have a boyfriend. He's an ex and a creep."

"Then I made the right call not to let you go with him, beautiful. But it's also why I left you at your hotel. I didn't need that kind of drama. Sorry." Leandro shrugs his shoulders, and I inwardly cringe.

Fucking Christos. Why can't he just remain out of my life instead of ruining all potential future boyfriends for me? But by the way Talon glowers at Leandro, I'm pretty sure he's never going to call me.

"Goddamn it, Leandro. You're so damn lucky. She is off-limits from now on. And because I dragged your ass into this mess, you're hired. She's going to need one helluva bodyguard, and you're the one man I trust." Talon drops his hands and finally puts space between himself and Leandro.

He automatically comes to my side and grasps my shoulder, guiding me a couple extra feet away. My body remains on autopilot, and I don't try to shrug from him despite being annoyed. It's hard for me to process what's happening. He was in charge of hiring me a bodyguard? He didn't even tell me. He had plenty of time to do so yesterday. Daddy never told me either. What pisses me off even more is that I didn't get a choice. I can't have this man as my bodyguard. I fucked him in a storage closet last night.

"I know you're about to argue with me, Stacia, but save your breath. You're in serious trouble. Not just with the Looking Glass. You're in trouble with your family and possibly soon to be with the police. If you want to save your ass, you better let me handle things. You obviously hit it off with Leandro, and I know you're going to try to rebel because I'm telling you who you can and can't be with, but that's just how it's going to be for now. Do you understand?" Talon keeps his voice low, the rumble tickling the hair over my ear.

Again, my body remains on autopilot, and I slowly bob my head, keeping my eyes directed at Leandro. He remains expressionless, and I wish I could listen to his thoughts. He probably thinks I'm crazy. Maybe an entitled brat. He definitely doesn't look at me the same way he had when we met last night.

It sucks. I liked him enough to fuck him, and that's going to hang over us. If he was still interested in me,

I'd ignore Talon and take advantage of his new close access as my bodyguard.

Now I'm pretty sure Leandro's going to be my cock-block to anyone else.

"Good, wild child. You've been through a lot. I care about you, and the last thing I want to see is you getting locked up. You'd never survive." Talon pulls me into his arms and hugs me.

My body finally relaxes, and I sink against him, inhaling a breath of his lavender laundry detergent along with something warmer—maybe a woodsy, smoky cologne.

"If you're going to force a new cock-block on me, you better prepare to hook up. I have needs, birdie." I exhale and pat his cheek, surprising him. "It's the least I can do for you. I know you desire me. And I'm pretty fucking sure you're going to be on Daddy's shit list when he finds out."

He chuckles and shakes his head. "I'm glad to see you're acting like yourself again. You had me worried."

Talon motions for me to sit on his leather couch. His apartment is exactly how I expected it to be. Tidy, clean, and full of art that borders on the edge of erotic. His eighty-inch TV hangs above a long stand and dozens of books of all genres line beneath it. He's always been a huge reader, and once even read what he described as wolf shifter porn for me because I said how much I loved it.

"All right, Leandro. Get your kit. I want you to run some blood panels on Stacia. I need to verify what she was given even if you think you know. You were both lucky. I've heard some fucked up shit about Juggernaut. I want to find out who the fuck slipped it into your drink." Talon wipes his hands down his face and rolls his shoulders as if the thought bothers him. And I know it does. He's always been anti-anything fun when it comes to drugs and alcohol.

"It's probably that bartender. What was her name, Stacia? Kat?" Leandro picks up his bag from where he left it by the door and saunters to the couch beside me. He sets it on top of the coffee table and opens it up, pulling out some medical supplies including a syringe.

What the fuck? What kind of bodyguard knows how to do this?

"It was Kitty, and she wouldn't risk her job or life like that. I'm a St. Germaine." I shift on the couch nervously, feeling queasy. I don't do needles well. When I was tattooed with our chapter's mark, I passed out.

I'm lucky that it didn't mess up the tattoo artist when she was outlining the heart key on my arm above my wrist.

"Then it was someone who has it out for you or your family," Leandro says, tying a band around my arm before putting a sand-filled ball in my hand to grip.

"There was a new server I didn't recognize." I bounce my bare feet, trying not to watch Leandro yet unable to look away.

Sucking in a short breath through my teeth, I throw myself back on the couch. Even just looking at the needle sends me reeling. Leandro quickly stands up and looks down on me, touching the back of his warm hand to my forehead. His dark chocolate eyes study mine, and I press my lips together.

"Why don't you lay back and close your eyes. I don't want you falling off the couch." Leandro stacks the pillows and pats his hand to them. "It'll take only a minute."

I just stare without moving.

"Come on, Stacia. I got you." Talon tosses the pillows to the floor and plops down beside me. He shifts me on the couch until I can rest my head on his lap. "This is exactly how I know Stacia didn't do it." He waves his hand at Leandro. "She passes out at even the thought of needles or blood. And there's no damn way she's strong enough to choke someone out. That guy experienced both things. Someone shot him up with something and then suffocated him to death." He combs my hair away and looks at me with his blue eyes. His dark blond hair hangs over his forehead, sweeping with his movements. "Isn't that right, wild child? You might have a reputation, but you are sweet as sugar. Now, keep your eyes on me. I'll get you through this."

He grabs my chin, not letting me look as he motions for Leandro to continue. My heart raps against my ribcage and sweat prickles on my forehead. I'm going to be sick. I know it.

"That's a good girl. Keep looking at me. You're doing excellent." Talon smears a tear off my cheek with the pad of his thumb. "He's almost done."

Shadows edge my vision and Talon disappears as darkness clings to me for an unknown amount of time. His warm touch brings me back, and I glare at him. His handsome face lights with a smile, and he sits me up, holding a glass of orange juice to my mouth.

"You're getting better," he says, making me take a sip. "You didn't throw up this time."

I groan and flick him. "Shut up and stop treating me like a child."

He clears his throat. "You're obviously not one, but I need to keep thinking that way, wild child. You're too damn lovable for your own good."

"You love me?" I tease, feeling a lot better already. "I knew it. We'll be banging in no time."

Leandro coughs and sets down a couple of things on the table, the clattering sound drawing my attention away from Talon's smile. Shit. I have to be careful about what I say in front of him. I'm sure he's going to be thinking about fucking me all the time. "I will get these to my contact ASAP. Do you need anything else before I go out? As soon as I get this handled, I'll start my shift."

Talon eases me off him and back on the couch. "Did you do as I ask and check yourself for injuries? Leandro can take care of mostly anything."

"I just have a couple bruises, but I'm fine." I motion toward my knees.

"That's from your fall last night. Have her ice them," Leandro says, still not looking at me or speaking to me. "Call me if you need anything."

A wave of wild emotions crashes over me, and I

watch in silence as Leandro leaves the apartment with his bag. I don't know how to think or feel about any of this. I don't know why I'm so torn by the fact that Talon arranged a new bodyguard for me. My dad might've ordered him to, but I just don't know. That's not part of his job as a business partner. I don't want to ask yet either.

Talon sucks in a deep breath and heads toward his kitchen table, where I spot a bunch of things laid out. He managed to swipe a couple items from my hotel room that he thought might allow him to figure out who the dead guy is, including his phone, wallet, and the guy's jacket.

"Talon? Do you have a picture of the man? Leandro reminded me of the confrontation we had with Christos. He was with someone. I didn't get a good look at the man at the hotel because I was too scared. But m aybe...what if it was him?" I comb my fingers through my damp hair, pushing my dark strands behind my ears. I stare at the small heart key tattoo above my wrist, waiting for my feet to obey my brain's command to stand up.

"Yeah, but why don't you wait for me to get into his phone? I'll be able to identify him and save yourself the trauma of looking at the douche." Talon reaches into the bag of ice he brought with us in the ice bucket and then transferred to his freezer.

I gag at the sight of the severed fingers. I had no idea he had cut them off the man, but I know why. The man has the fingerprint option on his phone. Thank the fucking universe it wasn't facial recognition.

Whoever killed him didn't take the phone or anything else, and Talon found it near the bed and under the sheet he used to cover him. He told me to wait by the door, and that's probably when he did this.

"This is why I've always told you to use only a passcode, wild child." Talon dries off the thumb and presses it to the phone, unlocking it. He swipes through the photos and holds it up to me, showing a couple of selfies of who I guess is the dead guy. "Is this him? His name is Brian Smithson."

I gingerly shuffle closer, trying not to stare at the bag of ice with the fingers. "What would you have done if the phone was locked and needed facial recognition?" I ask instead of answering his question about if I know him from last night.

"Do you really have to ask, wild child?" Talon wags the phone in my face. "Do you recognize him? Was he with Christos? It'll be a huge problem if he was."

I drag my finger across the phone, flipping through several more photos. From what I can tell, the man looks like he might be my dad's age with gray hair and leathery skin from tanning for far too many years. He doesn't appear to come from wealth either. There's a photo of him in a rundown house with bars on the window and then another of him in a white tank top and black Dickies. He's smoking a cigarette with an ugly tattoo crawling across his chest and down his biceps. He also has some sort of vine tattoo climbing up his neck. It's definitely not the guy that was with Christos, nor is it a man I would sleep with. He looks strung out on drugs in half the pictures, with red eyes and a missing tooth.

I whip my head back-and-forth. "Definitely not the guy. I can't believe he was in bed with me." I shiver, trying my best to suppress all my panicked thoughts. What if I was too drugged and I did sleep with him? I was naked after all.

But he wasn't.

Talon must realize that I'm having a panic attack, because he cups my cheeks and gets me to focus on him. "Hey, I know what you're thinking. From what

I can tell, that guy didn't touch you. Try not to think about it."

That's easy for him to say.

My mouth quivers. "What the fuck, birdie? I hate this. I hate that I don't remember. I hate that something obviously happened. I know I didn't kill him. Why the hell was he in my room? Who did it? Fuck." The words spill from my mouth, and Talon engulfs me in another hug, squeezing me tight and rubbing his big hand down my back.

"I hate this for you, but I promise, Stacia. I will figure it out. There's no way I'll let anything happen to you. Do you understand?" Talon doesn't let me go until I stop trembling and pull myself away.

I bounce on my feet. "But my dad—"

A bang on the door startles me, and I take a couple of steps back, expecting the police to break it down.

Talon strides to the door and looks through the peephole. "Shit. It's the other transfer. I forgot I had some assignments for him. Go to my room and wait there."

I don't hesitate and run to Talon's bedroom, closing the door but not completely.

I peek through the crack as Talon opens the door for

a familiar man. It's the guy who was with Christos last night.

Something dark comes over me, and I fling Talon's bedroom door open. "You! It's fucking you!" I yell, striding forward. "You did this!"

The guy doesn't have the chance to react before Talon grabs him and puts them into a chokehold. The man only struggles for a minute before he loses consciousness.

I hope Talon makes him pay.

6

Knave

Stacia

"Hey, Knave. Wake up." Talon smacks the man's cheek and shakes him. "Esteban, get the fuck up."

Knave must be his chapter nickname.

"Do you think he did this to help Christos get back at me?" I hug my arms around me, wishing Talon had choked him to death. Twisted? Absolutely. He probably deserves it, though.

Esteban snaps his eyes open and swings at Talon. He misses him by inches. Talon grabs Esteban's wrists and twists his arms up, pinning him down.

"Pinche pendejo." Esteban bares his teeth, his beautiful hazel eyes narrowing. "Let me go." A slight accent laces his command.

"Stop fighting, or I'll knock your ass out again." Talon leans down, getting in Esteban's face.

It's enough to get Esteban to comply. His gaze darts away from Talon's as he looks at me. I glower, refusing to look away.

"Where were you last night after you and Christos confronted me?" I ask, steeling myself against my fear. I don't need Talon to do anything except keep him subdued.

"I took that asshole back to the apartment. Talked some sense into him. You have him wound up, Princess. The guy is so fucking madly in love with you that it sent him over the edge, seeing you with someone else." Esteban remains placid, though the vein in his neck bulges.

"Violence has no place in her life. He fucked up and doesn't deserve Stacia. I heard about the sex tape. No good man would betray the love of his life like that. He's not in love with her. He's possessive and angry that she wouldn't tolerate that sort of behavior. And the next time I see him, he's going to regret it." Talon slams his palm against Esteban's chest, winding him.

He gets up and holds his hand out to me. "I promise you that, wild child. I'm pissed off for you."

"Ya cállate, mejor. Solo dices puras tonterías. Don't give me that shit. He did it to protect her." Esteban sits up on his elbows, breathing deeply. "You don't understand, viejo. You had it easy when you were initiated."

Esteban's comment sets Talon off, and he swings and punches Esteban in the jaw, sending him back to the floor. I latch my fingers to Talon's shirt and yank him before he decides to knock Esteban out again. I don't want to have this conversation with either of them. I don't want to have this conversation at all.

"Talon, I know you're protective of me, but this isn't getting us anywhere. We need to figure out who the hell the dead guy is." I narrow my eyes at Esteban, who hasn't stopped staring at me. It's like he's either trying to intimidate me because of Christos or he's checking me out. I can't honestly tell at this point. Talon has him up in arms and annoyed. "He has to know. He's lying about Christos. Christos isn't madly in love with me. He wants revenge. I embarrassed him by rejecting him at the meeting."

Esteban sighs. "Who the fuck are you talking about? What dead guy?" Not many people would interrupt a conversation that doesn't involve them, especially with the way Talon looks ready to beat the shit out of Esteban. I have to give him some credit. He is fearless. Not exactly smart but brave.

"This one." Talon pulls out the dead man's phone and shows Esteban the picture. "And if I discover that you're lying to me, you'll be buried in an unmarked grave. Understand?"

Esteban snatches the phone from Talon, which I'm pretty sure risks the state of his hand. Stupid yet courageous, once again. I don't think he would just test Talon to press his luck. It's more than that. I just can't put my finger on it.

Esteban releases a rumble that reverberates through me. "¡No mames! Smithson is dead? Are you sure? I just met with the gringo yesterday."

I throw my hand out. "Of course I'm sure he's dead. I woke up next to him. Someone is trying to set me up. Who is this fucker? He's not part of our chapter. Is he part of yours?"

"Fuck no. He's a new employee of mine. A distributor His Majesty set me up with." Esteban scrubs his hand across his hair. "Did he have anything on him? He was supposed to..." He doesn't finish his comment, but I'm pretty damn sure he's talking about something illegal.

"If he had anything, it was gone when I showed up. And I know for damn sure that Stacia didn't murder this guy. She was drugged last night. Did you have something to do with it? I know you split off from your father's empire and came here to get yours up and running, asshole. It was one of the reasons your transfer was accepted. We've been trying to get a handle on the underground. You're known for your reputation, Knave." Talon takes the phone back and tucks it into his suit jacket pocket.

I stare between the two of them, trying to read their silent conversation. I've never been involved much in the illegal affairs. I'm mostly just the face for Daddy, dancing in and out of the spotlight when needed and networking with Hollywood's finest through galas, events, parties, and more. I've always kept the attention off things.

No one cares about a boring businessman in Hollywood—not unless certain actions and behaviors come to light—so I take the honor and steal the spotlight. I'm the party girl who gets around. The one who decorates the covers of most tabloids. I also have so many connections among celebrities that all the newcomers want a piece of me. And sometimes, I give them a taste.

"I never approved of the distribution of any drugs in the club last night. You damn well know I wouldn't risk shit on a meeting night. I had strict orders about that. If Stacia was slipped something, it wasn't involving my business. It had to come from someone else. Do you know what it was?" Esteban locks me in his gaze, refusing to look away. I don't back down from his challenge either. "Are you sure it wasn't the douchebag from last night trying to get into your pants, Princess? It was very reckless of you to go off with a stranger."

His comment scrapes under my skin, peeling away yet another layer of anger simmering in my soul. How dare he try to reprimand me.

I don't get the chance to react before Talon grabs my hand, lacing his fingers with mine. He holds me back before I can act. I really want to slap Esteban. I'm not usually violent, but everything weighs heavy on me. I need answers. He claims that he's not involved, but if he knows the guy, then there must be a connection.

"Leandro would never. He has an impeccable record." Talon finally offers Esteban the chance to get up, realizing he better get some space between us, because the second I'm free, I might act. He motions to the couch. "You can meet him in a bit. He's taking care of Stacia's drug test. Until then, I want you to make a few phone calls. Don't let anyone know your employee is dead. I also want you to call Christos and make sure he didn't do this. I know you said you escorted him back to his apartment, but that means nothing. He could've gone back out. It's not that hard to find where Stacia stays during the meeting days. He probably knows her alias too."

He's right about that. I never did change my alias, and I always book the penthouse as Lydia Love. It's the name Christos teased me about for sounding like a porn star. He might be right, but I prefer Talon's comment about it being the perfect name for an erotica author instead. It was kind of a joke between us.

And I hate that Christos could've used that against me. I've been through enough with him. Now he's trying to crash back into my life to ruin me all over again. But I won't allow it. I'll destroy him before he can ever take another piece of me. He's far too careless. Anything he touches shatters. Luckily for me, I know how to repair myself. I'm just not sure I could survive a second calamity by his hands.

"Christos wouldn't have done this. He knows I'd kick his ass for touching my belongings, and all my employees are just that—mine. I don't pick up random addicts from the street. I spent a lot of time building my empire, so much so that I have surpassed what mi padre built. That's why I'm here and not in Mexico City. He feared I'd take it from him. I still might." Esteban cracks his knuckles and shakes out his shoulders. The more I look at him, the more ferocity I see in his gaze. A tattoo peeks out from the collar of his dress shirt, and I can't help but imagine what the rest of it looks like. I wonder where his chapter key is.

Fuck me. I shouldn't be thinking about what's beneath his clothes, even if it is art.

"I want to be certain. It's going to hit the media in a couple of hours. Someone wanted Stacia to get caught. We need to get ahead of things." Talon turns his attention to me and gives me a once-over. "Stacia, you need to call your dad. I know you're afraid, but it'll be worse if you don't. We might be in over our heads trying to take care of this alone. Someone is fucking with one of our empires. This could be about your father and not you. You could just have been a pawn caught up in the battle."

I hate that he's right. I have done nothing wrong to be framed like this. If it wasn't Christos like Esteban swears, then it's more. Someone else. And what better way to hurt Daddy than to try to hurt me. Except whoever it is doesn't know that the only way to hurt my dad is to hurt him. I'm expendable, even as his daughter.

I scrub my hands over my face. "What do I even say? This is all too much."

Talon engulfs me in a hug, squeezing me to him as if his strength can keep me together. It might be the only thing doing so. Because I just really want to fall apart. To curl up and cry. I want to shut the world out. What did I ever do to deserve all this bullshit?

Easing away, Talon cups my cheeks, forcing me to look into his eyes. We've always had a close relationship and have flirted for years, but something about him changes in this moment. I knew he cared about me, but I can actually feel it.

"You can handle anything, wild child. Things might seem like too much, but it'll get better. Tell your dad what happened without going into the details. Tell him what to expect and ask him what he wants you to do. Do not apologize or cry if you can help it. You need to stay strong in your convictions that you were not in the wrong." Talon rubs his lips together. "Do you understand?"

I swallow and blink my eyes, forcing my tears to stay put. I can feel the weight of Esteban's stare pouring into me, but I don't give him an ounce of my attention. He's already seen me in what might be my weakest moment apart from my break-up with Christos, and I can't allow him to witness any more of that. People use that shit against you, and I don't know Esteban. All I know is that he has a ruthless reputation.

Talon turns to Esteban. "If you make a sound, I'll ensure that the King's Court believes you were in on it." Protective looks sexy as hell on Talon, and I lean forward and snuggle my face to his broad chest, inhaling a breath of his cologne.

It takes everything in me to peel myself away, and he grabs my phone from among my belongings. I have at least a dozen missed calls from acquaintances and ten more from an unknown number. It could be anyone or anything, but I choose to ignore it all. I have to be selfish in this moment. The only important thing is getting my life back together before it completely crumbles apart.

I inhale a long, slow breath and hit my dad's contact. Talon doesn't move from my side, remaining close enough for me to bask in the scent of his strength and the shadow of his power. I bet he never imagined such a moment between us, and I wonder how far it'll push him away. Because our attraction is undeniable. It's always been present, despite the imaginary steel wall he created to keep me out. I'm supposedly untouchable, after all.

The line clicks, but my dad doesn't say a word. I only know he accepted my call because of his light breathing.

Annoyance rushes through me. I don't know if he's ever been this cold, and I know it's because I disappointed him, but he disappointed me as well.

"Daddy..." I clear my throat and rub my fingers together, my anxiety through the roof and tightening my chest. I know what I should say, but it's as if I lost my voice.

Don't cry. Don't fucking cry. I chant the words over and over as I try to gather my shaking nerves.

"Daddy, someone drugged me at the club last night, and I woke up in the penthouse with a dead man beside me. I think someone is trying to set our family up. What do you want me to do?" There. I said it. I told him what happened without accepting blame or pointing out the fact that I embarrassed him last night.

I expect him to start yelling. I expect him to hang up on me. What I don't expect is for him to release a long sigh and groan.

"Stacia, are you okay? Are you hurt?" Daddy asks, his deep voice cracking with emotions I'm not used to. "Where are you now?"

"I'm..." I flick my gaze to Talon. I don't want him to get in trouble.

He nods his head, encouraging me to speak.

I clear my throat for the millionth time. "I'm at Talon's apartment. Outside. He won't open the door if he's home." It's as if my lie comes out like the truth, the words easy to say as my protectiveness toward Talon clicks on to reciprocate his toward me. Because he shouldn't have anything to do with me while I am being shunned.

"You should've come home. You know what you did last night has consequences, Stacia. I understand why you did it, but you know our ways. Some things just have to be fucking done even if you don't want to. It's the cost of our lifestyle." Again, my dad's voice cracks, and he clears it. "I'm sorry for not thinking things through more clearly. I didn't expect for him to bombard you like that. I thought he was smarter. But regardless, I want you to know that you can always come home. I'm your dad. You don't need to drag Talon into things. He hates that shit."

Talon glares and shakes his head, denying my dad's comment. We both know how he hates our relationship. I think Dad feels threatened by his business partner, and he thinks that Talon might treat me like a daughter, totally missing the fact that it's not even close to being like that. For one, Talon is hot. He's never treated me like a daughter in any way and more like a friend. Yeah, he's older—not old enough to be my dad—but that doesn't mean shit. He's nothing like my dad. Daddy would have a coronary if he knew how often I thought about banging his business partner and friend.

Or the fact that I purposely tease Talon any chance I get.

"He was closer, and I thought that you guys might've been together. You always are after a meeting." I'm not wrong. I'm actually surprised that they weren't together.

"Talon had business to handle this morning with one of the heirs," Daddy says.

I can't stop myself from looking past Talon to stare at Esteban, quietly studying me. It's hard to forget he's in the room. There's something obnoxiously loud and distracting about his presence. I don't know what it is, but I don't like it. No one should be able to hold part of my attention without my permission.

"Oh." It's all I can manage to say.

"But since you're there, I'll call him and give him permission to speak with you. I want him to bring you straight to the Looking Glass. We'll handle everything else after our emergency meeting." Daddy grumbles under his breath something I can't make out. I think he's talking to someone else. "Be prepared, Stacia. You know we have another king in town, and you've given me no choice but to make an example to show that we don't approve of disrespect. But don't worry. I'll do my best to give you a choice with your consequence. I'll see you soon, daughter."

Daddy hangs up without another word, and I clutch my stomach as my heart sinks toward my feet. Fuck my life. Fuck Christos. I have never wanted to murder someone so much until this moment. I wish it was him who was found dead in my bed. It would've been the first time I'd hoped that I was at fault.

I turn away from Talon and Esteban, shuffling toward the bathroom. I need a moment alone. I need a moment to break.

Talon follows behind me, his shadow growing on the wall. "Stacia, wait. Let me—"

His phone rings, stopping him in his tracks.

I slam the bathroom door shut in his face and lock it.

Sliding to the floor, I curl in on myself. I never expected this day to come. I never expected to want to run away from my privileged life.

Unfortunately, I can't escape the Esoteric Society. I'm in for life.

It's either accept my punishment and move on or let this life consume me until I'm nothing.

But I'm stronger than that.

I'll prove that I'm unbreakable.

I will not let them push me down.

Time to Pay

Stacia

"We have to make a quick stop. Leandro is meeting us at Bitches Brew." Talon scours over his phone as Esteban drives the both of us. We sit in the backseat, treating him like a chauffeur with me ignoring his existence. For one, there was no way I was sitting next to him upfront. And two, Talon doesn't want even a foot between us. I can't help but wonder what's going through his mind. We managed to pull it off to where Daddy doesn't know he came to me and helped me. If he were to find out, Talon would also face some horrible consequences, considering I had been shunned.

"Are you sure that's a good idea? Maybe you should let him go and cut your losses. He's not one of us. I don't know why you'd expect some nobody asshole with a temper to protect Stacia. I might be willing to take over for the right price and the same benefits." Esteban speaks up for the first time from behind the wheel.

"Shut the fuck up, Knave. You're not getting anywhere near Stacia again. I don't trust you. I don't trust that you won't team up with Christos to make things worse. I know men like you. Stuck up, entitled, pieces of shit bastards who only know a life of privilege. You don't even know what it takes to make it in the real world. Unlike you, I was chosen and initiated. I wasn't born and just expected to do as your ancestors." Talon sits up straighter in the seat beside me. "Now, turn right and head to the end of the block. Bitches Brew is down the alley on the left. You will stay in the car."

And like that, Talon ends the conversation. I'm glad for it. Esteban's insinuation annoys me. He'll probably always see me as easy. I didn't know that Leandro was to be my new bodyguard. No one told me. No one ever tells me anything. It's none of his business if I feel like fucking a stranger. He can go fuck himself. I'm so sick of it. It's always do as Daddy says, behave, be obedient, tease but don't fuck, and don't get in trouble.

Maybe this lifestyle just isn't meant for me. I've always wanted to lead and take initiative regarding my family's business empire but maybe I should just give up my ambitions. I could learn not to care. I could just be the perfect little doll and let the Esoteric Society control me as much as it controls the world.

Except I can't. If I do as much, Daddy will throw me to the wolves of the world. I'd probably end up on my knees in front of Christos. It's the place many misogynist members think women belong.

Fuck that.

Esteban parks the car at the curb but doesn't shut off the engine, leaving it idling. Talon tips his head to the side, silently motioning for me to follow him out. He peers around the empty alleyway and to the back entrance of the coffee house. He slides on sunglasses and offers his hand to me as if he needs to ensure I won't run. His actions don't feel protective in this moment. It feels dominating and controlling, like he wants Esteban to know he can't have me, but also something else. Something darker. Authoritative. I don't know exactly what Daddy said to him during their short conversation, but it was enough to turn him rigid and cold. Closed off, even.

Talon smacks the roof of Esteban's Jaguar. "Keep a lookout. Call us if you notice something suspicious."

I stroll next to Talon, clinging onto his hand even though I know he won't let go of me. We head to the back door of Bitches Brew, and he knocks lightly in quick successions, creating an unfamiliar melody.

It takes a couple of minutes until I hear the locks whine open and then spot Leandro standing on the other side of the door. The barista rushes around the small room behind him, looking like they're not used to this sort of interruption.

Leandro's eyes meet mine, and he gives me a once-over as if he can't help himself. I shift under the intensity of his gaze, wondering if we would've fucked all night long if we hadn't been drugged. He looks like he has that sort of stamina. I know I do.

I shiver at just a thought, feeling warmth build between my legs. I can't believe he's going to be my bodyguard. I kind of wish that I could have someone else just so I could pursue something with this incredibly sexy man who is now completely invested in my life. Whether or not he wants to be is the question.

Leandro turns his gaze away and pulls an envelope from his jacket. He hands it to Talon. "These are the test results. I won't get anything from the DNA swabs for a few more days." Because even though I washed my hands and took a shower, Leandro was still able to scrape a tiny bit of blood from under my long and manicured nails. It made Talon swear, because he thought that I'd gotten everything until Leandro suggested running it in case.

"You're a good man." Talon offers Leandro a hand-shake. "We'll be in touch in a couple of hours. I have some business to take care of, and I'll be taking Stacia with me. I'd like you to keep an ear out at the hotel and with the local PD. I'm sure word will get out soon. Be ready to get out of here. I want you to pack Stacia a bag as well."

I jerk my attention to Talon. "What?"

"Would you prefer to get picked up and detained? You'll be considered the prime suspect. They'll ar-rest you first before even considering other options." Talon tightens his fingers around mine.

I hate that he's right, but the thought makes me uneasy. I'll be a fugitive. What if we can't find out the truth and I face even worse consequences? My heart flutters in panic. The Esoteric Society will go to great lengths to protect their own, but can I live my life like that? I'm innocent...I think.

"Consider it a vacation. You could use the time away from the spotlight. Settle your wild ass down." Talon squeezes my shoulder. "This is a good thing. Promise."

"I'll kick you in the dick if you're lying, birdie. I won't kiss it after either." I narrow my eyes at him, remaining straight-faced when all I want to do is laugh and cry at once.

"Jesus. She really is something, isn't she?" Leandro comments, keeping his voice low.

I glower at him, getting him to step back.

Talon bellows a laugh and whacks Leandro upside the head with the envelope. "Which is why you're the man for the job. She'll eat anyone else alive."

Heat warms my chest, crawling up my throat to settle in my cheeks. Nothing about this situation is amusing, but somehow, Talon still manages to find the light in the darkness of my collapsing world.

Talon doesn't give me long to think about things. He shakes Leandro's hand again and guides me back to the car. Before we rejoin Esteban, Talon rips open the envelope and looks over everything. He doesn't say anything as he reads, keeping it just out of view from me. His stern expression deepens, his forehead wrinkling with his rising anger. It's palatable enough for me to feel, and I inch away from him. It's not directed at me, but even just this close vicinity makes me uncomfortable. He's usually composed, so whatever he just learned must be bad. Really fucking bad.

"So what is it?" I ask, shifting on my feet.

Talon doesn't look at me, turning toward Esteban's Jaguar. "It's nothing to concern yourself over, Stacia. It's what I expected, and I will handle it from here."

He's gotta be shitting me. He can't just expect me to drop it. I was the one who was fucking drugged. It's my life on the line. Not his. He has no right to withhold information from me.

"Talon," I snap, trying to grab the papers from him.

He spins out of my reach and straightens his shoulders, squaring his body. "I said I'd handle it. Now get in the fucking car. You don't want to be late. It'll only make things worse."

And like that, he shuts me up. I'm irritated but lashing out anymore isn't going to change things. Talon is completely immune to any sort of arguing. He is set in his convictions. What he says goes. It's kind of like with my dad.

But it doesn't mean he won't feel the rage he ignited in me.

"Fucking ass," I mutter, ignoring his opening my door. I strut around the car, acting petty as hell, and I slide into the passenger seat next to Esteban.

I don't stare at the drug lord and sit back, crossing my arms over my chest. The raging emotions within this vehicle are thick enough to stab with a blade, but no one addresses it. Talon knows better. So does Esteban.

I'll just get to simmer in silence, hoping that I don't explode.

I need to get my shit together.

I need to steel myself toward whatever consequences that'll come my way.

Talon smacks the seat, startling me. "Head to the Looking Glass. If you're even a minute late, I'm holding you responsible."

Esteban tightens his fingers around the steering wheel and stomps the throttle, peeling away from the curb. A few people honk their horns as he cuts them off, heading onto the main street that'll take us to the night club. I slouch and stare out the window as the world blurs by. I feel sick to my stomach. I know it's everything adding up.

I hate Christos. This is all his fault. I will make him pay for this. I will not be the only one punished.

At least, that's what I have to tell myself.

Because men like him never get held responsible. He never holds himself accountable and still doesn't think that what he did to me was that bad. Apparently, he was 'doing me a favor.' He stole my right to decide about what kind collateral I'd give for the initiation I'd go through. Filming us having sex and handing it over to his chapter king without my consent messed me up. What was worse was that he was pissed off at me for not seeing things his way. He stalked and harassed me for months, refusing to believe that we were over. But then, one day, he just disappeared and relocated.

If only he stayed gone.

"Come on, wild child. We're here." Talon squeezes my elbow from the backseat.

I hadn't realized Esteban parked in the underground parking structure near the Looking Glass. I usually head through the main entrance from the street, allowing the paparazzi to always snap my picture, but this is different. I'm arriving as someone shunned.

I mindlessly stroll beside Talon with Esteban behind us, remaining utterly silent. I train my gaze toward the floor, refusing to look at anything or anyone. It's the only thing restraining the panic threatening to explode from my chest.

The scent of burning candles permeates the air. Esteban cuts off from us, vanishing into the shadows where dozens of people linger in wait. Talon presses his hand to the small of my back, forcing me to keep moving even though all I want to do is turn around and run. I thought this would be better than dealing with the cops, but I was wrong. I don't know what I was thinking. This is so much worse. Just being under the silent scrutiny and not knowing what's about to happen to me leaves me on the edge of losing my mind.

And then I see him.

Christos stands off to the side, right near the altar, the glow of candlelight showing off the fact that he props his mask on his forehead while everyone else remains obscured.

"Executioner, please prepare the Princess. I'll not be overseeing her punishment due to my ties, so you'll address His Majesty of the Rabbit Hole." My dad's voice bellows out, echoing across the spacious meeting room. I thought William would have returned to his chapter, but I guess he would want to stay to ensure my punishment for disrespecting an heir.

"Yes, Your Majesty," Talon says, deepening his voice. As my dad's business partner, Talon handles most of Daddy's dirty work and oversees the individual members while Daddy overlooks the entire chapter.

Talon pushes his fingers deeper into my back, nudging me to walk forward. My hands tremble, my body turning cold the closer I get to where the King's chamber is. I don't know exactly what Talon has to prepare me for, but whatever it is, it can't be good. He might take away my allowance in front of everyone, stealing away everything I need to survive. I could be forced into taking some shady ass job like a drug mule or madame of one of the sex clubs. I could be put on lockdown and forced to be a servant in one of the chapters. William could even demand I get transferred for a while.

"Princess, heir to His Majesty of the Looking Glass. You've been judged as disrespectful toward our traditions within the Esoteric Society. Because of your actions, you will stand before your chapter and not with them while the meeting is in session. Your discrepancies deem you undeserving of our ceremonial robes until you understand your place." William's voice booms from the doorway of Daddy's chambers as he enters the large room. "And to gain such awareness, you have to face the consequences of your actions. You will not have the luxury of private reprimand. However, because of your good record and previous obedience, I will allow you to pick your punishment from a short list I have found suitable."

What the actual fuck?

Talon growls under his breath, the sound vibrating against the back of my head as he stands close enough to touch. "You don't have to strip her to make a point."

"It's part of the punishment. She must bear the consequences of her disobedience. She does not look ashamed of her actions, and she needs to be humiliated," William snaps, smacking an ornate, ceremonial cane to the floor, one different from my dad's.

"Executioner, do your job and listen to His Majesty." Daddy speaks up from his spot near the altar, finally coming into view. "Princess, do as you're told. You cannot afford not to. Just be grateful that you aren't banished completely. Now strip. Bare yourself to the court and accept the consequences of your actions. This is your time of judgment."

I'm going to be sick.

I can't believe this is happening. I can't believe my dad is going along with this.

He turns away, his body language as unreadable as the mask he wears to hide his emotions. The coward. He won't stand up for me when I need him. No one will. Instead, he hides so he doesn't have to bear witness to me, because he can't leave the room. This is disgusting.

"If you don't strip, the Executioner will do it for you. And if he has to do that, you will face my list of consequences instead of making your decision." William hits his cane down again. "Get to it. We have dire matters to discuss, if I'm not mistaken. We can't move on until this is complete."

I can't decide what's worse. Stripping in front of people I have been around and have entrusted my life to for years or landing in prison. I'd have to strip bare there too. This is only for a meeting. I can handle it. I wear skimpy clothes all the time.

But what I wear is my choice. This, however, is not. I know there are some pervs among our chapter, and they will take great satisfaction in this moment.

"Fine. I'll do it." I press my lips together and straighten my shoulders, turning my back on everyone only to face Talon. His nostrils flare as our eyes meet. He looks ready to tackle me to stop me from pulling my shirt over my head, but he crosses his arms and flexes his muscles.

I swallow and close my eyes, inhaling a deep breath as I try to push away the world. I snap my eyes open again, holding onto Talon's stare as if we're alone.

I will not give anyone the satisfaction of seeing my eyes except for him.

"I'm so sorry," he mouths, his eyes flickering in the candlelight behind the half mask.

I dip my chin a little, linking my fingers to my shirt. I pull it over my head and drop it on the floor, biting my lip as I lose myself within the beautiful blue depths of Talon's eyes.

I strip out of my pants next, my whole body shaking. I can barely stay on my feet, the weight of everyone watching digging under my skin. I'm sure some people feel pity, like Bianca, who remains hidden by her parents, watching my humiliation without argument out of fear.

Tears prickle in the corners of my eyes, and I blink.

"Everything must go," William says, stepping forward. He surprises me by whacking the backs of my legs, sending me to my knees.

This is the first time I've ever wanted the ground to open up and swallow me whole. This is horrible. So fucking humiliating. So degrading.

"Is that really necessary?" The familiar voice surprises me. Christos steps forward, pulling down his hood and removing his mask to meet my gaze. "I already told you that my rejected welcome was warranted. You don't have to do this."

"How dare you interrupt. Justice must be served. If we allow one thing to slip, more will soon tumble behind it." William stomps forward, looming over me. "Now get back in line."

Confusion washes over me. Did Christos really just stand up on my behalf? He defended me? This is all a game to him. I know it. He's trying to make his way back into my life. Maybe he thinks I'll suddenly forgive him for everything he's done to me. But that's not how this works. He made the choice to ask me to welcome him with the White Queen's Kiss, fully knowing that I'd refuse. It's too late to be a Count in shining armor when he's the one responsible.

I regret ever giving him a piece of me. He shattered it and threw it in the trash. Now he's trying to take another.

William slams his cane down again, inches from my fingers. Next time, he won't miss. He's now let the power of his position get to his head, and he will be as vile as Daddy is when it comes to everyone's obedience. Except this is different. This involves me. If I make it hard, I'll embarrass Daddy even worse.

So I reach behind me, fumble with my bra, and then unclasp it.

I close my eyes as it drops before me, baring my breasts for William to see. Silence fills the air as he drinks in the sight of me. I feel like throwing up.

"While you finish, I will give you the mercy of choosing your punishment. You can either accept a lash from my cane for every hour you chose to avoid the consequences, or you can beg for forgiveness on your knees, the only way you have proved yourself worthy to the man you wronged." William shifts his cane, tapping it to the bottom of my chin. He guides my head up.

"No," Christos says, stepping out of line again. "I'll

not make her beg for the forgiveness I don't deserve."

My chest tightens, bile rising in my throat. He had just taken the easiest consequence and tore it away from me. Because I would've chosen that. I would've sucked his fucking cock to avoid the pain of being beaten naked in front of everyone.

"You bastard!" I scream, whipping my gaze to look at him. "I don't want to be beaten."

"You'll never forgive me if I let you degrade yourself for me, Princess." Christos braves taking another step closer.

"I'll never forgive you anyways." I swipe my hand across my cheeks.

"Enough!" William hollers, swinging the cane. He smacks Christos in the chest, but Christos manages to wrap his fingers around the cane, stopping him from hitting him harder. "If you don't want to participate, then the Princess can pick someone else. This must be done. It is her punishment."

A dozen thoughts flit in my head, and I turn toward Talon, considering how pissed off my dad would be if I chose to get on my knees for him. But then I think about what could be worse for Christos than if I chose the guy who seems like he might be one of his good friends. Now that's revenge. Maybe if I show Esteban a good time, he might help me more. I have nothing left to lose. If I have to do this, at least I can take some control back and use it to my advantage. I will not let this destroy me. I will not let William think for a second that he has any real power over me. I'm stealing my power back.

"I choose Knave. He can accept my apology on the Count's behalf." I shift my gaze to where Esteban stands, wearing his robe. He cocks his head, looking from me and to Christos. They have a silent conversation. Christos doesn't want him to participate, but from the way Esteban's eyes break away and he steps forward, he'd gladly fill Christos's place. My revenge is working. I have turned the game around and Christos is now losing.

"I accept, Your Majesty. This is the kind of welcoming I'd love from such an exquisite member. Now be a good girl, mamacita. I got you." Esteban shifts his robe and grabs his junk. He went from sexy to another perv in a matter of seconds, and I consider teaching him a lesson. He's playing the part the men here want. Someone demeaning me.

I glower at William and then at the rest of the utterly

quiet room. I'm sure there's a video camera ready to record this despicable moment. But it could've been worse. I may not have gotten the choice and had been beaten instead. I've seen it. I silently cried before, watching as my dad put someone in their place.

It's different when it's me and a guest leader.

This is worse than what my dad would've done.

I crawl forward on my knees, getting closer to Esteban. He looks down at me, his face hardening. Is that regret in his eyes? Maybe. He probably liked the idea for all of a second, and now he realizes just what he's involved in. At least, I'm going to pretend that's the case.

Goosebumps prickle over my bare chest, and I reach up and run my fingers over Esteban's belt, unfastening it for him.

The crowd shifts, some of our members turning away, giving me more respect than I'm sure William believes I deserve. Others take a step closer, ready to enjoy my humiliation, probably wishing that they could've been in Esteban's position. I know for a fact that Bianca's dad would've been first in line. He's always been grossly inappropriate.

I peek up at Esteban, meeting his hazel gaze. "You

better be fucking clean or I'll risk another round of punishment to ensure you never get off again."

"I am, Princess." He closes his mouth, tightening his jaw, watching as I unzip his pants and reach into his boxer briefs, pulling his flaccid cock free. Well, at least he hasn't gotten excited over the position I'm in yet. Maybe he won't get a boner at all, but the thought of putting a limp dick in my mouth makes this a bit worse.

Especially one the size of his. He has to be at least six inches soft. I wonder exactly how big he'll be when I turn him on.

"What's the matter, Knave? You can't get it up for the pretty Princess?" This comes from one of our oldest members, a man in his nineties who should've keeled over already. Mr. Clementine owns one of the biggest production companies in Hollywood. Our chapter has done a lot for him over the years. He should've been in prison a long time ago.

"Fuck off, viejo. I prefer that my women want me and not be coerced into it like you." Esteban grinds out the words, surprising me.

His reaction is enough to give me the confidence to continue. I stroke my fingers over the length of his cock, trying my best to ignore the fact that we have an audience.

He tips his head back and closes his eyes, no longer looking at me, but I continue to stare at him. I want him to feel the weight of my anger.

I lick my lips and prepare to give him what I'm sure might be the best blow job of his life, but two hands lock on to my shoulders before a robe drapes over me.

I stiffen at Christos's familiar cologne. His figure blocks out the candlelight, shadowing over Esteban.

"I'm volunteering to accept the Princess's consequence on her behalf just like Esteban is accepting my reward on my behalf. It is in our chapter's rulebook that anyone, at any time, can trade places as part of their SOS. I'm doing this for her, proving that I did not agree with the situation. She did nothing wrong. I'm the one who is wrong and should be punished." Christos lowers himself to his knees beside me, grabbing my chin to get me to look at him. "I'm so sorry, astéri mou. I'm so fucking sorry. I know you'll never forget what I've done, but I'll never stop trying to earn your forgiveness. You don't deserve this. I do."

William doesn't argue and only slams his cane down. "Proceed and strip, Count. We run fair consequences around here." The fucker. He's full of shit, and we all know it. If I were a man, I'd have never been given the option of getting on my knees. It would've been something else. He chose these two, knowing I'd be too afraid of getting beaten. True colors look awful on a man I had respected.

Christos strips beside me, showing off his muscular body. I shouldn't still be so attracted to him after everything. My confusion leaves my mind spinning.

"Jesus Christ, Count," Esteban mutters. "You're serious? Take the cane."

"And be down for weeks? Fuck no. At least you can imagine someone else. Now suck it up. You volunteered." Christos rolls his shoulders.

"You owe me," Esteban says, training his eyes on mine.

I gather my nerve and try to get to my feet. William slams the cane down, startling me. "Princess, you'll remain where you are and learn from this experience. Now appreciate the gift given to you."

I fall back on my ass and blink. Shadows crawl across the edges of my vision. I peer around at the crowd, inching closer. The red light of a camera blinks on. Someone's filming this to use as collateral to keep us in line.

"Proceed, Count," William says, adjusting his robe.

All I can do is watch in silence.

A part of me hates this whole situation, but another part of me craves this revenge. Christos deserves this. It's time he pays.

8

Suck It

Christos

This could've been worse. It's what I have to tell myself as I stare at Esteban's cock softening before me. I don't know what I'd prefer, gagging on his hard eight-incher or having it flaccid like a thick noodle resting on my tongue.

I shift, exhaling a long breath. Is that pre-cum? Shit. A drop gleams from his tip. Cringing, I drag my finger over it, swiping it with the pad of my thumb. This is bad enough as it is.

I flick my gaze to Stacia, wishing she'd look at me, but her eyes remain glued to Esteban. She smirks at him, her full lips as luscious as ever. It makes me want to punch him in the balls for not protesting when she picked him, but I can't blame him. Stacia's beyond a ten. I regret every second of my decision that caused her to break-up with me.

And then I was sent away before I could win her back. It only took His Majesty to need my skills to get a ticket to the area, and shocking enough, right into the same chapter as Stacia. It's like the universe decided to give me a second chance...and fuck me over to make me work for it.

I thought I was doing the right thing when I recorded our sex tape. I'd been given two choices—betray someone I love for initiation and earn my way up the ranks or take someone's life for a spot on a King's Court. At the time, I didn't have murder in me. The others facing initiation with me had the same choice. Let's just say, not all of them made it.

The initiation and collateral was too much. It was more than they were willing to give. Someone recruited for my chapter even committed suicide to escape.

I try not to think about the past. What mattered is that I didn't want Stacia in that position, and I took the opportunity to get us both initiated with the collateral since she was an heir to a King. I thought she'd be so happy not to have to face the darker side of the Esoteric Society.

I was wrong.

Not only did I lose her, but I also lost the chance to hold greater power.

If I had it, I wouldn't be on my knees, prolonging the act of sucking my friend's dick while a room full of people watch.

I was a dumbass for even thinking that Stacia would thank me. I was young. Still in college and madly in love with her. I still am. I had hoped she'd forgive me for giving the sex tape to the King of my chapter, but she didn't. She completely cut me from her life, which is why I couldn't resist the SOS from Kenneth St. Germaine. He thought I was unworthy of his daughter since I chose the easy way in. But it was more than that.

As for the Welcome Ceremony? It was a risk I had to take. I knew Stacia wouldn't want to see me, and I had to do something. I just didn't think that asking her to welcome me with the White Queen's Kiss and a night together would send her over the edge. I didn't realize that she would be put to shame because of it.

Which makes accepting this consequence that much easier.

"Any time now, Count. I'm losing patience," William mutters, stepping closer. The man has a chubby for power, getting off at forcing us into this position.

"Maybe you should learn about foreplay," I grumble to myself.

He taps his cane to the hard floor. "Five seconds or you'll forfeit the chance to accept the Princess's punishment."

Fuck me. Here I go.

I'll never take for granted what a woman does for a man. God, I just wish it were Stacia. I'd let her sit on my face as my punishment. But there's a lot of misogyny in this chapter.

Opening my mouth, I slowly suck in Esteban's cock, not bothering to put in a lot of effort. He tenses, his dick now hardening because of the sensation. Neither of us is attracted to the other, but we're best friends. It's taking one for the damn team.

"Look at him take that punishment," an unfamiliar voice mutters from the shadows.

I ease away and scowl. "Don't be jealous, old man."

"You don't get to stop until he finishes, so you better fucking put some effort into it, Count." This comes from another man, inching closer.

Damn it.

"Use your tongue," Stacia whispers, remaining by my side. The scent of her perfume wafts over me, and I close my eyes, reminding myself that I chose to do this for her.

"Keep talking, Princess," Esteban murmurs, breaking my concentration. "I'll do you a favor if you do."

"You wish it were me, don't you?" Stacia asks, surprising the hell out of me.

Esteban hums his agreement. "Fuck yeah, I do."

"Maybe it can be. On our terms." Stacia sighs under her breath, keeping her voice low so that the witnesses would strain to hear. "You'd have to get on your knees first."

"It would be my honor. Maldición, mamacita. You're so sexy. Christos fucked up losing you." Esteban groans as I bob my head, working him over more furiously, losing myself to my anger.

Because fuck him. He knows I'm still in love with Stacia. We have a code. Now, he's flirting with fire, and I'm prepared with the explosive to blow his ass up if he even tries.

"You'd treat me right, wouldn't you?" Stacia brushes her arm against mine.

I snap my eyes open, catching her caressing her knuckles to his leg. He's damn lucky I don't bite him. Because right now, I want to ensure he can never get his cock near my girl. She's mine. I'll win her back or die trying.

"Fuck yeah—" Esteban groans and grabs my head.

His cum floods my mouth in a shockwave of salty liquid I wasn't prepared for. I automatically swallow, regretting it immediately. Why the fuck didn't I think about this until it was too late? I was far too caught up on Stacia that I just wanted to get it over with.

I gag and spit, trying to rid my mouth of the taste of Esteban's load. I'll think twice about asking anyone to swallow no matter how hot it is to me.

"Damn." Stacia's soft voice pulls me from my haze of rage, disgust, and annoyance. The second our eyes meet, my heart rises from the pit of my stomach. I know that look. I've seen it a dozen times after pinning her down and sinking balls deep into her perfect pussy. She enjoyed it. Watching me fucking swallow turned her on. And damn, I wish I could slip my hand under her haphazardly placed robe and touch her warmth to confirm it for myself.

"This meeting is adjourned. Take note of the repercussions of stepping out of line. We follow a code for a reason. It's how our chapters thrives." His Majesty, Kenneth St. Germaine, speaks up before William can, and I snatch my clothes from the floor. "We'll see everyone in two weeks. Let's hope our next session will proceed without interruption or disobedience."

Esteban offers his hand out, passing me and helping Stacia from the floor. She wobbles on bare feet and shivers.

"And Princess, there are matters to discuss with the King's Court. Please get dressed and join us in the chamber room in ten minutes." William blows the candles out, blanketing the room in darkness. Figures silently exit the vast room, and light filters in from the stairs. I remain on my knees, trying to process what the hell happened.

I sucked my best friend's cock.

But what gets to me more is that my ex-girlfriend liked it.

This will hang over me as collateral, but who the fuck cares? This isn't the same era our parents grew up in. It shows exactly how outdated the Looking Glass chapter has become. How out of touch the kings of this area have become.

For the first time ever, I want to make changes.

"Hey, pendejo. You all right?" Esteban grips my shoulder and shakes me. "That was fucking wild."

"Wild?" I ask, my voice boiling with my anger. "Are you shitting me?"

I lose my composure, my rage controlling my body as my mind cowers. I lunge forward into Esteban, knocking him on his ass.

"Christos!" Stacia screams, thudding her feet on the cold floor, closing the space. "Stop it."

I grind my teeth and grab Esteban's shirt, fisting it in my hand. I hold him down as I swing and punch him in the jaw. He scowls and shoves me off, sending me sliding across the floor.

Stacia gets between us, raising each of her palms. "Stop it. I said fucking stop it! You're not going to fight each other. Haven't we all been punished enough? You know the King's Court will figure out a way to blame me. Taking my place only pissed off the court even more. You know they wanted me punished, not you."

Stacia trembles, her body shaking with her quivering mouth. A mouth so beautiful I can remember kissing it a dozen times. I still dream about her.

And then a tear splashes on her cheek, the warm tendril freezing me in place. The last time I saw her cry was when she found out that I filmed us fucking and turned it into the Rabbit Hole chapter I had belonged to before I was sent abroad and landed in Greece with family. Then the call to return came.

"Yeah, pinche pendejo. You need to chill." Esteban cups his jaw, rubbing the shadow turning into a bruise.

I clench my fingers into fists, wanting to punch him again. "This is your—"

Stacia slaps me, sending my head jerking to the side. "Stop being a prick. You chose to take my place. You're not going to fucking blame anyone. This is your fault."

"Damn straight." Esteban releases a groan.

Stacia points at him. "Just shut the fuck up and get out of here. Don't forget you owe me a favor. But right now, I just need you to leave."

I expect Esteban to argue. He's not used to being told what to do, especially in his line of work. No one gets away with pushing Esteban around, except for those on the King's Court, but he squares his shoulders and marches away without comment.

Stacia's always had a way with people. She could either have them wrapped around her finger, on their knees, or testing their last resolve. And right now, I'm feeling all three.

I bow my head, inhaling and exhaling, trying to get my anger under control. I've always had a bit of a short fuse, but I've been working on it. It was part of my sabbatical in Greece. I needed time to just figure my life out. I kind of lost control when Stacia left me. She was the one I had planned to marry. I even had the ring picked out for when we went through our initiation. She just wanted to wait until she graduated. Me? I wanted to marry her a month after we had been dating. She was it for me. She still is.

"Christos, I don't know what to say to you. Thank you does not feel right, all things considered." Stacia keeps her distance, crossing her arms over her chest, pulling the robe tighter.

"Don't say anything. I just want a minute to talk. There's so much I have to say to you. I'm hoping after all these years, you could show me some pity and give that to me. I know I don't deserve it but please. I just want to make things right." I step forward, trying to reach for her hands.

She recoils.

"I almost had to suck a cock or get caned because

of you. I don't think there's anything you can do to make things right, Christos. I just want you to leave me alone. I'm going through some major fucking shit right now, and I don't need this." Stacia swipes her hands across her cheeks. "The best thing you can do for me is to disappear. I mean it."

Fuck my life.

Something cracks inside me as my hope crumbles away as she takes another step back. I guess time doesn't heal anything when you fucked up like I have. I was stupid and ambitious. I was a cocky son of a bitch. I'm afraid there's nothing I can say now.

Tears blur my eyes, and I blink them away, refusing to cry in the meeting room. That's the last thing I fucking need. This place reeks of toxic masculinity, and it's enough to put me in my place.

I can drop to my knees though. I'm not afraid to grovel.

I clasp my hands together and crawl forward on my knees. "Stacia, please. I'm so fucking sorry. I regret everything I did. If I could go back and change things—"

"But you can't. You should've done right by me from the start. I trusted you. I loved you. And what did you do? You ruined me." Her voice cracks with her words. "Stop torturing me. Now go!"

Turning her back, she strides toward the closed door of the chamber room, where the King's Court waits for her.

I watch her go. I don't have a choice.

All of my efforts to try to fix things have failed.

I think I've lost Stacia forever.

The rosy light of the setting sun sobers my ass up enough from my anger to suck in a deep breath of air. Fuck the LA smog. It's hard to clear my head when all I want to do is cough.

"Are you ready to move on, Christos?" Esteban leans against the black brick wall of the Looking Glass. Dozens of street performers fill the sidewalk as pedestrians stroll down Sunset Boulevard in search of entertainment. "We have shit to do. I can move past things if you can. It'll be like it never happened."

"Just never bring it up again." I clench my jaw, trying to suppress the fact that it was only ten minutes ago that I had my best friend's cock in my mouth. It wasn't exactly the bonding experience I wanted. Sure, we'd joked about having threesomes with a chick, but it never included us together.

"Noted. But don't hold that shit against me. That was all your doing." Esteban pushes away from the wall and puts on a pair of sunglasses, stepping into the light.

"You shouldn't have agreed. Stacia is mine. You know I'm in love with her." Fucking asshole. I can't stop thinking about how it could've been her on her knees.

"Stop being delusional. You were turning into a stalking creep, Christos. That's not how you win her back. And you know what? I'm not going to deny her if she wants me. It would serve your ass right. Plus, she could use some fun after the bullshit of this morning." Esteban rubs his chin, cracking his neck. "Notice my face? I got fucking sucker punched by the Execution-er."

I furrow my brow, in confusion, helping to suppress my anger at Esteban. "What the fuck did you do?"

"He accused me of murder. Apparently, Stacia woke up next to a dead fucker, and he turned out to be one of my new dealers. That's why she's still in there.

There's a huge fucking mess that needs to be cleaned up."

What the hell is he talking about? Someone is dead? Holy fucking shit. Poor Stacia. I can't imagine what the fuck she went through. How was she involved with one of his dealers?

"That's not the worst of it. She was drugged." Esteban glances over his shoulder, double checking to make sure no one tries to sneak up behind him. No one ever realizes that he's a fucking drug lord, and runs an empire that His Majesty wants here. Because there's nothing easier than manipulating the people he needs if they have drug addictions and other problems. It's fucked up, but that's the dark world we live in. Give or take, and I'm one who would rather take than end up thrown out on the streets. I earned my place in the Esoteric Society. Sometimes we have to do things we don't want to, but in the end it's better.

Except for this fucked up shit right now.

Without responding to Esteban, I spin on my heels and march to the back exit of the Looking Glass. I don't care if Stacia demanded I leave her alone. I need to talk to her. I need to make sure she's OK. I want to offer her my help.

"Christos, where are you going? I said we had shit to do," Esteban calls from behind me.

"I need to check on Stacia." I attempt to open the back door, but it automatically locks from the inside, preventing me from accessing the club this way. Fuck me. I'm going to have to run around front.

"Pinche cabrón, no. What you need to do is give her space. She's meeting with the King's Court, and if they want to call us, they will. We need to get shit up and running. I'm not going to face a consequence because of you." Esteban grabs my shoulder, pulling me back.

I swing to punch him, but he expects it, and slams his fist into my gut. Bowing forward, I cough and spit as the air knocks from me.

"Don't make this hard. You're too obsessed and wrapped up in your emotions. Get your act together. Now. Let yourself cool off and then we'll see about Stacia." I hate that Esteban is right. He's always been a critical thinker and someone who goes through everything before making a decision. He has saved my ass more than once.

And he's right.

If I go running to Stacia now, I won't accomplish anything. I'll just piss her off even more.

"You'll be more of use with me," he adds. "I need to look into who was dealing last night. The Looking Glass was supposed to be off-limits. We know how important a clean reputation is. The King's Court might have my ass if I'm not prepared with answers. I'm not going to start off like this here. So come on. I need my Count."

"I'm going to kill whoever drugged her. You know that right?" I straighten my suit jacket, struggling to keep my heart from busting out of my chest.

"Killing is wasteful. You have to make them realize what fuck ups they are. Teach them a lesson so they can learn from it and be better employees." Esteban shifts his jacket, showing off a bejeweled hilt of a switchblade. He's always been a bit of a showoff.

"Then I'll make them wish they were dead," I respond, cracking my knuckles. I won't let anyone get away with thinking they can just mess with Stacia St. Germaine.

"That's what I'm talking about. See? The sabbatical was good for you. Now you're thinking things through. Maybe you'll get to join me on the King's Court, after all. This could be where we rise." Esteban wags his eyebrows, his face lighting with a smile.

"Fuck yeah. I've been waiting for this moment." I bump my knuckles to his.

He shoves me forward, getting me to head toward where he parked his car. "Good. Don't fuck it up."

I fuck up a lot of things in my life, but business isn't one of them. The Looking Glass chapter will be mine.

9

Reputation

Stacia

"If there is anything else you need to tell us, do so now. It's imperative that we have all of the details." Daddy sits on top of his desk, towering over me, while I hunker in the chair. I can't even look into his eyes after everything.

How he let William take control of the situation and humiliate me the way he did really fucked with me. I knew he wasn't the best father, but I thought he would at least stand up for me. Instead, he just abandoned me. I should've known. He's always put the chapter first.

"I know this is important, and I told you everything

I can remember. All I know is I didn't do it. I don't even know that guy." I motion toward the picture printout of the dead man that Talon took at the hotel. I had told the King's Court that I had taken it, so they wouldn't know that Talon showed up to help me when I was being shunned. "I've never seen him before. He's obviously not in any of my circles. Just look at him."

"Then how the hell was he in your penthouse room, Stacia?" He breaks his own rule by saying my real name within his chambers. "You left the crime scene, and we need something to feed to the police. We need to get a jump on it before the press finds out. You are lucky the Silver Screen Hotel management is on my payroll, and they were able to keep their bellhop from automatically calling the authorities." Daddy scoops up the picture of the dead guy and tosses it on my lap. "There has to be something more that you know."

"Take it easy, Your Majesty. I'm sure Princess is trying her best. She was out of it when she came to my door. You'll have to give her another day. Make sure the drugs are completely gone from her system." Talon touches my dad on the shoulder, drawing his attention away from me.

Daddy shoves him, but Talon only rocks back an inch, steeling himself in place. He is far more muscular than Daddy and younger, not exactly an even match. I'm sure Talon could knock him out. It's why he's the Looking Glass's enforcer. Why his nickname is the Executioner.

"Stacia should've never taken drugs." Daddy leans forward and snatches the front of my robe, dragging me out of the chair. He shakes me in front of him, not giving me a chance to stand on my feet. "You have a reputation to maintain. No daughter of mine will do drugs. Do you hear me?"

My fear gets the best of me, and I don't answer, my body cool and shaking. Daddy drops me to my knees. I hit the floor hard and cry out. He doesn't believe that I'm innocent. I already can tell.

I lick my lips. "I didn't take—"

"Shut the fuck up. I've had enough today. You have put everything at risk, and this is going to cost us a fucking fortune to cover up. Just get out of here. You better hope that we can get this under control. Our chapter will not go down because of your bad decisions." Daddy turns away from me and struts toward the corner of his chamber room. He pulls out his cell phone and dials. "Count, are you still around? I need you to take Princess somewhere for me. No one can know where she is right now."

What? He's got to be kidding me.

"Ken, I'll take Stacia. I need the heirs to do some runs for me." Talon shocks me by saying our names. Daddy started it, so he can't really say much. Standing over me, Talon offers his hand out, lifting me to my feet, even though I just want to curl up on the floor and disappear. "I have a house by the beach. It's under a family name."

Daddy grumbles into the phone and puts it away. "Fine. Make sure to get her bodyguard in order. I can't risk this getting out."

"Everything's handled. We'll find out who drugged Stacia and killed the bastard. It's a scandal we can spin positively. We've faced worse." Talon silently motions for me to walk to the door. "Trust our chapter. We have never let you down."

Daddy doesn't respond, and Talon doesn't wait.

I hope that he believes him.

I hope Talon is right.

"You need to sleep, Stacia. You've been up for almost thirty hours." Talon hovers in the doorway of the master suite of his beachfront mansion. I don't know what I was expecting, considering he doesn't live the same lavish lifestyle in the city, but it wasn't this Malibu estate.

I stare out the panoramic window at the dark beach. The only light sparkles from the moon. "I know that, but I can't. Every time I close my eyes…" I shudder and rest my elbows on my knees. "I don't want to sleep alone. Will you stay with me?"

Talon hovers in the doorway, pausing to think about my question. My heart pounds harder the longer he hesitates.

"Please," I say, my voice low and pleading. "I won't seduce you or anything."

A soft smile plays on his lips. "But I might try."

"Would that really be such a bad thing?" I scoot over and pat the bed. "Come on, birdie. Just lay with me. It might be the only way I can rest. You're the only one who seems to be on my side these days."

Talon meanders into the room, shutting the door behind him. He doesn't take his eyes off me as he crosses the space, his muscles rippling with his movements. The corded veins in his arms pulse, and I pull the blanket down, so he gets under it instead of lying on top. I don't want the barrier between us.

Talon silently climbs into bed and opens his arms, inviting me into them. His warmth is like a comforting blanket, and I want to bury myself against him and breathe in his intoxicating fragrance, like fruit and spices, with a hint of his lavender laundry soap—a cologne that will linger for days.

I rest my head on his chest and stroke my fingers over his torso, mapping out the grooves of his prominent abs through his shirt. I've only seen him without a shirt once at a pool party, but it's something I've never forgotten.

"You know, I was against the punishments they offered you. I almost punched William in the face for it. I would've risked death had Christos not stood up and took your place. I'm so fucking sorry, Stacia. The whole situation was fucked up." Talon mumbles the words, keeping his voice low as if he's afraid of someone overhearing him.

"I'm glad you didn't. I don't want you in that position ever. Not for me. I knew there would be consequences for my actions, and as much as I despise the idea, I can handle myself." I stroke my fingers up and down his stomach, enjoying how his muscles react to my touch.

"I know you can, wild child. And what you did, picking Knave—that was brilliant. That'll hurt Christos forever." Talon tilts his head, brushing his lips against my hair. "He's a piece of work."

"I won't lie. It was so fucking satisfying to watch." I tip my head up and meet his blue eyes. "It doesn't make up for what he did to me, but damn."

He chuckles. "Is that a new kink unlocked?"

Warmth pools between my legs as our conversation shifts from all the fucked up shit to something more personal. I think about his question for a moment. A part of me loved seeing Christos give Esteban a blow job. Partly, it was the act itself. Because Esteban is hotter than I'd like to admit, not to mention the size of his cock, completely smooth, his well-groomed body is something I appreciate. The other part of me loved that Christos did it for me. It had to take a lot for a straight man to agree to such an act in the presence of others. I can't help but wonder what went through his head. I mean, Esteban is bigger than him. That probably hurt his masculinity as much as me choosing

Esteban hurt his heart.

Revenge is fucking sweet.

"It definitely is a new kink for you. You're blushing. Your nipples are hard as fuck." Talon's blue eyes darken with both amusement and lust. He drags his gaze from mine to my boobs, staring at my pebbling nipples through my shirt. Fuck I love the way he does it.

"Maybe it's just your closeness, birdie," I say, my soft voice turning flirty. "Have you thought of that?"

He shifts slightly, playing with my dark hair, moving it off my shoulder. "You didn't react until I brought it up. You loved how the fucker deep throated him. How he didn't gag."

"Until he swallowed." A laugh escapes my lips.

"Damn, okay. New kink might not be your ex sucking cock. It's something darker. Huh, wild child? Does revenge turn you on?" Talon rubs his fingers over my arm, leaving a trail of goosebumps behind.

I can't stop from smiling. "It was just so perfect. Is that psychotic? I just...it felt so good that he had to do something humiliating. That he chose it."

"He could've taken the cane." Talon rolls onto his side, stroking his fingers over my cheek.

"What would have you chosen?" I prop up on

my elbow, facing him, watching as Talon's gaze trails down to my lips.

"For you, either one. I don't know if you realize this, but you've been my biggest challenge. I've wanted you since the day we met. It has taken everything in me to ignore my attraction. I have been staying away to help, but after how His fucking Majesty just stood by and...fuck Kenneth. I don't care anymore. He's lost all my respect."

Leaning closer, I close the space with only an inch between our mouths. I don't know if I should push him. I'm afraid that once everything settles, his mind will clear, and he might regret this. But I also want to do something to piss off my dad. Because Talon is right. He is the king of our chapter, and he could've stood up for me. He could've done something. Instead, he let a twisted, perverted man try to degrade me. He is just as responsible.

"And the fact that he even questioned you..." Talon clenches the blankets in his hand, his muscles tensing as his anger rises. "You didn't deserve that."

"It is what it is. I should've expected it." I tip my head slightly, bringing my hand up to comb my fingers through Talon's, soft dark blond hair. "But I don't want to think about it anymore. I just want to put it all behind me. I want to forget."

Talon stares at me in silence, a dozen emotions crossing his face. He wants to kiss me. He craves to kiss me. But a part of him resists.

Closing the space completely, I caress my lips to his, testing his reaction. He admitted he was afraid of seducing me, but how is it seduction when I'm ready and willing. I thought about this hundreds of times. And this kiss is just as sweet as the only other one we shared before.

He moans against my mouth, easing away. "Stacia. .."

I expect him to stop.

I expect a rejection to follow my name.

Talon does neither. He pushes me over and climbs on top of me, linking his fingers to the back of my neck to pull me closer, kissing me harder, deeper, his mouth going to war, but I'm not putting up a fight. I sink into the bed, savoring his weight on top of me.

"God, you're so beautiful. So sexy." Talon pushes himself up on one arm and grabs the hem of my night-shirt.

I raise my arms and let him pull it off me. He bows

down and kisses my clavicle, working his way to my breasts. He glides his tongue over my nipple as his hand drags down my stomach and into the waistband of my shorts. I arch my back under the sensation, kissing his neck and sucking his skin. I've never felt so hot in my life. Talon devours me like he might never get a chance at this moment again. He works his way lower, kissing the planes of my torso until he positions himself between my legs and tugs my panties and shorts off in one quick motion.

I lay bare before him, the heat of his kiss traveling down the rest of me, sending blooms of rosy color across my body.

"Tell me you want me," he says, with his palms on my knees, spreading my body as he drinks in the sight of my pussy. "I need to hear it, Stacia. I'm not going to touch you otherwise. I want you to be absolutely certain. Because if you let me, I'm going to want more of you. I won't want anyone else."

My chest rises and falls with my deep breathing, and I lean up and grab his shirt, trying to yank it over his head. He snatches my hands and restrains them, pushing me back to the bed, pinning me down, his body resting between my legs. His hard cock presses against me through the fabric of his pants, and I squirm, grinding my body as if it's the only way I'll find relief.

"Fuck me," I say, gliding my tongue over his neck and sucking him hard enough to leave a mark. "I want you to fuck me."

He releases my arms and grasps my chin. Holding me in place, he kisses me again, letting me rub my body to his without giving him more.

"Stop teasing me, Talon. You asked me to tell you that I wanted it. Now you're just torturing me. Come on. Fuck me." I reach between us and unbutton his pants, pulling his cock free. I stroke my fingers up and down his length, feeling as he drips his excitement on me.

He pulls away and stops me, only to press his hand to my stomach to pin me down as he repositions himself between my legs. He slides his middle finger inside me and uses his thumb to spread my body open. I gasp as his tongue caresses my clit, starting slowly as if he wants to take his time exploring every inch of me. I pant and squirm, but his other hand remains firmly right below my navel, pressing into my pelvis as he moves his middle finger inside me, creating sensations, unlike anything I've ever felt before while he kisses and sucks my clit like I'm the best thing he's ever tasted.

I rub my hands over his arms, tracing the bulging veins as I watch him eat me out, refusing to take my eyes away. He hums against my skin, staring at me, devouring my reaction as I throw myself back, clinging to the bed as he works me to my peak.

"I'm going to come. I'm going to come. Don't stop. Fuck." I chant as the sensation builds and builds, my body preparing to explode. "Fuck. Fuck, it feels so good. Fuck."

Talon hums again, keeping his even pace, his tongue rubbing against my clit at the same time his finger plays with my G-spot until my muscles tense, and I scream out with pleasure, my orgasm stealing my breath.

I practically fall apart, panting as my mind whirls. My legs tremble as he slows down, taking his time to finish, acting as if he might continue until I explode again.

I reach for him. "I can't handle another. Fuck me," I plead, my voice shaking.

Talon eases away, a smile playing on his face now damp with my excitement. "You can handle anything, Stacia. I'm not done with you yet. I warned you."

I don't even get a chance to react as he buries his face between my legs again, flicking his tongue over my clit in quick successions, building my body up again with the new sensation. I scream and shake, my muscles losing control as I ride on the high of lust created by Talon. He works me up and up, my heart threatening to explode along with another orgasm. But he stops short. He doesn't bring me to my peak and instead pulls away from me to grab my legs, spreading them wide, and thrusts inside me. He pins me in such a way that I gasp and huff with the pressure. This isn't a moment of slow sensuality. This is hot passion, and built-up desire from over the years, finally exploding between us. My eyes roll back into my head as he strums his finger over my clit, bouncing me against him and controlling my movements. My moans come in bursts, my voice ringing through the air. Talon doesn't hold back and moans with me, grunting with each thrust that takes me closer and closer to complete and utter satisfaction.

"You're going to come for me again, Stacia. I'm going to fuck you until you can't even stand up. You need it," he says, playing with my clit as he stretches out and pinches my nipple between his fingers. "You're going to melt for me. Come undone."

I moan my response, enjoying the sensation of his hips smacking my thighs, the softness of his balls tapping against my ass. I peek through my lashes, watching as he plays with me until I come again. The pleasure intensifies, and I bite my lip hard enough to taste blood, but I can't help it. It's as if pain and pleasure blend as one, distracting me from the rest of the world.

"I'll always give you what you need, Stacia. You are so fucking amazing. I regret wasting all this time. I won't deny you again." Talon bows forward and molds his lips to mine, pounding harder and harder into me as our sounds of passion fill the air until he thrusts hard and deep a few more times as he comes.

I cling onto him, continuing to kiss him, not letting him catch his breath. He gasps against my lips, sinking onto me, just letting his weight keep me down.

"Are you sure about that?" I ask after a minute, letting our emotions settle, knowing better than to get my hopes up. Because I know his position. I know my place. This could lead to far worse consequences if my dad were to find out.

He slides his arms under me and holds me closer while he flips over with me on top of him. "Absolutely. For as long as you want. Because fuck every-thing. I mean it. Fuck everything." He kisses me again, stroking his fingers up and down my spine.

"The Looking Glass? My dad?" I know I shouldn't ask him, but I can't help it. Talon feels like safety. He feels like the only one that would ever stand beside me and do anything.

"Especially His Majesty. He doesn't deserve his po-sition. He doesn't care about anything besides the power he gets from it. He's lost sight of our chapter's purpose," Talon responds, his voice breathy and deep.

All I can do is smile. I know he's right, but it's hard for me to believe him. Every man I've ever trusted has betrayed me.

I open my mouth to try to summon something to say, to tell him that maybe he should care just a little, considering the consequences, but his cell phone rings from his discarded pants, blaring through the air.

"You should get that," I say, knowing that he's not going to if I don't encourage him. "It could be impor-tant."

He sighs and shakes his head. "Leandro will leave a message. He has a key. Don't worry about it, wild child. I want you to let me take care of you."

So I give in. Talon and I shower together and return to the bed, more calm and relaxed than ever.

I close my eyes, but all I can see is the dead man.

However hard I try, it's not enough. This is just how it's going to be. As much as Talon wants to fix me, I don't think it's possible.

I'm broken.

10

Breaking News

Stacia

*U*nknown: *OMG, I just heard what happened. Are you okay? Juan gave me the number to reach you but said this was the one and only time I could until they figure shit out.*

Without having to ask, I know it's Bianca texting me from an unknown number. Very few people would have access to the burner phone Talon gave me yesterday. It only has two numbers programmed into it as well. His and Leandro's.

Me: I fucked Talon.

I don't know why I respond with that, but a part of me doesn't want to relive everything that happened. I'd prefer to cling onto my memory of the most amazing sex I've ever had. I ache in the best way, the reminder turning me on over and over again. Talon might be a hard ass, but he's an attentive lover unlike I've ever experienced.

Unknown: What?! Holy fuck! Are you insane? You're facing possible murder charges and you go and sleep with Talon?

I blink a few times. It wasn't the reaction I'd expected. Bianca always cheered me on my conquest in trying to seduce Talon.

Conquest... Oh, no. What if that was what this was?

Me: It just happened. He was there for me.

Unknown: Don't you think it's not a good time? What if you can't get out of this? Juan says it doesn't look good.

Me: What else does Juan say? He doesn't know shit. I didn't murder anyone. He's just being a dick to keep you away from me.

Unknown: I know that you'd never. I'm sorry. I'm just freaked out. I want you to be careful. What if it was Christos? He could go after someone else like Talon and blame you. I thought his acceptance of your punishment was convenient after I found out about you.

That was my first thought. And now that Bianca plants the idea back into my mind—she could be right. If Christos is behind this, he could hurt Talon.

Me: Shit. I need to confront him. He asked to talk to me, and I told him to fuck off.

Unknown: I don't know, Stacia. I don't feel right about it.

A knock on the door draws my attention away from my conversation with Bianca. I meet Talon's vivid blue gaze. He stands fully dressed in a suit, looking handsome as hell with his dark blond hair combed and styled like a damn cover model. But it also means he's going somewhere. He prefers casual to sophisticated, though he can pull both off. I realize I love him best naked, and seeing him ready to leave tightens my chest.

I crinkle my nose. "Where are you heading? I thought you'd be staying with me."

"I have errands to run." He remains in his spot instead of stepping closer like I expect him to. "Leandro's here, so you're safe."

I push to my feet, closing the space. "What kind of errands? Does it have to do with me?"

"Wild child," he says with a sigh, my nickname like a groan of annoyance. "It's better if you don't know all the details, but the DNA Leandro took isn't a match for the dead guy, so I'm looking into it more. I also have some shit to do for the business. You know how demanding my job can be. It's nothing too important or anything to worry about, and I won't be more than a couple of hours."

I slide my arms under his, hugging him. "Can't you have someone else handle things? Is there anything I can do to convince you to stay and—"

A strange alarm sounds, the noise coming from the hallway. Footsteps soon follow, and Talon pulls away and crosses his arms. I stand stunned, my lips parted, and my body turning rigid. He straightens his suit jacket and flicks his gaze away from me. I spot a familiar face pop up as Leandro reaches the landing. Shit. I don't know if I should be offended or relieved that Talon backed off...who am I kidding? I'm hurt. I know I fucked Leandro, so I should be thankful that I'm spared from the awkwardness, but Talon doesn't know that. I'm pretty sure I know the real reason Talon backs off. He doesn't want Leandro to know that we've been together. And what the fuck?

I decide to throw my fucks to the floor and close the space to Talon again, showing that Leandro was a night of fun. It wasn't anything serious, and I doubt he'll try anything again, considering he's been hired as my personal bodyguard.

"Please, don't go," I say, lowering my voice. I lift my hands to rest on his shoulders, and he steps away again.

The bastard pats me on the fucking head like I'm a child even though I've been a woman since before we met. I sense Leandro watching us without a word, probably realizing he just interrupted something.

My chest tightens with the pain of rejection. Inhaling a deep breath, I burn Talon a look, hoping he feels the fire of my gaze.

"You know what? Never fucking mind. I guess I should've expected this. The game's over and no longer fun for you." I clench my teeth, stopping my jaw from trembling.

"Stacia…" Talon says, messing with his tie.

I throw my hands out. "What?" I wait anxiously for him to come to his senses and tell me otherwise. I need him desperately. I'm afraid I'll fall apart otherwise. I refuse to be a dirty little secret. I'm worth more than that.

Scrubbing his jaw with his hand, he shakes his head. "Just text me if you need anything. I'll bring some things for dinner, okay?"

A part of me wants to scream and call him out. Another part of me wants to burst into tears, feeling as used as I did when Christos broke my heart.

But Leandro clears his throat, cutting the heavy silence. I don't want him to see me fall apart over another one of my bad choices. I guess it's better this way. Talon won't get dragged down with me if everything continues to spiral out of control.

"Okay," I manage to rasp out. "Whatever."

Without waiting, I spin around and head back into the master suite, slamming the door.

I slump onto the bed and cover my face, sucking in a few breaths.

I refuse to cry. I refuse to let this get to me.

I build an imaginary steel wall around me.

It's time I stop letting anyone in. It's the only way I'll never be left disappointed.

"Knock-knock, beautiful." Leandro's voice sounds through the door. "I have dinner. Don't make me unscrew the hinges and barge in. You gotta eat. You've already skipped lunch."

I remain curled up in bed with the blankets wrapped around me like a burrito. Am I being immature by ignoring Leandro? Most definitely. But I don't feel like eating or moving. I roll over and snatch my new phone off the nightstand, tapping my finger to the screen.

Me: I'm sick. Just put it in the fridge for later. Thanks.

Leandro: What are your symptoms? I'll bring you something.

Me: That's okay. I just want to rest.

Leandro: Vomiting? Diarrhea? Both?

Is he serious?

Me: Jesus, no. I wouldn't tell you if it was either.

Leandro: Headache? Stomachache? Nausea?

Damn, he's persistent.

Me: No. It's nothing. Just let me sleep.

Leandro: So you're fatigued. Sore throat? Cough? Congestion?

Me: It's the plague. Go away. I don't want you catching it.

Leandro: Well, I'm not letting you die on my watch. So open the door.

I toss the phone and flip over. There's no way in

hell I'm opening the door. He'll get bored and leave me alone. Pulling my knees to my chest, I hide under the pillow and try to ignore Leandro's knock. Like I assumed, he stops and the hallway goes quiet.

I grab the TV remote and turn it on, wanting to lose myself to mindless TV. I used to watch reality shows until I was on one and made to look like a huge slut, but that never bothered me. I've always hated that perception. It was when they couldn't get the reaction they wanted, and then they decided to bring on some other heiress to instigate me. It's not scandalous when you stand up and speak out about the double standards instead of crying with mascara on your face with the camera rolling.

I would never do that, and so that was that. The show runners moved on.

I stop on a cult documentary, wondering if people would think the Esoteric Society was a cult. My chapter checks quite a few culty boxes, but I knew what I was getting into with my initiation. I gave up nothing and gained more. Maybe I'm a bit brain washed, but my rosy glasses that I've looked at the world through for years are a permanent accessory.

The master door rattles as something buzzes against

it. I sit up on the bed and glower, realizing that Leandro didn't quiet down because he gave up. The bastard went to get tools. He wasn't joking about unscrewing the door hinges.

I don't even get a chance to yell at him to stop before he pulls the door off the frame and sets it aside. He covers his eyes with his hand instead of looking at me.

"Are you decent?" he asks, stepping in.

"No, I'm completely naked," I say, snapping with my annoyance.

Leandro drops his hand and smirks at me, giving me a long once over. "Damn. I was hoping you were telling the truth."

I grab a pillow and chuck it at him. He catches it with a laugh and sets it on the floor. I stare at him in shock. No other bodyguard would have acted this way. I don't know if I should be impressed or angry. Maybe a little bit of both.

"What the actual fuck?" I ask, wishing I was standing up so I could square my shoulders and silently threaten him with my body language. I can't exactly look tough, wrapped in blankets like a swaddled adult.

He reaches outside the door and grabs a tray with a couple takeout containers on top of it. "I told you

I'd barge in. You had the option of opening the door. Can you blame me? You said you were sick, and it's part of my job to take care of you. They hired me not only because of my skills in combat, weaponry, and protection, but I also have a medical background. So, if you're sick, I will do what I can to make you feel better."

I throw myself back, grab another pillow from beside me, and pull it over my head. What happened to the silent, serious guy that Talon turned him into the moment we both realized that I wasn't some chick he managed to pick up at the club?

"I brought a bunch of medicine if whatever your ailment is embarrasses you. But you don't have to worry, beautiful. I've seen a lot in my life. Nothing that comes out of you will scare me." Leandro's footsteps thump closer as he saunters to the bed. I listen as he sets the tray on the nightstand, but I refuse to look. I refuse to respond to his comment. Because there's no way in hell I'm going to let him see anything come out of me. Ever.

"Come on. Don't be shy. I thought we were already past that. You know I can't go anywhere, right? I know too much." The pillow shifts as Leandro tugs it away from my face, using his strength against me. "I've known Talon a long time and he's the type to kill to keep a secret. But don't worry. Yours is safe with me. I know you didn't commit a crime."

He says it in a way that I know he's joking, because Leandro doesn't know anything about the Esoteric Society. There's no possible way. Only members know. Not staff. Not other family members who aren't a part of things. Not friends. No one. He's just making a speculation, considering how aggressive Talon can be. I know they knew each other before this, because Talon was the one to choose Leandro. If I didn't want to be left alone, I'd ask more, but opening a conversation is the last thing I want.

"Well, at least you believe me. Not that it matters." I don't mean to sound like a bitch, but I really did just want him to leave.

"You're right. My opinion doesn't matter." Leandro starts opening up containers and prepping whatever is on the tray. "If you don't like what's here, you can blame Talon. He just dropped this off and left."

I grip the blankets in my fingers. "He came back and then left? He didn't even—" I snap my mouth shut, silencing the stream of thoughts racing through my mind. I can't believe Talon. What a fucking coward.

"He said things were taking longer than he expected, but he wanted to make sure you had something more than the leftovers. He'll be back either super late tonight or tomorrow morning." Leandro offers me the reusable to-go container, showing me the saucy, cheesy goodness of enchiladas. This proves that Talon knows he fucked up, because it's my favorite meal from my favorite hole-in-the-wall restaurant outside of LA.

"What things? What has he told you?" Maybe Leandro will shed light on whatever Talon is up to. If he's my bodyguard, he knows that he's going to have to build some sort of relationship with me. Even if it's not sexual, which I'm pretty sure will never happen again now that I know exactly where I stand in this world. I'm not going to drag Leandro into the bullshit of my life. He's already immersed in it, so I need to make sure he stays just outside of my personal bubble.

"He didn't say, and I didn't ask. It's none of my business. The only thing I need to concern myself over is you. Now eat. I'm sure you don't want me to hand-feed you." Leandro lifts an eyebrow, motioning toward my fork. "Don't think I won't."

A part of me wants to test him and see if he follows

through like he did with the door. I decided against it because I've already crossed enough lines.

Picking up the fork, I cut at the enchilada and then pop a bite in my mouth. Fucking Talon. The delicious, savory flavors burst over my tongue. I want so much to hate this food, but it's just too damn good.

It doesn't make up for things though. Talon showed me where I stand.

"Thank God. The last thing I wanted to do was risk you biting my hand off." Leandro smiles at me, shuffles toward the sitting area, and grabs a chair, dragging it to my bedside. "Now if you don't mind, I'm starving. There's too much lettuce in the fridge. I think Talon only knows how to feed rabbits."

"I'm guessing you didn't check the deep freezer?" I take another bite of food, turning my attention to watch Leandro bite into the biggest burrito I've ever seen.

He chuckles and covers his mouth. "Fuck no. It looked like somewhere someone stored bodies. Hide evidence..." He frowns for a second and takes another bite.

"Would've been nice if Talon managed to do that for me," I quip.

"Worthless CEO. Never getting his hands dirty." Leandro sets his burrito down on the wrapper.

If only that were the truth. Talon has done a lot of shady shit as the enforcer of the Looking Glass chapter.

"Right?" I say, trying to play along. "He's probably just out partying or some shit, putting me off on you."

He takes a sip from a soda cup. "He does seem like the type to get around. A man like him wouldn't be lonely..."

I frown at the thought. Even thinking that Talon could be out with another woman right now gets under my skin, flaring jealousy through me.

"Shit, beautiful. I didn't know you guys were a thing. I had assumed since we—fuck." Leandro sets his drink down and leans back in the chair, scrubbing his palms on his knees.

"No, we're not a thing. He made that clear. Yeah, I fucked him, but that's all it was." A part of me hates admitting that out loud, but the more I say it, the easier it will be in the long run.

Leandro falls silent, busying himself with eating the rest of his dinner. I don't try to speak either. I don't really have anything to say. So I continue to fork at my enchiladas until I finish and set the plate back on the tray.

Lowering myself back down on the bed, I pull the blanket up around me, cocooning myself to block the world out.

"Stacia, I know this isn't my place to talk, and it's definitely crossing a line, but I'm relieved there's nothing going on between you and Talon. He doesn't deserve someone like you." Leandro rests his hand on my side.

I turn back over. I can't help it. As much as I want to ignore him, I can't. What he says? It's crazy. He's relieved? He thinks Talon doesn't deserve me? It's hard for me to even form thoughts about it.

"I've known Talon a long time, Stacia. He's my high school buddy's older brother. And I know he's done some shit you don't want to be involved in," Leandro continues.

"You know I'm not exactly innocent, right? I'm not a murderer, but I'm not some sweet girl next door." I lick my lips, sucking my bottom one between my teeth. Why am I even having this conversation? Of course Leandro would be against Talon. I fucked him.

"You are still too good for him. And I'm not just saying that because I think you are beautiful, fun as hell, and…so damn sexy." Leandro smiles at me, almost shyly, like he's afraid I might react negatively.

I remain expressionless. I know I shouldn't devour his admission like I do, but I'm addicted to compliments. It makes me feel better when everything else feels like shit.

I open my mouth to tease him, maybe flirt with him a little bit, but the TV says my name, pulling my attention away.

"Breaking news. An unidentified man was discovered dead in the penthouse of the Silver Screen Hotel at 10:03AM. Authorities announced the room belonged to heiress Stacia St. Germaine. The authorities are currently looking to get in touch with the heiress—"

The TV clicks off, turning the screen black.

I jerk toward Leandro as he tucks the remote into his pocket. "Turn it back on."

Leandro shakes his head. "I have strict orders."

"You work for me. Now turn it back on. I need to see what's happening." I throw the blankets off me and lunge toward Leandro, trying to grab the remote from him.

He catches me only to set me on the floor and hops

to his feet. "I technically work for Talon at the moment. He thought it was best that there was no financial connection between the two of us in case."

"Just turn it back on," I beg, planting my palms to the floor and push up. "Please."

Leandro shakes his head again, strolling toward the TV. Pulling a knife from his pocket, he yanks out the plug and cuts the cord, preventing me from manually turning it on. Anger swells through me, but I remain in my place. I'll just look everything up on my phone.

"You don't need the kind of stress that comes with media speculation, Stacia. Why don't you go relax? I could draw you a bath or something." Leandro remains firm in his spot.

"Just get out." I turn my back on him and head to the bed. I lift up the blankets, searching for my phone, but it's not there.

Leandro clears his throat. "If you need to talk to someone, I will relay the messages. You are officially on lockdown until Talon gets back."

"You can't do this!" I yell, scooping up a pillow to pummel him with. "I'm not a prisoner."

"Exactly," he says, heading toward the doorless exit. "And we're going to keep it that way. So just relax and get some rest. We'll be done with everything soon."

Without waiting, Leandro fixes the door and starts screwing back the hinges. I just stand and burn daggers at him in silence. I hope he feels my anger.

I might as well be in prison.

At this point, I'm not sure I'll ever be able to live freely again.

11

Bad Guy

Stacia

My stomach flutters with nerves. Talon will be back any minute according to Leandro, and there was no fucking way I was going to let him see me like the hot mess I've been.

Leaning closer to the mirror, I apply my favorite shade of red to my lips and blow myself a kiss. It might be vain of me to think, but I'm hot as hell. Revenge in the form of hopefully making him regret how he just left and avoided me for far longer than he said—two full days instead of hours.

I've been bored out of my fucking mind and out of touch with the world. I couldn't lay in bed and zone out to the TV because of Leandro, and when I decided to finally leave the room, he controlled the remote and only streamed things as not to risk the news popping up.

The doorbell rings in several quick successions as Talon announces his arrival. I shouldn't be this nervous.

Fluffing my fingers through my dark brown hair, I force a smile on my face and take a deep breath. I'm going to pretend like nothing happened. Fixing my boobs to accentuate my cleavage, I give myself one more look in the mirror.

Leandro leans against the wall near the door, his arms folded over his chest. Goosebumps bloom across my skin in waves, and I strut closer, wishing I could throw on some stilettos to give me height. It might be a bit too much, though. I don't want Talon thinking I did this for him. Because really, it's for me. Maybe Leandro. He drinks me in from head to toe and whistles under his breath, not even hesitating to declare his attraction to me. I knew he wouldn't keep his professional boundaries with me.

"You know, one sure way to make your point to the bastard is if you put thoughts in his head." Leandro lowers his voice, his handsome smile curving with his mischievous thoughts.

"What kind of thoughts?" I close the space completely, using Leandro to give myself a few extra minutes to stabilize my confidence.

"Maybe leave a little of your lipstick right here." Leandro taps his cheek, his smile widening.

I giggle breathlessly, meeting his silent dare. Except I don't kiss his cheek. Cupping his face, I close the space and kiss him on the lips, humming under my breath as I test the seam of his mouth. He parts his lips without resisting, deepening our kiss, gliding his tongue over mine. Our first night together is a bit foggy, but his mouth against mine, how his tongue effortlessly explores mine, I remember how amazing a kisser he truly is. How fucking good a quickie we had.

He pulls back first for a second to look into my eyes but then he leans in and continues like he can't get enough.

Footsteps sound on the stairs, clomping loudly, and despite wanting Talon to capture us in this moment, Leandro pulls away and puts space between us. He swipes his hand across his mouth, smearing the lipstick without getting rid of it, and I straighten my shoulders.

"Stacia? You decent?" Talon calls out from the hall-way. "Where's Leandro?"

I bite my lip and smile at Leandro. He tugs at his collar and cracks his neck, his playful expression vanishing. I might've taken the kiss too far, yet he didn't resist. I'd do it all over again.

I quickly close the door completely. "Go away, birdie. We're bus—"

Leandro flies at me, covering my mouth with his hand. "Come on in, Talon."

"Don't you dare," I say in a sing-song voice. "You're not welcome here."

"I live here, wild child. Now stop acting like a brat. I've been running on no fucking sleep. We need to talk." Talon turns the knob, pushing the door open, forcing me out of the way.

His gaze falls on Leandro first since I'm off to the side, and fuck. I wish I could savor his expression forever. A thick vein pulses in his neck with the bulging of his muscles. Leandro stands tall, not letting Talon's jealously intimidate him.

"Are you fucking kidding me?" Talon shouts, fisting his hand.

He doesn't get a chance to step forward because Leandro lunges first, shoving Talon hard enough to send him reeling into the hallway. "Before you fucking start throwing punches, you better stop and think about shit."

"You crossed a line," Talon growls, straightening his jacket. It's now that I see a shadow on the floor just out of my view. Talon didn't come alone.

"Me?" Leandro retorts, laughing in exasperation. "You fucked her and then le—"

"Stop! Fuck!" I get in the doorway, separating Leandro and Talon from each other. I wanted to make Talon jealous and regret treating me like nothing happened. I didn't want him to get in a fight with my bodyguard. "I'm a consenting adult and there is no damn supposed line you two are accusing each other of crossing. What I do with who I choose is no one's business. I'm not with either of you. I'm just a stressed out, wanted woman, who feels like doing whoever she goddamn wants until I end up in prison."

Silence falls over us, and I steel myself, trying not to think about the words that spilled from my mouth.

"Stacia, you're not going to prison, okay?" Talon droops his shoulders, ruffling his fingers through his surprisingly unkempt hair.

Now that my adrenaline wanes, I give him a once-over, noticing he's in the same suit he left me in, unshaven with dark circles under his eyes—or maybe bruises. His lip is split too.

I try not to let his sudden broodiness get to me. "How can you say that? I saw the news. They said I'm wanted."

Groaning, Talon shuffles past me, heading to the sitting area. Leandro and I glance at each other in silence. Movement in the corner of my eye snags my attention, and I finally see who stands in the hallway lurking.

Esteban twists his lips to the side and shrugs without a word. He rests his back against the wall without asking to come in. So I shut the door in his face. I have no idea what he's doing here with Talon but my room thickens with enough testosterone as it is, and I don't want to exactly make eye contact with the man my ex sucked off while listening to my voice.

"Leandro, you weren't supposed to let her see the news until I returned. I didn't want the media speculation fucking with Stacia's head." Talon slumps in one of the chairs and rests his elbows on his knees.

I bite the inside of my lip, keeping my annoyance

under control. If Talon already didn't look so beaten and tired, I'd smack him for ordering Leandro to cut me off from the world.

Leandro lowers his shoulders, relaxing a bit. "I did everything in my power, but Stacia—"

"You're lucky she didn't eat you alive." Talon chuckles to himself, staring at the floor. Whatever anger that boiled on his sturdy surface dissipates as he gathers himself together.

I place my hands on my hips. "Stop talking about me like I'm not standing here. Come on, birdie. It's been fucking days. You can't do this type of shit and expect me to sit back placidly. I hate not knowing things. Where have you been and what the hell have you been doing?"

Talon turns his attention to Leandro. "Can you give us a minute?"

Shit. My nerves burst through me in waves, tensing my muscles. I thought I was prepared to confront Talon, but now that he asks to be alone with me...I'm panicking.

"Just tell me," I argue, blocking Leandro from leaving. "Tell me, and then you can go. Get some sleep."

Talon bobs his head, his face a series of lines with his

frown. Now's not the time to get into things with him. His current state might break the wall I built around myself to keep him out. I've just never seen him so…I can't explain it. Not weak. But maybe worried. For me.

"You don't have to worry because you're not wanted for murder. You're missing, and now the media reports possible foul play. A lot of people are worried about you."

Fuck my life.

I guess being missing is better than being wanted, but I can only imagine what my un-initiated family is going through. My mom—oh, no. If she thinks something happened to me, she might relapse. She's been doing so well at the posh treatment center in Monterey.

I comb my fingers through my hair and spin toward the wall. I've been worried about myself these last few days, thinking about the consequences when I should've been freaking out about how this affects everyone in my life.

"It's going to be okay. It's better this way. It'll give us a chance to figure out what the hell really happened and who did this." A warm hand touches my shoulder, Talon now standing behind me. I break under his touch, my body wanting to give out.

The door to the suite clicks closed as Leandro silently leaves. This is all too much. I want to be alone, but I also don't.

"You can't just keep me out of things. I need to know what is going on. This is my life. I should get a say, right?" I tremble with my words. When have I really, truly gotten a say in my life? I never even had a say in my initiation. My life was already built before me, and the gilded path I've been following turns out to be more treacherous. It's not made of gold, but of iron spikes, and I could trip and impale myself at any moment.

"I just want to protect you." Talon pulls at my shoulder, turning me around. His eyes meet mine, his intensity trapping me in place. It's the same look he gave me the moment he admitted how much he wanted me.

"Can you blame me if I struggle to believe you? Part of protecting me is keeping me informed. I'm not some outsider. I earned my damn place in the Esoteric Society. I'm the heir to the St. Germaine Empire. Don't you think that counts for something? You can't keep treating me like a naïve college student." I lower my voice to keep it from breaking. I can't help but think of the last moment we were together and how he so easily discarded me. Rejected me.

"I'm not treating you like a naïve kid, Stacia. I'm treating you with care and gentleness. I'm not a decent guy. I know you know this already, but I don't want to prove it to you. So please, give me a small break. I'm trying my best." Talon reaches up and grasps my chin. "I know some of this is because of how I left. I know I hurt you, but things are complicated."

"You patted me on the fucking head. You were too ashamed to even give me an ounce of affection in front of Leandro. And then you vanished for days. This is more than hurting me. I felt used." I turn my head, getting him to let go of me. It's the space I need to take a breath and to break away from our attraction keeping me frozen in place. "And what made it worse was that you just come stomping back in here, threatening Leandro like he's the one in the wrong. You made it clear. I'm not going to be your little secret. I'm not going to be something that complicates your life. I'm sorry if this isn't what you want to hear, and I'm sorry that I just can't accept your word and be understanding. I've already been hurt, and I need to be able to trust you. And right now, I can't. Not until you can trust that I can handle things."

My fucking eyes. I wish they wouldn't tear up. I don't want to cry in front of Talon, but I'm so confused and angry.

"I think it's best that you leave me alone, get some rest, and think about everything I've just said. But don't you dare, and I mean fucking dare, try to threaten another man I'm interested in because you're too cowardly to be with me how you want." I take a couple of steps away, keeping my eyes on Talon as I walk backward.

He shifts on his feet and scrubs his palms over his cheeks, uncomfortable with the fact that I'm crying while calling him out.

I expect him to argue with me. I expect him to try to give me a dozen excuses.

But instead, he once again doesn't meet my expectations. He turns around and leaves, not bothering to close the door.

I'm left standing in the middle of my bedroom with both Leandro and Esteban standing in the hallway. I don't know how to react, so I stride forward and slam the door in their faces.

I just want this whole fucking day to be over.

I refuse to stay in my room, keeping out of Talon's way. He can avoid me all he wants, but he claims I'm not a prisoner, so I'm not going to act like one.

Strolling down the stairs, I peek over the banister at the empty foyer. Only the light of the television flickers in the living room, but I don't hear any noise. Leandro is nowhere in sight, probably either patrolling the perimeter or sleeping. I'm not even sure what time it is without my phone.

The glow of a fire on the beach sparkles on the other side of the panoramic windows, and I spot a figure sitting on the sand. I grab a blanket off the back of the leather couch in the entertainment room and wrap it around my shoulders. I haven't been outside at all this whole time, only looking at the expansive ocean from the window. But it's dark out, and I don't think Leandro would've started a fire if he thought it would cause problems.

I exit through the glass back door and onto the stone walkway that disappears into the sand. The ocean roars as waves crash against the beach, and I tread my way toward the bonfire.

"Mamacita, did the Executioner let you leave your room?" Esteban asks from the sand, surprising me. I guess it wasn't Leandro, after all. "I'm sure you're bored out of your mind. Join me."

I hesitate, looking between the mansion and Esteban. Do I really want to start a conversation with him and open up that sort of door? I honestly don't know.

He pats the blanket beside him. "Siéntate. I have s'mores. You look like you could use something sweet."

Still, I don't move. Esteban wags his eyebrows, smiling at me. I'm tempted to turn around and run back into the house, but then again, being out here means that I won't have to deal with Talon or Leandro for that matter.

Heaving a sigh, I sashay forward, kicking sand. Esteban chuckles and scoots over a bit more. I lower myself beside him, keeping a foot of space between us before moving the box of graham crackers to create a tiny wall so he doesn't get tempted to lean in.

"Don't think I've chosen to join you because I'm interested. I'm just in desperate need of some fresh air." I curl my knees up and wrap my arms around them, resting my chin.

"It does seem quite intense inside. I can't imagine what it's like to have two men secretly vying for your attention, but also wanting to deny it to each other. It's a bit messy. At least with me, you don't have to worry." Esteban pops one of the marshmallows onto his wire stick and hangs it over the fire. "Toasted, chard, or completely burnt to a crisp?"

"Burnt." I keep my gaze turned to the fire, watching as the heat waves blur the whitecaps crashing into the shore.

"That's the best way, mamacita. I thought we'd have some things in common." Esteban pulls the flaming marshmallow from the fire and holds it in front of us, watching the flames eat away at the sugary outside, turning it black.

"If it's only how to make, s'mores, then don't get your hopes up. I am swearing off hot guys and any more trouble." I hold up the graham cracker and chocolate, letting Esteban put the marshmallow on top before I squeeze it together.

"So you think I'm hot." He smirks again, his hazel eyes dancing with firelight.

"And definitely trouble. Guys like you prey on people's weaknesses. I have already been through too much bullshit. You can thank Christos for that." I take a bite of the s'more, cracking the graham cracker in half. I end up just shoving the whole thing in my mouth, not even caring, because it's one way to shut myself up. I shouldn't have even brought Christos up. I don't even want to think about him. I know that Esteban is his best friend.

"I'd never thank Christos for anything...well, except maybe for that blow job. I didn't know he had it in him. He was surprisingly good." Esteban watches the side of my face, his intense gaze penetrating through me as if he can see what's on my mind.

"I'd have been better." My mouth betrays me with a smirk, and I grab one of the napkins and wipe my lips. "I'm glad you enjoyed it as much as I did. Though, I'm sure it was for different reasons."

Esteban bends closer, bumping me with his shoulder. "Are you sure about that, mamacita? I saw the way you smiled. How you couldn't take your eyes off us. I think it was more than a little payback."

Heat warms my chest, and I shake my head in denial, hiding my cheeks with my hair. "Whatever helps you sleep at night. Unless…you're into Christos too." Because I can already tell that Esteban is attracted to me. He wouldn't have invited me to join him just out of kindness. I don't know him well, but I know his type. He sees something he likes, and he'll go for it. It makes things a bit more exciting, though I know that nothing can happen between us. He's hot, but he's dangerous. I need to make smart choices in men, because clearly my attraction is often set to morally gray.

"He's not bad looking, but no. I'm not into Christos. He's…a bit unstable. The only one I'm into is you, mamacita. But I don't mind if you want to continue to fantasize about his chivalry. You have to truly love a woman to suck a cock on her behalf." Esteban smirks again with his words. "I can see the reason for his obsession."

I don't know how to respond, so I stare at the ocean before us, processing everything he's just said. "And what reason is that?"

"You're hypnotic. Not only muy bonita, but also confident. Not many women get initiated into the Esoteric Society. You must be algo especial. Extraordinaria. And it's obviously your strength and resilience. I overheard what you had told Talon about how things were going to work, and it takes a lot of bravery to stand up to someone like him." Esteban shifts beside me, leaning forward in an attempt to capture my gaze.

"That was a private moment," I say, building my wall up even higher as he tries to break it down.

"I'm not going to apologize for eavesdropping. I've already been pulled into this. I will stay on top of things. I don't blindly trust anyone, even those who are my superiors. This also involves my business. You were drugged, and I need to know by who just as much as you do. It doesn't look good if shit like this gets out to the media. I don't want my clients to be afraid. Especially if I need to entrust my product with new dealers." Esteban tightens his jaw with his words, going from soft and flirty to scary in a matter of seconds. He's one of those types. Charming and likable, but one wrong decision could have your life in his hands. That should be enough for me to stay away, but he's right. I need to know who drugged me, because that could help lead to the true killer.

I swallow my nerves. "Thanks for making things clear and—"

Someone catches my attention on the beach. Esteban frowns and swivels his torso, turning to glance at what I can't take my eyes off. This isn't exactly a spot for tourists or local beachgoers. It's more private with the mansions being within a gated community despite being on the beach. And it's late.

Esteban reaches into his jacket, surprising the hell out of me by sliding a gun from a holster on his side. "Why don't you go inside, mamacita? There shouldn't be anyone on this beach."

I slowly nod and get to my feet without arguing. Esteban soon follows suit, but instead of coming with me, he heads toward the figure.

I don't wait to find out what the person is doing here. I can't afford to be seen.

Reaching the door, I leave it cracked open and try to peer onto the beach, but Esteban disappears from my view.

A gunshot pops through the air, making me jump. I gasp and shut the door completely, locking it. I should run and find Talon or Leandro, but I'm paralyzed as I continue to stare, waiting for what happens next.

Esteban comes back into view, kicking up sand, pointing his gun toward the ground. He's alone.

Shit.

I don't wait for him to come back inside. The less I

know the better.

What the hell has my life turned into?

How can I be the one facing possible murder charges when I'm innocent and everyone around me isn't? Life just seems so fucking unfair.

It doesn't just seem it. It *is* unfair.

Maybe I should just be a bad guy too.

12

Boundaries

Stacia

Esteban didn't come chasing me last night, and I didn't seek him out either. And now, the two of us sit at the dining room table with Talon and Leandro.

And this is awkward as fuck.

I can tell that Talon and Leandro only behave for my sake. Talon still thinks he has a claim on me despite what I told him, and Leandro hates it.

And then there's Esteban, keeping his eyes glued on me, waiting for me to look at him.

I set my fork down and lean back in my chair. "Esteban, did you tell them that you killed some guy on the beach last night? What did you do with the body? Did you just let it drift out to sea?"

Leandro turns away from his breakfast and glowers at Esteban. A smile crosses my lips, and I fold my arms over my chest, squeezing the sides of my boobs just a little to accentuate my cleavage. I don't want him to be able to think straight. If it's going to be difficult for me being around the three of them, then they can suffer too.

"I didn't kill anyone, mamacita. Had you just stayed a moment longer, I could've told you as much." Esteban smirks right back at me. The cocky bastard. "I just threatened them to stay away. You should thank me. It was Christos. He followed us here."

My blood boils at the sound of his name. I can't believe he just said Christos was here last night. Now I'm glad I didn't hesitate on the beach. What the fuck is the asshole even thinking?

"That has to be against our code, Talon." I lean forward, finally speaking to him for the first time this morning. "You need to report it. He needs some consequences. He's just stepping over every damn boundary."

"I think Esteban did a fine job handling it. There's

no need to get the King's Court involved." Talon scoots his chair back. "Now, if you'll excuse me, I have work to do. I just got in more surveillance from your dad. Apparently, someone else was drugged last night."

"Wait. You knew? You knew that Christos was here?" I get up, blocking Talon's way.

"Did you even hear the other things I said, wild child?" Talon places his hands on my shoulders, physically, moving me out of his way. "If I can catch the asshole on camera, we'll have a lead."

Goddamn him. He makes me sound stupid. Of course, I heard him about the drugs, but I don't like the fact that once again, he chooses to leave me out of things. He doesn't consider Christos the same threat that I do.

"Talon, please. This is important to me." I try to block him again, but he picks me up off my feet, spins around, and sets me back down.

"We can discuss it later. Why don't you go watch TV or something." Talon looks at Esteban. "I need you with me on this one."

I throw my arms up. "Really?"

"Yes, really. Now, if you're a good girl, I'll tell Leandro to return your phone to you. Maybe you can call Bianca or something. She's been blowing up my damn line." Talon doesn't wait for me to argue and storms away, leaving me alone with Esteban and Leandro.

I flare my nostrils and chase after him, despite knowing that he's already made his decision. But I can't give up. He's going to know that he can't just do whatever the fuck he wants. That's not how this is going to work.

Except the fucker slams the door to his office and locks it. And there's no way I'm going back to the dining room with my hurt pride. So I head back to my room to hide like the chickenshit I keep turning into.

The familiar scent of citrus and spice waft over me first before I even have a chance to catch sight of Christos. He snatches my wrist and pulls me into my suite, quickly shutting and locking the door. His palm slaps across my lips as he holds me from behind, silencing me from screaming.

I thrash in his arms, trying to headbutt him, but all I do is hit his taut shoulder.

"Astéri mou, don't fight. I'm not going to hurt you, but I'm also not going to let you scream and let those idiots come confronting me. I just want to talk."

Christos murmurs against my ear, his warm breath tickling my skin.

"I don't want to talk," I mumble against his hand, trying my best to snap my teeth against the skin of his palm, but I can't get any leverage with the way he holds me.

"Then just listen to me. I've been so fucking worried about you. I know you don't want to hear it, but I love you, Stacia. Everything you're going through is fucking bullshit, and I can't just stand by and do nothing." Christos loosens his grip just a little to see if I continue to fight.

I manage to kick my foot up backward, but I miss my target, hitting him in the thigh instead of his balls. He growls under his breath and pushes me forward, half carrying me and half dragging me to the bathroom, where he shuts and locks the door with one hand.

"You asshole!" I scream, swinging my hand, trying to slap him.

He grabs my wrist and drags me closer, using the lack of space to overpower me. "I know, Stacia. You can hit me all you want, but please. Tell me everything that happened. Let me help you."

"The only way you can fucking help me is to take the blame and turn yourself in as the murderer." I give up on trying to fight and instead yank away. "It won't make me forgive you, but it'll be a fucking start."

Christos doesn't move, staring me up and down in silence as thoughts cloud his light brown eyes. "If that's what you need from me, and what you really want, then fine. I will turn myself in to the police."

I open and close my mouth in surprise. "What?"

"You heard me, astéri mou. If that's what I need to do to earn your forgiveness, I'll do it." Christos drops to his knees and crawls closer. He wraps his arms around me, hugging me from the floor. "Please, Stacia. I'll do anything."

I stand frozen with my arms up. How do I even respond? He just admitted that he's willing to go to prison for me, but he could be lying and manipulating me. Unfulfilled promises don't mean anything to me.

I link my fingers through his hair. "Christos...I...I don't want you to turn yourself in to the police. I just—"

The door to my bathroom flings open, smacking the wall. Leandro busts into the room, aiming a gun. "Let her the fuck go and don't move. I will shoot."

Christos eases his hands off me and raises them into the air. Everything happens so fast that I don't get a chance to call Leandro off. He grabs Christos, dragging him out of the bathroom. Shoving him to the floor with his knee on his spine, he then zip-ties his arms behind him.

"Are you okay, beautiful?" Leandro asks, pushing to his feet. "He didn't hurt you, right?"

"Of course, I didn't fucking hurt her!" Christos yells, Leandro's questions setting him off.

I shake my head, confirming Christos's comment. "That's Christos, Leandro."

"I know who he is." Leandro grasps my arm, tugging me away, putting space between Christos and us. He turns me slightly, so I face away. Leaning in, Leandro whispers, "If you want me to escort him out, just say the word. If you're allowing him to stay, I don't mind giving him a hard time for a bit. But you need to go grab Talon."

I pause, thinking over his words. Leandro knew who Christos was and still proceeded to tackle him and tie him up on my behalf. He'll even fuck with him if I ask him to. I've never felt as if someone was more on my side than I do in this moment.

Cupping Leandro's face, I run my fingers along his jaw. "Have I ever told you how much I appreciate you?" I raise my voice loud enough for Christos to hear. Then I kiss Leandro softly, humming in satisfaction, sensing Christos's glare. "Thank you, babe."

Leandro chuckles, realizing my intent. I'm beginning to think he gets off on me using him to make another man jealous. I can feel his hardening bulge against my leg as he hums in my ear. "It's my pleasure, beautiful."

"Holy fuck! Are you kidding me? *Him*?" Christos struggles to push up to his knees with his arms restrained. My kissing Leandro worked. He's utterly and completely jealous, and I can't help how much I enjoy it.

"You have no right to be angry with me, Christos. It's been years, and you're the one who fucked me over." I lace my fingers through Leandro's. Am I being a bitch? Absolutely. Do I care? Hell no.

Christos groans and shakes his head. "No, no, no, Stacia. I'm not angry. I'm just—" He slumps back to the floor, resting his cheek on the rug. "It's just so dangerous. You know why."

His words set me off, and I pull away from Leandro.

I stride forward, towering over him. "It's none of your business. You have absolutely no right telling me what is and isn't dangerous. You have no right to be jealous. And you damn well have no fucking right to judge me."

Christos sighs. "I—"

"Goddamn it, Christos! What the fuck did I tell you?" As if this situation couldn't get any worse, Esteban and Talon rush from the hallway. "You aren't welcome here unless Stacia agreed. Why can't you ever fucking listen?"

"Did you even ask her, asshole?" Christos asks, whipping his attention to me.

I stare with wide eyes.

"Obviously fucking not," he adds.

"That's because I told him not to, you dumb shit." Talon stomps to Christos, yanks him up by his arms, and hauls him to his feet. He pulls a switchblade from his pocket and jerks it up through the zip-ties, freeing Christos. "You're the reason Stacia is in this fucking position. Had you left her alone to begin with, she wouldn't have been drugged. You're damn lucky nothing worse happened to her or you'd be a dead man but keep this shit up and you will be one."

I hate how sexy protective looks on Talon after everything. There are too many attractive guys in one room for me to think straight, so I dodge past Esteban and bolt toward the stairs. It doesn't help that I fucked three of them and got turned on by the last watching my ex suck him off. What the hell is wrong with me?

"Stacia? Where are you going?" Talon calls from behind me, chasing after me without catching up, sending my heart racing.

"To get a fucking drink. I can't deal with this shit right now." I waltz into the pristine kitchen with stainless steel appliances and white cabinets. Sauntering around the island, I head to the wet bar where Talon has a collection of high-end bottles of alcohol.

I grab an ornate silver and glass bottle of vodka and pour a shot. It sinks smoothly to my stomach, warming my insides. Talon cocks his eyebrow at me, watching me in silence. I wave the bottle at him.

"Want one?" I ask, pouring a second shot. I down it, not waiting for Talon to respond.

Leandro shows up next with Esteban behind him. I spot Christos keeping his distance, choosing to stay in the dining room instead of joining us in the kitchen.

I pour another shot. "What about you, Esteban?"

Esteban takes it away before I can down it, tipping his head back and drinking it. He releases a breath and shakes his head. "I'm more of a tequila man, but it's pretty smooth."

"I'd expect it to be considering it cost a grand." Talon snatches the vodka bottle from me, but instead of putting it back on the shelf, he pours himself a glass in a short tumbler.

I snake my arm past him and grab the bottle again. "What about you, Leandro? Do you want one?"

"I don't drink on the job, beautiful. But thanks." Leandro moves to the high counter and takes a seat on a barstool.

"I'll take one, Stacia," Christos speaks up from the dining room, where he plops down in the chair.

"You ain't having shit, Count. You're not a house-guest." Talon snatches the bottle away from me and places it on a high shelf out of my reach. The bastard.

"You're really going to be an ass, Talon? You know we can get things done faster if you're not constantly having to come to my hotel. Don't you think it's smarter if we're all under the same roof? Someone could easily follow you like I did. I even got in without any of you fuckers realizing." Christos narrows his eyes at Leandro. "I thought you were supposed to be her bodyguard."

"I am, which is why I allowed you in so that I'd have the chance to fuck you up myself," Leandro retorts, remaining unfazed by the accusation and attempt to scrutinize his ability to protect me.

"Yeah fucking right." Christos gets to his feet and steps into the kitchen, puffing his chest out as if he can overpower Leandro, but we both know that Leandro has kicked his ass twice now. Once before he even knew I was his client.

Talon smacks his hand on the light gray streaked marble countertop. "That's enough. No more fucking fighting under my roof. If you're going to stay here, you better make sure it's okay with Stacia first. You are not to bother her or be distracted. We have shit to do and a business to run. We have people to track down. We found the fucker who drugged one of the girls last night."

My blood cools, despite my body warming because of the alcohol. He just said he found a possible lead and whoever has been drugging people at the Looking Glass.

The knowledge sobers me up enough to grab

Talon's arm, dragging his attention to me. "You found him? Who is it? Do we know him?"

Talon grinds his teeth, not responding to me right away.

I open my mouth to yell at him to stop keeping things for me, but I don't get the chance.

"We don't know yet, mamacita. But we will. I got an ID on him through one of my dealers." Esteban rolls his shoulders, his face hardening. "We will have him soon enough."

"And then what? Do you think it's somehow connected to the dead guy?" My legs tremble, my mind spinning. I grab onto the countertop to stabilize myself.

"You don't need to worry about that, wild child. It'll be handled. I told you I'd take care of things." Talon rests his hand on my shoulder before sliding it down my arm to lace around my waist. He manages to make my body relax, and I sink against him, wishing we could go back to when we first arrived. Because I hate this now. I hate how attracted I am to him, but also how many secrets he keeps for me. I hate that my attention continues to be pulled in every which way.

"We will take care of it," Christos says, staring at

me from the corner of my eye. I know he studies how Talon treats me, but he doesn't say anything. I doubt he will, considering Talon is part of the King's Court. "If you let me stay, astéri mou. Please. I just want to help you. I want to prove I'm worthy."

I close my eyes, trying to think things through. If I allow him to stay, it might open some doors I want to remain nailed shut and abandoned. However, he might've been right when he told Talon that things would be easier if they were here under one roof. They wouldn't risk people following them. Especially if I am currently considered missing. I'm sure there are tons of people theorizing what happened. I've seen many people across social media do even better work than the police, and for the first time, I'm afraid of them. You can't really buy off the public like you can the authorities. At least, that's what Daddy always said.

Opening my eyes, I peek at Talon and then at Leandro and Esteban before looking back at Talon. I half expect him to answer for me.

"It's up to you, wild child," Talon says, lowering his voice. "But I'm going to warn you that I will hurt him if he even tries anything. This isn't turning into an opportunity to win you back. Me and you have shit to talk about."

Wow. He did not just say that. I did not just love that he did either. Who am I kidding?

I slowly bob my head, glancing at Christos. "You can stay, but you have to stay down here. You can sleep on the couch. I don't want you sneaking around upstairs."

Christos shifts his jaw but doesn't argue. "I won't sneak around. You've cleared things up about your boundaries, and I can see things as they are."

I rub my lips together and ruffle my fingers through my hair. "Good. I'm fucking exhausted, so whatever it is you found out about the guy who drugged me can wait until morning, Talon. I don't want you discussing things without me."

"Stacia," he argues, straightening his shoulders.

I poke his chest. "No. That's how things are going to be. For all of you." I glance around even though I know everyone is listening. "Also, I don't want to see anyone throwing punches or getting jealous. None of you have a damn claim on me. Do you understand?"

I don't wait for them to answer and stroll out of the kitchen, leaving them in silence behind me.

I just hope we can figure things out and I can go

home and return to a life of normalcy.

Who knew I would miss such a thing?

I just want it all to be over.

13

Psycho

Esteban

"**E**sta loco," I mumble under my breath. "There's no fucking way he's getting away with coming into my damn territory and making my product look bad."

I rewind the video for the hundredth time, zooming in on a man in a barely club-passable suit slipping a bright red square of paper into a woman's drink. For one, I wouldn't sell such a shitty substance. I can tell from the square shape that it doesn't come from my employees. My product comes in a diamond, heart, spade, and clover shape, depending on where it's made and how pure the quality is.

"Kitty found the receipts with the time stamp of when he bought the victim the drink," Talon says, setting his phone in front of me. "The ID ties to a man in Culver City."

"There's no damn way that's our dude. Just look at him." Christos taps his finger on the screen, enlarging the picture of the ID. The bouncers scan and save every ID that passes through their verification machines. It's the best way to track patrons.

As for the man? Christos is right. He's not the one we want, but he can lead us to whoever sold him the shit.

No smart dealer would risk it in an establishment owned by a St. Germaine. This pinche cabrón probably couldn't get any pussy so he thought he could just take it. I can't wait to get my knife in him.

"I can have him located within the hour." I crack my knuckles, the idea of putting some pendejo in his place making my adrenaline pump.

Talon whacks me between the shoulders. I haven't seen him grin since we arrived, and having a lead helps with the situation. "Good. We'll head out in fifteen to be—"

"Head out where? What are you guys doing? I

thought we were supposed to go over everything together." Stacia stands akimbo in the doorway with Leandro behind her like a silent shadow. I love how sexy she looks, wearing short-shorts and a tank top, her dark hair extra pullable in her high ponytail.

"That was the plan until you decided to take your sweet time this morning. I figured I'd give you the fucking bullet points before we head out. Anything you need while we're gone?" Talon cracks his knuckles, standing tall, looming over Stacia's five and a half feet.

"Watch out, Executioner. She's going to take your cojones if you don't step back. I know her type. Más loca que una cabra." And I love it. Stacia looks sweet and innocent but I knew she had it in her to be crazy.

"Did you just call me a goat?" Stacia frowns, scrunching her nose.

I smirk at her. "It's something mi abuela used to say to me. It's not a bad thing, mamacita. Not in my eyes. I'd love to see you a little crazy, especially with the Executioner."

Talon takes advantage of her distraction. Grabbing his keys from his desk, he shoves them in his pocket and then shrugs into his suit jacket.

"Careful, Esteban. Don't egg her on," Christos warns, tapping a few keys on his laptop, sending the printer whirring to life.

"Oh, shut up. All of you. You're all going to be in trouble...except Leandro." Stacia smiles at her bodyguard.

In the corner of my eye, I watch as Talon opens his safe and pulls out a gun and a knife. He tucks them away in his holsters. "At least not from you." Talon eyes Leandro. "You should've kept her away until we were ready. Now you're going to have to restrain her so we can leave."

"Oh, fucking no you don't. I'm tired of sitting around here. I want to go. I'll stay in the car." Stacia saunters closer to Talon, resting her hands on his hips. "Please, birdie. You can update me in the car."

Talon sighs and shakes his head. "Absolutely not. We can't risk it."

Stacia pouts, her full lips completely kissable. Talon doesn't notice her hand sliding into his pocket until it's too late. Yanking out his key fob, she squeals and spins away, dodging past Leandro. Talon yells at him to grab her, but he only reaches out, brushing her arm. Talon shoves him into the wall and charges past him, running behind Stacia.

I meet Christos's gaze and howl a laugh. "Creo que estoy enamorado de ella. I know you think she's yours, pendejo, but goddamn. You have some competition."

Christos flares his nostrils and slams his palm to the table. "Fuck no."

"We can share," I tease, dodging out of the way.

"Christos, Esteban! Grab your shit. Leandro, load up. Stacia's coming with us. I swear to God if anyone sees her or shit happens, I'll take all your heads for not helping me. You dicks."

Tipping my head back, I laugh. "I'm definitely in love."

I stroll past Leandro and Talon in the hallway and head to the garage. Stacia sits in the front seat of the Astin Martin SUV, her lips curled with her pride. Cracking the window, she stretches up to speak to me. "How mad is he?"

"Pissed, but it's fine, mamacita. Open the door. I'll drive." I jog around the hood and wait for her to unlock the idling vehicle. I slide behind the wheel and reach out, touching her knee. "They don't give you enough credit. Big bad protectors. What Talon should be more concerned with is ensuring you can take care of yourself."

"If you can convince him that, I'll kiss you," she says, refusing to meet my gaze. She stares at the others getting ready to enter the garage.

"Don't think I won't do it. It might not be fair to you, though. I'm fucking sure he doesn't need convincing now." I motion to Talon, who stops at the backdoor, not even attempting to make either of us move.

But Leandro does, tapping his finger to her window. "Climb in back and put on these," he says, handing her a hoodie and sunglasses through the window.

"So this is happening?" Stacia asks, plopping down between Talon and Christos. "You're going to stop keeping shit from me?"

Talon dips his chin. "Like I had a choice." He smacks the driver's seat. "Drive, Knave. We've already wasted enough fucking time."

"Please, where are you taking me? I haven't done anything wrong," Bradley Thomas says, digging his fingers into his knees. The guy made it easy for us to pick him up, not even looking around on his walk from his apartment to the corner liquor store.

I glance at him in the rearview mirror, sitting in the middle of the backseat with a bag over his head. Stacia sits on Talon's lap, while Christos holds his gun to the man's chest.

"Like hell you didn't. We're going to cut your fucking dick off. We don't take kindly to rapists. You made a huge fucking mistake coming into our home and slipping drugs to unsuspecting women." Christos is the only one who speaks, lowering his voice to help obscure it.

"What! No. No. I haven't done anything. I'm not a fucking rapist. Any woman I've slept with wanted it. Who the fuck told you that? I don't even do drugs." Bradley tries to thrash, only to have Christos grab the bag tighter. He yanks it up to the man's nose and shoves the gun in his mouth deep enough to make him gag. Freezing, Bradley stops fighting, realizing he could lose his fucking head.

"Just shut up. We have evidence. But don't worry, asshole. If you can give us what we need, we will go easy on you." Christos pulls the gun from the man's mouth and clicks his seatbelt. "Now we're getting out. Don't you fucking make a sound. If you do, I'll stab you in the nuts. You can live without those."

Bradley trembles in the seat, shaking with his fear. He doesn't argue or risk going against Christos's instructions. Opening his door, Talon slides off the seat with Stacia, setting her on her feet outside the vehicle. Leandro fills the space on her other side, sandwiching her between them as if anyone would dare mess with us. No one would risk coming into my complex without notice. This is off-limits to anyone outside of my business, and the locals know better. I made it clear the moment I took over this territory on behalf of St. Germaine. He wanted someone from within the Esoteric Society, and he's been friends with my dad a long time. He knew it was better to have me expand the business rather than take over.

I don't show mercy. I've worked hard, making people fear me. It won't stop now.

"Just walk straight." Christos shoves the guy, making him stumble.

I catch him by the back of his shirt and pull him against my chest. He smells of rum and regrets, his odor enough to overpower the musk of the concrete around us. I guide the man to the metal door and use my phone to unlock it.

I yank the bag from his head and keep him in front of me, guiding him down the stairs. He sniffles and sobs. The second we clear the landing, and he realizes this could be the last place he ever sees, he tries to fight, full-blown crying.

"Please, don't do this. I'm not a bad man. I swear. I have a family." He wheezes with his words, digging his shoes into the slick floor with a drain in the center.

"Stop fucking lying. I know who you are, Bradley. You have a mom in an elderly care home that you're waiting on to die so you can inherit her money. You haven't visited her in three years, nor have you called her on more than just her birthday. I'm pretty sure she won't be missing you since you already act like she doesn't exist." Christos adjusts his mask, hiding his features. He takes over for me, not letting the man see my face as I take another mask and put it over my head, the full-face cover, hopefully, scary enough to leave this man a mess.

Stacia catches my attention from the corner of the room where she watches with wide eyes and Leandro trying to block her. Talon hands them both masks before putting on his own, and I help Christos restrain the man in a metal chair bolted to the floor.

I wonder if this might be too much for Stacia, because her complexion pales as she stares around my chamber. Leandro grips her, practically holding her up. I'd be lying if I said I've never tortured anyone, and I think she knows as much. I wonder how this whole thing will affect her. There's a reason Talon wanted to keep her out of things, but I'm pretty damn sure there's also a reason why he gave in and let her tag along. He wants to show her exactly who we are and what we have to do. He wants to teach her a silent lesson, so she doesn't ask again. Is it fucked up? Maybe. On the other hand, it's smart. But I think Talon underestimates her. From what I know of her now, she's tough as shit despite looking fragile. She just has to get past the shock.

If anything, this will desensitize her. She will come away from this stronger. Maybe even more willing to participate in getting shit done. I've only ever known her as the party girl and heiress of St. Germaine.

I'd like to see who she truly is.

"Please, what do you want?" Bradley wiggles his arms, testing the restraints.

"We want your dealer, pendejo. The asshole sold on

my territory. I want his fucking name." I reach into my jacket and pull out my blade, flipping the switch. I'll start small for now, but I have a whole collection of knives hidden in one of the cabinets, my favorite being, mi abuelo's machete. It was the first weapon I put in this room. I can't wait to christen the space with a bloody sacrifice, especially someone like Bradley.

"What are you talking about? I told you I don't do drugs." Bradley grinds his teeth, keeping his eyes on my weapon.

"Where the fuck did you buy the shit you put in the drink of one of our best customers at the Looking Glass? It wasn't something I sell. Cheap, diluted, and fucking lethal. She almost died." I step closer and press my blade to his neck, nicking his skin on purpose, watching the blood trickle to his collar.

Bradley hollers only to have Christos shove the bag into his mouth, gagging him. "Stop screaming and tell us, or we'll make an example out of you. No one fucks with women in our clubs." Yanking the bag from Bradley's mouth, Christos gets in his face and spits. "Now tell us. This is your last fucking chance. We don't have time."

He blubbers, gasping. "I don't—"

I swing my fist and punch the man in the face, cracking my knuckles against his jaw. "That's not a name," I growl, aiming my knife at his groin next. "You better fucking talk."

Bradley opens his mouth to holler again, and I jab down, sinking the tip of my blade in half an inch, just enough to paralyze him in fear.

"I don't know his real name. I have his number, though. He goes by Red. I can see if he will hook me up again. So you can't hurt me. I won't do it if you hurt me." Bradley bares his teeth, grinding them with his empty threat.

I stab him deeper, remaining expressionless as he howls in pain, unable to cup his junk. "Let's try that again. You're going to arrange a meeting no matter what. Do you understand? You're in my house. I make the rules here."

He heaves, his chest rising and falling with his deep breathing. Nodding his head, he agrees, finally coming to his good senses.

"Bueno. Arrange it now, and I'll think about whether or not we'll let you go." I swipe my blade across the zip tie, freeing one of his hands. "It'll all depend on what happens next. Do you understand?"

Bradley dips his chin in agreement. "I'll do whatever you want."

I grin, turning my attention to Talon. "Good. That's exactly what we want to hear."

"If you try anything stupid, you're not going to make it out of here. Call him. Leave it on speakerphone. See if he can give you the hookup tonight." Talon looms closer, taking over the situation. He pats my shoulder. "Go see if you can find anything on Red. Take Princess with you."

I leer at Bradley, stabbing my blade into the chair between his legs, startling him. Tipping my head back, I laugh and flip the blade closed. Stacia peeks at me from over Leandro's shoulder, and I ignore her bodyguard as I offer her my hand. She automatically slides her fingers through mine and allows me to tug her along to my office. She trembles but doesn't give much away. I can't tell if she fears me or is impressed. I guess I'll find out.

Leandro follows behind us, but I cut him off with my arm, forcing him to stop. He looks past me at the windowless room, made soundproof with extra insulation, and backs off. I think it's the only reason he does. He can guard the only way in or out. Not that we need it here.

"Enjoy the show," I mutter, starting to close the door on Leandro. He locks his gaze to mine, staring at me until the door clicks shut.

In here, Stacia won't hear anything. Talon can do whatever the hell he wants and clean it up before she realizes the extent of his darker side. He didn't receive the nickname the Executioner without good reason. I've heard the stories. He climbed the ladder in his chapter faster than any man. His cutthroat, power-hungry work ethic wouldn't allow anyone to step in front of him. And from how Stacia treats him, I'm nearly certain she doesn't realize how deadly that pendejo truly is—not that I don't respect him. He's loyal to those who earn it. Wanting to get his hands bloody might be the one thing holding him back. To be a true leader, he'll need to learn how to pass on the task. He's too controlling to think anyone else can do it right. It was obvious by him commanding me to look into this dealer.

Stacia puffs out a deep breath, shuddering in her spot. "Shit. That was intense," she whispers under her breath, barely loud enough for me to overhear.

I squeeze her fingers, drawing her attention to me.

"You're afraid." She'd be lying if she tried to deny it.

She doesn't, though. She thins her lips and nods. "You stabbed a guy like it was nothing. You were smiling."

Pulling her closer, I welcome her shivering body into my arms, wanting nothing more than to assure her that I save my twisted side for those who deserve it. "Mamacita, lo siento. I'm sorry. Forgive me, por favor. I didn't mean to frighten you."

Stacia sinks against me, my soft voice breaking her guard down enough for her body to realize I'm not a threat. Resting her head on my chest, she inhales slowly. The scent of her shampoo wafts around me with notes of grapefruit and vanilla, stirring something wild inside me.

"You didn't scare me," she whispers, trailing her hands along my sides. "I just—I don't know what I was expecting. I don't do well with blood, and I guess I was stupid not to consider you had a psychotic side. You'd have to, considering your...line of work."

"I'm a businessman in a treacherous industry. As long as the demand is there, someone has to supply it. It might as well be me. I have what it takes." I stroke my hand over her back, smoothing out the trembles.

"Does it bother you?"

"No..." Her voice trails off.

"I'd never hurt you, mamacita. But everyone else? They're fair game. No one drugs our members. No one sells on my territory. No one fucking tries to pull shit on me. Those who do will find themselves at the end of my blade." I ease away and touch her chin, glancing into her vibrant blue eyes.

"Is it weird if that makes me feel better?" Stacia offers me a waning smile, her eyes searching mine. "Not that I was worried about you. I just—everything feels so fucked up. That pervert drugged a girl with plans to fucking rape her. What if that were me? What if Leandro hadn't decided to ditch his meeting with Talon to leave with me? What if—"

I hug her close. "I know, Stacia. I know. I've thought about those things too. I let Christos take things too far that night with the confrontation. Had I kept better control over him, we'd...well, you'd have woken up alone with just a massive hangover."

She laughs breathlessly, pulling back to pat my chest. "That's ridiculous and crazy. I'm sure Christos can't be controlled."

"He sucked my cock, didn't he?" I raise my eyebrows, studying her as she glances down. The sudden intensity of her gaze, now lingering on my body, turns me on.

"Whatever you say," she says, surprising me by stepping even closer. Her hips brush mine, awakening my desire even more. I realize I might've made a mistake. She'll be the one controlling me by my damn dick.

"Mamacita, be careful. You look like you want to test me, and I have no restraint. I'd let you have your way, even if it was to only fuck with Christos. I'm a man with no shame." I caress my finger over her cheek, tracing her jaw.

She leans into me, tilting her head slightly, shifting her gaze to my mouth. We stand together in silence, and I count the seconds ticking by. I won't make the first move. If she wants me or even just wants to fuck with Christos, she's going to have to go first.

A knock on the door interrupts our battle of wills on who'll break first, and Stacia slides away from me. I scrub my fingers through my hair, turn my back on her and the door, and pull out my phone.

"Did he tell you anything? Are we meeting the dealer?" Stacia asks from behind me. I catch sight of Talon in the wall mirror, standing in the now open doorway.

"What's going on?"

Talon meets my gaze in the mirror. "I need you to trace the product," he says, not responding to Stacia. "Bradley was a dead end."

"What do you mean?" Stacia asks.

He tosses me a small, clear baggie. "It means there's more fucking work to do. Now, close your eyes, wild child. Don't open them until I say so. I know how you get with the sight of blood."

Stacia opens her mouth to argue but stops herself, paling as she glimpses at the bloody room behind Talon. Wobbling, she reaches for something to grab onto. "Shit."

I surprise her by scooping her into my arms, cradling her like my soon-to-be bride. "He's right, mamacita. You don't want to see this mess. Fuchi, guácala. Disgusting."

"Just get me out of here," Stacia says, squeezing her eyes shut.

"Anything for you," I say, peering at the body slumped on the floor. "Someone else will clean up this fucking mess, right Christos?"

Christos only scowls, remaining silent as I carry Stacia away.

14

Meeting

Stacia

Unknown: Meeting tonight. Everyone must attend.

Unknown: Wear appropriate attire.

I stomp toward my bedroom door only to nearly slam into Talon. He stands with his hand up, ready to knock. Stepping forward, Talon pushes me back into the room and closes the door. I swallow my nerves at his sudden closeness. He's either not going to let me avoid him much longer or he's going to tell me something I already know.

"I got the message about the meeting tonight," I say, holding my phone up.

Talon doesn't respond, closing the distance in brooding silence. I study his expression, his blue eyes roving to my lips. His hand slides around my waist, pulling me to him, pressing our hips together. Something warm and inviting erupts inside me, blowing away all my hesitation. Talon captures my mouth with his, kissing me like he's famished for my affection. I moan, slipping my tongue between his parted lips, all my pent-up annoyance and anger pouring out of me with my passion.

I jump into his arms, clutching the back of his neck, not letting him break away, even though he doesn't try. My heart pounds in erratic beats, my body buzzing with lust. I'm torn between wanting to pull away to slap him for all the bullshit and yanking his shirt off to kiss my way down his torso. I don't get a chance to decide as my back hits my bed and Talon drags me to the edge.

"I'm tired of this bullshit. I want you so fucking bad. I can't stand it. I know I piss you off, and that's not going to fucking change, but damn it. I need you to know how much I care about you." Talon kisses my shoulder, unfastening my jeans at the same time. I'm so caught up in my wild emotions and desire that all I do is lift my hips and let him yank them off me.

"You're an asshole," I say, gasping at the sensation of his mouth on my thigh. "Sweet talking me isn't going to just make up for things."

He slides his finger inside me, bending my knee to accommodate his broad shoulders. "I'm not making up for anything. I want you to fall apart for me. Let me remind you what you mean to me." Flicking his tongue across my clit, he sucks gently. I grab his hair, holding onto him with my trembling body. He peeks up, his eyes studying me. Desire weighs his eyelids, and he kisses and licks and sucks my body, working me up until I feel like I'll crumble before him.

He slides his other hand under my ass and carries me farther up the bed, dropping me onto the pillows. "You're so fucking wet for me, aren't you?"

"Mmmhmm, but this doesn't change anything. I'm not yours." I grip the blankets, arching my back as Talon sends me over the edge, my muscles spasming, my pussy clutching his fingers as he hums with satisfaction.

"Keep telling yourself that. You can try to make me jealous all you want, but that's not going to work anymore. I decided that it doesn't bother me. You get off on it. On this power. So I'll comply. I will just remind you every second about what you have with me. If you fuck someone else, I'll just fuck you twice as hard and longer. If you try to do it in front of me, don't think I won't join. You've buried yourself in my fucking soul, and there's no escaping you. You're my damn woman." Talon slides his belt off and unhooks his pants, kicking out of them. He grabs my shirt and drags it over my head, leaning down to suck my nipple into his mouth, the pressure making me moan and squirm.

"Don't think I'll be okay with you sleeping with someone else. You might have gotten over your jealousy, but I won't. I don't care if it's unfair, either." I link my fingers to the hem of his shirt, pulling it off of him so he lies naked on top of me.

He kisses me deeply, nipping my lip and stretching it, pinning me with his weight, letting me feel the length of his hard cock as he slides his shaft back-and-forth over my slick wetness without sinking inside me. "I don't want anyone else. I want you."

I smile and push him over, climbing on top of him. I align our bodies, sliding his cock inside me as I press my palms to his chest, slowly bouncing, just teasing him. His eyes roll back for a moment as he moans, digging his fingers into my hips, pushing me harder on him, still trying to take back control even with me on top. I let him, stretching my back as I rub my nipples, bouncing up and down at the fast pace he enjoys. Talon lives life hard and fast, pushing boundaries and crossing lines. He's seductive and powerful, everything that I need in this moment. And his power doesn't make me feel weak either. He makes me feel stronger than ever.

Groaning, Talon plays with my clit, thrusting from beneath me. I ride him until I gasp for breath, my body exploding with another orgasm. He flips me onto my back and stretches my legs up, pressing my feet to the headboard as he rocks his body at an intense pace, hitting the headboard against the wall loud enough that I'm sure everyone in the mansion can hear. The idea excites me, and I scratch my fingers into Talon's back and scream out, my pleasure ringing through the air.

Talon moans as he finishes, sliding his hand behind my neck and pulling me to him for a kiss. His tongue tangles with mine, enjoying every second as we come down from our high.

"That's my sexy fucking wild child. They're all going to think about me when they're with you now. They won't be able to forget it." Talon sinks onto me, combing his fingers through my hair, our bodies damp with sweat.

I smile and rub his shoulder. "I think you get off on torturing them."

He chuckles. "One of many things you'll learn about me. No more secrets. You've proven that I was an asshole and overprotective. I know you can handle anything. I know you can handle the whole fucking world."

"Keep your mask up and don't look at anyone. All you have to do is make it the ten feet it takes to reach the entrance of the VIP." Talon pulls strands of my blond wig over my shoulders, playing with the curls. "Christos and Esteban will be by your sides. Leandro, you have to stay in the club. Keep a watch on the bar. Call me if you see anything."

Leandro remains expressionless, but I know it bothers him that Talon commands him to stay in the club instead of joining us. But he can't go. He thinks we're having a meeting with just my dad. He knows nothing of the Esoteric Society, and it will always stay that way.

Esteban offers me his arm, and I take it, smirking at Talon, knowing that he's more aware than ever that I'm going to constantly push his buttons. Christos mutters something under his breath, crossing his arms. It makes it that much more satisfying. Esteban might be psychotic when it comes to his business, but he's been kind to me. He's also super fucking attractive, has a nice dick, and knows that I'm not interested in anything serious. He's down to help me torment Christos, even though he's his best friend.

I'm starting to believe their friendship is one of those 'keep your enemies closer' types of shit. Maybe sharing is caring. I don't really know or care.

Talon leads the way through the packed club. Patrons dance, laugh, and drink, and some do lines of coke, and who knows what else as they fill the booths with bottle service, since the VIP is completely out of the question for even some celebrities.

I try my best to keep my gaze on the floor, but a part of me wants to watch Leandro as he heads to the bar. Kitty is working tonight again, and I wonder if she knows what's up, since Talon made her go through receipts to find someone. Not that she would ask and risk losing her job. She not only gets a huge amount of money in tips, but Daddy pays all of the bartenders and servers big enough salaries that they can live comfortably in LA. And not just a tiny apartment in one of the towers.

We have nearly zero percent turnover.

"Princess, oh my fucking God. Get your ass over here. I fucking missed you." Bianca rushes to me, flinging her arms around my shoulders, and she nearly tackles me to the floor. Talon nudges us away from the landing of the staircase, making sure we're out of view as we make our way to the meeting room.

Esteban and Christos trail behind us, and Bianca peeks over her shoulder. "Please don't tell me the three of them are staying with you. What the fuck is going on with Christos? I thought you'd cut off his head after everything."

There's so much I want to tell her, but a part of me doesn't want to risk dragging her into things.

"If I cut off Christos's head, then he won't be able to see or hear me fucking the Executioner or his best friend." I glance over my shoulder and smile at Esteban.

"Ay, bitch. Both of them?" Bianca smiles wider, showing off her straight teeth. "Please tell me at once. Fuck, that would be so hot."

I'd laugh, the idea far more exciting than it should be. Talon threatened if he saw me with someone else that he would join. I'm not sure if he's really serious or not, because he'd probably wrestle someone and knock them out for my attention.

"Not yet, but Esteban is fucking sexy. He loves fucking with Christos's his head, so I might like that match." I tug Bianca further away from them and toward the dark room where Eduardo begins lighting candles.

I sigh in relief, knowing that William isn't attending the meeting tonight. Talon said he returned to the San Diego chapter.

I just don't think he wanted anything to do with the current mess.

"Princess, you're being summoned into the King's chambers." Talon's looming form materializes next to me, and I nearly jump out of my skin. For being so big, he can either sneak around easily or I'm just so unaware. Probably both. It's easy to get distracted with my best friend here.

I crinkle my nose and pop out my bottom lip, looking at Bianca. "I'll be back."

Talon touches his palm to the small on my back, guiding me toward the doorway to Daddy's chambers. It's the last place I want to be after everything. I'm still so fucking pissed off at him that I don't want to see him.

"Take a breath, wild child," Talon whispers, rubbing his fingers along my back. "It's going to be fine."

"You say that too much. You damn well know that nothing will be fine until we figure out who the hell killed that guy in my hotel room." I don't know why I say it, but I feel like I just have to put it out there. Being here at the Looking Glass leaves me on edge. The last time I was here, I was nearly forced into either being abused or coerced into sucking off someone to humiliate me.

"I only say it, because it's true. I won't stop until you actually believe me," Talon murmurs the words, keeping his voice low, so no one can overhear him.

I spot the other members of the King's Court surrounding my dad as he sits at his desk, flipping through some paperwork. I wish he were alone, so I could at least talk to him freely, but it's as if he doesn't want anything to do with me anymore. I'm probably an embarrassment that he just wants to discard. I doubt he'll even continue training me to one day take over our empire.

The thought angers me, and I bite my cheek and clench my fingers into fists.

"Good evening, Your Majesty," I say, bowing before him. "You've summoned me."

"Yes, Princess. As you know, the recent scandals have drawn some unwanted attention to our business endeavors. Business is down, and we've lost the trust of patrons." Daddy folds his hands together. "This is not good."

From the small look around the Looking Glass, I want to call bullshit on him. If anything, it's more crowded than I've seen in a while.

"You've always said even bad publicity is good," I say, keeping my eyes trained on the desk. "More people will start coming. We just need to live up to the expectations, don't you think? If I heard about something at a club, I'd want to check it out and see for myself."

"That only lasts as long as the story remains in the headlines. It's not an appropriate business model to follow. We need a good reason to keep people coming back. Women are nervous, but perhaps, if you bring people in, it might be different." Daddy clears his throat, trying to draw my attention to him. "Under a disguise, that is. Perhaps we also need to set a scene. Catch someone in the act so it hits the media. I want you in charge of that."

"We're trying to find the dealer," I argue, not exactly feeling his plan. I could easily get caught.

"You don't need to find a dealer. You just need to make one. I don't care who it is. I want someone's face tied to the drugging. Tonight. You can't leave until it's taken care of." Daddy straightens his back.

"You want me to frame an innocent man?" I ask, frowning at the idea. I, out of all people, know how shitty it is to be tied to something you haven't done.

"If you don't, I will give the media you. I don't have a choice. You can't just remain missing. We have excellent lawyers. I'm sure—"

"Are you blackmailing me?" My heart picks up pace, and I turn to look at the silent court around my father.

"No, but some feel that we need to test your alliance. It's time you step up and learn just what it takes to remain in the Esoteric Society. You are my daughter, so don't let me down." Standing up, Daddy doesn't let me argue and instead motions for his court to begin the meeting.

I stand in shock. Something has shifted in my dad, and I wish I could pinpoint what it is. He's still angry with me over embarrassing him in front of William, but I thought he'd be over it by now. Maybe he found out about Talon and hasn't said anything. Or maybe something's up with my mom. Regardless, I need a moment with him.

So I gather my nerve, rush to him before he can go into the meeting room, and yank him aside. I throw my arms around him in a hug, afraid that he might do something crazy.

"Please, Your Majesty. Just give me another minute of your time. Alone." I whisper the words in his ear, feeling his body tense next to mine. "Please, Daddy."

He sighs and waves to Talon, who shuts the door, cutting us off from the other members.

"Stacia, my Princess. I'm sorry I have to be so hard on you, but you're coming to an age where you're going to have to start relying on yourself. I'm not always going to be around to clean up your messes. I have a lot to focus on, and I can't keep having to worry about you." Daddy pulls away from me and rests his hand on my shoulder. "The stress of everything has been a lot on not only me and our other members. It's been a stress on our family. Your mother has relapsed again. She saw you on the news, and you know I couldn't tell her the truth."

Daddy bringing up my mom sinks into me. I haven't seen her in months, but that's only because she's not allowed visitors. And knowing that I'm the reason she succumbed to her addiction pains me on a deeper level.

"I'm sorry. I'm so sorry. I'll do whatever." I know it's not my fault, but it doesn't change that it still feels like it.

Daddy hugs me again. "I know you will. You've earned your place here, and I know you won't let me down again. Mistakes happened, but you have to learn from them and ensure they don't reoccur."

I can only nod my head, my voice refusing to come out. Daddy guides me toward the closed door and opens it, allowing in the soft light from the candles, illuminating our meeting.

I catch sight of Talon standing between Esteban and

Christos, the three of them brooding shadows among the dozens of masked members. Daddy has proven he chooses no favorites. And I must continue on as always.

"I call to order our meeting, welcoming you all into our sanctuary," Daddy says, taking his spot next to the altar.

I zone out as he leads a chant, vowing our loyalty, and lose myself to what's to come. I shouldn't have expected anything different. Talon gingerly holds my hand, standing close to me, and Esteban bumps his shoulder to mine. It's strange being surrounded by these men who have sworn their lives to our society, but also seem to have a new loyalty for me.

One I can't take for granted.

Because I'm going to need them. It's the only way I'm going to get through this unscathed.

"Now, if there is no other business to discuss, the meeting is adjourned," Daddy says, smacking his cane down.

I blink a few times, my mind refusing to come back to the present. I can't believe I missed out on the whole meeting, too busy thinking of myself.

Everyone breaks from the circle, mumbling as they

talk in groups about everything that went on tonight.

"Stacia, why would you offer to set someone up?" Christos asks, drawing my attention to him.

"Offer?" Now that he mentions it, Daddy spun the information to make me look better. He loves to make it seem like everyone has a choice, despite all of us knowing otherwise. When we need something, we have to do it.

"Esteban got a lead. We were going to fly out to Miami in the morning," Christos continues.

"What?" I hate that I can barely form sentences, but my mind swims with information.

"You need to tell His Majesty that we have a different plan. We're going to get this taken care of." Christos motions for me to walk toward my dad's chambers.

I shake my head. "I can't. I have to do this."

"No, you don't," he argues.

Annoyance rises through me. "Yes, I fucking do. I was commanded to. I didn't offer or volunteer. The club needs someone to blame, and it's my job to find them. Now, if you excuse me, I have work to do."

Christos grabs my arm. "I can do it for you."

As much as I want him to, I know better. It really does have to be me.

"You can't."

"Astéri mou—"

"Christos! I said I have to do it. Now move." I shove past him and head toward the stairs.

I don't look back.

15

The Task

Stacia

I don't even know where to begin. I can't exactly frame a man without any drugs or a plan. I should just leave and think things through, but I might chicken out if I do.

"Mamacita, Christos told me your assignment." Esteban leans his elbow on the bar next to me, playing with my blond wig with his free hand. "I owe you a favor, so here you go. You need to slip the baggy into someone's pocket. Make sure they're alone here. Someone wealthy. Maybe even one of those pinche celebrities over at the table service."

I stare at the clear baggy with heart-shaped papers

inside. Gingerly picking it up from the bar, I frown as I inspect them. "This is so wrong."

"Could be worse. They'll most likely be able to buy their way out of trouble. Bad press won't fuck with them. Not if you pick the right one." Esteban flicks his finger in the direction of the booths lining the walls, pointing out a blond guy surrounded by beautiful women. "I'm pretty sure that pendejo has a wife and kids at home."

"Who probably needs him. Look at how he keeps space between him and the women. This is for publicity." I know better than to trust everything I read in the tabloids, and that actor does whatever he's told. I know this because he asks for the club photographer, who always snaps pictures for him to release.

"Are you going to have an excuse for everyone? I know you don't want to do this, but I don't want to think about the consequences you'll have to face if you don't. What about that guy over there?" Esteban tilts his head, motioning to a man in a designer suit sitting alone at the end of the bar, cradling a tumbler of whiskey. "He doesn't look like he has any business being here."

I frown, staring in the direction of the man. This

should be easy. When it comes to me or someone else, I should choose myself. I have chosen myself dozens of times before. I don't know what my hang-up is. "No one has business being here."

"Stacia," he says, my name dripping with disappointment coming from his mouth. "I thought you had what it took. You were so tough at my office."

I roll my eyes. "That's not going to work. I don't suffer from a fragile ego."

He chuckles and slides his arm around my waist. "Then why don't you just let Christos do it and pretend it was you."

Narrowing my eyes, I glare at him. "I don't need his fucking help."

"Then take mine. What I have is exactly what you need. They're excellent quality, so if something happens, and whoever we target as his victim accidentally takes them, the chances of them hurting her are pretty low." Esteban scoops up the baggy of heart-shaped drugs again and sets it in my palm. "Just walk by him and stick them in his jacket pocket."

I mess with my wig. "Then what? Putting them in his pocket isn't going to do much."

Esteban wags his eyebrows. "What if you took him

a drink and said it belonged to that group? Then I will take them a drink from him."

I don't know how I feel about how easily Esteban comes up with this plan. I should be thankful, though. I didn't even really know where to begin. Why do I feel so bad about it?

"I don't know." I twist my lips to the side. "We don't know anything about him."

"And it's best to keep it that way. You need to harden yourself, or else you'll be riddled with guilt forever. Think about yourself. That guy...you know he'll get off easy. Just look at him. The rich never suffer the same consequences." Esteban motions for Kitty, and she greets us with a smile. "I'm going to need a round of mixed drinks for the ladies over there. And another whiskey for my girl here."

I shift in my seat, hiding my face. I know that Kitty probably knows that I'm not missing, but I don't want to draw any more attention to myself. She shouldn't be put in this position.

"You got it, handsome." Kitty starts collecting glasses and setting them on the bar quickly, putting together Drink Me Elixirs.

My stomach twists at the sight, and I try not to react.

I don't think I'll drink another one again after what happened to me.

"Gracias, gatita." Esteban slips her several hundreds and gathers all the glasses in his hands, managing to carry five at once. He winks at me and nods his head toward the man. "You're up, mamacita. Just make sure he sees the women after I leave."

I rub my lips together, bobbing my head, summoning my courage to follow through. I just have to stop thinking about it. It's the only way I'm going to get shit done. Grabbing the glass of whiskey, I straighten my shoulders and strut toward the man.

I exhale a deep breath, lowering my voice, hopefully disguising it enough. "Hey, handsome," I say, copying Kitty with her compliment. "The ladies over there bought you a drink. Are you alone tonight?"

The man tips his head up from his glass and looks at me, his face not lighting up like I expect from a man who just got hit on by a beautiful woman.

"Unfortunately, yes. My girlfriend dumped me." The man swigs the rest of his whiskey and takes the one I offer him. "I had planned on proposing to her."

Aw man. This is definitely going to be kicking a man when he's down. I push through my awkwardness and lean in close, half hugging him. "Oh, handsome. It's a good thing there's a table of pretty ladies over there waiting to distract you."

I peek over, watching Esteban slip away, disappearing into the crowd. Touching the man's chin, I get him to follow my line of sight, where the women all lift their drinks with huge smiles on their faces. He chuckles, lightening up.

"See? It looks like they want your company. Why don't you join them?" I hug him with one arm, quickly dropping the baggy into his pocket.

"You're right. Fuck Trinity. All she wanted was my money, anyway. Ungrateful bitch calling the cops." The man bangs his fist on the bar, his eyes glassy with intoxication. "I didn't even hit her that hard."

My eyes widen with his comment, my heart sinking to my stomach. I can't believe I felt bad about this for even a second. He's moping because he assaulted his girlfriend and is mad she stood up for herself and called for help.

"I'm sure you didn't," I bite out, struggling to keep my cool. I want this asshole out of here. I want him to know that shit guys deserve shit lives.

"Damn straight. I bet those ladies are ten times better too." The guy stands up from the barstool.

I pat his back. "I know. They're so hot. Go have fun. That's what the Looking Glass is for. Forget reality and enter the world of your own desire." I sound like an infomercial for the club, but in a way, I'm right. This has always been a place for people to come and ignore the world outside. If only I could do so now.

The man grins and holds up his glass of whiskey, whistling at the ladies in the booth. They all cheer, drunk and high on their excitement, and he manages to slide into the booth with them. It'll be a rude awakening when they sober up and realize just how ugly the man truly is. Because no one with an attitude like his could ever be attractive.

"Mamacita, you did good. Look at that asshole. Even if you didn't plant any Jabberwocky on him, he'd probably still try to force himself on one of those ladies. I can see it in his eyes. I'm good at reading people, and he's a disgrace of a man." Esteban materializes beside me, sliding his hand around my back, leaning in to whisper in my ear.

"You're right. He's an abuser. He deserves what he gets. I know men like him. They think they're untouchable. And the police are useless when it comes to the victims. I've seen it." Because a lot of shit goes down around me. At college. At clubs. I'm only safe because my dad owns this place, and I have his entire team watching my back.

Not many have that luxury.

"I'm glad you finally see it my way. It won't be long. The woman to his right was only drinking water, so I slipped something in her drink. They'll all know something is wrong and call for help." Esteban squeezes my side, humming in my ear.

"You really thought this through, haven't you?" Slipping the sober girl something is the surest way of getting her friends to notice. As for the rest of them, they could play it off as them drinking too much. It wouldn't be the case if it was their designated driver.

Excitement blooms through me, heating my chest. I turn and hug Esteban, so thankful that he demanded to help me and wouldn't let me be stubborn about it. His hand draws down my lower back, and he pulls me in closer, meeting my gaze. I bite my lip, his closeness, setting off my desire. So I kiss him. I mold my lips to his, wanting so badly to thank him in the best way I know how.

Tightening his arms around me, Esteban spins me

slightly and sets me on the barstool, getting between my legs, ignoring the fact that the whole fucking club could watch us. I don't even care. It excites me. And damn, he's an amazing kisser. Our tongues graze together, dancing with our passion, set off by the thrill of the night. I comb my fingers through his hair, deepening our kiss, wishing that we could go somewhere private, so I could experience more of him. Because I'm so fucking tired of the bullshit. I just want to have a night of fun. I want a night to forget about everything.

"Take me to the car," I murmur through kisses, reaching between us to rub my fingers over his hard-on. "I want to fuck you."

Esteban groans against my lips, his breath warm against my mouth. He eases away, meeting my eyes again, studying my face as if he needs to see the truth of my words in my stare.

"Mamacita, we have to make sure things unfold as we intend." Esteban tucks my hair behind my ear, leaning in to kiss me again. "Just give it a couple more minutes. Then we'll really have something to celebrate."

I scrunch my nose, wishing he had just given in to me with reckless abandon, the same recklessness I want to explore. I'm so tired of being restrained. I'm so tired of being the heiress of the St. Germain Empire. I just want to be invisible and free, and that's how I feel right now. I don't feel like me. I feel like some random party girl having the night of her life.

I stroke him harder, exploring the length of his desire. And damn, I almost forgot how big he is. I want to get on my knees for him and give him a better experience than the last time I had to kneel before him. "Are you sure we have to? If you don't want to go to the car, there's a storage closet by the bar we can go to." The same one where I fucked Leandro.

"Stacia—"

"Natalia! Oh, my God. Natalia! Someone help us!" The scream rips over the music, cutting off Esteban.

I whip my attention to the group of girls behind us, spotting the one beside the man rolling her head, struggling to keep upright.

"What's wrong with her?" another of her friends asks. "She looks drunk."

"Holy fucking shit. She's been drugged. Look at my nail polish." The girl at the end holds up Natalia's glass of water in one hand while showing the change in color of her nail polish on her index finger. I'd seen the nail polish that reacts to drugs like that at college, but it's been a while. I should've known that these women would be smart, considering that something happened recently at the club.

The man at the table stands up, his eyes widening. He moves past the girl and starts heading toward the dance floor.

"Stop him! We think he drugged our friend!" the girl with the nail polish yells, pointing at the bastard we set up.

Tony materializes next to him, parting the crowd with his hulking body. He grabs the man by his suit jacket, stopping him from trying to run.

The man holds his hands up. "Let me go. I didn't do anything."

"That'll be up to the cops to decide. Just hang out with me for a moment, buddy, and we'll get this sorted out." Tony tightens his grip on the man.

The man swings and tries to punch Tony in the face, but he's too quick, spinning him around and smashing him against the bar.

Esteban links his fingers through mine, tugging me away from the scene. I don't resist, following behind him like a shadow as people gather around and watch the drama unfold. The girls at the table continue to yell as another bouncer comes up and assists them.

My body trembles with adrenaline, and Esteban pulls me in closer, heading toward the hallway with the bathrooms, where we can also find an emergency exit. We both have the pin to get out without the alarm going off, and I know it's the best way. There's too much going on. I'm sure there will be at least a hundred videos from shaky cell phones of drunk patrons showing up on the internet as we speak. The last thing I need is someone to notice me. I'm wearing a wig, but my face is the same.

I jog in my heels, trying to match Esteban's pace. He spins me against the wall and laughs, kissing me again when we're out of the crowd.

"That was fucking awesome. Perfecto," he says, cupping my cheeks. "The media will be all over this. Tony will be a hero."

I smile, holding onto his dress shirt. "He'll love it. I still can't believe that worked."

"Now we celebrate," Esteban says, lifting me off my feet.

He blindly carries me, kissing me with enough passion to steal my breath away. My adrenaline pumps through my veins, sending me on a high I never want to come down from. We're both so caught up with each other that it takes me a few seconds to realize a camera flashes behind us. The light pops, again and again, illuminating the dimly lit hallway.

I pull away from Esteban, peering over his shoulders as a man stands ten feet away, holding a camera fit for a paparazzi. But he's no one I recognize. I've never seen this man around here before. The bouncers never let paps inside.

"Stacia St. Germaine. Is that you?" the man asks, aiming his camera at me again. "I'd like a moment of your time. I have some questions."

Esteban stiffens and sets me on my feet, blocking me protectively. "Pinche pendejo. Get the fuck away from my girl."

"So she is Stacia?" the man asks, not taking his eyes from me.

"I don't know what the fuck you're talking about. You need to give me that camera. Now. No one can take photos here, you damn pap. If you give it to me willingly, I won't destroy it." Esteban reaches into his jacket, surely putting his hand on his gun. I know he always carries one along with a knife.

"I'm not a paparazzi. I just wanna talk. Give me ten minutes," the man says.

I pull the strands of my wig around my face, hoping it hides me more. Esteban stands tall, creating a wall between me and the man. Peeking behind me, I judge the distance between me and the door. Five feet. I just have to make it five feet, and I'll be out of here.

"I don't care who the fuck you are. You're mistaken. This is my girl, and you're bothering us. Give me the camera. Now." Esteban steps forward as the man steps back. "Don't make me hurt you."

Holy shit.

I wouldn't put it past him to do as much.

"Please, just do as he says. I'm not whoever you think I am." My voice cracks with my pleas. I don't want any more shit going down tonight. The place will soon be surrounded with cops. I just need to get out of here.

"You've been filed as a missing person, but I was hired to investigate, and I knew things weren't adding up. Ms. St. Germaine, please. Let's just have a conversation. I'm not a cop. I just want some answers. I have a question about the dead man in your hotel room. You know about him, right?" The man holds one hand up, clutching his camera with the other.

My heart pounds, the beats ricocheting through my head. I clutch my hands together, trying to get my body to stop shaking. But I can't.

"You don't know what you're talking about. Give me the camera now." Esteban pulls his gun from his holster, aiming it at the man. "This is your last chance."

Without hesitating, the man spins and rushes toward the men's room, shoving the door open. Instead of chasing after him, Esteban spins, picks me up, and tosses me on his shoulder before pounding his finger to the keypad, opening the door. I realize why immediately.

Sirens ring through the air, echoing as the police show up at the club. Right now, they're the biggest threat. I'm not supposed to be here. I'm missing, after all.

"Fuck," I say, hanging like a ragdoll as Esteban rushes toward where Talon parked the SUV.

"Don't worry, mamacita. I got you. It's going to be okay. You have to trust me."

I swallow my nerves, not responding as Esteban opens the SUV and sets me in the front.

He pulls out his phone and yells something into it. I sink into my seat, my body draining of its adrenaline.

Stomping the throttle, Esteban drives away, not even caring about the flashing blue and red lights.

It's all I can stare at. They blur together, blending with the nightlife.

Everything will come crashing down at any minute. I know it.

The next time I see the red and blue lights, they will be coming for me.

16

Possession

Stacia

"I swear to fucking God. If anything happens to Stacia under your care, I'll impale all of you no matter who's at fault." Talon hands a duffle bag to a silent flight attendant, the man sweating profusely as if Talon threatens him and not Esteban and Christos. "I hope to have an ID on the PI within a few days. Once I do, it'll be safer to come home."

"We'll consider this a little work vacation. It's been a while since I've visited mis primos." Esteban slides his arm around my waist, staying by my side. I can't bring myself to look at anyone, really. I feel at fault that the PI spotted me at the Looking Glass.

Talon turns to me. Holding his hand out, he coaxes me forward. My feet automatically shuffle into his space and away from Esteban. Talon touches the small of my back, guiding me far enough away to stay out of listening range.

He shifts us so that our backs face the others as they get ready to board the small private jet. "I hate that I can't come with you, but I'm going to trust you will take care of yourself. Please keep your disguise on at all times. I don't know what the PI wants, but I swear I'll find out. No one will know that you aren't missing. Just behave. Try not to drink. Don't do drugs. All that bullshit."

"What about sex? Are you going to tell me to wear a chastity belt?" A bubble of laughter escapes my mouth.

"I know it won't be with a stranger, so I'll allow it." He eyes the private jet, probably imagining what he'd do to me if he could follow. "Be smart about things."

I smile wider. "Are you really telling me to make good choices, birdie?"

"Fuck yeah. I know you. Just try to behave. Don't go flashing your tits or pussy. And you know what? I changed my mind. Don't go fucking anyone. I can't join from across the country." Talon grazes his fingers over my jaw. Leaning in, he presses his lips to mine, purposely kissing me deep and with enough passion to send tingles right between my legs. He's making a show out of it because of Esteban. Esteban hasn't left my side since the club and our kiss. I know it's annoying Talon, and Christos looks ready to have a coronary because of it. At least one of those is satisfying.

As for Leandro? He remains expressionless and professional. I can't tell what's on his mind. He's been distant lately.

"Ew, bitch. You better not start fucking right here." Bianca's playful voice sounds through the air.

I break away from Talon and jerk my attention to her. What is she doing here? I was nearly certain that her parents were going to demand we don't see each other outside of our meetings. They still treat her like a child, controlling her finances and life. They hold everything over her head to get her to comply.

"Bianca! What the fuck are you doing here?" I ask, moving away from Talon. I never had a chance to even tell her goodbye after the meeting before the police showed up.

"What do you think? You can't fly to fucking Florida without me. Juan doesn't know you're going, and Christos asked him if I could tag along to meet some of the heirs at the Miami chapter." Bianca beams, her white teeth bright against the color of her burgundy lipstick.

I shift my gaze to Christos. "You arranged this?" I can't believe he did this. It's a pretty big risk to be entrusted with the safety of one of the King's Court's daughters, let alone two.

He shrugs, scrubbing his fingers through his hair. "I thought you could use the company."

"Don't let him think he can get in your chonies. He invited her because he wanted another cock-block. She's supposed to ensure we don't hook up." Esteban wiggles his fingers at me, trying to get me to close the space to him again. "He's threatened because he knows that I'm better for you than he is, and he's afraid to admit it."

"You have a job, Knave. You better fucking keep your head on straight and your cock in your pants." Talon points at him, glowering. "Do you understand?"

Esteban challenges him with a smile. "If she comes on to me, I won't deny her. If you're so fucking worried, then tag along. If not, mind your fucking business, Executioner. She made it clear that she's a free spirit and will do whatever she wants. I fully support her decision." Esteban winks at me and moves out of the way before Talon can whack him upside the head. He moves toward the stairs, leading up to the door of the jet.

I cover my eyes, my cheeks flaming. "That's enough. We're not having this conversation any longer."

"Yeah, we better fucking not. You're gonna make me jealous with your abundance of dick, you lucky bitch. And here I am going to end up hiding in the lavatory, so I don't scar myself for life if you all decide to have an orgy or some shit." Bianca tips her head back, screeching a laugh.

Christos mutters something under his breath and joins Esteban, getting Bianca to follow him. Leandro remains utterly silent with his arms crossed at the bottom of the stairs. He doesn't approach me, but I know he's waiting for me to board before he does.

Talon snatches my wrist, spinning me into his arms for another hug. "Please be careful, Stacia. It kills me that I can't be there, and not only because I want to keep you to myself. I just struggle trusting you with anyone else now."

"Then maybe you should hurry up and find that PI, so I don't have to stay there long." I clutch his cheeks and kiss him sensually, not getting carried away, just savoring the taste of his affection.

Talon breaks away first and spins me around, smacking my ass to get me to walk toward Leandro. I smile over my shoulder and blow a kiss like I always do whenever I walk away from him and know that he's watching me leave. He's lucky that I'm not wearing a dress. Or maybe he's unlucky. I can't flash him my ass as I ascend the stairs.

Leandro trails behind me, boarding last and the flight attendant secures the door. The captain and first officer greet us with a smile, standing outside the cockpit. I walk into the main cabin and peer around at the luxurious space with reclining seats, tables, and giant flatscreen TVs. This is far better than first class on any commercial airline.

I spot Esteban and Christos hunched over, staring at a phone. Glancing up, Christos gives me a look that speaks volumes. My heart jumps at the same time the plane engine hums to life.

I rush and sit beside Bianca while Leandro sits behind us, keeping to himself.

"What's wrong? You're making a face," I ask, leaning forward, lowering my voice.

Esteban sighs and holds his phone out. "They released the charges about the guy." He means the one I framed.

I read the list over and over again. I can't believe my eyes. "Murder? I don't understand."

"The woman died this morning," Christos replies, lowering his voice. "She overdosed."

I gasp and cover my mouth.

Shit. That wasn't supposed to happen. This is all my fault.

"Are you kidding me?" My chest heaves and my stomach twists. She would still be alive if we didn't have to frame the guy. If *I* didn't have to frame that guy.

Esteban reaches over and touches my leg. "Something's not right. The amount I slipped in the drink wasn't enough to do that."

"How can you be sure? She died. We fucked up." I pull away from Esteban and turn in my seat, unable to get up as the plane moves across the runway, preparing to takeoff.

"You have to believe me. There's no way she could've died. Not because of the drugs." Esteban squeezes my knee.

"I have a friend at the precinct who will look into it more. They'll be able to get the toxicity reports." Christos leans closer but doesn't touch me. "It's going to be okay."

Then why doesn't it feel that way?

I don't argue. My mind and body shut down as I replay everything over and over again. Someone lost their life. A woman is dead because of me. It's as simple as that. I have to accept the blame.

Maybe I deserve what's coming to me.

Maybe I should just give up now.

Is all this really worth it?

I don't know.

Closing my eyes, I shut out the world. I lose myself to my inner darkness. It's who I am now. It's who I will always be.

Clouds fill the horizon, casting gray light over the ocean. Yachts line the harbor docks, creating a picturesque sight of Miami. There's something more relaxed about the atmosphere compared to the beaches of LA.

"No, acosador. You're staying here. Stacia is safe with me. It would be an insult to mis primos if I allowed you to come." Esteban holds his hand up to Leandro. "You can keep watch here. Ensure no one comes on the dock."

Leandro steps in front of me. "If I don't go, Stacia doesn't go either. I have orders. She's not leaving my sight."

I rest my hand on Leandro's shoulder, pulling him back just a bit. I wouldn't put it past Esteban to start throwing punches. And the last thing we need is to make a scene.

"I'll be fine with Esteban. We're only meeting his family. Why don't you go find Christos and Bianca? I bet Bianca would appreciate someone else interrupting the awkwardness." Because we still haven't had a chance to talk about everything that went down in the meeting room, and Leandro doesn't know about that. He won't ever.

Leandro shifts his body to look at me. "I don't know, beautiful. If something were to happen to you on my watch—"

"It wouldn't be your watch. It would be mine. And I would take full responsibility. I can even put it in fucking writing if you want, acosador." Esteban holds out his arm for me. "Come on, mamacita. I can't wait for you to meet mi familia."

I gingerly take Esteban's hand, offering Leandro a small smile.

He groans under his breath, but he doesn't stop us. Instead, he yells, "I'll kill you myself, Esteban. And stop calling me a stalker. That's you and Christos. Yo soy el protector, jefe."

Esteban howls a laugh and shakes his head, pulling me along with him. I peek behind me, catching Leandro's gaze as he stays on the dock. He's not going far. I doubt he'll actually go to Christos and Bianca as they wait at the beach café around the corner. Esteban hugs me close, sliding his arm around my waist. We stroll together, matching each other's movements, as if we are one entity. My blond wig blows in the sea breeze, but it does nothing to cool the humidity. Perspiration prickles along my neck, and I wish I could just yank off this wig.

"You drive me loco, mamacita. I can't tell if you like

me or if you just like fucking with them." Esteban keeps his voice low. "I was hoping we'd finish what we started back at the club on the plane."

Heat rises from my chest and into my cheeks. How am I supposed to even respond to this?

"Esteban, I'm not into being possessed by any of you. I'm sorry if you don't like that. I'm choosing not to be monogamous."

"You didn't respond to my comment. I'm not going to lie. I'm so fucking attracted to you. So much so that I'm willing to ignore the fact that you have Talon by the balls and Christos by his fucking soul. Even tu acosador looks like he's ready for you to put a ring on his cock." Esteban stares at the side of my face, waiting for me to look at him. "I don't even care if you fuck them. I want to fuck you too. But no more pendejos. You can have your fill of us."

I don't even know what to think or how to react. I should feel like a whore, but I don't. If anything, I feel amazing. I just don't want him to know that I love the idea of having four sexy men here for me in every way I could want. But it's complicated. I don't even know why I included Christos. He's wearing me down, and I need to keep my space. They could all very well be the end of me. They claim that they're okay with my decision to not be in a relationship, but how long can that last? One of them could eventually lash out and hurt the others...or me. Not to mention how unfair it might be to them.

Because I wasn't lying when I told Talon I wasn't okay if he pursued anyone else. I'm greedy like that.

"Stacia, please say something," Esteban says, slowing our pace.

I keep my eyes trained ahead of me, staring at a couple of smaller yachts as we head toward one twice the size of the rest at the end of the long dock.

I huff a breath through my lips, gathering my courage to speak my mind. "I'm having a blast with you, Esteban. You're an amazing kisser, and if you don't care about the others, then we're good. I like you. I just don't want the attachment. I don't know what's happening in my life, and I'd prefer just to...I don't know."

He chuckles and spins me toward him, stopping to kiss me. I sigh against his lips, the sensation of his mouth setting off my desire. "I'm good with that. I don't need anything else."

I giggle and pat his chest, easing away. "But like I told

Talon, if you plan to be with me, you can't be with anyone else."

Esteban raises an eyebrow. "You say that like I want anyone else, mamacita. No. I just want you. It's too hard in this world."

"So you want to be with me because it's easy?" I tease, circling my fingers over his jaw. "I guess I should make things a bit harder, huh?"

Esteban practically purrs, pulling me close so that our bodies are flush together. He flexes his cock, pressing it against my hip. "No. It's already so fucking hard."

"Esteban!" A loud whistle rings through the air, drawing our attention away from each other. "¡Apúrate!"

A handsome man with dark hair and sunglasses waves his hands over his head as he stands on the sundeck of the last yacht with *Queen of Hearts* written across it. It's obvious that Esteban's cousin belongs to the Miami chapter of the Esoteric Society.

"¡Cállate!" Esteban shouts back, draping his arm across my shoulders. He tugs me along to where the ramp waits on the dock to let us aboard the yacht.

The man meets us on the deck with a handsome

smile. Breaking away from me, Esteban closes the space to his cousin and engulfs him in a hug. Esteban smacks the man on the back hard enough to make him huff.

"Mi primo, introduce me to your beautiful girl. I thought you were coming alone." The man pulls away from Esteban and holds his hand out to me. "Enchanted to meet you, miss…"

"Stacia St. Germaine," Esteban finishes for him. "Mamacita, this is my cousin, Chiquito Vargas."

I raise an eyebrow. "Chiquito—"

Barking a laugh, Esteban play-fights him. "It's my nickname for him. Don't call him anything else. I never want to hear his real name on your lips."

"Pendejo," Chiquito mutters, shaking his head. "You'll never let that go, will you? It's not my fault that chica said my name and not yours."

Wow. I side-eye Esteban, engrossed in their playful yet competitive banter. I pick up that Esteban's not saying his name because of something in their past. Sounds like a woman called him by his cousin's name or something.

"Really, Esteban?" I ask, smirking.

"Pinche cabrón, primo." Esteban chuckles and returns to my side, hooking his arm around my waist. "We were kids."

"Exactly. That's why—"

"All right, that's enough. I have too much shit to do to reminisce with you. I brought you something. Let's go inside." Esteban tips his head, motioning toward the salon.

Chiquito's expression hardens, and he gives Esteban a long look. Leading the way inside, Chiquito motions for us to sit on a leather sectional facing the panoramic window with a view of the harbor. Reaching into his jacket, Esteban pulls out a small baggy and drops it onto the coffee table. The sight of the drugs is like a slap to the face, reminding me that someone died.

"Where the fuck did you get this bullshit? It's been a while since I've seen a batch." Chiquito tosses it back to Esteban. "My DEA contact confiscated shit similar to this from a drug mule posed as a tourist."

"Can you put me in touch? Someone's trying to fuck with my territory. I need to find out if it's an operation we need to worry about." Esteban pockets the bag of drugs again. He rubs his palm over my knee, smoothing away my anxiety. I expect him to divulge to his cousin everything else going on, but he doesn't.

Chiquito pulls out his phone. He taps his screen a couple of times, and Esteban's phone chimes. "Whatever you need, primo. I just sent you the files I have on the mule. He's still local."

"He's not in jail?" I ask, unable to keep my question to myself.

He shakes his head. "He comes from a wealthy family. According to my contact, the product mysteriously disappeared from evidence. The gringo's lawyer got the charges knocked down to possession."

Shit. Who the hell are we dealing with?

"I owe you, primo," Esteban says. The two of them hug as I watch silently, a dozen thoughts flitting through my head. He offers his hand out to me. "Come on, mamacita. Let's get this asshole."

I only nod. I hope we really can. I'm tired of false leads and disappointment.

I just want my life back.

Whatever is left of it, at least.

17

Drug Mule

Stacia

"Where are we going?" I stand outside the rental car, folding my arms over my chest. "What about the others?"

"What about them?" Esteban opens the passenger's side door for me and waits for me to get in.

If my feet weren't hurting in my heels, I'd protest. But I'm tired. The stroll from the harbor was a lot longer than I expected, and now I know why. Esteban wasn't taking me to the beach café to join Bianca and Christos.

"Bianca doesn't want to deal with this shit. Check your phone, mamacita. She texted us." Esteban closes the door and strides around the hood of the car. He climbs behind the wheel and starts the engine, lurching away from the curb without waiting for me to protest.

"They'll meet up with us for dinner. This is a good thing." Esteban puts on his sunglasses and motions for me to do the same.

"How so? You don't think we need help?" I sit back in the seat, wondering how pissed off Leandro will be. I'm sure he was behind us, keeping his distance and probably didn't expect Esteban to take off.

"Because I get some alone time with you. You look stunning. I want to take you out to get your mind off things." Esteban grins and switches lanes, turning left at the end of the block.

"What about Leandro?" I ask, pulling my phone from my purse. He wasn't lying about the text messages.

He chuckles. "Again, what about him? I'm sure he's tracking us."

My phone buzzes in my hand, and I spot another text on the screen. Bianca didn't just text me. She created a group chat with all of us, including Leandro.

Bianca: What's taking so long?

Bianca: When are you guys coming back?

Bianca: There's only so much I can talk to Christos about.

Bianca: Bitch, respond.

Christos: Please do. I'm the one suffering.

Leandro: FYI they're not heading your way.

Christos: You fucker. Bianca's here for Stacia.

Bianca: Yeah fucking right. Don't buy it, bitch. He thought I'd be a distraction. He knows you won't fuck him but you definitely will bang Esteban.

Leandro: …

Bianca: Enjoy the show. I'm going shopping. Christos is buying.

Christos: You have until dinner, asshole.

Leandro: Won't be too long. Esteban underestimates my capabilities.

I laugh at the conversation unfolding. Esteban slows down, stopping at a red light. Turning in my seat, I stare out the back window, wondering where Leandro might be and if he has a car or something I don't know about. I don't see him, though. Esteban might've been right about him tracking us.

"We should probably find them, Esteban. I feel bad." I rest my back in the seat, staring at the beautiful view of the ocean as the sun breaks through the clouds, lighting the sea aglow with the fiery colors of sunset. It's been a while since I've paid attention, and I appreciate the beauty more than ever.

"They'll be fine. I promise. I want you just to relax and let me take care of this. It'll be a quick errand to find this guy, and then we'll do something fun." Esteban holds out his hand, silently asking me to take his. I do so without hesitating, giving up on arguing. There is no point. Esteban is the type that if he has something on his mind, then it's set. I need to compromise in this situation because he doesn't even have to do any of this. I should just be thankful.

"Whatever you say," I say, forcing myself to smile.

"Bueno. You have to learn to trust me. I owed you a favor, mamacita. This impacts me as much as it does you. My business is important, and I will not just stand by as someone tries to fuck it up. I've been working for this my whole damn life. I'm not going to let it slip through my fingers." Esteban jerks the car, drifting around the corner and heading right. He follows the navigation until we end up a couple of miles from the harbor at a hotel on the ocean. A valet opens my door and Esteban comes around to help me out.

Esteban tips the man a wad of cash, and I keep my sunglasses on through the luxurious lobby of the five-star hotel. When he said we'd do something fun, I didn't expect for him to bring me to a hotel. We're staying at a different one already.

The concierge smiles at us from behind the counter, already prepared with a hotel key. "Welcome, Mr. and Mrs. Castillo. Congratulations on your nuptials. We hope you enjoy your stay at The Salazar in the honeymoon suite. We have everything prepared as requested."

Esteban grins and kisses my cheek. "Gracias."

I lower my brow, eyeing Esteban in my peripheral vision. I can't believe he booked a suite as if we're newlyweds. Crazy bastard. I don't even know how to react. Pulling me in close, we walk in sync toward the gleaming metal and mirror elevators, passing a swanky restaurant and bar.

"What is all this?" I ask, whispering in Esteban's ear. "I thought we were supposed to find out who the mule is."

Esteban holds his finger up over his lips. "Shh, mamacita. We are doing just that. We might as well have a good time."

The elevator dings at the top floor, where two penthouse suites take up the level at opposite ends of a hall. Butterflies swarm in my stomach, igniting my nerves. The last time I stayed in a penthouse, I woke up coming down from a high and next to a dead guy. It haunts me.

Stopping in front of the heavy wooden door, Esteban waves the key card and unlocks it. He surprises me by scooping me off my feet and carrying me over the threshold into a room of silvers, turquoise, and whites, complementing the endless ocean view on the other side of the glass wall.

The exhilaration of the moment consumes me, and I find my mouth against Esteban's, kissing him sensually and slowly, testing his reaction. He groans and adjusts me, wrapping my legs around him. I cling on, hooking myself to him by my ankles, throwing my caution and nerves to the floor.

"We only have half an hour until the mule arrives," Esteban murmurs, tangling his fingers into my wig. "We can't get carried away."

"What if I said that this might be your one chance to fuck me?" Because now that I'm alone with Esteban, no longer worried about being seen, I can't help getting caught up in the lust he awakens in me.

"You're lying. I'll ensure it." Esteban carries me into the bedroom suite with another view of the crystalline ocean, lit up with streaks of white from the sun dipping toward the horizon. "Just know, if you're serious, don't plan on meeting up with the others. They'll be on their own the rest of the night."

"They'll be fine," I say, kissing him deeper, tangling my tongue with his.

"Goddamn." Esteban sets me on the edge of the bed, kissing me as he reaches under my dress for my non-existent panties. He moans, sliding his fingers over my pussy, my desire hot and buzzing through me. "Muy sexy. Eres divina. I can't wait to taste you."

Esteban pulls me to the edge of the bed and buries his head under the hem of my dress, licking up my thigh at a slow enough pace to make me squirm. My breathing quickens with his warm breath, his fingers kneading into my legs as he spreads me wider.

"Oh, fuck." I grip the duvet, arching my back as Esteban slides a finger inside me at the same time he rolls his tongue over my clit, sucking it softly. "Esteban."

I moan, tightening my thighs around his head. He purrs, gliding his tongue in even strokes over my body.

I rock against him, riding him how I like, savoring how he reads my body and adds pressure with another finger.

He works me over, humming his satisfaction every time I moan, my legs shaking, my body demanding to reach its peak. I yank up the hem of my dress and grab Esteban's light brown hair, playing with the tresses. He licks and sucks, kissing my clit as he fucks me with his fingers until I scream out, my muscles spasming.

He doesn't stop, only moving his fingers away from my body to unfasten his pants, not letting my body relax, prolonging the intensity of my pleasure. Freeing his cock, he kicks out of his pants and rubs the length of his shaft. I reach out and grab him by the hips, taking control. I glide my tongue over his tip and down his shaft, blindly grabbing at his shirt to get him to take it off. He pulls my dress off next, leaving me exposed in front of him. His eyes rove across my body, drinking me in for only a moment until he scoops me up and tosses me toward the middle of the bed. Laughter bubbles from my lips, and Esteban captures the lightness of my voice with his mouth, silencing me. He climbs on top of me, taking control in the way I love, his hands mapping my body as he spreads me wide to settle between my legs.

"I've been dreaming of this moment," Esteban says, kissing my neck and rolling my nipple under his fingers. "Ever since you were on your knees before me. I knew I had to have you."

"Stop trying to make me fall in love with you," I respond, scratching my nails into his back. "Just shut up and fuck me. Fuck me until I forget. I don't want to think about anything except this moment."

He grunts at my nails biting his skin and captures my mouth, nipping my lip hard enough to make me moan. Aligning our bodies, he thrusts inside me, growling in my ear, the noise so sexy. I love hearing his pleasure, feeling his muscles rippling and tightening around me.

Clinging onto his back, I brace myself in place, screaming my bliss every time he thrusts hard and deep, faster and faster, stealing my breath and thoughts away until all I feel and think about is pleasure. He grabs my hips and lifts me higher, dragging a pillow beneath me, switching our position to better watch me. Esteban kneels, using my legs for leverage, and I arch and close my eyes. No one's ever fucked me like this—just raw and hard, fast and rough, treating the moment like a one-night thing despite the both of us knowing otherwise. Esteban awakens something different inside me. The casual attraction and honesty get to me in a good way. Knowing that crossing this line adds to the revenge I've desired to inflict on Christos for so long only makes it that much better.

Rubbing his fingers over my clit, he adds to my pleasure again. "You're so fucking wet. So hot. Look at you take me."

My body explodes with another orgasm, my pussy clutching onto Esteban, pulsing through his thrusting, his moans mirroring mine. Sweat sparkles on our bodies, the heat of our desire potent in the air. We watch each other panting, never taking our gazes away, enjoying the spontaneity and pent-up lust we've carried toward each other for weeks.

"You're so fucking perfect, Stacia. I will make you fall in love with me," he mutters as if talking to himself. "I'm patient."

"You're crazy." I lean up and press my hand to his mouth.

"Estoy loco por ti," he mumbles against my palm and then glides his tongue over my fingers, sucking one into his mouth.

Moaning, he draws firmer circles over my clit, stopping me from saying anything else as I explode with another orgasm. He pounds into me over and over until he grunts and pulls out, coming all over my hips and stomach.

He licks his lips, appreciating the view of me, and I snatch his hands and pull him onto me, only to have him roll until I'm lying on top, his cock resting between my legs, our hearts pounding against each other.

We don't move for what feels like forever until Esteban's phone chimes. He growls under his breath and lifts me up, carrying me to the gigantic two-person shower.

Turning on the water, he lets steam fill the air. "I want you to take your time. I'll handle the bastard. He's here."

I blink a few times, opening my mouth to argue, but Esteban kisses me.

"It won't take long. I need you to stay hidden in case." Esteban pulls me into his arms, hugging me again. "I got this."

"Just be careful," I say, standing before him as he quickly cleans up and throws on a robe. I'm sure he'll adorn himself with a weapon.

"Always am." Esteban kisses my temple and leaves the bathroom.

As much as I want to lock the door, I keep it cracked open and listen for sounds of an altercation. I take off my wig, unpinning it, and set it on the counter. I unravel my dark hair from the cap and let it fall across my shoulders. I take the fastest shower of my life, quickly rinsing away the passion.

I wrap a towel around myself, shivering in the cold air seeping in from the partially open door. I know I should worry about someone barging in, but I realize that I'm more freaked out at the idea of something happening to Esteban. I know I told him that he needed to stop trying to make me fall in love with him, and I don't know if it's because I'm coming down from the wave of our fuck session, or what, but I don't want anything happening to him. I've seen for myself the dangers he faces. He's not exactly the CEO of a safe business. He's a drug lord, and probably on the top of a dozen hit lists. It's only his membership to the Esoteric Society that really keeps the law off his back and adds protection to his lethal life.

"I told you I'm innocent. I had no fucking idea about the damn drugs. Someone snuck them into my bag." An unfamiliar voice echoes through the air.

I can't hear Esteban clearly, but he does mutter something.

"LA? I've never been to fucking LA. I don't know anything about this bullshit. Whoever you got your information from was wrong. Now I suggest you let me leave. You don't want any trouble." Something crashes, and the man hollers.

"You're lying. Whatever they are paying you, I will give you double. You were already on the DEA's list. They are watching you. I can get them off your back. I just need to know who the fuck you're working for," Esteban says, matching the man's energy.

"I don't know who they are. I've only talked to them on the phone. They left the product for me in a rental car. They set me up. They wanted me to get caught."

"What for?" Esteban asks.

I crack the door open more, trying to get a view of the two of them, but they're not in the bedroom. Their voices echo through the open door leading into the sitting room.

I clutch my towel and tiptoe into the suite, looking around for my dress. I quickly put it back on and quietly make my way to the door.

The guy groans. "I don't fucking know. The product they gave was complete shit anyway."

Esteban appears in my view, and he glances at me and shakes his head. "I want their information."

"I don't have it," the guy argues.

Lunging forward, Esteban grabs the man and drags him to the floor. He kicks him in the stomach and flips him on his back, surprising him with a gun he pulls from the robe pocket. "You better tell me fucking now. Someone is trying to get into my territory, copying my shit with a deadly product. I can't have my customers worrying about their lives when they're just chasing a damn high."

The man cowers on the floor, covering his face protectively as if his hands could really shield him from a bullet. He wears a suit without a tie and looks like many of the wealthy businessmen that fly through LA.

"You have five seconds. Don't make me rip the answers out of you." Esteban waves his gun at the man without clicking off the safety. I don't think he will shoot him here. But the guy doesn't know it.

"He goes by the Carpenter. He wants to fix things." The man heaves a breath, rolling over and away from Esteban. "You think you're tough, but this guy will kill anyone who gets in his way."

"So will I." Esteban turns his attention toward me and motions for me to cover my eyes.

I don't.

Instead, I step out of the room.

"Stop, Knave. We can use him. He can send his boss a message." I know I shouldn't get involved, but all I can think about is how the hell we'll get out of this if there's a body. I'm already in enough trouble as it is.

"This will be a message." Esteban aims to gun at the man.

The man holds his arms up, sobbing for his life. "Please, listen to her. I'm better alive. I'll do whatever you want."

Esteban shakes his head. "No."

He steps forward and presses the gun to the man's head, raising his eyebrows at me because I refuse to look away.

And then he pulls the trigger.

The man screams out as nothing happens. Esteban's gun isn't loaded. But it's enough to make the man pee himself, and I step away and frown.

Laughing, Esteban loads his gun in front of the man and waves it. "Pinche pendejo. Is that piss? Get the fuck up. You're going to take me to your boss. Tell him I want to make him a deal."

The man bobs his head up and down, scrambling to get to his feet. He tugs his phone from his pocket and taps the screen a couple of times. "Okay, I—"

Someone pounds on the suite door, cutting the man off. I flip my attention to Esteban and back to the door.

"Jefe, open up. We gotta go," Leandro yells, pounding the wood again. "There's an armed man coming up the stairs."

Esteban glowers and turns his gun on the man. Without waiting for him to plead for his life, Esteban pulls the trigger and shoots the man between the eyes, startling me.

The world blurs with my shock, and a second later, I find myself being dragged toward the door. Leandro lifts me up, throwing me onto his shoulder protective-ly.

Another gunshot rings through the air.

"Take Stacia to the car. I'll be there in five. We've been set up. I'm not allowing this Carpenter cabrón think he can get away with this shit," Esteban says, moving the body of the other man out of the way of the stairwell.

"Esteban, please. No. Just come with us," I plead, my chest tightening with my fear.

He leans in and kisses me. "I'll be fine, mamacita. I'll see you soon."

He doesn't wait for me to respond and heads back to the suite to probably wait for another asshole to come.

Leandro carries me away.

I fear that I'll never see Esteban alive again.

Hitman

Stacia

"Cia, fuck bitch. Are you okay? What's happening? Christos demanded I stay here and bailed on me." Bianca throws her arms around me, hugging me.

I stand frozen, still reeling about what happened at the hotel.

"She's in shock. Just give her some space. Can you get a glass of water?" Leandro guides me toward the couch in the sitting room of the family suite at our hotel near the airport.

He grabs a blanket and wraps it around my shoulders, sitting close to me. "Just focus on getting your breathing under control. I know you're afraid. Esteban was stupid for putting you through that. He's too full of himself. Thinks he's invincible. He could've gotten you killed."

My hands quiver and I don't respond, waiting for Bianca to return from the small kitchenette. She brings me a bottle of water and cracks it open, pouring it into a glass. Plopping down on my other side, she ignores Leandro about giving me space and smothers me with her arms, pulling me into her boobs.

It's enough to make me laugh, my voice raspy.

"That's better. Now take a drink and tell me what the hell is going on. This was supposed to be a vacation and keeping off the radar of the media." Bianca helps me take a drink of water until I clutch the glass myself.

I want to tell her that it feels like another assignment given to us by the King's Court, but I know better than to say anything in front of Leandro.

"I think we found out who's been trying to deal shitty product in LA." I lick my lips and sink back on the couch, resting my head on the cool wall.

"Whoever it is, is out of their damn mind, trying to mess with..." Bianca shuts her mouth, flicking her gaze to Leandro and back to me. "Leandro and Christos better take care of it, is all I mean. I don't want to worry about fucking overdosing on shit product. It's like they purposely want to kill people."

Except the woman who died had some of Esteban's product. Yet he denies that's why she died.

I guess we'll never really know.

All of our phones buzz, drawing our attention away from each other. I pull mine from my purse and glance at the screen.

Esteban: We're back. Open the door. We had to rush through the lobby. Christos doesn't have his room key.

I hop to my feet before Leandro and Bianca and rush across the room, yanking the door open. Leandro grabs me and holds me back protectively, and I realize what a stupid mistake I made. I didn't even bother to look through the peephole to make sure it was really Esteban.

"What the fuck? Give her to me." Esteban closes the space and practically rips me away from Leandro to engulf me in a hug. "Come here, mamacita. I'm okay."

"Don't get fucking pissed at me for doing my job. The job you have made difficult." Leandro fists his hand, looking ready to punch Esteban.

Christos gets between us and him, surprising the

hell out of me. "That's enough. We don't have time to fight. We have bigger fucking problems."

His words send a wave of ice through me, and I shiver, peeking at Esteban. But he doesn't react, keeping his face expressionless.

"There's been a hit put on Stacia. We managed to get that out of one of the bastards, who somehow knew we were here. We think it was the PI. He must've told whoever hired him that Stacia isn't missing. It's the only thing that makes sense," Christos adds, tightening his jaw.

"So it wasn't even about the drugs?" A million thoughts swirl through my mind. I struggle to comprehend everything going on. But a hit on my head? What the actual fuck? I didn't do anything. How can someone want me dead?

Esteban touches my cheeks, resting his forehead to mine. "Just take a breath. We're going to figure things out. I have an ID that we can look into. We just need to head back to LA."

I squeeze my eyes shut. We were supposed to stay until Talon found the PI and ensured he didn't tell anyone. But if there's a hit on me? It means he failed. I wonder if he even knows.

A hand touches my back. "We're going to get the shit in control. No one can get within reach of you, astéri mou. It'll be safer in LA. We own the city."

"Sorry if I have a hard time believing you, Christos," I snap, struggling to keep myself together.

"If you don't believe him, then believe me. We're here for you. We're all in this together." Esteban kisses me, not even caring that he makes Christos and Leandro frown.

I sigh. "I wish we didn't have to be. This isn't something I want bringing people together. Because if it doesn't work out, we might all just fall apart."

Where is my strength when I need it? Where is my hope?

I'm beginning to think it died with that man.

It's hard for me to be positive when the world burns around me.

I'll just have to figure out how to put out the flames. If I don't, it'll be worse than going to prison. I'll lose my life.

This will have been for nothing.

"You fucked him, didn't you?" Talon eyes Esteban from over my shoulder. "He's far too happy after dealing with the shitshow he warned me about."

Fiery blush flames across my cheeks at his question. He's not angry, but his bold curiosity reminds me of his comment about letting me be with whoever I want as long as he gets to join in. I've never had a threesome before and the idea...it surprisingly turns me on.

I cover his mouth with my hand, my heart jumping in excitement. "Stop it. That's personal."

"Not when it comes to me, wild child. I want to know, so I can knock him down a notch if he even thinks you're his alone. I had you first." Talon kisses my palm, his voice loud and vibrating over my skin.

Esteban chuckles from behind me.

"You hear that, fucker? Don't get any ideas." Talon slides his hand down my spine and squeezes my ass at the same time he kisses me, plunging his tongue into my mouth to make a show of it.

"That's a lot of talk for someone who technically didn't have her first." Christos remains expressionless, but I can tell it bothers him that Esteban and Talon are so casual about my relationship with them.

I square my shoulders and look at him. "Don't even

start. I'm a free woman, and I will do whatever I want. Whomever I want. As much as I want."

"Which you have every right to do. He's only complaining because he wants you too, mamacita. And I'm pretty sure your little stalker does as well." Esteban presses against me from behind, sandwiching me to Talon. "It's almost as if he knows what he's missing."

Holy fuck. I loved the heat of their bodies around me.

"You fucked him too, didn't you?" he whispers lowly, his words only a breath in my ear.

Shit. I shiver and don't deny it.

"I don't think so. He hasn't said anything." Because Leandro has stepped back after becoming my bodyguard. I had fun with him. I enjoy kissing him and teasing Talon, but I'm just not sure he wants in on this mess.

"He'd be in denial if he didn't." Esteban kisses the nape of my neck, and I groan at the attention.

"Or maybe he's just a smart man." Talon eases away from me, gazing at Leandro helping Bianca put her things in the back of the car.

Heat continues to burn across my skin. I can't handle another moment of them casually discussing everyone's feelings for me. "That's enough. I just want to get out of here, go home, and eat a bucket of ice cream before sleeping for a year. It's the only way I think I can recover from everything."

"That sounds like a fantastic idea, wild child." Talon looks at the others. "It'll give us time to catch up. Esteban has shit to do. And Leandro can take Bianca home."

"I'm not a chauffeur," Leandro says, speaking up, clearly eavesdropping on our conversation.

Talon sighs. "For now, you are. I have things under control—"

"But do you? Stacia has a hit on her. I need to stay close to ensure her safety." Leandro tosses the final bag into the trunk and slams it shut. Bianca stares at us with wide eyes from the passenger seat. "The last time I trusted somebody with her, she almost got killed. She's my client, and you pay me to ensure she doesn't get within reach of some asshole who wants to hurt her."

Talon puffs out his chest, fisting his hands. He steps away from me, challenging Leandro with his height. "Don't undermine me—"

I scramble to get between the two of them, their building rage like a burning fuse on a bomb. They might not intend to, but if they explode, it could hurt someone else in the process. That someone else being me.

I press my hands to Leandro's chest, nudging him back. "Please, take Bianca home for me. You're the only one I trust with her life. I don't want her to get hurt in the crossfire."

Leandro loosens his muscles, drooping his shoulders in defeat. "Beautiful, I just worry. I know you're brave and plenty capable of handling yourself, but I also know that Talon is enamored by you. I can't blame him, but I will fault him if something happens."

"I will go with them. Esteban doesn't need my help." Christos scrubs his hand through his hair. "You won't have to worry about me being distracted."

It's enough to get Leandro to back off completely and return to the car and Bianca. Esteban kisses me one more time and strolls toward a second car waiting for him, leaving me, Talon and Christos with the SUV.

I stand awkwardly, watching Leandro drive Bianca away. She stares at me through the window, until they turn and head out of the private hangar.

Esteban sticks his hand out the window and waves at me before flipping off Christos and Talon. I meander away from them and slide into the front seat, resting my head back. It's going to be a long drive with the two of them.

Talon hops behind the wheel and starts the engine. He rests his hand on my knee and offers me a small smile. "You don't know how much I've missed you, Stacia. I worried about you the entire time, and nearly lost my shit when Esteban messaged me. He was reckless."

"He couldn't have expected that, Talon," I say, glancing out the windshield.

"I'm going to cock-block him for the rest of time. You're lucky that Leandro is excellent at his job." Talon puts the car in drive and accelerates, keeping his voice low as if he doesn't want to give Christos a reason to join in the conversation.

He doesn't even try, putting on his sunglasses and ignoring the world. A part of me feels bad for him. I know I shouldn't. I know he deserves what he gets, but he's been trying his best. I'm just not sure I can ever truly forgive him or trust him.

"Can we just move on? I don't want to have to constantly intercept." I shift in my seat, staring at the side of Talon's face.

"He was that good in bed?" he asks, smirking.

I open and close my mouth, my face burning again, surely as red as a tomato.

Christos smacks the back of Talon's seat, clearly unable to ignore our conversation. "She doesn't have to fucking answer that, Talon. I don't know where you get off on thinking—"

The horn blares and Talon slams the brakes, screeching to a stop as another black SUV cuts us off at the gate. The back window rolls down, and I stare frozen at the bright flash of a camera.

"Shit, get down," Talon growls, hitting the high beams.

But it's too late. The photographer snaps a dozen more pictures, capturing me.

This is worse than the PI. This is the paparazzi, and my appearance will be splashed across every front page of every tabloid and website.

"He's a dead man," Christos says, pulling a gun from his holster. Rolling down the back window, he leans out and aims.

The paparazzi's SUV jolts forward as they slam the accelerator, driving away.

"We have to follow him," Christos says, smacking

the back of Talon's seat again.

"And do what? Kill him? You were out of line, Christos. We have an appearance to maintain. You could've made things worse." Talon reaches back and grabs the front of Christos's shirt. "Calm the fuck down and put in an alert to the Looking Glass. We need to stay on top of this."

"We need to handle it ourselves," Christos argues, pulling away from Talon.

I scream in frustration, shocking both of them into silence. "Just take me home. Take me home, so I can figure this out myself."

Christos touches my shoulder. "Stacia—"

I yank away from him. "Now! Do it now!"

Culty

Leandro

*B*eautiful: *Someone tipped off the paps. They got a picture of me.*

"Can you drop me off at the Looking Glass? Apparently, my parents want to meet there." Bianca pulls my attention away from my phone, hooked to the dash.

I glance at her in my peripheral vision. The Looking Glass isn't exactly what I'd consider a good meeting spot, especially in the afternoon.

"What kind of business do your parents do? The Looking Glass isn't even open. Do they work with Mr. St. Germaine?" I stare at the road ahead of me, the line of cars slowing as a tour bus blocks the way, allowing people to snap pictures of a temporary movie set.

"No, but they're in the industry." Bianca doesn't explain anymore, hunching down in her seat as she taps away at her phone.

"Film or drugs? I knew Talon was into some shady shit, but this is beyond what I had expected." I remain stoic, my curiosity turning me bold. When I agreed to be Stacia's bodyguard, I thought it would be against the paparazzi and the occasional stalker. She's known as a party girl, but she's more famous because of her wealth. As far as I knew, she tried the celebrity life and backed out of it. She graduated from one of the most prestigious universities in California and is supposed to take over the family business. If her father ever decides to give it up.

"Film," Bianca says, nonchalantly. "Talon isn't really into the drug scene either, just so you know. You can blame Esteban and Christos for that. Mr. St. Germaine hired them to better control the club scene. You know how it is. Rock stars and celebrities. Wealthy people who just want to have a good time. Keep them happy and business thrives. It's better to have a tap on the market and complete control than to give away any sort of profit to somebody who could destroy you."

Her words surprise me. I thought she was basically Stacia's sidekick, but Bianca knows a lot more than she lets on.

"A lot of these production deals depend on keeping clients happy, no matter what it is." She finally looks up at me from her phone, probably sensing that I'm staring at her, waiting because of the red light. "I wouldn't think too much about it, to be honest. It's safer that way."

I cock an eyebrow and turn my attention back to my phone as it lights up with another text message.

Beautiful: We have to stop by the Looking Glass. My dad wants to see me. Talon says to go back to Malibu and wait for us. Take the night off.

I usually wouldn't question orders, but something is definitely up, especially if I'm dropping off Bianca as well. There's no point in driving to Malibu if we're all at the same place. I can just wait around. It's better this way. As much as Talon swears he can protect Stacia, it is my responsibility. Not to mention that I don't trust the company he keeps.

I fucking hate that Stacia continues to fall for Esteban's charm. He seems like the type to discard someone once he gets bored. He loves the chase and competition. He's not exactly an upstanding citizen. His drugs caused the death of an innocent bystander. He could've very well also been responsible for drugging us. I've seen the toxicity reports, and they mirror what I know about the Jabberwocky drugs. Doesn't matter how pure he claims his to be.

"Go ahead and pull around the back and into the private structure. You can drop me off there." Bianca motions to the side street, coming up past the nondescript building of the Looking Glass. During the day, it looks like nothing special with black painted bricks and windows. It's not until night falls that it lights up.

I do as she says and maneuver the vehicle down the ramp and into the underground garage. I pull around to the elevator, stopping in front of it. Bianca doesn't wait for me to get out, and a man in a suit comes from another car. He looks to be twice her age, and I suspect that might be Juan. Strolling to my window, he holds out a hundred-dollar bill.

"I don't accept tips. Do you need help with her luggage?" I ask, cutting the engine.

The man frowns, and I realize he probably doesn't know who I am. I'm not some driver.

"That would be great, Leandro. Come on, Juan.

That's Stacia's bodyguard and not a driver. You should know that." Bianca offers me a weak smile.

"I don't have time to memorize the help." He turns to me and motions to his car. "You can put everything in the trunk and close up before you leave. We have business to attend to. Thank you for bringing my daughter home."

Juan nudges Bianca, getting her to walk toward the elevator. I stand in annoyance, glancing from my car to Juan's. If Bianca wasn't Stacia's best friend, I'd just leave her stuff on the ground, but I'm a better man than that, despite me wanting to run a key over the perfect paint of Juan's Porsche.

Another vehicle comes into the garage and parks by Juan. I recognize the actress immediately as the star of the latest blockbuster with her picture glowing across every damn billboard in the city. She ignores me as she walks by and heads to the elevator, pulling something that looks like a masquerade mask from her purse.

What the actual fuck?

I finish loading Juan's Porsche and shut the hatch. I return to my vehicle and climb behind the wheel, keeping the engine off as another car pulls into the garage.

"I told you we wouldn't be fucking late. I've about had it with His Majesty calling these spontaneous gatherings. His daughter needs to be controlled better. I don't know why we even humor this bullshit." A man in a suit steps from his Lamborghini and walks around to help the woman from the passenger seat.

"Give the girl a break. You remember what it was like being fresh out of college and free. She'll mature up once this is behind her. I think it should just be a learning experience and not something that will ruin her life. I highly doubt she has it in her to actually murder someone." The woman grasps the man's face and presses a kiss to his forehead. "Now don't argue in there or I won't fuck you for a week. If you argue, you know the meeting lasts longer than it should. Just let His Majesty handle it. This is all a formality anyways."

What the actual fuck? His Majesty? Surely they can't be talking about Stacia's father. What a fucking pretentious bastard if he's making all these people refer to him as some sort of royalty. He's a shady as fuck businessman with far too much money to even know what to do with.

I lean back in my seat, leaving the window cracked, and I stare in silence as another couple of cars come in and overdressed people head to the elevator. I spot a familiar vehicle, and Esteban gets out and rushes to the elevator without glancing around.

Beautiful: Are you ignoring my messages?

My phone buzzes with the text message, and I quickly snatch it off the dashboard and duck down, spotting Talon's familiar SUV. A part of me wants Stacia to catch me so I can confront her, but the nosy part of me wants to know what the hell is going on. This is not just Stacia meeting her father here. This is some sort of group meeting among the rich and famous. And I want to know more. My curiosity won't let me go.

I quickly tap my finger across my screen.

Me: Sorry, beautiful. I was driving and just stopped to grab something to eat. Are you sure you don't want me to stay around and wait? I'm a few blocks away from the Looking Glass.

Beautiful: Talon says to go back to Malibu.

Me: Is that what you want for me to do?

A car door slams, and Talon and Christos exit the vehicle while Stacia remains inside. Talon doesn't help her out, and instead strides toward the elevator. Christos is the one to stay behind, and I frown as I peek over the dashboard, spying as he waits for her to open the door.

Beautiful: I wish you could come back and be here for me, but it's not allowed. I'll talk to you later, okay? Maybe do something fun for yourself. Consider this a day off.

Me: I'll see you tonight, beautiful. Maybe we can watch a movie. You deserve some time away from the chaos.

I know better than to say as much, but I can't help myself. I see how possessive and manipulative those around Stacia are, and it pisses me off to no end that it takes them pushing her to the edge to get her to finally stand up for herself. I think it's one of the reasons why she messes with both Talon and Esteban. She hasn't said as much, but she enjoys the power of her sexuality, and takes advantage of it as her way of maintaining control. I understand it, and I'd be a dick if I even thought anything less of her because of it, which I don't. But a part of me wants her to myself. I think she doesn't realize what she does to all of us, and I don't want to push her or pressure her. I don't want to deal with Talon either.

I know I should just let it all go and think of her as

the one-night stand she should be.

If only it were that simple.

Stacia exits the SUV, clearly after responding to me, and I gawk at Christos as he grabs a bag from the backseat. He pulls out a full-face mask, the silver gleaming in the harsh lights overhead. And then Stacia joins him, flipping on a diamond-encrusted masquerade mask, covering her face, but not really disguising who she is. It's weird as fuck.

There's no fucking way I'm leaving now. I knew that Talon was into shady shit, and I also knew that they had some private meetings. But masks? This is a little bit culty.

Stacia and Christos enter the elevator, standing close as the door shuts. I exit my vehicle and stroll toward the entrance, peering at the empty stairwell. I need to make sure no one comes in while I head up. I should mind my own business. I am paid to mind my own business. But there's something about all of this that I want to unravel. Maybe if I do, I can help Stacia out. There has to be more to this whole situation. I don't think a drug lord would frame the daughter of a wealthy businessman without reason. And knowing that someone hired a hitman? There is a whole shit ton more to this, but I need to figure out. Stacia is my top priority, and I don't think those protective—or more like obsessed—men around her have her best interest at heart.

There's no point in disguising myself, so I enter the elevator and head up to an unmarked level. A man waits on the other side, and I grab him and yank him in, forcing him to his knees as I lock him in a choke-hold. He's obviously not a security guard. I don't know who he is, but I take his mask and black robe, shrugging it on.

This is definitely a cult. There's no other explanation.

The elevator returns to the parking garage, and I pop my trunk and put the man in. It's not my vehicle anyways, belonging to Talon. He can deal with the shit later. I just need to know more so I can approach him about all of this. It's fucking nuts.

I make my way back upstairs, and I enter a dimly lit room with only candlelight. Voices hum through the air, and I stand beside a man in a mask and robe, acting as if I belong.

A gong sounds to the air, vibrating over my skin. The group chants something, unfamiliar, their haunting voices creeping me the fuck out. I peer around the room, drinking in each figure, trying to find Stacia, but it's hard with so many people. A part of me knows I should bail out of here. I should pretend that I never saw any of this, because this seems like the kind of cult that will kill you. Yet I'm not in the mood to make wise decisions. I want to know what I'm dealing with. What Stacia's dealing with.

"I call order to the Looking Glass chapter. Tonight, we must skip our rituals and jump right into business. It has come to my attention that things are not going as planned. We need to act fast to prevent a scandal involving Princess. Because she is connected to me, I cannot do as some of you suggest and let it play out as part of God's will. We need to clean up this mess immediately." A man with a crown and a mask with horns steps forward from what looks like a sacrificial altar, but there is nobody waiting to play sacrifice. Yet.

"Your Majesty, might I suggest we do the same as whoever is trying to set us up and frame someone again? It worked quite well with that drugging situation." This comes from somewhere among the crowd, the voice too soft to pinpoint.

"I agree. Which is why I brought you all together for

approval. I know some of you believe that Princess is getting special treatment because she is my daughter, and I want to prove that it is not the case. We would stand beside any of you in this situation, which is part of our foundation as the Esoteric Society. The Princess is in need, and we must all do our parts, but it will not go without challenges. So tonight, I want to put forth a task. If Princess does not complete the task, then we will move forward with letting her take the blame so we can move on. Is that acceptable?" His Majesty says, motioning to the crowd. "Everyone who agrees, say ay."

"Ay," dozens of voices respond, filling the room.

His Majesty raises a cane. "Those who disagree and want to try another approach, say nay."

"Nay," only a handful of voices say, some of them familiar, belonging to Christos, Esteban, Talon, and Bianca along with some unrecognizable but confident women.

His Majesty smacks his cane down. "Majority rules. Princess, you must complete this task within the week to ensure your freedom. We can no longer put the Looking Glass chapter in jeopardy."

"You want me to frame another person? Who? How

the fuck am I supposed to do that?" Stacia's familiar voice rings out as she steps toward the center of the haphazard circle. "There has to be something else we can do."

A figure rushes from the crowd and grabs onto Stacia, smacking her across the face, sending her masquerade mask flying. I force my feet to stay in place, my body wanting nothing more than to grab the fucker and break his neck.

"Do not question His Majesty's authority!" A man yells, grabbing Stacia by her hair. I realize it's one of the men from the parking garage.

Another man comes from the crowd and grabs him, yanking him back. "Touch her again, and you'll lose your hand."

It's Christos.

The man sneers. "You son of a—"

"Order! There will not be violence in my court. Princess, your task is settled. If you choose to call an SOS on any of our members, remember, you must return the favor. Do you understand?" His Majesty asks, bringing his cane down again.

"Yes, Your Majesty," Stacia says, cowering on the floor. "I won't let you down."

"Meeting adjourned. Will the King's Court please head to my chambers? Everyone else is dismissed." And like that, His Majesty vanishes into another room, and someone blows out the candles.

The crowd disperses, and I stay among the group, moving along and choosing to take the stairs, along with a dozen others. I can't see Stacia in the crowd, so I do my best to keep my gaze trained down, not making conversation, though somebody murmurs about the annoyance of this interruption.

My nerves tighten my muscles, and I push past someone as they take off their robe and hang it by the door. I leave mine on and ignore him, jogging into the parking garage. I spot the man I'd shoved in my trunk, standing in the elevator, yelling into his cell phone.

I shove another man down and run toward my car, turning on the engine. Fuck me. I've been exposed. If I'm caught, I'm a dead man.

But I'm not giving up now.

Someone honks their horn, and I ignore them, hitting the throttle and smashing the corner of their vehicle before they can trap me in.

My tires squeal and smoke fills the air. A man jumps out of my way, realizing I'm not going to brake for him. I'd rather just run them over and deal with that later.

A chime rings through the air, and I glance at my phone, spotting Stacia's name.

Beautiful: Don't go to Malibu. Get out of the city. I'll contact you soon as I can.

Me: What the fuck, Stacia? What is all of this? You're in a fucking cult.

Beautiful: It's not a cult. I can explain everything. You just have to go.

As much as I want to argue, I don't. Instead, I drive. I run a dozen red lights and don't stop until I hit the freeway.

I don't look in my rearview mirror.

I can't look back.

Exposed

Stacia

I tug at my hair, wringing the strands with my fingers. What the actual fuck? Why didn't I pay better attention in the parking garage? How did Leandro even make it into the meeting room? I have so many questions.

Bianca bounces on her feet. "I'm so sorry, Stacia. I asked him to drop me off here. I should've had him park on the street, but I had all my stuff and—"

"Maybe he didn't see much. The meeting was short. We can cover it up. Jasper said he didn't get a good look at the intruder. The court thinks he was with PI or paps." Christos rubs his fingers over his chin, eyeing the closed door of Daddy's chambers.

Leandro: Someone was following me but I lost them. I'm ditching my phone and the car.

My heart sinks to my stomach at Leandro's text message.

Me: There's a lot of things I can't explain. It's dangerous.

Christos snatches my phone away and glares at the screen. "Astéri mou, are you crazy? You have to stop texting him right now. If someone catches you—"

The door to Daddy's chamber swings open, and Christos pockets my phone, keeping it away from me. Talon fills the doorway, his eyes hooded with worry and exhaustion, but he doesn't give anything else away.

"Princess, the King's Court will see you now. We got surveillance of the intruder, and it turns out to be your bodyguard." Talon tightens his jaw.

I try not to react, though I feel as if I might pass out at any second. Christos presses his hand to my lower back, guiding me forward until I start walking on my own. Talon blocks him and Esteban, not allowing them to pass the threshold. I'm going to be sick. I know what happens to those who discover the Esoteric Society. Leandro isn't someone they would offer a spot to.

"You have to do something, birdie," I whisper, keeping my voice low. "They're going to kill him."

"Just stay calm and agree to whatever they ask. We will figure this out," he responds, nudging me forward until I stand before Daddy.

I drop to my knees and bow my head, showing my respect and my regret.

"Do you know why we have called you before us, Princess?" Daddy asks, looming over me.

I shake my head, choosing not to give answers just in case they don't already have them. I'm not going to incriminate myself or give them reason to think that I brought Leandro into this and broke the rules.

"It seems that your bodyguard couldn't mind his own damn business, and we have a problem." Daddy reaches out and touches my chin, forcing my head up to meet his eyes. "You're lucky that I love you, daughter. I am constantly having to challenge the others on my court. They want the bodyguard dead, and they want you to do it."

My chest squeezes, stealing my breath away. He did not just say what I think he did. "What? No."

"Shut up and listen, Stacia," Daddy says, again

breaking our rule about using our real names. It shows that Daddy is beyond this bullshit as much as I am.

I snap my mouth shut and turn my gaze to look at Talon, who clenches his fingers into fists without a word.

"It would be in your best interest to listen. And I mean really listen. I don't know what kind of bullshit you've got yourself caught up in, but I cannot stand by as someone threatens our chapter. This is not only our livelihood, but it is also our lives. There's a lot at stake, and we need to handle your bodyguard immediately. Obviously, I understand that you're not a killer. It has been very clear since even before your initiation, but we can't just let him go. The court has agreed to accept my compromise, and you will frame Leandro for all these murders. Do you understand? It is the only way this can happen or he's a dead man." Daddy steps away from me and returns to his desk, slouching in the rolling chair.

Tears fill my eyes, but I don't argue with him. Talon warned me to just agree. If I try to argue, it'll get worse. This is a small mercy I must take. Because Daddy is right. If I were anyone else, I'd probably lose my head as well.

"I understand and will take care of it," I say, keeping my voice low to stop it from shaking.

"You better. You have until the end of the week. I can't buy any more time from the authorities." Daddy turns toward his court. "Is that satisfactory?" he asks them, acting like they have a choice. Daddy is the king of our chapter for a reason. He is a ruthless man, and he will fight anyone who tries to go against him. But he's also a smart man, which is why he gives into such compromises.

"Yes," Daddy's court says in unison.

"Excellent. This meeting is adjourned. Everything said within these walls must stay within these walls. We cannot risk this getting out. It is one of the benefits of being on the King's Court. Does everyone agree?" Daddy looks around those closest to him, including Talon.

"Agree," everyone says.

Daddy peers at me in silence.

"Agree," I whisper, hanging my head.

"Good. You are all free to go." Daddy smacks his hands together, the sound shocking through me. I don't move from my spot until he vanishes from the room with his most trusted following behind him.

Talon silently goes with them.

I peek up and watch him go, leaving me alone in the King's chamber. I don't know what to do as my world continues to fall apart around me. It was one thing, framing a man who abused his girlfriend and who was an entitled bastard. It's another to frame a man that I like and enjoy the company of. A man who has proven he'd die to protect me.

I hate my life.

I hate this fucking secret society.

The benefits no longer outweigh the danger. I don't gain anything anymore, and it feels as if I'm losing everything.

My life. My friends. The men I care about. My innocence.

It's something that can't be maintained any longer. I can't just be the party girl and the heir of the St. Germaine empire. I have to be more. I have to do more.

I can't let the Looking Glass chapter destroy me. I just can't. I refuse to frame Leandro.

I need to figure out who really killed those people. And quickly. Because time is running out.

"Astéri mou, let me help you. You can't just stay here." Christos materializes beside me, kneeling on the ground. "Tell me what happened and what we need to do."

I shake my head, tears burning my eyes. "We have to get out of here. We have to run away. I can't do what they've asked of me."

Christos lifts me off the floor, carrying me through the dark, empty meeting room. I have no idea where Esteban and Bianca went, but they were probably ordered to vacate the building. Rubbing his hand up and down my spine, he smooths out my trembles, caring for me in a way I haven't let him do in so long. Something about his familiarity helps settle the erratic beats of my heart, but my mind still begs me to keep my guard up.

"If you want to run, then we'll run. I have a place in Greece we can stay, off the radar, and away from the Esoteric Society." Christos whispers the words in my ear so quietly that I struggle to hear them. "I'll take care of you. Nothing will get between us again."

He cracks the foundation of the wall I built between us. My heart flutters with his words. He'd so easily give up his life as he knows it to ensure mine doesn't end. But how long can we run for? How long can we hide? I wouldn't be just giving up the Esoteric Society.

I'd have to give up everything, including the men I've grown to appreciate and cherish. Perhaps love, if I'm even capable of such things.

And what about Leandro?

"Christos, I'm just so scared. I can't do this. Any of this." I bury my face in the crook of his neck, not even caring if my tears dampen his button-down.

"Don't talk like that. I know you're capable of doing anything. You just need a moment to collect yourself. I'm going to get you out of here, okay?" Christos doesn't wait for me to respond and carries me to the elevator and down to the parking garage. Esteban stands at his car, leaning against the door, and he doesn't say anything while he opens the passenger side while Christos sets me on the front seat.

Bianca must've left with Juan, and I doubt he will let her come in contact with me anytime soon. She'll have to sneak around like she's done before, but it makes me feel like crap.

I lose myself to my thoughts, not paying attention as Christos drives with Esteban in the backseat. Pulling into a gated community, Christos navigates through the cookie-cutter streets with identical condos. I had expected him to take us back to Malibu, but we're somewhere else.

"What's going on?" I ask, straightening in the seat. "I thought we were going back to Malibu."

Esteban peeks his head between the front seats. "No, mamacita. It's too dangerous. I finally got a contact for the drugs, and we need to take care of that first."

"You can wait in the car, astéri mou," Christos says, parking in front of a stone pathway leading to a wrought iron gate, surrounding a patio.

Hydrangeas bloom in pink and blue colors, and a mermaid waterfall fountain trickles off to the side. I spot a sunflower flag hanging by the door and wonder what the fuck kind of drug lord lives here.

I start to grab the handle, ignoring Christos's suggestion. "I need to move. I can't just act like nothing is happening."

He touches my knee. "Please, Stacia. Just wait here," he says with such desperation that I decide not to argue and slouch back down in my seat. I don't need to prove that I can handle everything all the time. Not with Christos. Not with Esteban either. It's just hard to get it out of my head. It's hard to allow others to take care of me when I've had to take care of myself for so long.

"Bueno, mamacita. We'll hurry." Esteban exits the

vehicle.

Christos joins him, glancing at me over his shoulder as they walk up the strangely quaint entry to the condo. I huddle down in the seat, wishing I had chosen to duck in the back. I want to be able to see without being seen. The back windows are tinted darker.

A buzzing noise hums through the car, and I pull up the center consul, finding where Christos stored my phone after he had hidden it to help me. I quickly scoop it up, flicking, my gaze between the screen and the door.

Unknown: Get out of there. Do it now.

My stomach twists at the text.

Unknown: It's a set up. It's another hit on you.

A feminine voice screams out, and I scramble in my seat to get a better view. An elderly woman cowers back, holding up a cane as Esteban and Christos tower over her. There's no fucking way she is a drug lord.

Unknown: Get out!

I reach over and slam my palm to the horn, blaring it in a long succession. Christos spins and looks at me, fear crossing his face.

"Duck!" he yells, his voice echoing through the closed window.

I don't have time to react as he yanks a gun from his jacket, aims, and shoots. I startle and screech, dropping to the floor and trying to shove myself under the dash the best I can.

My body jerks at the sound of another gunshot, and someone smacks into the window, trying to yank open the door. I push open the passenger side and manage to crawl out, keeping down. I can't stay in a vehicle with someone trying to break in. Not if I want to survive.

"Stacia, over here," Esteban says, motioning for me to run toward him while Christos shoots at a man in a mask.

I run, hunkering down. The old woman continues to scream and tries to attack Esteban with her cane. He grabs onto it and yanks it away. She hobbles down the hall and out of view. I knew this wasn't the house of a drug lord. This is all set up. But by who?

"Get inside. There's a back door that leads to a garage. Here are the keys." Esteban hands me a set of keys with a fuzzy ball on them.

"The hit is still on me. This was a set up," I say, hurrying inside, my nerves frayed because of the gunshots between a hitman and Christos with just a few cars between them.

"I know. The old lady said someone paid her twenty grand to use her house as a front." Esteban pulls me inside, shutting the door. "I want you to get out of here. Wait for us to call. We need to find out about this fucking hit."

I know better than to argue and let him lead the way to the back door. I step into the garage and click the alarm on the car. Esteban is too engrossed with me that he doesn't see the old woman coming up behind him.

"Esteban!" I scream, rushing forward. I grab onto his jacket and yank, but I'm too slow. The old woman manages to stab him with a kitchen knife.

Esteban stumbles toward me, and I grab a wrench from a toolbox by the door, chucking it at the woman, getting her to fall back. Blood coats Esteban's hand, and he wobbles on his feet.

"Fuck. Get in the car. I'll get help." I practically drag him and shove him into the passenger side. I hit the button to open the garage door, listening to another round of gunfire, echoing through the air, coming from the front.

But I can't stay for Christos. Not when Esteban's bleeding out in front of me. He'll be okay. I know he will. The hitman isn't after him but me.

"You can't take me to a hospital," Esteban groans, heaving deep breaths.

I tug up his shirt and pull it off, using it to stanch the bleeding the best I can. I back out of the garage, steering one-handed, and then put the car in drive. My body trembles with fear. I can't see how bad Esteban's wound is because of the blood. There's so much of it.

"Where do we go?" I ask, swinging around the corner, sending the back-end fishtailing for a second.

"Call Talon." Esteban sucks in a breath between his teeth.

I wiggle in my seat, managing to pull my phone from my back pocket. It nearly slips from my sticky fingers. I force myself to pull over just outside the complex, my mind racing. If I don't, I'm going to crash this car and make things worse.

"You better not fucking die on me, Esteban," I mutter, wiping my hand on my pants. "I mean it."

He chuckles and moans. "It's only a flesh wound. Looks worse than it is. Just call Talon."

A message on my screen catches my attention.

Unknown: Tell me you got out. Tell me you're safe.

I know the unknown message belongs to Leandro. He promised he'd get in touch.

Me: Esteban was stabbed. I don't know what to do. He said no hospitals.

Unknown: Meet me in the parking lot of Fourth and Grand with the pharmacy. It's five away from you.

Me: You're tracking me.

Unknown: It's my job. Now focus on driving safe. Don't speed. Don't draw attention.

Me: Coming.

Esteban leans back in the seat, grinding his teeth. I pull back onto the road and follow the directions Leandro gave me. My head pounds with every passing second. My heart screams to hurry up but my mind knows better. Like Leandro said, I can't draw attention. I can't think about Christos either.

Fuck, Christos.

Not thinking about him seems to be an impossible task. What if he gets hurt or worse? As much as I don't want to care about him, I do. We have so much history, which is why it hurts so badly.

My phone vibrates again, buzzing on my lap. I scoop it up, exhaling a breath of relief at the sight of Christos's name flashing on the screen. I swallow the lump in my throat and answer, my hand shaking against my ear.

I clear my throat. "Christos?"

Christos releases a breath of relief. "Astéri mou, are you okay? There's blood all over—"

"Esteban was stabbed. I'm getting him help." I glance in my rearview mirror at the empty street behind me. "I'm sorry I left you."

"I would've been pissed if you stayed. I pacified the man. He's in the trunk. I swear I'm getting answers for you, Stacia. This will be over soon." Christos lowers his voice. "I just need you to be strong."

"And I need you to be safe. Don't do anything stupid, Christos. I mean it. Call Talon and no one else." I peek at Esteban, his eyes blinking as if he struggles to stay awake. "I have to go. I'll keep you updated."

"You better." Christos hangs up first, the silence cutting through the line as heavy as my fear hanging over me like a cold cloak.

I reach over and rest my hand on Esteban's knee, smoothing circles over and over again. "Almost there. Just hang on."

I spot the mom-and-pop pharmacy on the corner and pull into the empty parking lot. Boards cover the windows and spray paint decorates the cinderblock façade. This can't be right. Maybe Leandro fucked up.

Esteban gasps, startling me, his groan ringing through the car. I hit the brakes and throw the gear into park, turning in my seat. His eyes roll, his body slackening. He's lost too much blood.

"Esteban! Esteban, wake the fuck up! Stay with me!" I scream, tears burning my eyes.

He doesn't move or respond.

I'm afraid I just heard him take his last breath.

21

Promises

Stacia

"Please, Esteban," I cry, shaking him.

The passenger side door opens, startling me, and I scream out only to gasp a breath at the sight of Leandro. His brow furrows as he assesses the situation, and he shoves his hands under Esteban and lifts him from the car.

"He's breathing. In shock. Get the side door for me," Leandro says, jogging fast enough for me to have to run to keep up.

Forcing my legs to hustle, I bolt to the side door and hoist it open. A chain clatters against the heavy metal. I'm pretty sure it's been cut off since the rest of the place looks abandoned. I wonder how Leandro found this place or knew we could use it.

"I have everything set up over here." A woman in scrubs stands at a metal table covered in plastic. Bright light shines from her medical glasses, blinding me. "What's your blood type, Leandro? He's going to need a transfusion."

"AB." Leandro sets Esteban on the table and runs to wash his hands at the sink of what must've been a break room. He grabs a mask and gloves, suiting up. "Stacia's O-negative."

"All right, girlie. You're a universal donor. Your friend's going to need you." The woman cuts open Esteban's shirt, getting a view of the stab wound. She flashes her light in Esteban's eyes. "Sir? Can you hear me? You're lucky as hell you weren't stabbed a little more to the right. You'd be dead."

My body chills with her words. I should've driven faster. I should've done something. What if he does die? I can't think about that.

"Stacia, come lay down and let me get you hooked up. I know this shit makes you queasy, but it's going to be okay. We need to get him stabilized so Dr. Silva can get him sutured up." Leandro motions for me to lay beside Esteban, and I lace my fingers through his, hoping he knows I'm here.

"Esteban, I'm not going anywhere," I say softly, squeezing his fingers. My heart jumps at the sight of the IV line, and I turn my gaze away.

Fuck. Don't pass out. Don't fucking pass out.

"You're going to feel a pinch," Leandro says getting me hooked up to the line. "Don't think about it. Listen to my voice. You're saving his life."

I close my eyes and imagine being somewhere else, anywhere else. I Imagine being back in Florida, staring at the aqua water with Esteban.

Even though that trip was shitty, coming back here, it's been worse. So much worse than I imagined.

"Look at you, beautiful. You're not even pale. I think you're getting desensitized." Leandro moves to join the doctor.

The doctor and Leandro quietly work through things, and I feel Esteban's fingers tighten around mine. I don't know how much time has passed, but it hasn't been that long, and I'm so relieved to feel his movement.

"Mamacita," Esteban murmurs, rubbing his thumb over mine.

I open my eyes and meet his. I offer him a small smile and squeeze his fingers. "You scared me. You're supposed to be a big bad drug lord, and a fucking grandma almost took you out."

Esteban chuckles and groans. "Don't remind me."

"Oh, I'm going to hang this over your head forever. It'll be my own personal collateral to ensure you stay by my side." I puff a breath through my lips, my bunched nerves finally relaxing.

The doctor shuts off her bright light and peels off her gloves. "Make sure he gets rest. I wrote a prescription for pain meds. I want you to keep an eye on his sutures. Keep them clean. I'll check back in with you in a couple days, brother."

Brother? I didn't know Leandro had another sibling—a sister. I only knew about his older brother, who's estranged. But why would I? It's never come up. It seems that he knows everything about me, but I still have so much to learn.

"Just send me a bill. Thanks again, sis." Leandro begins cleaning up all of the bloody gauze and evidence that something went down here.

The doctor doesn't give me another look and grabs her bag and exits the building, vanishing before I even have a chance to thank her.

"We're going to have to move him," Leandro says, grabbing my attention. "I want you to pull my car around. We're going to leave that junker you brought here." He hands me the keys. "It's the silver sedan parked on the street."

Leandro helps me to my feet, double checking to make sure I'm not going to fall on my ass because of my blood donation. I'm too numb to even think about it. I can't believe everything that has happened today. I just need to power through and ignore the world. I just need to get somewhere safe, and I know Leandro will take me there.

"And Stacia?" he adds, stopping me from rushing out the door. "You did good. We have a lot to talk about, but I want you to know that I'm here. I don't care what kind of shit you're wrapped up in. I'm here and I'm not going anywhere."

My heart flutters with his words. A part of me wants to tell him that he should leave. He should run away from me and never look back. But another part of me never wants to let him go. Because it's dangerous being around me.

I don't think I'll ever be safe again.

"No one will find you here. I doubt they'll be looking in this area, either." Leandro leads me into the quaint living room of a house about an hour outside LA in a suburban city off the 210 Freeway.

"My dad threatened to send me to a private school out here." I smirk and look around the room, catching sight of some framed family pictures scattered across a decorative table against the wall. "Is this your house? You always seemed like you'd have a bachelor pad, in some high-rise apartment."

Leandro chuckles, turning his attention to the hallway, where he set up Esteban to rest. "It's a bit unbelievable to think that the heiress of the St. Germaine fortune would be at a boarding school in the IE. I would guess Switzerland. Maybe England. Not the Inland Empire."

I laugh and shake my head. "Like I said, it was a threat. And you didn't answer my question."

"Technically, yes, this is my place, but I haven't lived here since high school. My parents left it to me and my siblings, and we just haven't figured out what we wanted to do. My sister and I have busy lives and my brother doesn't want to hassle with anything." Leandro's face darkens with his words. "Anyone looking for me would have to do a lot of digging to find this location. I took on an alias when I got into protection detail."

"So Leandro isn't your real name?" I ask, raising my eyebrows.

"Is Stacia yours?" Leandro steps closer, peering down at me. His eyes shift back-and-forth, searching my face for whatever silent questions that whirl through his mind. I knew this was coming. He saw things he shouldn't have, and now I'm going to have to explain everything. But a part of me hesitates. It has been ingrained in my mind that if the secret of the Looking Glass ever got out, there would be lethal consequences.

But what do I have to lose at this point? Leandro deserves to know what he truly got himself into when he took the job as my bodyguard.

Slowly bobbing my head, I confirm my answer to his question. "I'm Stacia St. Germaine, and the daughter of Kenneth St. Germaine, the current king of the Looking Glass chapter of the Esoteric Society."

Leandro twists his lips, tightening his jaw. "Do you know how strange that sounds? A secret society?"

I understand why he questions things. It does sound crazy. It is crazy. "Are you sure you want to know more? They've killed people for less. Right now, they have their mind set on you. I've been instructed to frame you for the murders. It's either that or death." My voice shakes with the admission. It's hard to even say this out loud.

Leandro squeezes his eyes shut and moves to sit on the couch. He covers his face with his hands and breathes out a low, long sigh. I'm sure this was the last thing he expected, taking me on as a client, and it would've probably been easier on him if he just thought I was involved in a drug cartel or some shit.

"I won't ruin your life. It's not worth it to me. I care about you." I sit beside him and half-hug him, seeing if he'll allow me to touch him.

He leans into me more, sliding his arm around me to pull me close. "I'm not afraid of them. I'm afraid for you. What I saw was absolutely insane. And with the hitman? Stacia, this isn't random. This isn't some bullshit cartel or business deal gone wrong trying to get retaliation. I don't have proof, but it's the most logical thing. Especially after what happened with Esteban."

I rest my head on his shoulder without responding. I don't know exactly what to say. He's right, and I know it deep down. This is far beyond some random bullshit. This has to be an insider. Someone is manipulating our entire chapter, forcing my father into doing things he wouldn't normally do, but he wants to take care of me.

Leandro rubs his hand up and down my arm, not pushing me to say anymore. "I know this is a hell of a lot to deal with, which is why I chose to stick around. I'm not going to stand by and let a bunch of entitled pricks try to ruin your life or mine. They've underestimated me if they think they'd get rid of me so easily."

I tilt my head and meet his gaze. "But why? Why risk it? You should get out while you can. If we can't find you—"

Leandro cuts me off with a kiss that sends shockwaves through my body. I devour his sudden affection and groan, shifting to slide onto his lap. His actions speak volumes. He stays because of me. He risks everything because of me. Why he chooses so? Especially because he knows that I am messing around with both

Talon and Esteban is beyond me.

I don't want to think about it though. I want to lose myself in this moment and drown in his attention. Because this moment is only filled with our vulnerability and need for closeness. This isn't manipulation. This isn't having fun. This moment runs far deeper because we both know what's at stake, yet we throw our caution to the ground.

"You drive me wild, beautiful. I've been a jealous man without your attention. I tried to pull away. I tried to just get my job done and ignore the fact that you were showing others attention, but you're too damn irresistible. I don't care if I'm not the only one. What I care about is if I'm not one at all." Leandro combs his fingers through my hair, kissing along my jaw and down my neck. "I've never stopped thinking about you. How your lips taste. How your body feels. I couldn't imagine not having you again."

Excitement rises from my middle to bloom over my heart, sending it beating chaotically. I feel so incredibly special and sexy in this moment. Not many men would handle my refusal to choose just one of them, and I'm so very lucky that they're learning to be okay with it. For me. They think I am worth it.

I grip his shirt, pulling the fabric. "I know that it's frustrating, but I do like you, Leandro. I just happen to like others. I love your attention. I love all your affection. It's hard to explain, but if you are truly okay with it—"

He shuts me up again with another kiss, sliding his tongue into my mouth as his fingers grip my shirt, and he pulls it over my head. "You don't have to explain anything. I'm all in. I told you I'm not going anywhere, and I am a man of my word."

Sliding off his lap, I get to my knees and unbutton his jeans, pulling them down to free his cock. He grabs my hair and pulls me closer, and I slide my tongue over his tip before I suck him into my mouth, loving how raspy and sexy his moan is. My name like a whispered plea of desperation coming from his mouth.

Leandro doesn't let me suck him off for long, pulling me up onto my feet, so he can undress me completely. I stand exposed in front of him, my nipples hard, my body warm and ready, my lust as intense as my need for him.

He eases my leg up, making me balance as he sits on the end of the couch, pulling my body to his, as he glides his tongue over my clit, turning my knees weak.

Rolling his tongue over my body, he sucks and licks me in a way that leaves my nails biting into his broad shoulders.

I tip my head back, letting my hair cascade as Leandro works me over. Neither of us sees the door open, but I don't react as Talon fills the frame, holding a set of keys in his hand. I knew he goes way back with Leandro, and I should've expected him to show up here, but now that he has...and the way he watches Leandro eat me out without moving...

Fuck me.

"Leandro—" I scream out his name with my orgasm, pushing him back on the couch as I smother his face with my body.

"What did I say, Stacia?" Talon asks, his deep voice rumbling through the air with the slam of the door.

Leandro grips my hips with his fingers, but I don't move off him.

"You said if you caught me fucking someone else that you would join us," I say, my chest heaving with my deep breathing, my lust overpowering everything.

"So what are you doing now?" Talon skulks closer, his arms rippling as he flexes his muscles.

I swallow and slide back, meeting with Leandro's

gaze. "I'm sorry. This is—"

"Going to be fucking fun. I already told you I was okay with this, Stacia. I know this asshole well enough to know that he stands by his word." Leandro sits up, sliding me down his body until his cock rest between my legs. "But he's going to learn that I was here first. I fucked you first. Now, he's going to watch me fuck you hard. He's going to enjoy every second of it."

Talon grabs a fist full of my hair and tips my head back, crashing his mouth to mine. "You lied to me."

I moan in confirmation. "It was none of your business."

Talon tightens his fingers through my hair, holding my head in place, watching me pant. "It is now, and I'm not waiting."

I nod, keeping my eyes on his. "Make me come."

Leandro adjusts me on his body, pressing his cock between my legs. I gasp as he slides into me, the sensation turning my mind to mush.

Bouncing me up and down, Leandro guides my movements, as Talon grabs my breasts and pinches my nipples. My moans come in quick bursts, and Talon surprises me by moving between Leandro's legs so that we're sitting up on the couch with me on my knees on his lap.

"Like I said, I'm not waiting, Stacia. You knew what would happen if I caught you having fun without me. Your ass is mine. You've teased me too long about it with those damn plugs. I know you're ready." Talon lifts my hair to glide his tongue over my shoulder.

My body tingles at his suggestion, his hand sliding down my spine until he draws a circle around my ass, the sensation making me clench.

"I am," I gasp, feeling the pressure of his finger sliding into my ass, slickened by my desire. "But make me fucking come."

He releases a rumbling moan and sucks my shoulder hard, teasing my body as Leandro slows down, sensually rocking our bodies together.

"I'm going to make you feel so good," Talon murmurs, continuing to play with me.

Leandro kisses my neck, pushing my body down harder, deeper. "You better. You'll find what you need in my bag. Take it slow."

Talon spanks my ass and vanishes for only a minute, returning to stand beside us and in my view. I pant and bounce, watching as he undresses, kicking out of his clothes, exposing just how hard watching me with

Leandro makes him. I reach out and grab his hard-on, pulling him to me, opening my mouth to suck him in. He thrusts deep into my throat, holding my head, dominating me how he likes. It turns me on, feeling him pull my hair and fuck my mouth until he breaks away to kiss me again like he can't get enough. Like he only cares about us and the pleasure unfolding between us.

"You're our woman, you know. Ours to protect. To pleasure. To punish for making us get on our k nees..." Talon spanks me again, positioning himself behind me. He massages my ass, opening and closing my cheeks, teasing me with his tip.

Leandro stops completely and cups my face, holding me in place to watch my expression. Reaching between us, he strokes his fingers over my clit, adding pleasure to the blip of pain that makes me suck in a breath.

"Relax, beautiful. Don't resist. Let your body welcome him." Leandro continues rubbing my most sensitive spot, his eyes boring into mine.

"Goddamn, you're so sexy. Look at you take me," Talon says, slowly pushing deeper, gentle yet passionate, his pleasure vibrating across my shoulder.

I moan and close my eyes, focusing on the sensations stealing my thoughts away. Leandro and Talon move in sync, taking their time to enjoy me, kissing me and complimenting me, ensuring I get my fill of pleasure. My body aches in a good way with each thrust, each bite and kiss and caress until another orgasm bursts through me, and I cry out in bliss.

"Give her another," Talon demands, sucking my shoulder, fucking me harder and faster, his muscles tensing.

Leandro pins me to him, bouncing me enough as he draws circles over my clit, sending my eyes rolling. He grunts as he cums, only slowing his body but maintaining the perfect speed and pressure with his hand. My slick body sings, climbing higher and higher until I hit my peak once again, and I shout and cling onto Leandro, barely able to keep my head up.

Talon rests on top of me, sandwiching me to Leandro on the couch, his hips bumping my ass as his mouth finds my ear and sucks on my lobe. He moans heavily as he finishes, his hands continuing to roam and trace over my skin like he can't get enough.

I sink into Leandro, my chest rising and falling with my deep breathing. My mind catches up with me, and

I squeeze my eyes shut and shiver. I can't believe I just did that. I let two gorgeous men fuck me at once—but not only that. I fucking liked it. Loved it even. I've never felt so damn sexy and wanted in my life. Two men care about me enough to get past their jealously and team up to give me what I want. How can I be so lucky and cursed at once? My life outside these walls might be spiraling out of control but I've found the best and safest shelter right here.

"You better have a big enough tub for all of us," Talon says, sliding his arms around my stomach, pulling me up to carry me like a blushing bride. "There's no fucking way I'm letting her crash after this. She's going to ride this high forever."

"Master suite is upstairs. Let me grab a few things from the kitchen, and I'll be right up." Leandro stretches his arms over his head, smiling at me, not even caring that we're all naked and glistening together. He kisses my temple and straightens his back, letting Talon carry me to the stairs.

"You're so goddamn perfect, Stacia. I'll be a fucking dead man before I let anything else bad happen to you. This shit ends today. I promise." Talon brushes his lips to mine. "You'll see. I want you to relax and not worry about a thing anymore."

"You make it sound so easy," I say, resting my head on his bare shoulder.

"Because it is." Talon meets my gaze. "A hit on you is a hit on the St. Germaine empire and the Looking Glass. Someone wants to destroy it all, and now that we have the hitman, the court won't be able to turn their backs and demand you clean up for them."

"I want to talk to him," I say, sobering up from the high of passion. "I should be the one to get answers."

"I don't want you to worry about it. We'll have the name by tonight. Christos is working on it." Talon adjusts me in his arms.

"Talon, please. We had an agreement. You wouldn't leave me out of things. This guy tried to kill me. Esteban was injured because of this. I want him to pay." I purse my lips, my anger rising.

"How can I deny you, wild child? Shit. I'll hold the fucker down for you. No one's getting away with this. I swear on my life."

And I believe him.

22

Bloody Times

Stacia

"I'm starting to get why Daddy wanted me to maintain the party girl persona and just promote the club," I say, standing outside an old factory on the outskirts of LA. Half of the chain-link fence lies in a crumpled mess, clearly cut and driven through several times. The barbed wire does nothing to keep anyone out, but I don't think anyone but criminals and vagabonds would want to be here. This is where the Looking Glass members do a lot of their shady business. At least, that's according to Talon.

"You don't have to go in. I'm sure Christos has already cut the answers right off the man's tongue."

Talon hugs me close, refusing to put even a foot of space between us.

Leandro argued with him over letting me come along, but I needed somebody to stay with Esteban, and Leandro needs to remain hidden. I know it bugs him, because he wants to protect me, but right now, he's the one who needs the true protection. I'm not going to let him go down because of all this bullshit. I won't.

"I can handle it, Talon. Just lead away." I clutch onto his arm, pulling him forward until he stops dragging his feet and guides me toward the rolling metal door, half open where semis used to load and unload whatever product that was made here.

Two men stand in the entry, parting ways at the sight of me and Talon. I don't have to ask to know that they work for Christos. I don't know his real business, but I know he launders money and controls a couple businesses for Esteban. That's how they got to know each other and became best friends.

A man howls, his voice ringing through the air, bouncing off the walls of this vast, empty space. My steps falter at hearing his pain, and I swallow the bile trying to sneak up my throat. I thought I had finally gained a stronger stomach than this, but there's just something about another human's agony that I can't seem to handle. But this guy tried to kill me. He doesn't deserve my sympathy.

"Stacia, turn around. You're losing color." Talon tries to spin me away, but I plant my feet to the concrete floor.

"I'm fine. Stop treating me like I'm some fragile little girl. You just fucked the hell out of me. I'm strong enough, and you know it." I jab my finger to his chest. "You might call me a wild child, but I'm a woman fucking scorned. I am handling this."

Talon offers me a wicked smile, his handsome features lighting up. "Bossy is sexy on you, but only because I want to spank you again. Keep talking to me like that, and you won't be able to walk normal for a week."

Heat crawls up my chest only to have another scream splash the warmth away. I square my shoulders, glowering at Talon as I push past him, heading in the direction where I'm pretty sure the man is located.

Talon doesn't let me get far on my own and hooks his arm around my waist, pulling me to him protectively. He leans in and nips my ear, releasing a sexy growl that I struggle to ignore. But I think he wants to distract me. He wants me to turn around and run away. Even if he thinks I can handle myself, I know he'd prefer to do everything for me. That's just him. He doesn't want me thinking that I need to prove myself. But it's not about that. It's about making a goddamn point. I might be an heiress. I might be known for reality TV, drinking too much, and partying, but I am far more than that. I have a business degree. I know my way around sleazy men and how to manipulate them despite their misogyny and fragile masculinity. There's power in my fucking pussy, and it's those who act like their weak nut sacks are made of steel that will fall before me.

"If you throw up or pass out, I will fucking spank you for ignoring me," Talon mutters, strutting toward the open door of a dark room that looks to be an old office.

"Keep threatening me and you're going to find out what it's like to experience my true wrath. Don't think I won't fuck you senseless." I smirk at his softening expression. "I have my own collection of cocks, you know. It's only fair to let me use them."

He tips his head back with a laugh, his voice booming through the air. Christos materializes in the dark doorway, hearing our arrival.

I gape at the blood splashed across his plastic apron. "What in the fucking serial killer attire is this?" Because it's unlike anything I've ever seen or expected to see on Christos.

Talon practically cackles, far more amused by this whole situation than he should be. But then again, he's known as the Executioner at the Looking Glass. I've always known he had a dark side. I just have never truly seen it for myself.

"I thought you were going to convince her to stay with Esteban." Christos yanks the apron off and drops it to the floor. He wipes his bloody hands on his dark jeans, though it does nothing for the sticky stains on his skin. "He's not responding to any of my methods. Whoever hired him knew exactly what he was paying for. This guy is willing to die to keep secrets."

I rub my throat, praying that the lump stays down. I don't even want to know what his supposed methods are. I can already imagine a bunch of disturbing things flitting through my mind.

"You just haven't asked the right questions. You have to negotiate. If he thinks he's going to die regardless, why would he help you?" Talon says, scooping the bloody apron off the floor. He tosses it back to Christos. "Let this be a lesson to both of you, considering you are going to be part of the King's Court soon enough."

It takes everything in me not to frown. The last place I want to end up is on the Looking Glass King's Court, especially after they demanded I frame Leandro for murders he'd never commit.

"Stacia, I want you front and center. I want him to see that he failed." Talon takes my hand and pulls me along, forcing my feet to work. The potent stench of sweat and body odor wafts through the air. I grab the front of my shirt and pull it up over my nose. I can't help it. It might even smell like death in here.

"Do we have a name?" Talon asks, continuing to take charge of the situation as if he's done this a million times. And he might have. I should be unnerved, but ultimately, I'm grateful. I don't think I could do this without him.

"No. This guy is either the dumbest asshole on Earth or he's a professional. Someone had to pay him a lot of money." Christos closes rank by my side, his presence comforting, something changing between us.

I no longer recoil anytime I'm near him. He's done so much to earn my trust that I'm open to giving him more.

"All right. That's fine. We don't need his fucking name. We just need whoever hired him." Talon cracks the knuckles on his free hand and rolls his shoulders. "I want you to go in there and hurt him. However, you please, wild child. Women know how to bring a man down best."

I swallow my nerves and brace myself. I want to be strong in this moment. I want to prove to more than Christos and Talon that I'm capable. I want to prove it to myself. I can be gentle yet ruthless. I can take care of shit just as well as they can. I never want them to think that I need them. They should know that they're in my life because I want them here.

A low groan echoes through the dimly lit room, and I spot a man zip tied to a metal chair. It reminds me of a couple of movies I've seen where the good guys get captured and tortured. But this isn't the case. We are the good guys. Well, at least to me. Sometimes it's okay to be an antihero when it's my fucking life.

I like having men who will destroy the world to save me.

I like being the most important thing regardless of the consequences of everything and anything else.

I take my fingers away from Talon and sashay forward without hesitation. The man in the chair whips his head up and tightens his jaw, the gesture being the only reaction he gives me.

Fisting my hand, I close the space completely and punch him right between the legs, feeling the softness of his junk crush beneath my force. He howls in pain but doesn't beg for mercy. So I do it again and again, not even bothering to ask him any questions.

"What the fuck!" the man hollers, trying to cross his legs to protect himself.

"You've already proven that you're not going to cooperate, so I'm going to punch your dick until there's nothing left. I have had a long fucking day, and this is therapeutic." I slam my hand down again, stopping and just smashing it. Tipping my head up, I meet the guy's eyes. "How much was my death worth? How much were you fucking paid?"

I don't think a woman has ever challenged him like this, because he opens and closes his mouth in surprise, like he can't believe I'm manhandling him.

I grab him by the neck and squeeze. "If you tell me,

I'll just end your life. If you don't, we're going to find out how long you can live after I pulverize your dick. We're going to learn how long it takes to bleed out when I rip off the tip. I'll use my fingernails."

"I don't know yet! I don't get paid until the job is done. All I have is the down payment. I don't ask for names for a reason." The man rocks back-and-forth, trying to move the chair.

I turned to Christos. "Pull it out. I'm not giving him the satisfaction of even a second of gentle touch."

Christos whistles between his teeth. "Damn, astéri mou. You're vicious."

"That's what happens when someone fucks with my life...or refuses to give me answers. My dad always taught me to do whatever I have to by any means necessary. Even if it means literally destroying this ass-hole's balls." Narrowing my eyes, I stare at the hitman, waiting for him to react.

"And here I thought I was going to have to teach you, wild child." Talon claps, rubbing his hands to-gether. "Do as she asked, Count. My woman isn't go-ing for gentle. Pull his limp dick out and hold it while she rips it off."

"Maybe I'll skin it first. I'm due for a mani anyway. My manicurist is exceptional at getting things out from under my nails." I giggle, my voice surely as crazy as I feel in this moment. A part of me disconnects, summoning the deadly entity I was instructed to nurture and grow to protect myself and my family's business.

The hitman grinds his teeth, bucking against the chair. It wobbles, threatening to tumble backward with the asshole in it. So I shove him. He howls as he falls on his back, crushing his arms. I bite the inside of my lip, stopping myself from reacting. If I react, he might know I'm on the fence about following through. I just want goddamn answers.

Christos wags his eyebrows at me, grabbing at the hitman's pants. He unbuttons them and tries to remain expressionless as he exposes the man's cock. I scrunch my face at the sight of the barely inch nubbin peeking through a bush of pubic hair long enough that I can't even see the man's scrotum.

Christos eyes me and I stare right back at him, a dozen silent thoughts swirling between us. He cracks first, bursting with loud laughter as we kneel beside this man and stare at the poor excuse for a dick between his legs.

"How do you suggest I hold this for you. I'm going to need some tweezers or something. I'm pretty sure my fingers are thicker than that thing as long," Christos says, his voice cracking with his laughter.

"Hurry up with your fun, you sexy little psycho." Talon stands over us, peering down. "We don't have all day. I'm sure he's not going to talk either. We need to just move on."

"Yeah, this is more about revenge for trying to kill me. But I wanted to give him the option. You know I have a kind heart. He can only blame himself for what he's about to experience. It would be so easy just to give us some answers and let him move on into what I'm sure will be a lot of ass fucking in hell. He's definitely going to end up as a bottom, considering...that." I usually don't make fun of a man's size, but he seems like he has fragile masculinity. Got to be a tough guy to make up for something.

Christos chuckles and grabs the man's cock, stretching it out by the head. The man screams, his voice grating on my eardrums. He continues to thrash, trying everything he can to escape us.

I can't believe I'm doing this. I was hoping he'd just talk already. But Talon was right. He's not going to say anything. And I don't want to be caught lying.

"Can you shut him up?" I ask, peeking up at Talon. "Give me something he can choke on."

"Why don't you just cut it off and shove it in his mouth?" Talon crosses his arms.

What a twisted bastard. I gasp a laugh in surprise. "Because he can just swallow it. Come on, killer. Help me out. I thought you wanted me to learn your ways."

"I think you have surpassed me. Just have your fun." Talon steps back, putting more space between us. Something indecipherable crosses his face. I think he wants to know if I'll actually follow through with my threat as well.

"Hurry up, Princess. The fucker is getting a boner." Christos grimaces.

I flick the man's shaft, making him howl again. "Then we will fucking kill it. Last chance, asshole. You have to give us something. We can end this really quickly."

Again, the man doesn't talk. All he does is thrash.

Damn it.

I slowly, begrudgingly, continue on my mission to inflict pain and hope that he will actually talk. Using my thumb and index finger, I pinch his foreskin with my nails, putting enough pressure to make him freeze.

"I don't have a fucking name! All I have is a wire transfer. It's in my phone. Please, don't fucking do this, you sick bitch. You said if I talked, you wouldn't." The man snaps his teeth at me, turning rabid, like an animal now shoved in the corner.

"I've already looked at it. It gives us nothing," Christos says, stretching the guy even more. "He has a contact, Princess. He's not saying everything."

The man hollers again. "Check my bank account. I'll give you the password. It'll give more than the fucking email. I swear."

"What kind of fucking hitman are you, leaving a trail?" Talon asks, looking around the small room until he finds the table of the man's belongings.

"I'm just a desperate man who needs fucking money. I owe a debt. It was either this or losing my fucking arm. And you fuckers? You want to take my dick. Just let me give you what I can. The Executioner will kill me if you don't, so please just give me this mercy." The man stretches his neck, looking at me.

I freeze. Did he just say what I think he did?

"Please," he begs, his mouth quivering. "Just check. *5T7EDw!* with a lowercase w. You'll see what you nee—"

A gunshot booms out, and I startle, staring at the bullet hole oozing from the hitman's head. I whip my attention from him and gawk at Talon, standing feet away with his gun still aimed. My mind races, my heart thudding hard enough to hurt my chest.

I huff a shaking breath. "Did he say Execute—"

"Stacia, I—"

"Holy fucking shit. I'm in." Christos's voice cuts off Talon. I hadn't even realized he moved, grabbing the man's phone. "Carrington Credit Union from Lewis Smith of Hawk Enterprises. Who the fuck..." His voice trails off.

"That's a mistake. There's no fucking way," I say, stumbling to my feet. I shuffle the few steps to Christos, feeling as if I might die if I don't verify the words for myself.

Talon steps closer, towering beside me. "Stacia—"

I snatch the phone from Christos, holding out the screen to Talon. "Someone is fucking framing you. I can't believe this shit. The fucking idiot. How unbelievable for them to use your alias to hire a hitman to kill me."

Christos remains utterly silent, hovering close

enough that our arms brush together. I reach out and lace my hand with his, my body shivering as my adrenaline slips away as fast as the hitman lost his life.

"We need to call my dad. This is all so crazy." I shift on my feet, staring at Talon's expressionless face. "Why would someone do this?"

Talon tucks his gun away, his face hardening into a series of lines. "No one hacked me, wild child."

I whip my head back-and-forth. "I know it's hard to believe but look. It's an Esoteric Society bank and your company. It's your alias."

"Nobody hacked me, Stacia," Talon repeats, snatching the phone from my hand. He tucks it into his pocket. Turning to Christos, he says, "Take her back to Leandro's. I'll take care of everything here."

What in the actual hell? He's too calm. Too emotionless. Talon just saw for himself that someone is trying to frame him for a hit on me, and now he just wants us to leave? I don't understand.

Christos tugs me back only to step in front of me. "Talon, what the fuck do you mean when you say no one hacked you?"

"Don't worry about it. Just take her back to Leandro's." Talon turns away, shutting down any sort of conversation.

Christos doesn't accept it and shoves his hands into Talon's back. "I will fucking worry about it! What the fuck is going on?" Yanking his gun from his jacket, he aims it at Talon. "Tell us."

"Christos, what the hell?" I ask, rushing to get between them. "You can't pull a gun on him."

"Stacia, don't you get it? He just said he wasn't hacked. He's not flipping the fuck out about being framed." Christos growls the words, pushing against me.

"He's in shock," I argue, spinning to face Talon. "Right?"

Talon slowly shakes his head, breaking his eyes from mine. "I'm sorry, Stacia. You were never supposed to find out. You were never in any real danger, and I had to do this. I needed a way to shake the King's Court to weaken the alliance toward your father so I could challenge him."

My head spins as I try to process his words. What is he talking about?

"You hired the hitman!" Christos yells, dragging me away. "You should've told us. You could've gotten Stacia killed!"

"Why are you lying?" I whisper, my blood cooling. I can't wrap my mind around this. It doesn't make sense. "You wouldn't do this. I know you wouldn't..." Tears fill my eyes, my heart refusing to chill out.

Talon rubs the back of his neck. "I'm sorry, Stacia. There's a lot you don't know—"

Christos swings his arm, punching Talon in the face, jerking his head to the side. "You bastard! You're dead!"

Talon doesn't fight back, letting Christos punch him again.

A small sob escapes my mouth. I don't understand any of this. Talon just admitted that he hired a hitman to come after me. He admitted it was to go against the King's Court to weaken them. He wants to challenge them.

Christos abandons his mission to knock Talon out and rushes to me, engulfing me in his arms. I let him pick me up, my feet refusing to move. My eyes betraying me with burning tears when all I want to do is shut down and match Talon's emotionless attitude with my own.

"Did you murder the man at my hotel too?" I ask, lowering my voice to stop it from cracking.

He doesn't respond.

"You're why they targeted Leandro! You brought him into this, knowing the possibility of him finding out." I hold his gaze, though my tears make it hard to see. "You can't possibly tell me this was all for a power move?"

Talon sighs. "We'll talk about this later."

"No. We'll talk now, because I don't believe any of this. I know you. You wouldn't have even considered risking my life. I know you're not responsible for Esteban getting hurt." I clench my teeth.

"Collateral damage, wild child. You can't possibly think I'd care if one of the guys you're fucking dies." Talon flinches at my reaction. Now I know he's lying. The man I've grown close to, the one who would kill to protect me, wouldn't jeopardize the state of my heart.

"This is unbelievable! You're lying, Talon. I know you're fucking lying. Why won't you just admit it? You wouldn't do this." A part of me can't deny the evidence, but deep down, I know something is off. It feels too wrong to be true.

"I'm sorry, Stacia. I'm not a good man. I have priorities, and I needed you to accomplish them. You knew the risk of being around me. I use people. It's what I do, but I swear this wasn't for nothing. I'm taking care of it. I promise. This will all work out." Talon strides toward the door, not waiting for Christos to carry me away. He glances at us over his shoulder. "Just go back to Leandro. Stay low until I call."

Without waiting for me to respond, Talon disappears, leaving me alone with Christos and a dead man hired to kill me.

"He's lying," I whisper to Christos. "I know it."

Christos hugs me tighter. "But what if he's not? If he didn't do it, he'd deny it, astéri mou."

"There's more to it. I know it, and I'm going to find out." I ease away from him. "You can either help me or just leave. I'm not going back to Leandro's. I'm going to the Looking Glass."

"Stacia," Christos says, slumping his shoulders.

I purse my lips. "I'll owe you. Whatever you want."

Christos grabs my hand. "That's not necessary. I'll help you regardless. I'm never leaving you again. I'm always here. No matter what."

And I believe him. It's my faith in him that pushes me forward. He might've betrayed me before, but he's changed. I've changed. We're in all this shit together.

23

Betrayal

Stacia

Daddy's going to kill me for breaking into his office, but I don't know how else to approach him. He ignored my last ten phone calls, and no one on the staff of the Looking Glass will tell me where he is. So now I wait at his desk, hoping he'll see me on one of his security cameras, and finally show his fucking face.

It only takes ten minutes for the office door to swing open. Daddy greets me with a scowl, angry enough that I nearly lose my resolve. I hate admitting that he scares me. Something has definitely shifted between us, and he no longer looks at me as if I'm his pride and joy. He looks at me like he just wishes I was dead.

"Are you fucking stupid, Stacia? You're risking everything we have by being here. You are wanted by the police because of your fuck up. You can't show your face until you give them the true killer. What have you been doing? I haven't heard a word about where you are with your task." Daddy strides forward, not even bothering to shut the door. He's that bold and dangerous. The staff knows to stay out of his way.

I hate being alone with him.

I hate feeling so small in his toxic presence.

Standing up, I straighten my shoulders, trying to give myself more height so he doesn't loom over me. I don't speak, just staring at him, mirroring his same leering expression. But I know I'm far from intimidating. I've given him no reason to be afraid of me.

That's not the route I should take, and I know it. It's just hard for me to cower and pretend that I don't want to smack him for being so awful. For putting me in this position.

I need to be the perfect, obedient daughter, who loves her father and would do anything to please him.

I throw my arms around him, burying my face in his chest. "I'm so sorry, Daddy. I know I'm not supposed to be here, but it's important. You weren't responding to my phone calls, and I've been worried sick about you. I thought something happened. I was nearly killed by a hitman."

Daddy turns rigid, his muscles tightening with my words. He doesn't bring his arms up to hug me back and instead grabs my shoulder, forcing me away from him. "Goddamn it. I was afraid of something like this happening. I've been looking into Smithson, and it turns out, he wasn't loyal. His people think you had something to do with this death. I suspect this has to do with that...but there's more."

Stepping forward, I clutch the front of his suit, peering into his eyes. I remind myself of Talon and the situation. I think about how he didn't deny his part, claiming that he wasn't framed. It's still hard for me to even think it's true. I might be stupid for it, but I can't help it. I've fallen in love with that man. But there's also Daddy. I'm torn between my family and my place and everything. Because if Talon challenges Daddy, one of them is a dead man.

"I know there's more." I try not to think about his comment about Smithson, the dead man that started all of this. It's weird for Daddy to spill that kind of information without being asked. "It's worse than that. I discovered it was an inside job. The hitman was hired by someone with a bank account linked to the society." My voice cracks, my nerve faltering. I'm not going to disclose that I found the account connected to Talon. Daddy's not the type to look into things. He knows that Talon isn't exactly a man who can be framed. Christos believes him. I just can't.

"Now what I discovered makes sense. What do you know?" Daddy clenches his jaw. What he discovered? He knows things and hasn't told me? Of course he hasn't. If it's Talon...it's not. It can't be.

"I think this is all a setup as a power-play. The drugs. The murder. And now the hit on me. I think you need to look into things. I need my bodyguard, and I can't do that with this fucking task hanging over my head. Don't you think it's better to have someone who knows everything protecting me?" I finally drop my hands from Daddy's jacket, his scrutiny stabbing me too deeply that I can't stay this close any longer. I can't look at him either.

He remains silent and expressionless, not reacting to anything I say. It pisses me off.

"Say something. Please. I don't understand. If you know something, why aren't you more enraged?

Someone is fucking with our lives, using me. Do you even care?" I ask, tugging at my wig. I'm growing to hate the disguise, and I just want things to go back to how they were, but I know that's not possible.

Even if I'm no longer tasked with framing Leandro, I still have to figure out the situation with Talon. I'm drowning in all of these problems, and I can't even ask for a life raft. The Esoteric Society would prefer I either sink or learn to fucking swim in rough waters.

"Your Majesty," I snap, no longer able to maintain my desperate daughter personality. "You have to do something. Call order to the court. Tell them that I need my bodyguard. You need to figure out who is after us."

Finally, Daddy reacts. His aged face deepens with wrinkles, his eyes turning into slits. I don't even have a chance to brace myself as he charges me and grabs me by my throat, lifting me off my feet. He drops me onto the chair and towers over me, his broad body blocking any sort of escape path I can find. If he decides that he's going to hurt me, there's nothing I can really do.

I can't fight from this position. I can't do anything except pray. What happened to the man who promised me an empire? How can the scandals have rattled him so much that he's willing to practically disown me? He knows I'm innocent, yet he's treating me like I'm guilty. He's treating me like I'm the one responsible for all of our chapter's problems.

"I need you to shut up and listen to me, Stacia. This shit didn't start happening until Christos showed up. So I've done some investigating. He's the one behind all of this, starting with drugging you. He set up our club. He killed the patron, pumping more drugs in her system to make sure she'd overdose. Hired the hitman so he could get in your head. He is so damn obsessed with you that he'll do anything to make you his, even if it means destroying our entire chapter. This is your fault, you know. Why couldn't you just thank him for arranging both of your initiations? He saved you the trouble, considering half our chapter didn't agree you were worthy. You guys would be married, and there would be no problems. You would've been a step closer to taking control of our family business. You'd be just years away from controlling the Looking Glass as Queen. But obviously you can't see past your own fucking feelings. You act as if he showed the entire world the two of you fucking. The fact that you consider him choosing that over the other task presented to you guys as a betrayal... You're a disgrace and a disappointment. And now I'm left cleaning up your mess again and again." Daddy growls with his words, his accusations and comments burning through me, destroying every ounce of respect I had for this man. He's lying. Christos isn't behind this. I know that, because I know whose account is supposedly linked to it.

Now I realize why. He isn't worried about such a challenge because he doesn't see it as a threat. And why? I think he might be the one truly behind it. He's manipulating me. He's gaslighting me and making me feel as if I'm the reason for all of this when we both know I'm not. His explanations are too easy and un-founded.

I can't believe this...yet I can.

What I don't understand is why. Why go through the trouble? Why hurt his own flesh and blood?

"Did you know that I'm the one who presented the offer? I'm not usually allowed to say, but I thought it would be best for you. You didn't have it in you to accept a real task, and it was the only way to ensure your spot." Daddy steps back and crosses his arms, shaking his head. "You two had it so easy. He denied the challenge for a spot on a King's Court. And this is how he repays me? He's a dead man."

My mouth dries. I can't speak. I can't think. All these years, Daddy fed me lies. He never once implied I'd been almost rejected.

Christos saved my life.

"I think I know a way to change things for you, Stacia," Daddy continues, his voice softening in his true manipulative fashion. He thinks my silence means I believe him. "I will call order to the court and present them with this information. It'll be an easy task. You can get the revenge you crave while we also deliver punishment. No one will stand in my way. Christos will fall. He deserves such a fate."

I open and close my mouth in shock. He's so far deep into ruining our lives, and so sure I'll believe him. What kind of proof does he have that he thinks he can convince the entire King's Court?

So I gather my bravado and ask, "What kind of proof do you have? These are serious allegations. I only have the accounts attached to the hit."

Daddy sighs and goes to his desk, clicking on his computer. He brings something up on the screen, and I stare in shock. It's the email trail with the hitman, who I assume are some dealers, and even the vow Christos signed long ago. Daddy also brings up screenshots of the account information and the start of a wire transfer. But something's different. It isn't Talon's alias. It's Christos's. Now I know this is all completely wrong.

Now I wonder if Talon was telling the truth. Maybe it wasn't Daddy. But...no. That still doesn't make sense. Why would my dad cover up for Talon supposedly betraying our family? The only explanation I can think of is that Daddy doesn't want Talon to know he knows the truth. Maybe he's using Christos as a cover for Talon's behavior. He could be doing this to prepare for when Talon comes after him. Maybe he thinks I'll tell Talon.

And now I'm stuck in the middle of everything.

"Is this proof enough for you, daughter?" Daddy asks, clicking out of the screen.

I just nod my head. I have nothing else to say. I need to get out of here. I need to tell Christos what's happening. I need to find Talon and warn him.

But mostly, I need to figure out what to do next. I can't stand the thought of something happening to anyone because of this.

I stand up from the chair, half expecting Daddy to shove me down, but he doesn't. He lets me have my space.

"Now that you see, will you please stop taking these risks and putting our name in jeopardy? You need to hide and pretend that this is not happening. I'll have Talon bring you in when the time comes, okay?" Daddy asks, remaining stern-faced toward the situation.

I nod my head in silence and walk toward the door.

He stops me and kisses the top of my head. "I know this is tough, but it is what it is. I will handle it and will take care of those against us. Then we can move on."

Again, I bob my head in agreement.

I leave Daddy standing in the office staring behind me.

I feel as if my world is about to implode.

I'm afraid there won't be any survivors.

Christos parks in the garage of Leandro's house, and I finally intake a deep breath. I haven't said anything since leaving the Looking Glass, and he hasn't pried. He knows that I need time to process. He's always been good about that.

But now he looks at me, the anticipation for answers clear on his face.

"Why didn't you tell me that my dad arranged your initiation?" I ask, keeping my voice low. "He said that he made it so that neither of us had to do something worse and that I fucked up by being ungrateful. He thought we would be married and happy because of it."

Christos purses his lips and frowns. "What do you mean he arranged it? The initiation was given to me by William. I had been given a choice after one of the other new recruits... God this is fucked up. I don't even want to think about it. I love you, Stacia. I love you so damn much, but I know I failed you. I just couldn't do the other thing they had demanded. It's why I'll probably never be the king of a chapter. It all came down to testing my loyalty. It was either that or lose you completely. Because you were marked. You were marked as a victim to be sacrificed as an initiation for someone else. You weren't chosen at first."

My heart sinks to my stomach. Daddy said I wasn't chosen, but he never said I had been marked. I didn't think that still happened. I've heard rumors about those seeking power killing as part of their initiation ...but the King's Court picking me as sacrifice? What the actual fuck?

"From what I know, another guy showed up. A relative or something. I don't exactly know who he was, but he was also considered an heir. He was to be groomed to be a King like me but for the Looking Glass. But he died before he could be initiated. I don't know all the details. I just know that his death fucked things up. He committed suicide to escape. So William gave me this offer, thinking I might follow the same fate. I didn't know it was you until then. He said I could do this and solidify both of our places. He never mentioned your dad." Christos frowns and leans closer, pushing my hair behind my ear.

I'm more confused than ever. "So what was your other choice?" I know the answer deep down, but I need to hear it.

"To finish what the other heir couldn't. It would've solidified my path to take over. I chose to betray you instead, and then...it ended up being for nothing. I lost you anyway." Christos closes the space, resting his forehead to mine. "I'm so sorry, astéri mou. I couldn't tell you any of this. You know the consequences if I did. It would've jeopardized both of our lives. So I risked losing you to save you. I prayed you'd forgive me...but I did lose you. I wouldn't change it though."

My heart hammers at his admission, and I close my eyes, sharing his breath. I wish with everything in me that I had known what was happening. I was too naïve. It was too easy to just get angry and throw Christos away. Then he accepted it. He left. But something must've changed. My dad was the one who brought him back.

Daddy knew what kind of effect it would have on me, and he did it anyway. I think he did it on purpose. Shit.

"You didn't lose me," I murmur, wanting nothing more than to forget the shitty situation. I want to forget all the treachery and the lies spun like spiderwebs catching me as the prey. I can't escape. But I can at least learn to cut myself free. To fight back.

"But I did. You obviously have your heart open for others, astéri mou." Christos grazes his lips to mine with his words.

"I do, but that doesn't mean it's not open for you too. I wish things could've been different, but then..." I let my voice trail off, closing the space to his mouth completely, kissing him softly, gingerly, waiting for his reaction.

He slides his tongue over mine, deepening our kiss, giving in to my need instead of sending me away despite everything.

Heat blooms between us, and I drag my hands over the front of his shirt, unbuttoning it as quickly as I can, wanting nothing more than to feel his skin against mine. To remember what it's like to be with Christos with his love for me. With his loyalty.

Pushing back his seat, Christos makes room so I can slide on his lap. His fingers latch onto my shirt, and he pulls it over my head, breaking away from my mouth to kiss my cleavage. I reach between us and unfasten his belt and pants, pulling his cock free to stroke my fingers over the hard length, already stiff and ready for me.

"I love you, Stacia. I've been begging the universe for this moment again. I will not take you for granted. I will stand by your side, no matter what. I love you," Christos says, pulling my pants down and stretching my legs up to undress me completely.

I lace my arms around his neck and kiss him again, grinding my wetness over his length, just savoring the sensation of being so close.

He doesn't let me tease him for long and lifts me up only to align our bodies and pull me down onto his erection, the particular pressure recognizable enough to make me gasp. Our tongues fight for control, and I hold his face, stealing every one of his moans as I bounce, the weight of the situation releasing with my movements. I just want him to fuck all our pain away. Our heartache. Now that we're so close and the truth begins to piece our relationship back together, I just want to lose myself in this moment.

Christos rubs my clit, adding to my pleasure, and I break from his mouth and pant, moving faster. My moans come in loud bursts, and he sucks on my throat, leaving his mark. It feels so good being with him again. He was always an exceptional lover, always ensuring that I got my fill of pleasure before him.

An orgasm builds, sending electric shockwaves through my body, tensing my muscles. I gasp as I reach my peak and crash my mouth back to Christos's, slowing down only to have him take over my movements, lifting and dropping me over and over, his thrusts turning my body into mush and lengthening my orgasm.

My knees shake from the pleasure, and I fall against him, pressing my boobs into his warm chest, lying flat with the seat completely reclined. Christos thrusts a couple more times, kissing me with so much passion that I can feel his love in every molecule of my body. He comes with a sexy moan, slowing down until we are left with just our heavy breathing and hearts beating. Then it's just me and him together, the world feeling like it can't reach us inside the car.

"I hope you know how hard it is for me not to make you scream like that again. I never want to leave this space. I'm afraid that if we do, it'll be over. You're all I've ever wanted, Stacia." Christos kisses my neck, stroking his hand along my spine. "Please let this be real."

"It's real, Christos. You might have hurt me, but I've healed. You've proven that you're still worthy of my love. I wish we could've changed things. I wish we could get these years back. Things would've been different, though. We would've continued living behind rose-colored glass, unable to see the wicked world outside of each other. Now that we know it's there, we can face it. I'm not going to let the King's Court destroy us. I'm going to figure out what my dad is hiding. He can't hide the truth any longer." I rest my head on Christos, listening to his beating heart.

"You're right. He wants to remain in the past, and I think he knows just how powerful you can be. He's threatened by it, and he's not ready to give up his reign. He knows that you can easily take it, especially with me by your side. With Esteban and Talon too." Christos tilts his head, meeting my gaze. "I'm sure that this is what it's all about. It's starting to make more sense."

I should've known. I should've seen it from a mile away. My dad has been manipulating me like he has everyone else. He's a coward. I'm going to prove as much.

His kingdom will fall.

24

True Executioner

Talon

I'm a dick. I knew Stacia wouldn't believe that I put a hit on her, but I had to go along with it. I can't trust that we're not being watched. I so blindly agreed to trust the King's Court that I missed what was happening.

Because I'm not the only one on the account tied to that alias. I share it with Stacia's father. We're business partners, after all, working under one entity. He was the one to put a hit on her. He wanted me to know as well. He wouldn't have been so obvious otherwise.

And now I have to go in and confront him. He's called the King's Court to his chambers. I know Stacia came to visit him, and she left in anger. The bastard thinks I'm stupid, but I heard everything. He's twisting one hell of a lie. Stacia truly proved her loyalty to me by not telling her father that she knew about the account. Loyalty I don't deserve. Not after blatantly making her feel as if she doesn't know me.

And now I must deal with this aftermath. He blamed Christos, but I doubt she believes that either. Maybe she'll finally see things as they are. Our chapter is on the verge of falling apart.

I just need to figure out why he did it. I'm not going to act stupid anymore. I'm not going to fake it until he messes up. He's gone too far. There's only so much I can ignore to keep the peace. He started a war.

I slip into my robe and pull my ceremonial mask down, even though we're just gathering in the King's chambers. The other members of our court already wait around, muttering under their breaths to each other about having to come in yet again. They obviously just like to reap the benefits of being part of our chapter without actually doing the work. They get a vote without having to do anything except pay their dues.

"It's about time you showed up, Executioner.

Where have you been?" Juan leans back in his chair, staring me down through his full-faced black mask.

"I had shit to do. Unlike you fuckers, I'm more than just a handsome face around here. I had to arrange a couple of things." I clomp forward with my annoyance.

"How is Princess?" Kenneth asks, speaking up from behind his big desk. He damn well knows how she is. He sent her my way, though I don't think he realizes she didn't return to me like he probably had hoped. After all, he has some twisted plan, and we're all about to partake in it.

"I haven't seen Stacia since earlier today." I cross my arms over my chest, remaining standing instead of joining everyone as they sit around, drinking alcohol from crystal tumblers, acting as if this is just us meeting for drinks.

Kenneth sits forward, locking his attention to me. He realizes something is wrong, because I heard it for myself that he wanted Stacia to come to me, and she obviously didn't.

"What do you mean you haven't seen her? You're supposed to be watching her and ensuring that she follows through with her task." A vein pops up in

Kenneth's neck, throbbing with his anger. I imagine pressing my fingers to the spot, squeezing tightly until he blacks out. Until I murder him. Because that's how this is going to end.

"I've been fucking dealing with a hitman." I step forward, enjoying the fact that Kenneth is too damn proud to stand up and face me, which allows me to loom over him.

"Which is why I have called the session in order. It has come to my attention that one of our heirs has betrayed us." Kenneth talks over me, pulling something from a folder. He sets down an email trail and bank transfers. I've seen them before, on the hitman's phone, but these have been altered.

He's really going all out, trying to blame Christos. He thinks I'm some sort of fool.

"Christos hired a hitman to kill my legacy. But I think it goes deeper than that. He's trying to destroy my reputation in the process. He's taking advantage of the scandal, and I want to put a stop to it." Kenneth raises an eyebrow, keeping his gaze trained on me as he lies through his clenched teeth.

"Now why would he do that? He's obviously obsessed with the Princess." Juan speaks up from his spot, choosing not to accept Kenneth at face value. He's always been an asshole, but he's a smart man. He hasn't gotten to where he belongs because he's just a follower.

"I don't know. Maybe because he can't have her? Maybe he's still embarrassed over the punishment? He sucked a cock on her behalf, and she still won't give him the time of day. I'd consider that a bit ungrateful," another member says, butting in. Stanley adjusts his mask, pulling it up to take a sip of alcohol.

I tighten my fists, shaking with my rage at his fucked up assessment of the woman I love.

"That seems fair. Perhaps you should do something about it, Ken. She's screwed up and needs to know her place. I think it will be easy enough to move past this with Christos. He's quite valuable to our chapter. I've seen quite an increase in clients because of him. He knows the extortion business well," Deidre says, resting his elbows on his knees. "It all comes down to your disobedient child who I still believe never deserved a spot in this chapter. But you were far too obsessed with having an heir, considering what happened to Sebastian."

Sebastian? I recognize the name, but I can't put a

story or face to it. This must've been right before I came from New York as Kenneth's business partner, bringing a slew of celebrities and wealthy clients with me.

Kenneth slams his palms on his desk. "Enough! Had the hit been on any of you, things would be different. I'm asking to vote on his execution. We cannot tolerate someone trying to gain power by going rogue. I don't think he'll stop even if I demanded Stacia to be a good girl for him. She's too wild and unpredictable."

"Whatever you want, Your Majesty. You obviously have your mind set, and you only bring attention to this, because you have to," Juan says, shaking his head, his face expressionless through his mask.

Stanley sets his tumbler of whiskey down. "I agree. We can find another. My nephew will be graduating soon, and he—"

I step forward and snatch the papers from the desk, crumpling them up and throwing them in Kenneth's face. "You goddamn liar! I'm not going to stand here while you arrange an innocent man's execution. He's done nothing but obey. And this proof is bullshit. You know it, and I know it. Why are you doing it? You used our joint account. Did you think I wouldn't find out?"

Silence falls through the room as Kenneth leans back in his chair, a smile breaking across his face, unobscured by the fact that he wears only a masquerade mask, always more bold than the others on his court.

"I *knew* you'd find out, Executioner. I did it on purpose to ensure it." Kenneth reaches into his desk, pulling out a blade. He stabs it into the wood, letting it stand on its tip. "You've crossed the line. Did you really think I wouldn't know that you were fucking her? Be thankful that I didn't really pin this on you and just wanted to mess with your head for betraying me to fuck that whore. That disgrace." Kenneth turns to the others. "You all were right. Having no heir would've been better than claiming the slut. She deserves to be banished for everything she has done. I'm no longer protecting her."

Juan shifts in his seat. "Kenneth, I thought you got over it? You don't need to be blood to be family. You can't possibly hold this against her. She's Bianca's best friend. She—"

Kenneth throws his glass in Juan's face, shutting him up. "This meeting is adjourned. My decision stands. Christos will take the fall for the murders, and Stacia is disinherited, excommunicated, and renounced as an heir."

My blood boils with my rage. What he declares? It's Stacia's execution.

"Are you out of your goddamn mind, Kenneth?" I ask, bubbling with a fury that'll unleash at any second. "That doesn't solve any of our problems. What the hell are you so afraid of that you're willing to doom the next generation of our chapter? Your own flesh and blood."

"Stacia isn't my daughter!" Kenneth hollers, launching from his chair. I dodge out of the way, his knife missing me by inches.

Grabbing the back of his robe, I twist the fabric tight enough to make him gasp. He loses his footing and falls to his knees. I throw an uppercut into his chin, sending his mask flying off. The crunch of bones against my fist satisfies me on a deep-seated level. I want his head.

"Are you fucking kidding me? That's what this is all about?" From the tension in the room, the others must've known the truth. "How long have you known? Your sudden need to destroy everything we've built proves it hasn't been forever."

"It doesn't matter," Kenneth snaps, trying to grab at

my robe. "Now if you don't stop this shit, I'll consider it treason."

I shove him hard and knock him on his back. "Don't you fucking threaten me. You're the one who has already committed treason. You hired a hitman without the consent of the court to kill Stacia. You—"

"I'm the fucking king of this chapter!" Kenneth shouts, cutting me off. He sits back up, but I don't let him get off the floor. No one intervenes. No one tries to get between us. I wouldn't expect them to either. "Stacia has proven incapable of following our rules and leaves our secret in danger. Do you really think a sex tape for the fucking whore is enough to keep her quiet and compliant? No. We've all made a vow to protect this chapter no matter the cost. If you have a problem—"

I lock my fingers to his neck, squeezing tightly. He grips my wrists. There's no overpowering me. I'm ten times stronger and more fit. I've gained the Executioner's name for a reason.

"Executioner, stop. You'll leave me no choice. If you want to challenge the king's authority, then you must do so properly. The same will be decided regarding Stacia and Christos. We will put it to a vote." Juan touches the cool barrel of a gun to my temple.

I've never believed in manifestation until now. My lie to Stacia now comes to fruition as I stand before the King's Court ready to challenge the man I trusted with my life and business. We've both changed over the last few weeks, all because of Stacia. I couldn't fight my attraction any longer, helping me see things more clearly. And Kenneth? Well, however the hell he discovered that Stacia wasn't his biological daughter turned him into a true fucking monster.

"Talon," Juan warns, pushing the barrel more firmly to my skin. "You have five seconds. Agree to handle the situation appropriately or die."

I release Kenneth and spit in his face. It takes everything in me not to take my chances against Juan. I don't know if he truly has it in him but finding out would be my greatest mistake. Stacia needs me. She needs to know the truth. I can't let her succumb to the deadly betrayal her father blames her for. She is innocent on every level.

"I fully intend to challenge the leadership of this chapter. Call in an SOS to the Rabbit Hole. We need a witness." I tug off my mask and glower at Kenneth. "I suggest you change your mind about all of this and renounce your own fucking reign. If you don't, I won't make it a swift death. You'll suffer for all your wrongdoings."

I don't wait for the others to respond and spin, striding toward the door. I exit the King's chambers and look around the quiet meeting room. The next time I return, everything will change. If it doesn't, then I'll die fighting for it otherwise. There are no other options.

"Why are you creeping, you bastard?" Leandro stomps through the pebble garden, crunching them with his boots.

I turn away from the crack in the curtains, where I get a clear view of Stacia sitting in bed with Esteban and Christos at a desk, hunched over his computer with a phone beside it. It looks like he continues to search through the hitman's phone, trying to find something, anything that'll give them answers.

Unfortunately, everything still ties to me unless they know the truth otherwise.

"I'm not sure if I'm welcome here, but I need to talk

to Stacia." I swivel on my feet, meeting Leandro's gaze. "Did they update you on everything?"

"You mean about you claiming to have been behind the hitman? Yeah. But we know you're full of shit. I recognized the account. It's the one St. Germaine paid me with. I know both of you share it, but I didn't tell Stacia that and thought I'd give you the opportunity. St. Germaine fucked up enough already. He underestimated the fact that Stacia isn't his sweet little girl anymore, showing her forged documents that said something else. It's a lot of bullshit, and I'm fucking tired." Leandro taps his finger on the glass, grabbing everyone's attention inside. "Now stop being a fucking coward. It's unbecoming of you. You're supposed to be a hard ass."

I punch him in the arm, but he doesn't budge, matching me in strength. I respect him immensely for hanging around despite all the bullshit. Many would've run. They would've tried to get in touch with the police. But we own this area. The police are on our payroll. He wouldn't have gone far if he had tried.

"Yeah, fucking yeah. I've just had a long day. Shit is fucked up, dude." I scrub my palms against my beard, trying my best not to get angry all over again. Leandro wouldn't take kindly to me busting the window to get rid of the rage brewing inside me.

"And the day is not fucking over. I'm so upset with you, birdie." Stacia saunters around the corner of the house, her fists on her hips and her arms akimbo. She looks sexy as hell, wearing just a long T-shirt, and I bet if I got close enough, I'd be able to smell one of these bastards all over her. Maybe even all of them.

I'm jealous that I wasn't here to partake in such incredible bonding experiences. I hadn't realized that I might have a cuckold kink. I love hearing Stacia moan in pleasure, no matter where it comes from. And seeing her get fucked? I get a damn boner just thinking about it.

I open my arms, too exhausted to put up a hard front toward the woman who makes me weak in my knees. She doesn't hesitate and falls into my embrace, resting her head against my chest.

"I want you to tell me everything. You know I don't fucking believe you about hiring a hitman. I know Daddy was involved. I confronted him, and he blamed it on Christos. Can you believe that?" Stacia tips her head back, her blue eyes sparkling in the soft light of the sun peeking through the heavy clouds. "He said a whole bunch of fucked up things. Something isn't right, Talon."

If only I had the nerve to tell her right here, right now, but a part of me knows that she needs to learn it for herself. It might break her, and I don't want to be the one to give her that sort of news. Am I an asshole for trying to save myself? Fuck yeah, I am. But her tears ruin me. She needs the jagged edge of her father's betrayal to find what she needs to fight back harder. Because shit is about to explode.

"I know, wild child. I didn't want to admit this before, because I think our businesses have been jeopardized, but the alias on the wire transfer? Your father and I own it jointly." My chest rises and falls with my quick breathing, and I wait for her to smack me and turn away.

But she doesn't. Her eyes search mine, peering into my very being, determined to find answers I hold back.

"That's what I don't understand. He hired a fucking hitman to kill me. So fucked up." Stacia closes her eyes, thinning her lips in an attempt to stop her jaw from trembling.

"It is," I confirm, reaching up to brush a warm tear

from beneath her eye.

"But why?" Stacia clings onto the front of my shirt, begging me with her watery eyes to give her answers.

I swallow and tighten my jaw, resisting the urge to lay it all out for her. To be the man to deliver news that might break her heart more so than knowing that her father hired a man to kill her.

"I don't have all the answers, but I know who does. I think it's time we visit your mom, Stacia. When's the last time you saw her?" I ask, turning my attention to Leandro as he remains a silent shadow behind her.

Stacia lifts and drops her shoulders, shaking her head. "I don't know. She's been in rehab. I guess it's been months. I haven't talked to her since a couple days before I had to hide."

"Then we should go tonight. I'll arrange everything. Pack a bag in case." I turn to Leandro. "I need you to watch Kenneth. Make sure he doesn't do anything stupid. And if he does, call me."

Leandro looks like he wants to argue but decides against it, nodding his head and then turning around to walk away, giving Stacia and I a moment alone.

I ensure it by tugging her away from the window until I press her back to the cinderblock wall, separating the yard from the neighbor's. I cup her cheeks and lean in, kissing her trembling mouth, trying to empower her like she needs.

"I'm sorry for trying to deny your trust in me. I'm not a good man, Stacia, but you're right. I would never do anything to hurt you. I only do things to protect you." I rest my cheek against hers, inhaling soft breaths of her citrusy fragrance. "I love you, wild child. It's never been more clear to me."

Stacia hugs me tighter, pressing flush against me. "I love you too, birdie. But you have some fucking making up to do. I thought I was going crazy. I was so confused. And then I felt abandoned."

I sigh, my chest heavy with her words. "I plan on it. I promise. As soon as all the shit is over, I will bow at your feet. I'll treat you as you deserve. You'll be my beautiful Queen."

Stacia smiles, her face lighting up at my words. She kisses me again, the weight of her body keeping me grounded. Because another part of me wants to explode. I want to ruin the world for this woman. And maybe I will. She deserves to watch those who have tried to destroy her break.

I'll be the true Executioner.

25

Secrets

Stacia

"I just need a second. Stay here." I stand outside the door to my wing of the St. Germaine mansion. I haven't lived here in weeks, and it already doesn't feel like home anymore. Nowhere does, really.

Talon looks ready to follow me, so I raise my palm to him and pat his chest. It's better for me to go in alone in case one of the household staff happens to come by my suite. We double-checked to make sure Daddy wasn't home, not that he would be. I'm pretty sure he spends most of his days sleeping in the city at one of his swanky apartments. It's easier for business, he used to say, considering that he would leave me alone for days at a time and then weeks when I was still a teenager.

"You better hurry your ass up." Talon leans against the railing, peering around the vibrant, robust gardens, scenting the air with a plethora of floral fragrances.

I turn away from him without comment and rush into my wing, taking the stairs up to my master suite, where I have a safe with legal documents. I'm going to need proof of my power of attorney. My mom arranged it when I turned twenty-one. It was one of those little secrets we kept. It wasn't that she didn't trust Daddy. It was because he had already seemed to dust his hands of her because of her struggle with her addiction.

I haven't enacted my right involving her healthcare, since she's still continuing to make good choices. It's when she stops that I'll intervene.

Opening the door to my bedroom, I halt in my tracks. The place has been completely destroyed. Broken furniture lies in sporadic piles across the spacious room, and all my wall art has been ripped and broken. Part of my curtains hang in tattered pieces, the plush fabric singed from being burned. I stare at the ashes of a pile of my clothes, and I realize that the sprinklers must've turned on to put it out. Water spots stain my bed, and the hint of mildew hangs in the air. All my electronics have been smashed, and the only thing that seems to be in place is my small bookcase behind locked glass. My dad either ran out of time or energy, leaving the place in shambles.

I rest my palm on my chest, feeling the beats of my nervous heart. If I even had an ounce of hope to ever come back here, it's now gone. What have I done so wrong to deserve this? Daddy knows I'm innocent. He knows I would never do something to purposely tarnish our good standing and reputation.

I just want it all to make sense.

Strolling around the disaster, I make my way to my wall safe within my bathroom. Daddy didn't know I had it installed a while ago, and it seems like he didn't bother to take out his anger on my bathroom. The Gothic painting of a woman holding a bleeding heart remains perfectly hung as I left it, and I unlatch the side of it from the wall and swing it open to find my safe.

I pound my finger against the keypad, just wanting to grab everything and run, so I never have to look at this place again. It beeps as the lock slides open, and I find the lockbox within it holding everything important I need.

I tuck it under my arm and spin away, jogging through my trashed bedroom and back out to where Talon remains exactly where I left him.

"What's wrong?" he asks, his brow furrowing with his concern. "Did something happen?"

"It doesn't matter. It's not important. I have what I need, so let's go." There's no point in spilling my feelings to Talon right now. We don't have time for this.

I grab his hand and pull him along, getting him to move instead of allowing him even a second to interrogate me. Because I'm obviously shaken. I feel sick to my stomach. And every second that passes makes it harder and harder for me to breathe easy. I just need to get out of here.

Talon reaches the car first and opens my door, and I enter the code for my lockbox, popping it open. My hands shake as I pull out document after document until I find my mom's healthcare power of attorney legal contract, naming me as her surrogate. I find the number to the posh rehab facility in Monterey, disguised as a spa, and I inhale a couple of deep breaths before I connect the line.

"Divine Health and Wellness, this is Tami. How can I help you?" a woman asks, her cheerful voice mirroring what I would expect from someone well-trained in customer service.

"Hi, Tami. This is Stacia St. Germaine. I wanted to set up a visitation with my mother. Her name is Evelyn St. Germaine." I peek at Talon in my peripheral vision. He doesn't drive or anything, just waiting patiently for me to finish.

"I'm sorry, Ms. St. Germaine. It looks like Evelyn was checked out of the facility two months ago," the woman says.

I frown and clutch my lockbox. "That's impossible. She had a court order. She couldn't have checked out."

The clicking of fingers tapping a keyboard sound through the line. "I wish I could give you more information, but it seems her power of attorney had arranged something else. You might want to ask Mr. Kenneth St. Germaine."

My blood cools, my chest tightening. "Mr. Kenneth St. Germain is not my mother's power of attorney. I am. He has no legal binding in making her medical decisions."

Silence greets me.

"Let me speak to your manager. This was a big mistake. I need whatever information you have regarding my mother." My fingers tremble, my mind whirling.

"I'm sorry, Ms. St. Germaine. If you could, please come down to the facility. We can—"

I hang up the phone with a shriek, knowing damn well that my father probably paid big money to move my mom.

Talon slides his arm around my shoulder. "I should've fucking known this would happen. I'm sorry, Stacia. Don't worry. We'll find your mother."

I clench my teeth together hard enough to make my jaw ache. "I want to find my dad. I need to fucking face him. He can't do this, and I'm going to tell him as much."

Sighing, Talon pulls out his phone and taps the screen a couple of times. "If you're sure, I'll take you to him. I've been tracking the fucker. It looks like he's out of the city. Do you have any houses in Orange County?"

"It's where my mom grew up. Daddy owns the townhouse complex, but I've never been." I lean back in my seat, closing my eyes and inhaling a deep breath through my nose, settling my nerves. "Do you think he took her there?"

Talon starts the car. "If he did, we're going to find out. We're going to get you answers. Promise."

"That's his car. If she's been out of rehab for months, why didn't he take her home? Why is he even here?" I unbuckle my seatbelt, wishing with everything in me that this wasn't real.

"Because he's been caught. It's as simple as that. He's trying to hide his messes. I'm sorry, wild child. I want to tell you what I know, but I refuse to be the one to deliver this kind of news. I don't know all of it." Talon takes my hand and kisses my knuckles. "Regardless, we're in this together. We're going to fix this shit."

Talon said that my mom had some answers, but I'm afraid for her now. Because, obviously, Daddy knows that he's been caught. Talon told me as much. He told me about their confrontation in the King's chambers and how he decided to go with his fake reasoning to me about the account and make it a reality, challenging my dad. He just has to wait for the summoning.

And maybe that's why my dad has become so desperate.

There's only one way to get real answers and that is to cut them out of him. Because there's no way he will just freely give them.

Talon's words trigger something dark inside me, and I peer at the condo as if I have x-ray vision and can see through the walls. If Talon is afraid to tell me, then it must be bad. And it has something to do with my mother.

"Do you have everything we need?" I ask, not wanting to say the words out loud. Like I said though, I'll get answers from my dad by any means necessary. He's proven how ruthless he can be. He hired a fucking hitman to kill me. And for what?

Talon reaches into the backseat and pulls out a duffel bag. He unzips it and shows me its contents. I wish Christos, Esteban, and Leandro were all here with me to help give me more strength than Talon does alone, because I feel so much stronger when I'm with them all, but this will have to do.

"You don't have to do anything you don't want to, wild child. And I should let you know, if we do this, it will jeopardize my chance to take over. I mean, if we get caught. But I don't give a fuck. I'll take every damn fucker down who tries to hurt us. I'm not scared. They put me in my position for a reason." Talon closes the bag and opens his door. "Let's see if we can get your mom first. It'll be better that way."

He's right. As much as I want to run in with my knives ready, I need to think about my mom. She's an innocent bystander in all of this. She's been kept in the dark about the Looking Glass and the workings of the Esoteric Society. I think it's one of those things that threw her deeper into her addiction. It's hard to trust someone who will kill to keep others' secrets.

We creep around to the sliding glass door within a walled courtyard, and Talon helps me up and over. Fear ignites in my heart, the scream of my mom muffling through the door. I'm afraid we're too late. I'm afraid my dad has decided to do something despicable and unthinkable.

Talon moves me out of the way and grabs a knife from the duffel bag, shoving it into the small space where the lock is to pop it open. It's obvious that my dad doesn't stay here, because he doesn't truly protect himself with extra security, which makes this so much easier. I bet he didn't even expect us to show up. But, he made a fucking bad decision, and we're going to take advantage of it.

"Shut the fuck up, Evelyn. If you don't, I will do it for you, you fucking whore." Daddy growls the words, his anger palpable.

My mom sobs in response, the fear in her voice hurting me deeply. Talon holds me back, stopping me from running in to save my mom. He pulls out his cell phone and begins recording.

I spot my father striding across the dirty living room of the condo to where my mom sits in a worn recliner.

"This is all your damn fault, slut. You couldn't just keep your damn legs closed. You fucking lied to me for years! Years! And now your bastard daughter will try to destroy everything." Dad slams his fist into the arm of the chair, startling my mom and making her cry harder. "The rehab just called saying she's looking for you. You fucking bitch. You gave her power of attorney, and now it's going to fucking make things worse. You need to void it immediately. She can't have anything to use against me."

"No," Mom says softly. "You can't make me. You're no longer my husband. You have no say in my life anymore. Now leave or I'll call the cops."

My dad swings his arm and slaps Mom across the face. "I own the cops. You're a fucking dead woman. My son died because of your bitch daughter. Had I known she wasn't mine, I'd have done things differently. I wouldn't have given Sebastian the choice. He killed himself because he couldn't go through with killing her when she was marked as not being a suitable heir. She's only alive because I thought she was mine. You're a lying fucking slut. Give me what I need, or I will kill you just like I killed that fucking worthless piece of shit man you opened your legs for."

"What?" Mom asks, her whole body trembling. "You killed Garett? You said it was an overdose. You said everything was going to be fine."

"It was supposed to be, but Stacia messed it all up." My dad rubs his hands over his face.

"What is that supposed to mean, Ken? What did you do? What did you fucking do?" Mom pushes from her chair, her anger giving her the strength to confront my father.

"You know, I thought I could live with knowing that Stacia wasn't mine, but she had to go and disrespect me in front of an important ally. I knew she would never be anything like me no matter how hard I tried, so I punished her for it. I punished her fucking sperm donor as well. He had no idea what was coming when he thought Stacia wanted to meet him. It was so fucking satisfying, watching the light leave his eyes. Stacia was too fucking drugged to do anything, acting just like you."

Mom swings at my dad, trying to smack him, but he grabs her wrist and throws her back to the chair. My mind spins with his revelation. He's always been bold. He wants people to know his viciousness. He wants people to be afraid of him and what he can do. It's how he's gotten so much power. His power must end.

"You fucking bitch. You fucking slut. Never try to lay a hand on me!" Daddy wraps his hands around my mom's throat, squeezing the scream out of her. She falls silent, opening and closing her mouth, gasping for breath. I can't stay still any longer, and I grab the tire iron from Talon and rush forward. I swing it at the back of my dad's head, hitting him hard enough to send him sprawling away from mom.

"You fucking monster!" I scream, swinging the tire iron at my dad again. Or at the man who raised me, considering he obviously doesn't see me as his daughter. At least because I'm not his biological daughter.

I can barely comprehend everything. He said that my mom cheated on him. And it sounds like it was the same man that I found dead in my bed. He was responsible for this all along. He's been playing me since the beginning. I had no idea that refusing to welcome Christos into our chapter would turn this man insane. It was all his fault to begin with. I know that now. He's unhinged and out of control.

Then something else clicks. He said his son died because of me, but I don't have a brother. What if he was the heir Christos mentioned? The one who committed suicide because he couldn't follow through with sacrificing me.

And then Daddy found out I wasn't his kid, after all.

This is so fucking twisted.

I have to end him. If I don't, he will destroy my entire world.

"Stacia, get your mom. I'll take care of this," Talon says, helping Mom to her feet. She sobs at the sight of me, her face red and puffy with her fear and sadness.

It's enough to get me to stop swinging, and I rush to my mom and slide my arms around her, half dragging her and half carrying her toward the front door of the condo.

"Oh, baby. I'm so sorry, my baby. I didn't intend for this to ever happen. He wasn't supposed to find out," Mom says, her tears pouring down her face. "I'm so sorry."

I don't respond as I rush her toward the car, leaving Talon behind to face my dad. I want so badly to go back in and go after him, but my mom doesn't let me go.

And then a gunshot rings through the air, and I stare at the entrance to the condo, holding my breath. I expect Talon to come out, covered in blood, ready to announce that he took care of my dad, but he doesn't.

Another pop shatters the quiet, and I push my mom into the backseat of Talon's car.

"Stacia, get in!" Talon yells, swiveling and pointing a gun at the condo. "He has a gun and he's not going down willingly."

I scream as I spot my dad running out the door behind Talon. I brace for him to shoot Talon in the back, but he's out of bullets. Talon swivels and aims, pulling his trigger. It misses Daddy by inches, pene-trating the stucco wall of the building. My dad ducks, taking shelter behind some thick hedges.

"Hurry! The cops are already on the way. I hear the sirens. We'll deal with him later." Talon jumps into the passenger seat, slamming the door shut. "Drive!"

I stomp the throttle without hesitation, sending my mom forward against the seats. Her cries echo through the air, and I try my best to tune them out, focusing on getting as far away as possible.

My knuckles turn white as I clutch the steering wheel, turning onto the main street, only to step on the gas pedal harder, sending us accelerating well past the speed limit.

"Pull over up here. I need to make some phone calls," Talon says, motioning to a busy parking lot at a strip mall.

"He's going to turn me in to the police. I know he is." I flutter my eyelashes, clearing the unshed tears away. "He's going to put me in prison. He has the money and power to make it happen. Fuck!"

I smack my hands on the steering wheel, my breath coming in heavy pants, my whole body now strung out on adrenaline.

Talon grabs my chin, turning me toward him. "We have the evidence we need to put him away. This is not going to fall on you. Do you understand?"

I heave a breath, shuddering as it escapes me. "Yes."

Talon strokes his fingers over my cheek, soothing me the best he can. "Good. Now let me drive. I want you in the backseat with your mom. Stay low. We're going to get her somewhere safe. And then Kenneth St. Germaine is going to get what he deserves. That fucking king will fall."

Demented Reign

Stacia

"I love you, baby. I am so sorry for all of this. I've just been so afraid of Kenneth that I didn't really know what to do. I thought that things were going to be okay. I had apologized. I had admitted that I was young and stupid, I was caught up on drugs, and I've made some bad choices. I thought Kenneth had forgiven me. We came to an agreement to move past things because he wasn't exactly faithful." Mom curls her knees to her chest, sitting up in the bed of one of the guest rooms in Leandro's home. "But I guess that didn't matter, considering what happened to Sebastian. I knew Ken had struggled over his death, but he had you. This secret took that away. I feel horrible."

"Wait, who is Sebastian?" I ask, my mind still reeling from the information. It sounds as if Daddy only found out about my mom's unfaithfulness recently. It explains why something as little as embarrassing him sent him over the edge. He's always been a little unhinged.

"He was your half-brother from your father's own discrepancies. Kenneth wasn't exactly a saint, despite his last name. That's why I thought we could get through this. We had both made mistakes, but he was upset I didn't tell him when Sebastian came into his life right before you graduated college. Your father had an affair with some lawyer in San Diego, and I guess the kid found out. I don't know much about it. Your father was so happy to have a son. It was all so...I can't explain it. It made me feel like utter shit, and it's what made me spiral and end up back in rehab. The guilt. Then he killed himself, and a part of me knows Kenneth blames himself." Mom rests her chin on her knees, her eyes glassy.

"This is too much," I say, squeezing my eyes shut. I know every family has skeletons in the closet, but it seems like I found an entire cemetery. Now I know that the heir Christos spoke of was Sebastian. He was given the task to sacrifice me, because I was deemed unworthy. His suicide saved my life. He saved me. This is so twisted. My mom doesn't even know the extent of it. She'll live her life just assuming Dad lost it because he found out I wasn't his. I'm certain he's had a psychotic break because he lost his heir and then learned that the one he had left—me—isn't even his blood.

"I know, baby. I don't have all the answers. Kenneth is a very secretive man. I know he was trying to protect me from his criminal activities. I just wish it didn't turn out this way. I know it doesn't seem like it, but he did love you. He didn't want you to know, because he didn't want you to think anything differently of him." Mom sighs, her breath heavy with her exhaustion.

She's making excuses for him even now. She needs so much help, and I don't know if just talking about it's going to do anything.

"Why don't you get some rest?" I say, standing up from the loveseat. I can't sit here and listen to her for another moment if she's falling into old habits again. My dad tried to kill her. He wanted to kill me. He killed my biological dad. This shit has changed me.

I need to get ahead of it now.

Mom squeezes my hand. "Okay, Stacia. I am tired."

I kiss her forehead and shuffle my way across the room, feeling as if the weight of the universe crashes down on me. Talon waits for me in the hallway, and then engulfs me in a hug, pulling me off my feet. He kisses me softly, trying his best to smother away the confusion and hurt, the anger and betrayal, the best he can.

Carrying me to the living room, Talon holds me close as he makes his way to the couch. The TV blares with the news, and I hear the newscaster say my name.

"Again, if you have any information regarding Stacia St. Germaine, please call the LAPD immediately. She is suspected to be armed and dangerous, working alongside known murderer Christos Makris. They were last seen together, leaving her father's Hollywood club after she broke in and held up the staff, trying to get money."

I gawk in shock and horror as a blurry surveillance photo of me appears on the screen, leaving the Looking Glass with Christos after I confronted my dad in his office.

This is his way of getting ahead of the game of cat and mouse we currently play. He thinks I'm the mouse, but I am the feline, and my claws are sharper than ever. I'm not a house cat. I'm a fucking wild animal with a thirst to kill that only murdering him will quench.

"What are we going to do? We can't go to the police. He already has them wrapped around his finger." Christos sits beside Esteban on the loveseat. Leandro perches on the armrest of the couch, looking at me and Talon. They were all waiting for us when we got back, and this is the first time I've gotten to sit down because of my mom. But Talon should've caught them up already.

"We need to take it to social media. You know he owns the fucking news stations too." I comb my fingers through my messy hair, trying my best to fix it. "We need to post the video we took, Talon. We can edit it to remove anything incriminating about us or the Looking Glass. I'll have Bianca help. We can send it to all the paparazzi and some influencers."

Talon kisses my cheek. "You're wickedly good at this."

"A true leader, right? I always knew Stacia would be a motherfucking excellent Queen." Christos stands and strides to my side, holding his arms open.

I pull him closer, making Talon laugh as he loses his footing and ends up on top of me, sandwiching me between them. It's the first time I've laughed all day, and it feels incredible. My world is on the verge of imploding, but when I'm with my guys, I feel unstoppable. Invincible.

I feel as if everything will be okay.

Talon works on editing the video he took of my parents fighting and my dad's admission, and I try my best to ignore the sound of Mom's screams on camera. Christos hugs me close, snuggling his face to the crook of my shoulder, begging for the attention I've denied him over and over again until the truth finally set us both free.

Leandro helps Esteban from the loveseat, and I watch as the two of them head toward Leandro's office with the promise of making contact with every pap and celebrity unaffiliated with the Esoteric Society that Esteban knows. I just hope it works.

It's easy to pay off the police when you're as wealthy as my dad, but he doesn't stand a chance when the public will demand he gets held accountable. It's the best I can hope for.

My phone buzzes, drawing my attention. I hadn't

expected messages to come in so soon. I know that Esteban is probably tapping at lightning speed, and those who know me would reach out.

Bianca: Holy shit, bitch! Esteban said not to bother you, but he can suck my big imaginary dick. I heard what happened. Juan knew it would come out, so he told me what he knew. WTAF! Are you okay?

I'm not surprised by Bianca's message. Juan might be hot and cold with me, but he loves Bianca, and he wouldn't let her get blindsided like this. If only he'd have spoken up for me. Talon mentioned that he knew about my brother. He knew that I wasn't Kenneth's daughter.

Me: I honestly don't know. He tried to kill my mom. If I hadn't wanted to confront him, she would be dead.

Bianca: He's a fucking asshole, and he doesn't deserve being in his position of power. Juan said that he's been acting off lately, and he worries about our chapter. If the Esoteric Society suspects that things will get out, they'll send other enforcers in to fix things.

And by fixings, she pretty much means they'll kill us all and take control. Because being part of the Esoteric Society means that they also have access to everyone's assets. Leandro wasn't really wrong in thinking that the Looking Glass might be a façade for a cult because, in all honesty, it does check quite a few boxes.

Bianca: Juan also said that there's going to be a summons soon. You know what that means.

Me: That I better hurry up and get this fucking video out there.

Bianca: Are you sure about it? You know how dangerous it is bringing the spotlight on any member of our society. Once it's out there, you can't take it back. Maybe there's another way.

Me: You know there's not. You saw the news, didn't you? They have twisted it to make me the suspect. This is the proof I need to exonerate myself. This will fix everything.

Bianca: Just stay safe. Take care of yourself. I don't trust half of the King's Court. You know how much they hate change.

Me: Well, they're going to have to either adapt or die. This bullshit has gone on long enough.

Bianca: Amen, bitch. Take that fucker down. I'll be cheering for you.

Me: Love you, bitch.

I clutch my phone, staring at the screen, waiting for the backlight to turn off. Christos kisses my neck, bringing my mind away from my conversation with Bianca and to what unfolds in front of us. Talon hooks his phone to a projector, lighting up the wall with the video of Kenneth screaming at my mom. He sends me the file, and my hand buzzes again, my screen lighting up with a memory I wish I could forget, but a memory I need to replay and rewatch over and over again, hoping that it picks up and gets the truth out there.

Esteban shuffles from the hallway with Leandro, and the two of them stare at the projection on the wall. My dad's voice booms out, exclaiming that he killed my biological dad, and now that I hear it again, my chest aches and my head pounds. He stole away any possible chance I'd ever have of meeting the man that my mom liked enough to betray Kenneth with and have me.

Anger flourishes through me once again, and I dig my nails into my palm. Christos eases my fingers off my phone, taking it away before I break it with my anger.

"Mamacita, I'm sorry. I should've known something. He was put on my staff by His Majesty. I should've looked more into it. I took Kenneth's word for it that he was a good dealer." Esteban frowns, clutching his side, the wound still tender but healing well.

"You don't have to apologize. It wasn't your fault at all. You couldn't have possibly known any of this. Fuck, I didn't even suspect it." I hang my head, letting my hair veil my face. "I just wish I had."

"We all wish it, Stacia," Christos says quietly, hugging me closer. "No one informed the new recruits that Sebastian was related to you or Kenneth. Had I known, I would've told you. I didn't know him for long, but he couldn't complete the task, thankfully."

I still can't believe it, and I feel so cheated because of Kenneth. He was a hypocrite and a fucking bastard. Sebastian was to be initiated before Kenneth found out that I wasn't really his. That had played a big part in things. I'm sure it's what destroyed things now.

"I'm done, wild child. Let's get this out there quickly. I just got a summons. We're all to meet at the Looking Glass." Talon flicks his gaze to Leandro. "I'm to bring you."

My heartbeat skips, and I wish I could get the world to stop spinning for a moment. To stop time from ticking long enough for me to figure everything out, instead of constantly having to aim and shoot blindly, hoping that I hit my target and not face the ricochet of an out of control bullet.

"Let me do the honors," I say shifting, opening my hand for Talon to give me the phone.

"All you have to do is hit send. It will go to the massive list Esteban put together. And then you can share it with the rest of the world." Talon scoots closer, sitting beside me, his closeness giving me the strength to find the courage to put this into the world. Because once it's out there, my life will change forever. I don't know what kind of consequences we'll face or what will happen with Kenneth, but there's no turning back.

I'm tired of being the villain of his fucking story.

He will get what I owe to him.

He will never recover from this.

I tap the phone, praying to the universe that it gets where it needs to go. It's quite anti-climactic, watching things send out without the world exploding around me or fireworks shooting into the air to celebrate our success. Instead, the room falls silent. It feels surreal. It's one of those things that I'll have to have patience for, despite my need for instant gratification.

"I guess that's all we can do for now," I say, pushing on Talon's and Christos's knees to help me get to my feet.

"Let's just hope this is it." Christos stands and hugs me from behind, brushing my hair away from my shoulder.

Glass shatters from somewhere in the house, shock panicking me. One of the front windows explodes next, and I scream at the sight of a Molotov cocktail burning across the floor. I screech, the sound startling and ear piercing, and Talon pulls a gun from his jacket and rushes next to another window, slowly moving the curtain to peek out. Leandro runs to put out the fire with an extinguisher, and Esteban clicks on his phone.

"No!" my mom screams, her voice ringing from up-stairs.

"Mom!" I jerk away from Christos at the sound of her panic. "Mom!"

More glass shatters, and someone jumps from the second story outside the front door. No one can stop me before I bolt to it and swing it open, my body freezing at the sight of my mom face down on the concrete patio. Blood pools from her head, and she doesn't move.

Talon vanishes, running upstairs, and Christos snatches me by the waist and yanks me back.

That's when I see him.

Kenneth aims a gun from an idling car on the street with a man in a mask. It's someone from the King's Court, but I can't tell who it is from here.

Esteban shoots through the doorway, his aim good enough to send the driver screeching away with bullet holes on the side of the vehicle.

"Mom?" I ask, tears burning my eyes. I elbow Christos in the stomach, getting him to release me. I don't care if it's dangerous outside. I have to get to my mom. She needs me.

"Call an ambulance," Christos says, coming up to my side. "Stacia, be careful. They could come back around."

"Let them!" I scream, dropping to my knees. I touch my fingers to my mom's bent neck, knowing that it's already too late, but I refuse to believe it. I refuse to accept that Kenneth managed to find us. I shouldn't have expected anything less. He has eyes everywhere.

Sirens echo in the distance, and Talon hops down the stairs two at a time, returning to the living room. He bolts to me and lifts me off my feet, dragging me away from my mom. I kick and thrash, begging with everything in me for him to just let me go.

"Come on, Stacia. We have to get out of here. The cops are on their way, and there's nothing we can do for your mom. I'm so sorry. I should've double-checked the room. It looks like she had her phone on her, and she called him. He had someone come in and push her when we were dealing with the attack." Talon adjusts me in his arms, holding me against him, waiting for me to calm down and hug him with my whole body.

"What do you mean she called him?" I ask, my voice cracking.

"She texted him too. She wanted him to show mercy on you. She begged him to leave you alone and punish her instead. She was trying to protect you, Stacia." Talon chokes up with the words, and it's the first time I've ever seen him with such emotion. "I'm so sorry."

My mind and body shut down, and I rest my chin on Talon's shoulder, unable to say anything else. I don't fight him either, letting him carry me toward the garage. Christos and Esteban follow us, but Leandro remains on the porch, kneeling next to my mom's body.

"I'll make sure she's taken care of, beautiful," Leandro says, his voice hard to hear over the sirens. "I'll give the police everything they need. They won't be able to deny it. We're outside of LA County. It'll take time if they try to cover things up."

"Thank you," I whisper, closing my eyes as the garage door shuts.

Christos gets behind the wheel with Esteban in the front seat. Talon slides into the back with me on his lap, holding me close and not letting me go.

I thought we had won.

I thought this was all going to be over.

I should've known better. There's only one way things can truly end in my favor.

I must kill the king of the Looking Glass.

It's only with his death that we'll ever escape his demented reign.

27

The Summons

Stacia

"**I** always knew that douchebag was a psycho. If you look at the clip again, you can tell how calculated his actions are."

I swipe my finger across the screen, sending another social media influencer's speculation into the oblivion of the internet. It's all that I see online, on TV, and even on the radio and every social media site.

"Breaking news, Kenneth St. Germaine was detained this morning from his yacht at the Manhattan Beach Harbor. He faces murder and attempted murder charges along with aggravated assault, and a long list of other felonies." Again, another influencer, who has taken to social media to pass along the news, appears on my screen.

"Shit," Esteban says, looking over my shoulder at my phone. "It's fucking working. That video is everywhere."

"Can you believe that this asshole already posted bail? He hadn't even been detained for four hours. That's what you call privilege, people. This man murdered someone. The evidence is clear, yet he still gets a damn trial. If we don't speak out, he'll get away with it." I freeze, staring at the video of one of my favorite influencers. I can't believe I heard it from her first. And it's so fucked up. She's right though, men like my dad get away with everything. I just hope this time is different. They know I'm not the killer, but now I'm the daughter of one.

A knock on the door draws my attention from my phone. Esteban gets up, moving more slowly than usual, his healing taking time, though I know he would rather just push through the pain to get shit done. It bothers him that he's not out with the others, dealing with Looking Glass stuff.

Glancing through the peephole, Esteban sighs and opens the door. He unlocks it and cracks it open, not letting me see who's on the other side.

"What the fuck is this about? We are heading to the Looking Glass in an hour. There's no need to harass us," Esteban mutters, swiveling to glance at me.

I tuck my phone away and get to my feet. I can already tell that this has to do with our chapter. My dad's arrest has left us in chaos and peril.

"Due to this scandal, our meeting location has been changed." A familiar man stands outside, stretching to look over Esteban and at me. He's one of the members of the King's Court. Deidre, I think. He never talked to me much. "You know the rules. Word of mouth only. We can't let that shit get out. There's already so much damage control we have to do."

"It's such an honor to be personally summoned by the Joker, pendejo." Esteban moves out of the way, his sarcasm heavy and his deep voice. "Talon could've told us. He's on his way back now."

"Actually, he's not. He's traveling with William Blackstone now. His entourage follows him. It's my duty as the messenger to ensure everyone shows." He turns in my direction, narrowing his eyes. "Including His Majesty."

His silent threat strikes fear in my heart. He purposely mentions my dad, or should I say, Kenneth, and I know it's to get under my skin. If Kenneth is removed from his position, and Talon takes over, Deidre can lose his position within the King's Court. It is better for him if that doesn't happen.

"Give me the address, and we'll be there on time," Esteban says, balling his hands. "We don't need an escort."

"Blackstone says otherwise. He's tasked me with bringing you in and is currently acting as temporary king. I will not disobey his order and neither should you. Gather your things. I just want to get this over with and move on. You don't know how difficult it has been managing my business when everyone's concerned about the St. Germaine state of affairs." Deidre tightens his jaw, looking ready to grab Esteban by the collar to drag him out of the apartment.

"Fine, whatever. But I'm driving." Esteban peeks over his shoulder at me. "Message Christos and let him know." I know Esteban says it because he doesn't trust Deidre, and frankly, neither do I. Anyone who is close to Kenneth that hasn't spoken up against him is not my ally.

Pulling my phone out, I quickly shoot Christos a

text message.

Me: Kenneth posted bail. He's going to be at the meeting. Deidre is at the door, demanding we go with him.

Christos: I heard from William. I'll track your phone.

Me: I'll see you soon.

Christos: Love you, babe.

Babe? Shit. Christos has never in his life called me that.

Deidre clears his throat, his gruff voice grating on my nerves, stopping me from replying. "We don't have all day. Traffic is bad, and we have to do some rerouting to ensure no one's following you. That's the last thing we fucking need. More paparazzi. More bullshit."

I square my shoulders, my anger taking over me. "You can only blame your fucking king. None of this is my fault. Stop treating it that way."

Esteban shoves his hand against Deidre, keeping him from entering the apartment to confront me. Deidre steps back, raising his hands in surrender. I realize that Esteban reached for a weapon, threatening him.

I stroll forward and wrap my arms around Esteban from behind, getting him to calm down before he murders someone on the front porch. We have enough to deal with, and right now, the only thing I worry about is seeing my dad again. Fuck, I can't get that out of my head. He raised me, but he also ruined me. He wants to kill me. He killed my mom.

I shove the thought away, blinking my eyes to clear the tears. I still can't believe it. I try my best to pretend that she's still in rehab somewhere, and not in the morgue. They won't release her body until the investigation is complete. Because they also want to tie that to my dad. He hired someone to break into Leandro's house. Luckily, Leandro had quite a bit of proof, considering they were trying to burn the whole place down. His surveillance was enough to prove he was innocent.

"Whatever. Let's just get this over with. I don't want to be late. I want to watch the Executioner fall." Deidre smirks with his words, knowing that he's trying to get under my skin. Talon told me that they all know we have started something together, and I'm sure it's going to be a problem if my dad—Kenneth—doesn't end up behind bars for the rest of his life.

Esteban blocks me from trying to slap Deidre, and he spins on his heels and strides away, heading toward the apartment complex parking lot. Esteban pushes me against the door, cupping my face with his hand.

He kisses me without a word, caressing his lips to mine, slowly and sensually until my racing heart subsides. "They're going to do whatever they can to get to you, and you can't let them. They thrive on reactions. They hope we'll fuck up, so we need to be careful."

"I think they have Christos's phone," I murmur, whispering the words. "This is a trap."

"I know it is, but they don't know we expect it. Just keep pretending. Punishment is best served as a surprise in situations like this." Esteban presses harder into me. "Be brave, mamacita."

I groan and kiss him harder, hooking my arms around him, wishing that a simple kiss could truly stop time. But Deidre honks his horn, and we have no choice but to follow him. At least Esteban's driving. I wouldn't trust the ride if he wasn't. I'm already nervous enough as it is.

Before we reach the car, Esteban hands me a knife, a money clip full of cash with a baggie of drugs, and a set of keys with a tracking chip on them. I hide the money clip my bra because I don't have a purse and put the knife and keys in my pocket.

"If anything goes down, I want you to run. Those are keys to a spare vehicle and an apartment in Palm Springs. Run and don't stop. This is part of a challenge. I just know," Esteban says, glowering at Deidre as he blares the horn again, standing outside the car and leaning in through the window.

"I want the same for you. Don't be a hero. You're already still healing." I gently caress my fingers along his shirt without touching his injury. "I want you alive. Promise me."

"No. If it comes between me and you, you're the one who's getting out of here." Esteban kisses me again and turns me toward the car. "Now sit in the back. If the Joker even looks like he's going to fuck with me, I want you to stab him in the jugular. And then grab the seatbelt and choke him."

I shiver at the thought of taking a man's life. I know I have it in me. Self-preservation really pushes me to my limits. I had no idea that I was so ruthless until it was me against the world.

"I have your back." I ease away from him and climb into the backseat of the car, glowering at Deidre. I slam the door, not letting him get into the back with me, and he rolls his eyes and heads around to the passenger side.

Silence hangs heavy in the air as Esteban pulls out of the spot and drives. I count each second passing, staring out the window as Deidre gives Esteban directions. Two miles turn to three, and we navigate through the city until we reach the 101.

My phone buzzes from my pocket, and I pull it out and answer the call from Talon.

"Stacia, get out. This is part of the challenge. Kenneth has been given the opportunity to keep his position if he takes care of you first—" Talon hollers in pain, and something crashes. He grunts in the phone. "Hurry and get here. I have to surrender, or they'll kill me."

Goosebumps prickle over my skin as the line drops. They have Talon. William turned this into another challenge I can't fucking fail.

My heart hammers and I reach forward and grab the seatbelt stretching it quickly to wrap around Deidre's neck. I hold the knife against his throat, keeping him in place.

"Stop the car." I leverage my strength with my knees, choking Deidre. "They've changed the rules."

"What?" Esteban asks.

"You heard me. We have to run. Daddy's been tasked to kill me before the meeting. If he does, the challenge is off." I grip tighter to the seatbelt.

Esteban slams the brakes, stopping the vehicle before we turn onto the on-ramp of the freeway. He grabs my wrist and forces the knife into Deidre's neck, stabbing him. I screech as warm blood coats my fingers, but I don't have time to even think about what's going on. Esteban throws open the driver's side door and quickly snatches me from the back, leaving Deidre bleeding out in the front seat.

"I'm going to kill that fucker," Esteban growls, squeezing my hand as he practically drags me to the tree-lined landscape and away from the road. We make it up the steep hill leading back to the busy street, only to see a black SUV with tinted windows crawl by our car.

"Fuck. What are we going to do?" I ask, keeping my voice a whisper, even though I know the men in the car can't hear me. They pull over and get out, sending ice through my veins.

Esteban doesn't wait to see what happens, forcing me to run with him away from the scene. My shoes slap on the pavement, and I search our surroundings, afraid that some monster will come popping out at any second. I can't believe this is happening. I can't believe Kenneth was given the option and Talon now relies on me. The fucking bastard.

"Just another block, mamacita. We need to get somewhere public, and there's a mall coming up." Esteban herds me along, making sure I don't slow down.

He grabs his phone from his pocket and taps the screen with one finger, sending ringing through the air from the speaker. The line clicks and a soft hello follows only to have Esteban yell, "Bianca, are you there?" He pauses. "Bueno. I need the location. We're not backing down. You can tell them as much. Tell them if they proceed without us or hurt anyone Stacia loves, the secret's out. I have shit ready to send to the world."

"Esteban," I say, my heart beating wildly. "Demand we talk to them. We need to be sure they're alive."

"You heard her, Bianca," Esteban snaps, hitting the speaker button. He slows down when we reach a crowded intersection. "We expected the worst, mamacita. If we're going down, we're taking the fuckers down with us. We knew Kenneth wasn't going to just give up." Esteban keeps his voice low.

"Here's the location. I'm handing you to Talon now," Juan says, his voice cutting over Bianca's. A notification blinks on his screen with a pin on a map, and I try my best to focus on it as we run.

"That's only a couple blocks away. We're coming," Esteban says, breathing heavily with effort. I'm sure the run strains his body more than mine, but we can't stop. If we stop, another hitman could catch up. There could be others around here.

"No. Don't bring her. It's too late. Just send the proof out," Talon says, speaking up. "Take her out of here."

Rage rushes through me, and I snatch the phone from Esteban. "I can't just run. You know I can't, Talon. I need to be there for the challenge. I'm not letting Daddy get away with this."

"Wild child," Talon argues, his voice raising with his frustration. "It's not going to end how we want. Just stay away."

"Fuck you. I can't run anymore." I gasp a couple of breaths, my stamina faltering.

"If you come here, they will sentence you to death, Stacia. I don't want to risk your life." Talon groans, his deep voice reverberating through my bones. "Kenneth, is still King until—"

"Please, Talon. I have a plan. I'm done running. I'm done fucking hiding. I'm taking my life back." I clutch the phone. "I can't let them think they can push me around. You have to trust me. I know how to handle men like them." And more importantly, though I don't say this, I need revenge. I'm not letting Daddy's privilege and entitlement let him get away with murdering my mom. Murdering my biological dad.

If I don't stop him, he will murder me in time. I know it.

All this bullshit ends here.

28

The Challenge

Stacia

Well, if this doesn't scream cult, then I don't know what does. Now that I see things from the outside, I realize just how fucked up everything is within our chapter of the Esoteric Society. I was initiated thinking that this would help me my whole life. I'd get everything I need, from wealth and fame, to protection and close friendships. I could get away with things others couldn't and live an elite lifestyle.

But now I'm staring at what might as well be an aisle in which I walk my own death march.

Boards cover the stain-glass windows from the outside, creating an eerie vibe to the old, abandoned church. Candles light the altar up ahead, and dozens of people fill the pews.

Instead of all being on an equal level, like meetings at the Looking Glass, the King's Court stands higher than the rest, speaking volumes. We look ready to worship them and not vow loyalty to each other.

This is so twisted and fucked up.

"Welcome, Princess. Knave. It is incredible to find you've made it among us." Is he kidding me? His voice might be friendly, but wicked darkness lies in William's eyes. "Hand over all your weapons. This is a neutral territory, and violence won't be tolerated. You've earned your right to be here, making His Majesty fail to hold reign by defeating him at his own task." He holds up a robe, waiting for Esteban to give him his weapons, adding them to the basket far too full for comfort. Looks like everyone here was prepared for a massacre, and it's the first time we've all been stripped of any sort of additional power.

William looks at me in silence.

I open my arms. "I don't have anything on me."

"Then I'm going to need to check." William twists his lips with a leer, his eyes turning heavy with lust. I don't know how I could've ever thought he was a good man. He's just as bad as Kenneth.

Esteban opens his mouth to argue, but I pull out the money clip from my bra and then yank up my shirt, flashing William my boobs.

"Like I said, I have no fucking weapons. Now, unless you plan to strip down every fucking man in here and stick your finger in his ass, then you better step back and let me in." I stand up taller, daring him to respond.

He only chuckles and hands me the robe. "It seems the circumstances have given you a lot of nerve."

"You mean my dad murdering people and blaming me? It's giving me a lot more than nerve. I want him out." My chest heaves with my anger, but Esteban slides his fingers through mine, keeping me in control.

"It'll take a lot more than just desire to see that happen. Now be a good girl and join the others. We have some business to attend to." William motions for me and Esteban to head toward the group gathered in front of the altar.

My heart weighs heavy in my chest like a stone, hardened from the worst kind of betrayal. A betrayal that has turned me into a scorned woman with a taste for destruction. All I can think about is how I'm going to destroy the one man I was supposed to love unconditionally. A man who is supposed to love me the same. But now he stands above us, lost to a God complex and narcissism, manipulating everyone he can.

"Princess! We've been waiting for you." Kenneth opens his arms wide, reaching toward the ceiling. He hides behind a full mask and robe.

The edges of my vision crowd with shadows, my anger making it hard to see straight. If I ever loved this man like a father, that love died with my mom. He has shown who he truly is. I was unlucky under his spell, his charm and power enough to blind me toward his monstrosities.

"Are you sure about that? I heard you failed your fucking task. Does everyone else know?" I raise my voice, listening to it echo through the vaulted room. "Did you really think you could hire someone to kill me and then just act as if none of this has ever happened?"

Kenneth glowers at me, only his eyes visible through the painted metal of his mask, the design disturbing with its devil horns. I used to think it was unique, but now I realize it's the perfect replica of who that man is on the inside.

Honestly, though, I think the devil might be kinder.

At least he was once an angel. Kenneth is far from that. He's never had a good side now that I see things clearly. He was a hypocrite toward my mom, angry that she cheated on him when it was obvious that he cheated first. And as for the brother I never knew? He had to have seen this man in all his frightening glory. It was enough for him to choose death. He sacrificed himself to save me. I wish I had the chance to know him.

I try not to be distracted by the thought and wonder how things would be different had he been just like Kenneth.

"You need to be held accountable for jeopardizing the Looking Glass chapter. You're a traitor! I demand, there be action against you." I search the crowd, spotting Bianca's familiar mask. I look for Talon and Christos but don't see them. Of course, I don't. I know they're being kept elsewhere. It's why Talon wanted me to run. But I have collateral. We will use it if we have to.

"Come up here and say that to my face, Princess. I know you like to hide behind the men you whore yourself out to for protection. I always knew Talon was weak, easily persuaded by pussy." Kenneth turns to Esteban and points at him. "And look where it has gotten you, Knave. You could've had everything. I was giving you the opportunity of your lifetime, and now it's going to disappear. Someone like you is easily replaceable."

Esteban pushes past me, finding his strength to stride forward as if he's not healing from a stab wound. The crowd erupts in mumbles, and someone shouts that this whole situation is bullshit. Another yells to kill Esteban so they can finish the meeting and get home.

I scream out, using my voice to bring order to the meeting. "You have been challenged for your position, King," I say, grabbing onto the back of Esteban's robe, keeping him from doing something that could get him hurt. "You're stalling like the coward you are. It is in our doctrine, that if a king is no longer fit to lead that someone can prove worthy to be his predecessor. Where is the Executioner? I know you have him. You better fucking follow our bylaws or all of this is over. For everyone. I'd rather fucking die than see you continue your reign."

"Hurry the fuck up, Your Majesty. I don't trust her. Just give her what she wants. Show us what kind of man you are," someone yells.

Silence fills the air with his comment, and everybody looks around, clearly curious as to what will happen next. If Kenneth will be brave enough to face a true king.

I turn and look at William. "You're here to ensure it is a fair challenge. Where is the Executioner? Don't think I won't take you down too. We're not stupid. You think you have shit against us, but we're not fucking threatened anymore."

William adjusts his mask, showing off his wide smile. "You've been mistaken, Princess. I'm not here to ensure a fair challenge. I'm here to see to it that the one worthy of leading as a king of the Esoteric Society remains on the throne. Not all challenges are accepted. As a proctor, and the current one overseeing the Looking Glass, I have denied the request. I think you're only bluffing. You're not brave enough to die for your convictions."

Goosebumps prickle all over my skin, my anger melting into fear.

"But don't worry, Princess. The Executioner has been given a second chance to prove that he's not the traitor he's been accused of being. We have a witness that must be taken care of. And as for you, Princess?

It's up to you to beg for mercy. You must convince this entire room that you're still worthy, despite the scandal surrounding you. Had you just been an obedient heir, we wouldn't be in this mess." William strides closer, his robe billowing behind him. I can't believe what he's saying. This all comes back to the last time he was here. He's still pissed off that he didn't get his way, and that Christos stepped up and took the punishment, fighting for justice on my behalf, standing up against a misogynistic, perverted bastard.

"What?" I can't help asking. My voice cracks, and I clear my throat, wishing I could summon the hope I need to get through this.

Because in this moment, it feels as if everything is falling apart. I thought these men would adhere to the rules of the Esoteric Society and take care of the threat of exposure, but maybe that was my problem. Maybe there are no rules. Maybe they have created their own. Every chapter controls its own people. Only the wealth and ability to call for help from another chapter is what really brings everyone together.

William motions toward one of the cloaked figures at the end of the pew, and he heads toward an old confessional with a scratched-up façade. He pulls open the first door, revealing two figures. I recognize Talon's muscular build and tall frame. Christos sits on the bench, crammed with him.

The sight of Talon helps me summon my bravery. "This is your last chance. You'll be all over the news. The Society of—"

"We control the world!" William shouts. "You have nothing!"

He says it with such certainty that I believe him.

Trusting that a psycho even had an ounce of fear will be my downfall.

Our downfall.

Because the cloaked man drags Talon out and then grabs Christos too, shoving him hard enough to make him fall to his knees.

"No," I whisper, touching the front of my robe. I feel the hardness of Esteban's money clip and remember that I have a set of keys in my pocket still. They're not conventional weapons, but I have to think on my feet. I won't go down without a fight.

"Bring the witness forward. It's time to set an example," William commands, surprising me by sliding his arm around my waist, pulling me into him. I didn't even see him move, my gaze locked onto the confessionals.

I tense at his closeness, smelling the rancid scent of his breath. With his other hand, he shoves Esteban forward, sending him reeling onto the platform. The audience remains seated, watching as if we're a personal show here for their entertainment.

I look over my shoulder, catching Bianca's gaze. She pouts her bottom lip. I know she wants to stand up and shout against this madness, but she's also fearful for her own life. I wouldn't want her to do so anyway. She doesn't deserve falling to the consequences created by my wicked family. Our wicked king.

"We are gathered here today to solidify our vows to the Looking Glass chapter," Kenneth says, his voice is booming through the nave of the cathedral. "As you all know, our secrecy has been put at risk and my own position as your ruler has been jeopardized because of this. It is with great sadness that I must have our very own enforcer stand before us today to prove his loyalty."

The robed member tugs the bag off Talon's head. I gasp at the sight of his black eye and split lip, clearly showing he has been beaten before he was bound and imprisoned. He underestimated everyone and the rules and order he swore his life to. Or maybe he was blinded by his feelings for me. He only cared about my safety and didn't think about himself.

He shifts on his feet and stares at the crowd, his eyes locking onto mine. "I'm sorry, wild child," he mouths, thinning his lips.

A part of me doesn't believe he was taken down so easily, but the proof stands before me.

Christos growls as His Majesty rips the bag off Christos's head, purposely rough. He punches him in the stomach, sending him to his knees.

"And bring the witness." Kenneth points toward another confessional, and a second guy opens the accordion door and grabs Leandro.

Fuck me. He wasn't supposed to be here. He had stayed to take care of my mom's body. He wasn't going to be spotted. He was supposed to stay out of the way until everything was done, and now he's here, being called a witness. And there's only one outcome for such a title.

He's about to die.

"Executioner, it's time to live up to your name and secure the secret of the Looking Glass. If you shall fail, you will face the same fate. It is your task to clean up this mess. First, the witness, and then the traitor. He did not accept his challenge to plead for mercy." Kenneth stands behind Leandro, grabbing his hair and tipping his head back, just to spit in his face. "Off with his head."

The last time I heard him say those words, I witnessed a man die before me. He wasn't decapitated, but Kenneth found it funny, considering the history of our founding chapter.

They wouldn't dare give Talon a weapon. They're too chickenshit.

They're going to make him kill Leandro with his bare hands.

I need to give them a minute to think. I need to buy some time. I will not just stand idly by and wait my turn. That is not what I was raised to do. I'm not a docile Princess. I'm a goddamn warrior, and I'm ready to fight to be Queen.

All I have to do is figure out how to intervene without ending up with a knife in my back. I touch my pocket through my robe, feeling the keys. And then I touch the money clip again, remembering that it's not just cash. Esteban's been carrying the drugs he confiscated like a trinket or a prize like a serial killer takes from a victim.

Now I know what I need to do.

"Stop!" I scream, shoving past one of the King's Court members. I fall to my knees before Kenneth, letting my fear and anger burst from me in a wail of a sob. "Please! Stop! You don't have to do this. I'm begging you, don't make him do this."

Kenneth surprises me by grabbing my hair and yanking me up. "You're going to have to do more than that, Princess. You're a whore, so fucking act like one. Show us what you're willing to do, and I'll consider sparing one of them. But there are no guarantees."

My stomach twists at his suggestion. How fucking disgusting. He's not insinuating that I do something to him, is he?

"You will have to prove worthy to the entire King's Court any way we want." Kenneth yanks me higher off the ground, leering at me, his eyes lined with hatred.

"Get your fucking hands off her!" Esteban yells, rushing toward us. A man charges him, knocking him off his feet.

He pulls out a blade and aims it at his throat.

My ears ring, and I struggle to breathe. If I give in, it'll just prolong my agony. They want to humiliate me before they take everything away. They will not show me mercy. Kenneth isn't capable of it.

But he doesn't know that I'm not the daughter he raised. I'm the woman forged from the aftermath of his wrongdoings. I'm as sharp and deadly as the blade he uses to cut people down. But I won't crumble. I won't give in.

I'd rather die trying than let him ever think that he is above me.

I thrash, screaming, doing my best to keep his attention away from the fact that I pull the keys from my pocket. I jab my hand forward and managed to sink the car key through his eye, making him recoil and trip over the altar of candles. The room erupts in chaos as Talon and Christos take advantage of the situation, freeing Leandro from the binds.

Smoke billows from some of the knocked-over candles, catching fire to the altar cloth. I press my weight on Kenneth, but I'm not heavy enough to pin him down. He locks his fingers around my wrists and yanks, pulling the keys from his eye hard enough to send them flying. With his other hand, he grabs me by the throat and squeezes, his mask now askew, his vision blocked but his mouth showing.

So I make my move, taking the opportunity I need. I pull the drugs from the baggie and jam the stack of red squares into his mouth, using my fingers to shove them down his throat, covering his mouth with my hand until they dissolve and he has to swallow.

He continues to squeeze, managing to grab me with both hands, and I open and close my mouth, trying to scream for help. People fight around me, and smoke clouds the room. This is it. I wasn't quick enough. Maybe the drugs won't work.

I close my eyes and prepare to die.

Water splashes across me, shocking my body, and I open my eyes and gasp for breath, Kenneth now beneath me with his eyes rolling and his body convulsing. I don't know how long I blacked out for, maybe seconds. Possibly a minute.

"Stacia! Stacia!" Leandro yells, calling my name from somewhere behind me. People scream, and the crowd disperses, no longer entertained by the fucked up situation.

I raise my hand up, my body shaking as I struggle to breathe from being choked, and from the smoky air, turning black as the sprinklers put out the fire.

"She's over there. Hurry and grab her. The police are

coming, and we can't be caught here." Talon materializes a few feet away from me and Leandro rushes to scoop me up into his arms.

I can barely comprehend the chaos. I don't even see where the members of the King's Court disappear to. I don't know where William Blackstone is either. All I see are those who rush toward the exits, probably thankful that they get to go home. They probably won't even think twice about everything that happened as long as no one messes with their lives.

"Kill him," Esteban says, his arm slung around Christos's shoulders. "You have to make sure he doesn't make it out alive."

Talon stands over Kenneth, looking down at him, his body now still and unmoving. Blood gushes from his eye and ears, with his mouth stained red. Reaching down, Talon presses his fingers into His Majesty's throat, checking for a pulse.

"He's already dead," Talon says, getting to his feet. "Let the police find him. They can see what a psycho he is."

"What about the evidence? Everyone in the robes?" I ask, a part of me fearing the repercussions of this side of us coming to light. A side that should have always remained in the darkness.

"Who fucking cares. Let them think whatever they want." Leandro adjusts me in his arms and motions toward an emergency exit leading from the altar.

"It'll be covered up by morning. I can assure you that. The Esoteric Society will always remain a mystery and an urban legend to those outside of our courts." Talon pushes open the door, looking around at the massacre in the church. He proved his name worthy. He showed everyone the dangerous man he really is.

As for me? I'm no longer a good little Princess Kenneth tried to force me to be. I'm not just a body for him to treat like a piece in a game. I'm not a weak little prey being hunted for power. I'm the true predator. The true Queen.

And I am here to take control. The Looking Glass chapter will never be the same. We will move forward. I didn't almost lose everything just to give it away.

I have proven my worth.

As I stand by the sides of the men who cherish and adore me. The men who respect me. I know I'm fit to rule.

Long may we reign.

The Vow

Stacia

"Did you see the news?" Leandro asks, heading into the guest bedroom I've claimed within the St. Germaine estate. "His death was ruled an overdose. There isn't a single mention of all the bullshit, including the fact that you keyed him in the eye. Fucking crazy. I just can't wrap my mind around how powerful this cult is."

"It's not a cult." I laugh, tossing a pillow at him. "You'll see, Protector. Just wait until the next meeting."

Leandro's face darkens, his smile fading. I know a part of him despises the idea that I don't just turn my back and walk away from all of this, but there's too much I want to change in the world. I can't do that without the Looking Glass chapter and Kenneth's financial empire, which now belongs to me as the last St. Germaine.

I roll off the bed and sashay toward him, shaking my hips and giving him a view of my cleavage from my nighty. He had commanded that I rest for a day as he monitored my breathing, but that day turned into two, and I finally have been catching up on sleep while Talon, Christos, and Esteban solidify our new stronghold on power.

He can't resist me and opens his arms, letting me stroll into his embrace. His dark expression turns to lust, and he meets me for a passionate kiss, giving me life instead of taking my breath. Electricity courses through my veins, buzzing across my skin and down my body to heat between my legs. I've been yearning for a moment of affection, especially because my guys have been treating me as if I'm porcelain instead of made of bulletproof glass.

He moans against my mouth, pressing his hips to mine, so I can feel the hardness of his length on my pelvis. I reach down and stroke my fingers over his cock, wanting nothing more than to give in to his every desire.

"You might want to reconsider if you are even a little bit exhausted, wild child," Talon says, standing in the doorway to the bedroom. "I'm not alone out here, and you know the rule."

I lift my eyebrows and laugh, my voice tinkling through the air, breathy with the thrill of his suggestion.

I curl and uncurl my finger, holding onto Leandro, still teasing him with my free hand. "And I have put a new rule into effect as Queen. If you want to be on my court, you must bow before me," I tease, biting my lip at that suggestion.

"Dios mío, mamacita. I'll kiss you from your feet to your pussy. You don't have to command me twice." Esteban dodges past Talon, smacking him on the back with a laugh.

Nerves dance across my muscles, but I don't deny them. If they are okay with listening to my commands, acting as my equals when it comes to my love, then I will give them what they want. I'm not afraid. They will never break me to their wills. They will always lift me up and ensure the world is mine.

"Fuck, how is this going to even work?" Christos asks, following behind Talon as he slams the door, despite no one being on the estate besides us. I retired the staff early, wanting nothing more than to repay those who worked for someone like Kenneth.

Esteban chuckles and stops behind me, only to grab my wrist and spin me around. He brings his finger to my lips. "Uno." Lacing his fingers through mine, he holds up my arm next. "Dos." Tingles burst between my legs as he drags his finger down my arm and across my chest, dipping it between my cleavage to draw a line down my torso to my pelvis. He slips his finger inside my thong and touches between my legs. "Tres." He takes a moment to stroke me, sending my legs trembling, my body wanting to crumble to the floor with his attention. He slowly drops to his knees and guides me to turn back toward Leandro. He then takes his slick finger, wet from my body, and he gently slides it into my ass, making me moan. "Quattro."

"Damn. I call dibs on quattro." Christos says, coming up to my side. He kisses my shoulder and works his way down, kneeling beside Esteban, who tugs my thong down and spanks my ass. Christos kisses the hotspot, and I moan, clutching onto Leandro.

"Only if you're good with this, Stacia. If it's too much—"

I shut up Leandro with a kiss, smiling against his mouth. "Give me what I want. Bow down and I'm yours."

Leandro hums under his breath, lifting my hair to kiss my throat. It's as if the playfulness leaves the room, stripped away with my nighty as the four men I care about most in the world smother me with their attention, their muscular bodies like a protective wall around me, their hands made to make me feel good. Their mouths perfect for kissing away my doubt and filling me with the devotion they carry. Their hearts being everything I could ever want, holding me as their equal and treating me as the most important thing in their world. And as for their souls? They're vowed to me through this bond we share, this life we had to destroy so we could rebuild it the way we wanted.

And they're mine. All fucking mine.

I grab Leandro's shirt and pull it over his head, guiding him close to kiss between my legs, only letting him tease me for a minute. I reach out for Talon next, wiggling my fingers and getting him to step close. He kisses me, flicking his tongue across mine, tasting my mouth as he cups my breast and rolls my pebbling nipple between his fingers, sending another wave of desire through me. I yank his shirt up, pulling it off him, and he hooks his arm around my waist and lifts me up, tossing me to the bed.

"Undress for her," Talon says, remaining dominant in his desires, but it's only for the control of my pleasure, ensuring that I get everything I could ever want.

I arch my back, letting Esteban take off my panties completely, and I rest on my elbows, smiling as each of them strips down naked for me, without shame, fully intent on sharing me in unimaginable ways.

Crawling forward, Esteban lifts my legs up, resting them on his shoulders as he bows down and drags his tongue across the seam of my body, gliding his tongue over my clit, only to suck it sensually into his mouth, making me moan so loud that my voice echoes through the room.

I grab at Christos, pulling him forward until he is close enough for me to reach. I lace my fingers around his cock and guide him to my mouth, getting him to straddle my face in a way that he can thrust into my throat the way he prefers. Talon shifts on the bed, grabbing my nipple before he leans down and sucks it into his mouth. I blindly reach for his dick, letting him guide my hand over his length, just wanting to give as much pleasure as I take.

I moan, my voice vibrating on Christos's cock, and he pulls out and smiles at me, caressing his finger to my cheek.

A shockwave of ecstasy builds between my legs, Esteban bringing me to my peak so quickly that all I can do is scream out and stretch, grabbing the blankets for something to hold onto. My pent-up desire explodes, and I sit up and grab at Talon's hips, pulling him to my mouth to suck him. I rub my fingers over his balls, feeling the tightness, and then I do the same to Leandro as he rubs his own dick, turned on by the sight of me laying before them.

"Lay on top of me, Stacia. I want those fucking perky tits right on my chest." Talon lies back on the bed and gets me to climb on top of him, and Esteban pulls me down until I feel Talon's cock between my legs.

"God, I'm so lucky. You're the sexiest woman in the universe." Talon adjusts his body and slides inside me, groaning at the heat of my wetness. I pant and close my eyes, savoring the sensation of our bodies meeting.

Talon bounces me slightly, controlling my movements until Christos pulls me up away from Talon to kiss my throat.

"I love you, astéri mou. You're my everything. My star. My Queen. My soul." Christos nudges me back down, resting his palms on my ass cheek as cool liquid splashes across my body. I moan at the sensation of his finger teasing me, testing me and preparing me for the ache that'll leave me begging for more. Because it's not only about my pleasure. It's about theirs too, and the thought of getting off the four men who cherish me most turns me on even more.

"Pinche cabrón, you're so fucking lucky," Esteban says, tilting my head to watch my face. "Look at her face. She loves it."

I gasp as Christos pushes inside, going slow, letting me get used to his body. Esteban shifts up, guiding his cock into my mouth, letting me suck on him as Leandro slides his hand between me and Talon and strokes my clit.

My eyes roll with my pleasure, and I lose myself to the sensations, my body humming, and my muscles tensing, a good ache, radiating between my legs as another orgasm builds, and I pull away from Esteban to scream out in bliss.

Leandro takes Esteban's place, and I stroke his balls as I lick his tip, slobbering over him to get him extra wet. He strokes his cock, looking down at me with heavy-lidded eyes, his handsome face devouring me in ways that make my body sing.

Talon groans beneath me, grabbing my hips and holding me in place, thrusting into me, harder and faster, getting Christos to work in sync until Christos pulls out to come on my back. Talon flips me off and onto my back, stretching my leg as he rocks his hips harder and harder, adding pressure to my clit with his thumb until I scream again. He grunts, pulling me close, holding me in place, coming inside me.

I pant, my heart racing, my body caught up on adrenaline that makes even the lightest stroke of Leandro's fingers on my nipples feel like electricity.

He pulls me up and Esteban squirts lube over Leandro's cock for him, not even caring that he has to stroke him to prep him for what he wants. Leandro eases me up and presses his tip against my ass, slowly sliding in until I'm sitting on him completely. He sucks on my shoulder, giving me a hickey, and Esteban stands at the edge of the bed, watching as Leandro fucks my ass. Licking his lips, Esteban closes the space and grabs my legs, holding them up and spreading me wider. He aligns his body and sinks inside me, not even caring about the mess Talon left behind. He clenches his jaw and uses my legs to brace himself, swinging hard and deep, pinning me to Leandro as he braces, bouncing me in a way that gets me going. My moans are like bursts of screams, ringing over and over again, my pleasure so loud that it might linger in my ears for days.

Talon and Christos take turns, kissing me and stroking my nipples, showering me with their attention as Esteban and Leandro fuck me in such a way that someone's going to have to carry me after. But I don't care. It's worth it, and I would do it again and again, this moment bringing us closer together.

Our bonds will never break. This is our vow to each other.

"I'm going to come," Esteban mutters, thrusting hard as he continues to play with my clit, my body swollen and aching in the best way possible, and another orgasm rips through me. I pull him forward, pressing my mouth to his shoulder as he grunts, his body exploding with his passion.

Leandro slows, taking his time to enjoy me as the others watch until he finishes, leaving me breathless and completely malleable on his lap, my muscles relaxed, my need satiated and my heart full.

The four of us lie on the bed together, me sprawled across Talon and Leandro, holding onto Esteban and Christos's hands, just listening to our hearts beating and our heavy breathing in perfect sync, the weight of the world no longer pressing down on us.

I've never felt so free.

I've never felt so strong and powerful.

But it's more than just a feeling. It's a certainty that I know deep in my bones.

We're worthy of this power, and we won't take it for granted. We will make the most of it. We will be the change that the world needs.

Our future might be full of secrets, but behind the Looking Glass, the world will thrive.

Our lives will flourish.

Together.

That I vow.

Fame

Stacia

"Are you sure you're ready for a meeting? We could skip two more weeks and still be okay. The chapter is fine, and everyone has settled down since the aftermath of the bastard." Talon adjusts my robe, pulling the hem up as I stand in the Queen's chamber, every aspect of Kenneth and his court now gone. This isn't a place for secret meetings or plotting. It is a sanctuary to reflect and remember what our purpose is from here. The weight of darkness still hangs over us, and our business still might be morally gray, but we use it to our advantage to better those who need more and deserve more.

Like the rehab center I have created free of charge and with the best care for those who need it, named for my mother. I refuse to let the world forget her, even if she had long been thrown out by the world because of her disease.

And as for the Looking Glass chapter, we no longer have wealth as part of the stipulation to grow among the elites. We want those who aren't afraid of using their voices, working hard to create change. We need those who can build a path that others can follow without worrying about a minefield left behind by those who would rather kill to get ahead than realize that we're all in this together.

"I just don't want you to get stressed out. I know it's hard being here." Talon glides his fingers under my robe and across my stomach, resting his palm just below my navel. "Stress isn't good for the baby."

I drape my arms around his neck and pull him in to kiss me. "The last thing I am is stressed, birdie. I'm excited. I don't want to put this off again. It's time to step up, don't you think?"

"They already know you're the perfect Queen, and they're thrilled to have you back. But let me be nervous. I prefer to hide you from the world." Talon kisses me softly. "Don't fault me for wanting to protect you."

"William arrived. He will bear witness to the shift in power." Leandro remains expressionless standing in the doorway, keeping it mostly closed so no one can see into the brightly lit sanctuary of our office, now full of color and plants and light, unlike the dark tomb, Kenneth had created.

I tense at William's name, just the thought of him igniting rage inside me. But it has to be this way. We don't have a choice otherwise. His signature is necessary in the declaration of a new ruler of our chapter.

"We'll be right out," Talon says, turning toward me. He sighs and rests his head on my shoulder, bowing into me. "I can handle this."

I shake my head. "I don't want to give him a reason to doubt me. If it were up to him, he'd take over our chapter and combine it with his."

"Fuck that. He doesn't have the finances. Me and you—Christos, Esteban, and Leandro—we have a motherfucking empire. Our reach goes beyond the Looking Glass. We'll make it known." Talon pulls away from me and helps me adjust my diamond-encrusted masquerade mask.

I take a deep breath and twine my fingers through

his, letting him guide me toward the meeting room. Bianca waits outside the door. She smiles at me, taking her place at my side, her Duchess nickname, showing that she is no longer just the heir of Juan. She has surpassed him in power. And from the grin on his face as he stands next to Marge-Louise proves that he doesn't care. He might have his flaws, but he loves his daughter.

I touch my stomach. The kind of love I already feel with the life inside me growing every day, getting as powerful as the rest of us. My future heir. She will be raised far better than I was, doted on, and guided, taught and shown the love that she deserves and more.

"I call to order this meeting and have come to issue the initiation for Her Majesty," William says, his voice laced with annoyance. Hatred even. He'd prefer to see me begging on my knees, instead of standing before him, my head high and my shoulders back, embodying more power than he will ever know. He is just as weak and limp as his small dick.

"Please step forward, Your Majesty. As it is customary, the Queen must pass the initiation to claim her leadership position. Do you accept the challenge?" William says, twisting his lips to the side. I want so badly to smack the smugness off his face, but Talon squeezes my hand, keeping me in control.

"I'm taking the initiation for her," Talon says, speaking up. "As acting enforcer, it's in my right to do so for the person I vow my loyalty to."

William sneers, shaking his head. "That only works for an initiation to be an heir. If she wants to be Queen, she must complete the challenge."

I tug from Talon's hand, stepping in front of him before he lunges at William. "I accept the challenge," I say, my voice coming out strong, echoing over the silent room. A couple members mutter under their breaths from the front row, and I make a point to look at them, spotting a few men that want nothing more than what William wants. I know these are the men that helped Kenneth and managed to escape, though they still claimed that they were following orders. They didn't want to be deemed traitors, and they accept that power now belongs to me.

Except I don't believe them.

I will prove a point.

"You are tasked with sacrificing one of our very own to prove to the Esoteric Society that you are worthy to lead and are capable of making the most difficult decisions for the greater good of our people." William turns toward the altar and tugs off a cloth covering a jewel-encrusted gun, one that has probably been in this chapter for a century.

My heart hammers, and I turn my attention to the crowd, looking at everyone. Nerves hang heavy in the air, and I smell the sweat of those who fear that I will choose them.

I gingerly lift the heavy gun, allowing Talon to adjust it for me, making sure it's loaded correctly and ready to fire. He stands behind me, acting as my instructor, and he turns me toward the crowd. I lift my arms, letting him hold my hands to help brace me.

I smile and slightly swivel, aiming the gun at the men I know who want to run, thinking they're next. I take pleasure in their fear, stopping on each man in the front row, one by one until I turned back to William.

"I've made my decision," I say.

I pull the trigger without waiting for him to plea for his life, shooting him in the head, watching as his body falls to the floor. The deafening silence rings in my ears, and I let Talon take the gun from me.

"My initiation is complete, and I swear my loyalty to this chapter, hoping we can forge through this and make our world a better place. This isn't about the elite and entitled. It's about speaking for the voiceless and helping those who need it. Any way we can." I tip my head down and take the ceremonial crown from the table. Bianca helps put it on my head, and Christos hands me my scepter, adorned with glittering rubies as red as the blood on my hands.

"Bow to Her Majesty," Talon exclaims, smiling widely, his eyes shining through his mask.

Esteban, Christos, and Leandro kneel first, followed by Bianca and others in the crowd follow suit.

"We'd like to transfer to another chapter," a man says, speaking up. "You're not our Queen."

I remain expressionless and turn toward the men, still standing, refusing to ever bow at my feet, wanting to cling to the past as I blast our way to the future.

So there's only one thing I can do. If they don't want to join us, then they will be left behind.

Turning to Talon, I nod my head.

He doesn't hesitate and shoots each standing man with perfect accuracy, sending them sprawling to the floor.

I turn to the crowd and slam my scepter down, the noise booming through the air.

"I'm calling order to our first meeting under my reign. Welcome to the Looking Glass. From here on out, we vow to help the world. We will not leave destruction in our paths. We will only plant seeds for a better future and a better life. Do you accept this vow?"

"I do," the crowd says in unison, the voices filled with excitement instead of the monotonous tone I had grown used to.

I turn to Talon and hold out my hand, and he comes to my side. Leandro, Christos, and Esteban fill the space around me, circling me in their strength and love and devotion.

I'm their Queen and they're my kings. My knights. My protectors. My everything.

And together, we will rise in fame and fortune. We will be known for the good we leave behind. We will never fall. Never bow. Never break.

The world isn't ours for the taking. The world will be what we make of it. It'll be a better place, full of wonder, love, and light, and everything I imagined it to be. It'll be perfect.

~The End~

More Books

OMEGAVERSE SERIES

Saint Vista Pack Regimes

Bonds of Steele Omegaverse

PARANORMAL

The Seven Sinners of Hell's Kingdon

The Pack Mates of Lunar Crest

The Wolfpacks of Shadow Moon Island

The Fated Mate of the Dragon Clans

The Divine Vampire Heirs

The Royale Vampire Heirs

The Academy of Vampire Heirs

La Vega Vampire Showstoppers

Rise from the Flames

About Ginna Moran

GINNA MORAN IS the *USA Today* Bestselling author of over seventy novels including the popular The Pack Mates of Lunar Crest and The Seven Sinners of Hell's Kingdom reverse harem novels.

She always carried a fascination for all things paranormal and wrote her first unpublished manuscript at age eighteen. Her love of the supernatural grew stronger through her adult life, and she now spends her days with different creatures of the night. Whether it's vampires, werewolves, dragons, fae, angels, demons, or mermaids, Ginna loves creating and living in worlds from her dreams.

Aside from Ginna's professional life, she enjoys binge-watching TV, crafting and design, playing pretend with her daughter, and cuddling with her dog. Some of her favorite things include chocolate, mermaids, anything that glitters, learning new things, cheesy jokes, and organizing her bookshelf.

Ginna is currently hard at work on her next novel and the one after, and the one after that.